Not What I Expected

The Unpredictable Road from Womanhood to Motherhood

Donya Currie Arias
Hildie S. Block
Editors

ISBN: 0-931181-26-7
First Edition
Published in the USA
Copyright © 2007, Donya Currie Arias and Hildie S. Block
All rights revert to the individual authors.

Book design by Nita Congress.
Cover art by Dale Shimato.
Cover design by Chuck Arias.
Printed by Main Street Rag Publishing, Charlotte, NC.

Paycock Press
3819 North 13th Street
Arlington, VA 22201
www.gargoylemagazine.com

Credit Where Credit Is Due

"Just Talk" by Hildie S. Block first appeared in *Motherverse*, Winter 2006. "Croup" by Jody Bolz first appeared in the *Crab Orchard Review*. "Holy Places" by Stephany Brown was previously published in *If I Had My Life to Live Over* (Papier Mache Press, 1992) and in *The Next Parish Over: A Collection of Irish-American Writing* (New Rivers Press, 1993). "Changing Color" by Carole Burns first appeared in *Enhanced Gravity* (Paycock Press, 2006). "Natural Disasters" by Bonnie Jo Campbell first appeared in *Mid American Review*. "A Fine Day," © Carol Carpenter, was previously published in *Iowa Woman*. "Children," © Grace Cavalieri, first appeared in the *Patterson Literary Review* and *Cuffed Frays* (Argonne Press). "Early," © Cindy Dale, was previously published in *Zoetrope All-Story*. "Nightcap," © Amy Farnsworth, was published in her chapbook *Bodies of Water, Bodies of Light*. "Mother Notes for Elaine," © Peggy Garrison, was originally published in *IKON*. "As Soon as the Baby Moves," © Jacqueline Jules, was published in *Potpourri*, November 1992. "Prepared Childbirth," © Jacqueline Jules, was originally published in *Nomad's Chair*, Summer 1994. "You're So Lucky," © Suzanne Kamata, first appeared in *New York Stories*. "Spock Addendum for Maura," © Jackie Kudler, was published in *Sacred Precinct* (Sixteen Rivers Press). "Hurricane Season," © Margaret McMullen, was published in *Southern California Anthology* (University of Southern California, 2002). "Card Party" by Judith Montgomery was first published in the *Formalist*, vol. 8, no. 2, and was reprinted in the chapbook *Passion* (Defined Providence Press, 1999). "Night Terrors" by Judith Montgomery was first published in *The Anthology of New England Writers 2001*. "Cropped Roots," © Teresa Méndez-Quigley, first appeared in *Mad Poets Review*, 2000 annual issue. "Latitudes," © K.W. Oxnard, first appeared in *Mediphors*, Spring/Summer 1996. "The Calling," © Andrea Potos, appeared in the anthology *Mother-as-Writer: A Delicate Balance* (Xlibris, 2002). "Now I Lay Me Down to Wait" by Elizabeth Roca first appeared in *Brain, Child: The Magazine for Thinking Mothers*, Spring 2001; and in the anthology *Brain, Child's Greatest Hits, 2000–2003*. "Our Beloved, Jacob," © Kirsten Rogers, was first published in *Quills and Pixels*, 2003. "The Strong Pull of a Handful of Tiny Cells" by Robyn Samuels, © *Los Angeles Times* 2001. "Slow Dance," © Kathleen Walsh Spencer, was first published in *Welcome Home*, July 1999. "A Butterfly's Wings," © Lynn Stearns, was first published in *FlashPoint*, Fall 2001. "Mother and Son" by Lynn Tait was previously published in *Quills Canadian Poetry Magazine*. "The Naming," © Hilary Tham, first appeared in *Bad Names for Women* (Word Works, 1989). "How to Hold a Son," © Amy Unsworth. 2002. Some sections of "Tug and Pull" by Donna Vitucci first appeared online at literarymama.com. "Pearl in a Foul Oyster World," © Phylis Warady, was published in *Purpose*, March 1986; *Tyro*, October 1991; and *The Writing Parent*, December 1999/January 2000.

Acknowledgments

We'd like to thank our husbands and children for giving us the time, energy, and material for this book. To the contributors and all submitters for touching our hearts and bearing with us. Special thanks to Richard Peabody for his undying efforts to bring light to the Washington area literary scene. And to "go-ddess" Nita Congress who worked her magic on the final draft and made it look like a "real" book. Thank you.

Contents

Introduction ix

pregnant

Now I Lay Me Down to Wait, elizabeth roca 3
Pregnant, judith laura 20
Untitled, karen massey 21
The Orchard, wende mccabe-teichert 22
September 12, 4 am, kristin stitz 23
The Corridor, brenda-fay glik 26
A Butterfly's Wings, lynn stearns 28
Pickled Pregnancy Test, patricia gavin 30
I Knew All Along, cathy warner 32
The Stitching of a Baseball Thrown at Noon, janice levy 43

birth

Birth, patricia gray 51
from "I Married a Mexican Teenager," susan mckinney de ortega 52
Prepared Childbirth, jacqueline jules 56
The Demon Who Delivered Me My Daughter, viva hammer 57
seeing, barbara a. rouillard 64
You're So Lucky, suzanne kamata 66
My Daughter, dewi l. faulkner 79

Latitudes, k.w. oxnard 87
Interphase, darcy cummings 100

infertility in progress

Infertility in Progress, anne hasselbrack 103
A Personal Relationship with God, tessa dratt 104
The Barren Season, mary doroshenk 114
Let's Make a Baby!, lisa rhoades 116
The Strong Pull of a Handful of Tiny Cells, robyn samuels 117
Cropped Roots, teresa méndez-quigley 122

becoming mom

On Becoming a Mother, polly b. dredge 125
becoming mom, barbara gibson 131
Purple Fleece and Motherhood, katherine mikkelson 133
Watching Her Child Become a Work of Art, lyn lifshin 136
Holy Places, stephany brown 137
Second Child, sarah kennedy 147
Night Terrors, judith h. montgomery 149
Suddenly I Am My Mother, sandra perlman 150
Ice Ages, molly ruskin 151
Slow Dance, kathleen walsh spencer 153
50-50, katy mckinney 154
Milk, arlene eager 155
Bret-at-Six Remembers My Womb, marion cohen 157
Untitled, franka arabia 158
The Naming, hilary tham 159
Newborn Baby without the Picket Fence, nicole braun 160
Snow, Fall, judith arcana 164
Hurricane Season, margaret mcmullan 165

Dancing Partner, dianne smaniotto 178

lost children

As Soon as the Baby Moves, jacqueline jules 181
First Child, kate banigan-white 183
Miscarriage, laurie king-billman 192
Changing Color, carole burns 193
Premature, corrine de winter 204
Our Beloved, Jacob, kirsten swain rogers 205
The Not Named: Mothers Who Grieve for Lost Children, sharon winn 213

a mother's needs

A Mother's Needs, jacqueline jules 219
Just Talk, hildie s. block 220
Untitled, holly smith 224
Sunday, Four O'Clock, terry scheidt 225
On Mothering and Writing, rachel hall 226
At the Waterloo Poetry Festival with My Daughter, jill stein 240
A Sweet-Loving Mother, maureen egan 241
Mother Notes for Elaine, peggy garrison 244
Nightcap, annie farnsworth 246
Tug and Pull, donna d. vitucci 247
The Calling, andrea potos 265
Night Vision, kathryn leenay 266
Nap Time, ethney mcmahon 269
Not a Poem, katherine grace bond 270
Stopping by the Bathroom on a Busy Evening, katherine grace bond 271
A Fine Day, carol carpenter 272
Whiteout, sharon charde 281

worry

Card Party, judith h. montgomery ... 285
Natural Disasters, bonnie jo campbell ... 286
Baby Dreams, donya currie arias ... 288
Croup, jody bolz ... 292
Early, cindy dale ... 295

after

After, marilyn rauth ... 309
Vasectomy Saves Woman, susan kushner resnick ... 311
Mother and Son, lynn tait ... 317
On a Son's Leaving after Thanksgiving, mary ann larkin ... 319
Children, grace cavalieri ... 320
On Guard, terri watrous berry ... 322
How to Hold a Son, amy unsworth ... 324

lessons

Today We Learned to Blink, margaret grosh ... 329
Pearl in a Foul Oyster World, phylis warady ... 330
Arabic, clarinda harriss ... 333
There's No Place Like Home, amy hirshberg lederman ... 335
The Vine, mary-sherman willis ... 340
Lessons from Ben, Just Turned 3, katy mckinney ... 341
Camping with Lucy, claire tristram ... 343
Postpartum Day Two, patricia gavin ... 348
Spock Addendum for Maura, jacqueline kudler ... 349
Domestic Bliss, christina daub ... 351

Our Contributors ... 355

Introduction

The two of us (and our husbands) have five children, ranging from three to eight years old. As educated, intelligent, and conscientious women, we read and studied to prepare ourselves for motherhood. We liked the cheerful reassurance of such titles as *What to Expect When You're Expecting* and the many similarly styled childbirth and parenting books radiating optimism and confidence, predicated on complete knowability and predictability.

Then we had our kids.

Then we learned that, in pregnancy, birthing, motherhood, and after, *nothing* goes as expected. And nothing can prepare you for the sleepless nights, the wracking pains, the wordless agonies, the endless worries, the exquisite moments, the unexpected bliss.

"Why didn't anybody tell us?" we wondered. Well, for one thing, when you're busy being a mother, it's tough to find the time to write about what it's like to be a mother. As writing moms, we rarely suffer from writer's block, but almost constantly from writer's interruption. But the stories are there, inside, and they must be given voice. This intense emotional experience is the one not found in parenting books that recommend only to "be consistent" and "use discipline."

And that's the reason for this book. The stories the eighty-plus contributors to *Not What I Expected* tell are poignant and heart-breaking, joyful and tear-jerking. In selecting these works from among more than a thousand submissions, we looked not for the most familiar names, but for the most familiar messages—the ones that resonated with emotion, truths, and moments that change a person forever.

###

In "Pregnant," the authors touch on the pregnancy experience, from a poem that marvels in the flutter of first kicks to an essay written to a baby in the womb the day after the September 11 terror attacks to a gripping account of a woman's months spent on bed rest trying to save her twins.

In "Birth," the works all touch on first-person birthing experiences, some with a contraction-by-contraction account. Two women give birth in foreign lands, a son grows older and wiser, labor pains come with the force of an earthquake, a mother bonds with her newborn.

"Infertility in Progress" takes us along on the journeys some mothers have faced in yearning for a baby that might never be born. A woman contemplates surrogate parenthood, another struggles to decide what to do with frozen embryos, and the promise of a new pregnancy is met with joy—and fear.

"Becoming Mom" tells of ways women's lives change when they become mothers, whether at the moment of actual birth or adoption or one day when mothering suddenly clicked. One author tells us how "each change in my child requires a change in me," others weave awesome tales of adoption, bringing a second child into the world, learning to adapt to diapers, spit-up and middle-of-the-night feedings.

"Lost Children" might be the most difficult section to read because it deals with child death, something that is so wrong and earth-shattering we all reel from it. As Donya's aunt recently said when her friend's teenage son died of cancer, every time a child dies, a piece of every mother's heart breaks. The works in this section are brave and honest as they peel away the layers of grief and lay it out for us to read.

"A Mother's Needs" might well be titled "frustration." Sometimes the joy of parenthood isn't enough to overshadow our desires for a moment alone, a clear, adult thought, or a warm, unrushed meal. A lawyer struggles to leave for work as her daughter begs her not to go. A mom locks herself in the bathroom just to have an uninterrupted conversation—with herself. A new mom wonders why her baby cries so much. Another eats the cake she had packed in her son's lunch box, only to feel guilt when he asks for it later.

What mother doesn't "Worry" about a million times a day? In this section the authors contemplate many things that can go wrong in the life of a child, from birth defects to childhood injuries to illness to premature birth.

"After" looks at the time after children have grown, after a baby no longer relies on us for literal nourishment but still needs us in other ways. That can be liberating, heart-wrenching, or both.

In "Lessons," a teenage son teaches a mother about her own hypocrisy, a powerful career woman learns the value of an infant's blinking eyes, an alcoholic learns suddenly what it's like to bear the responsibility of motherhood. Here the authors illustrate ways we teach our children and our children teach us.

Finally, what's "domestic bliss"? We learn it can be cat puke on the living room rug, an older child's forgotten homework, a suckling newborn, and a sip of lukewarm coffee.

†††

We created this book to hold these stories. Depending on where you are on the road to pregnancy and parenthood, you might not have known about some of these pathways and byways; you might not want to look at some of the signposts; you might not care for some of the scenery. But we assure you, as you journey down your road, you will nod in recognition, sigh or weep in sympathy, laugh out loud, as you find familiar terrain in this book.

Will it prepare you? Will you know what to expect next?

No. But you'll learn that we're all in the same clueless condition, muddling through, struggling bravely, making little decisions with big consequences and big decisions with uncertain information, trying our best, giving our all, guessing, second guessing. And then being rewarded with a wet baby kiss, a grubby little hand on the leg, a truce with a teenage rebel, a flashed smile from a confident young face uplifted at graduation, a look of relief from a harried parent dropping off the grandchild.

In the words of Ralph Waldo Emerson, "We find delight in the beauty and happiness of children that makes the heart too big for the body." This book is dedicated to children everywhere and to the indelible marks they've left on our lives.

pregnant

photo by n. laquis harkins

elizabeth roca

Now I Lay Me Down to Wait

The worst thing anyone said to me during my pregnancy was partly my own fault. I was lying on an examining table in a paper gown, listening to my obstetrician, Dr. S, estimate the severity of my pre-term labor. I was seventeen weeks pregnant and had been experiencing strong, irregular contractions—up to eight in half an hour—for the last week. In the course of three days I had gone from working a forty-hour week to working half time to complete, flat-out bed rest. The contractions had not yet caused my cervix to dilate, but sonograms showed that it was beginning to efface. Terbutaline, indomethacin, and nifedipine, drugs often successful at halting pre-term labor, had slowed the contractions but not stopped them, and had added the unpleasant side effects of racing heart, tremor, breathlessness, flushing, and anxiety, although it was difficult for me to distinguish the drug-induced anxiety from my own, natural anxiety. No one could explain why I had gone into such early labor, except that I was carrying twins, the result of my third in vitro fertilization attempt.

After eighteen months of infertility and the accompanying rigorous treatment, I felt I should know what Dr. S really thought of my situation. I didn't quite have the courage to ask bluntly, "Am I going to miscarry?" Instead I said, "Do you think this pregnancy will continue?" Everything is in the phrasing, I realized later. "Am I going to miscarry?" would have been asking for an honest assessment. But my question, tentatively phrased as it was, was begging for reassurance. Dr. S, a young, talkative man, said, "You're young, you're healthy. I'm sure you will have a baby someday, but I'm not sure you will have these babies."

Anyone whose pregnancy has been threatened knows that each one is unique. These babies were not interchangeable with the baby of any future pregnancy, or any baby I might adopt, or any other baby at all. I wanted them fiercely, with all their already formed characteristics; the thought of losing them made me gasp. I heard little of what Dr. S said next. The only other phrase I remember is, "Eventually you will have a family, and that is your goal." I think now he was trying to get me to see the big picture, because he could offer no reassurance in the short term. His words made me cry. They jolted me out of the dreamy haze of pregnancy that I was trying so hard to maintain.

Some women experience pre-term contractions without knowing it, but I knew immediately. My husband and I were eating dinner in a tapas restaurant in Washington, D.C., when I felt a sensation that was unique but instantly familiar: a half-painful tightening of my lower abdomen, drawing in toward my navel.

"Hm," he said. "Wonder why?"

"Because it's twins, maybe? Early Braxton-Hicks?"

"Well," he said, "call the doctor tomorrow."

That was our last restaurant meal for the next four months. It was, in fact, the last day for four months that I stood upright for any length of time. And it was the last day for a long, long time that we were able to say the word "contraction" without gritting our teeth.

We wanted this pregnancy, my husband and I. I wanted it on my own, horribly. Over four or so years, I had wanted to become pregnant so badly it became difficult to think or talk or breathe normally; all of me was involved in the effort to push away the despair and rage I felt at leading a life so different from the one I wanted to lead. When I finally got pregnant, I became afraid. Afraid to believe in the pregnancy, afraid something would go wrong. It was, I felt, my luck or fate not to have a baby. Being pregnant with twins, a piece of news that elicited congratulations from everyone I told, frightened me more. Twice the risk, twice the loss.

Now that something was going wrong, I was living in a state of unsurprised dread. If I passed my hand over my belly, I contracted. Traveling to the doctor's office and sitting in the waiting room made me contract frantically, until I came to dread my appointments. A contraction I had during a sonogram showed funneling—the amniotic sac of the lower baby was pushed down into my cervix, which pinched it into a funnel shape. If that happened often enough, the sac would break. I was put on bed rest in the hope that less activity would still the contractions, and—although this theory was a point of debate among doctors—that keeping the weight of the pregnancy off my cervix would prevent it from dilating and effacing as quickly. Dr. S also put a nylon stitch, or cerclage, in my cervix to try to hold it shut. "Better to do it before it starts to happen on its own," he said. The epidural I received for the procedure stopped my contractions for a few hours. Then they started up again.

Contractions were the rhythm of my days. Dr. S felt I should have no more than four an hour, which was just possible if I lay absolutely motionless. If I moved at all, even to talk on the phone, I contracted more frequently. Going to the kitchen for food, which I tried during my first couple of days on bed rest, provoked a series of contractions that took hours to quiet. My husband began preparing my day's food before he went to work: healthy, simple things like yogurt with raisins and soy cheese sandwiches and celery stuffed with peanut butter. He left it in insulated packs set on the floor near the bed, along with quart bottles of water. Being well hydrated helps smooth out the uterus's activity, so Dr. S told me to "flood myself," and I drank up to six quarts a day. But bending over or crouching down to retrieve the food made me contract, so my husband began setting the bags on my dresser.

Sitting up to eat caused contractions, so I learned to eat lying down—slowly, and sometimes dropping food on my pillow. I got up only to use the bathroom and to shower.

Being on my feet for the length of a shower caused contractions, of course, so I began showering every other day, then every third day. Drinking all that water kept me peeing often, and I used trips to the bathroom to do something else so I wouldn't be upright too long. I got up to pee, and brushed my teeth. Fifteen minutes later I got up again, and brushed my hair. On the next trip I got a sandwich from my food bag, and so on.

I watched an awful lot of television and stroked the cat, who pressed against me, the only one happy to have me on bed rest. I talked on the phone with my friends and coworkers, who were worried and sympathetic. They understood if I started to contract and cut the call short. I cried and brooded, thinking of how far I still had to go in this pregnancy. The distance between seventeen weeks and forty weeks seemed insurmountable. Even twenty-four weeks, the point (according to Dr. S) at which the babies would reach viability, seemed unreachably far. Twenty-eight weeks was the magic number, when the babies would be mostly developed and would have a ninety-percent chance of surviving.

My mother visited a couple of times a week, bringing food and videos, and I was grateful for her company. After she left, I waited for my husband to come home from work, when he would fix us a frozen dinner and stretch out next to me to watch TV.

"I could never do that," a few people said when I described my regime. "That would be torture." At the beginning it was, especially when I wanted to do something small, like write a thank you note, and realized I would have to ask someone else to buy note cards, fetch a stamp, get my address book, and mail the damn thing. Usually that person was my husband, and he was already working full time and doing all the household chores. Little by little I gave up needs until my main interests were showering and eating. I tried to read sometimes, but my concentration was jolted by each contraction.

I didn't go as crazy as someone more social might. Still, I was sad and scared.

Each day took so long to pass, and the babies needed so many days before they could live outside my body. When I first went into pre-term labor they were tiny, measured in centimeters rather than in pounds and ounces, barely formed. I was hoping the bed rest would slow the progress of the labor to match their progress, but with each trip to the bathroom, a feeling of pressure in my bowels increased. When I asked Dr. S about this sensation, he said, "That's caused by the weight of the pregnancy on your cervix and rectum. It's not a good sign."

The babies were tiny, but already they were too much weight for my body to contain. I despaired when I thought of taking them to term, when they would be so much heavier than they were now. Also dawning was the realization that in order to maintain my pregnancy, I would have to give up almost everything pleasurable about it. During my fertility treatments I had longed to wear maternity clothes, to walk around with a big round belly and chat about my symptoms in the office lunchroom. All of that was out of the question now, and although I felt these were petty desires, I wept at their loss.

When the pregnancy was twenty-three weeks along I went into labor, and my husband drove me to the hospital, half a mile from our house. By the time I was admitted to the prenatal triage unit I was contracting every two minutes. I was given shots of terbutaline to slow the contractions back to their usual level and put in a room in the antepartum ward, which was my home for the next ten weeks.

Being on bed rest in the hospital was preferable to being on bed rest at home. I was relieved to be in a place where my condition was scrutinized minutely, with sonograms, biophysical profiles, daily monitoring sessions, and visits from the staff perinatologists as well as whichever obstetrician from my group was on duty. At first the obstetricians wanted to send me home, considering my pregnancy insufficiently endangered to warrant a prolonged hospital stay. But the perinatologists overruled them. I'm just as glad not to know what argument they used, but I imagine it was something along the lines of what one perinatologist, Dr. B, said to me my second day in the hospital: "Twins born at this stage usually don't survive."

That was the second-worst thing anyone said during my pregnancy and, of course, it made me cry. But I came to like Dr. B, an excellent doctor whose abrupt bedside manner resulted, I decided, from a combination of shyness and a desire to give his patients all the available information. I also liked his partner, Dr. M, an easygoing, fatherly man. I had mixed feelings about the five obstetricians in my group, some of whom were less friendly. Being in the hospital was like working one of the retail jobs I had held in high school and college: You saw the most varied parade of personalities.

Unfortunately, the show came with a stunning lack of privacy. Anyone was allowed to walk into my room and start talking to me, often without knocking. Doctors and nurses were to be expected, as was the technician who took my vital signs and changed my sheets. The room was only semiprivate, so I had fifteen roommates in ten weeks, and those roommates had visitors. But there was also housekeeping staff, food service staff, nutritionists, a mailman, chaplains, phlebotomists, and someone whose job it was to empty the sharps container on the wall. My feeling of invasion was increased by my inability to leave the room myself, or even to go sit in the bathroom, since I had been reduced to using a bedside commode. Anything anyone wanted to say to me, I had to lie and listen to. I sent away the physical therapist, whose exercises made me contract, and I sent away the neonatologist, whose description of babies born mid-pregnancy (intravenous nutrition, breathing assistance, brain hemorrhages) reduced me to a contracting, weepy mess, but otherwise I lay and smiled and said "please" and "thank you." These people were helping me keep my babies, and I wanted their good will.

I was put on a terbutaline pump, which delivered liquid terbutaline subcutaneously in a constant flow, with large doses given at regular intervals. The only problem with terbutaline is that the user eventually becomes immune to its effect. The remedy is a "mag wash," or a course of intravenous magnesium sulfate, which usually lasts twenty-four hours and clears out the body's receptors, rendering the terbutaline effective again. No one can predict how long it takes for any given patient to build up the immunity, so my contractions were closely observed. They remained as constant as ever, growing increasingly strong and painful. At first the nurses panicked when my hour-long monitoring sessions showed six or more contractions, but gradually they became used to my irritable uterus and offered me warm support.

I was magged, as the perinatologists said, about two weeks after I arrived at the hospital. Again, I had started labor. The mag stopped that, returning my contractions to their usual level once I had been put back on the terbutaline pump. That lasted nearly four weeks, a long time for a mag wash. Then it stopped working. I went into labor at two a.m. and had to be magged a second time. Everyone has different reactions to mag, but none of them are pleasant. I was constantly nauseous, my skin felt hot and flushed, my vision doubled, and I was too weak to sit up or roll over without help. I raised my hand once to scratch my face, and my hand fell back limply and whacked me in the eye.

Being on mag was like being in a sour dream. I felt I could deal with everything else, but the nausea and that scary weakness were too much for me. For weeks I had been sustained by the feeling that I was on bed rest by choice—that, if necessary, I could get up and walk out of the hospital like any healthy person. Mag made me feel sick and feeble, like someone truly ill. After the second round I swore I wouldn't let them mag me again, no matter what.

My friends and coworkers sent cards, flowers, food, and anything they could think of that might amuse a person with extremely limited mobility: books, videos, crossword puzzles, and all kinds of children's toys, including coloring books, Silly Putty, and a handheld, computerized Yahtzee game. The toys turned out to be popular with my visitors, who would sit on the commode lid and color or play Yahtzee.

My two mainstays were my mother and my husband. My mother visited nearly every day, and I had cause to remember that one of her best qualities is a willingness to perform boring, thankless tasks that are nevertheless vital to the person for whom they are done. She made innumerable trips down to the cafeteria to bring me treats such as cookies or fruit smoothies. Whenever I mentioned a project I thought might be diverting, like a latch hook kit, she went out and found it for me. When I showered—ten minutes, every other day—she arrived with her own thick, fluffy towels to substitute for the hospital's skimpy ones and stood outside the shower stall with my toiletries, handing them in one by one. On the day I hit week twenty-eight, a Wednesday, she brought an index card with a brightly colored 28! and taped it to the wall. I was so pleased by this that on each successive Wednesday she brought another card with that week's number and taped it below the previous one. One week when she knew she wouldn't be able to come on Wednesday, she brought the card in on Tuesday in a sealed envelope and left it with me. At midnight I opened the envelope and stuck the card on the wall, where it made a spot of warm color.

If my mother was good at remembering the little things, my husband was good in a crisis. He spent my mag washes sitting next to my bed, alternately holding my feet for comfort and wiping my face with a cool, wet washcloth. He held plastic pans for me to be sick in and emptied them in the bathroom. He lived alone in our house for those ten weeks and never complained about loneliness, or about having to handle himself all the housekeeping and financial tasks we usually shared. Except for one evening when he worked late, he came to the hospital every day of my seventy-five-day stay. He was sometimes exhausted and depressed, but he never left me alone. "Go home," I'd say. "You're tired."

"I want to be where you are," he'd reply. I never argued. I wanted him to be where I was, too. I missed him most right after he left at eight p.m., when visiting hours ended. We had slept in the same bed almost every night for eight years, and when the room was dark I felt his absence.

As the weeks dragged by, my situation became less dismal. My basic regime remained the same, but I received wheelchair privileges, which meant that a visitor could take me for a wheelchair ride around the hospital. At first my mother came and took me to the gift shop, where I bought birthday cards for my husband and some friends; later we went by the nursery and looked through the window. Sitting upright was painful, I found; after half an hour I was glad to crawl back into bed.

Some occasions were actually fun. On Halloween my mother brought in little pumpkins and paints to decorate them, and my husband brought a mechanical bat that, when hung from the ceiling, flew in circles. The nurses loved it. For my husband's birthday in early November my parents brought in a Chinese meal and gifts I had asked them to buy, and we sang "Happy Birthday" around a fruit tart topped with an unlit candle.

An unexpected benefit of bed rest was the lack of the usual physical discomforts of pregnancy. I had no trouble with retained fluids, and because I bore my full weight so seldom I rarely noticed the extra twenty-five pounds I was carrying. If I had still been commuting to work by Metro I would have been worn out; as it was, I was physically rested, if not mentally content. And I had spent almost no money on maternity clothes, although I did own a nice collection of size-large pajamas.

The twenty-eighth week was wonderful. My friends called and congratulated me, and several nurses stopped by, all smiles. Twenty-eight weeks was no longer an unimaginable summit, and it no longer seemed good enough. I wanted to get the babies further, far enough to come home right away instead of spending time in the hospital.

That week one of the things I had been dreading happened. A new patient was wheeled into my room by a nurse one evening. I couldn't see past the curtain that divided the room, but I heard her settle into bed. After the nurse left, I introduced myself. Her name was Sharon. She told me that she was nineteen weeks pregnant and that her water had broken that afternoon. "I was on the toilet," she said, "and I heard this pop, and water sprayed everywhere. It just kept gushing and gushing."

That sounded awful to me, but her voice was upbeat, so I said, "Maybe they can do something about it."

"I don't know," she said. Then someone came with a wheelchair to take her for a sonogram. When she returned to the room, she told me that the doctor had said they would have to wait and see if the amniotic fluid would replenish itself, or if the hole was too big for the sac to hold liquid anymore. This was Friday; they were planning to check her again on Monday.

Sharon was neither friendly nor unfriendly to me over the next two days. I had the impression that she was saving her energy, more even than I had to save mine. Asking about her feelings or about the baby seemed too intimate, and any other conversation would have been inane, so I didn't try to talk to her. We said good morning and that was about it. Her husband, Christian, on the other hand, poked his head around the curtain and said hello and asked how I was feeling. I knew that, for whatever reason, he liked me, and I liked him. His round, young face with its large dark eyes looked worried and sad, and I felt anxious for him.

People came to visit Sharon, bearing flowers and balloons with religious mottoes printed on them. One evening a group of women came and sat and ate food out of paper bags and talked—loudly and long past visiting hours. Their conversation centered on keeping faithful in the midst of adversity. "I feel strong," Sharon told them. "I don't know why, but I feel right. Christian keeps worrying—he's bringing me down. What's meant to happen, will happen. I know there's a plan for me and my baby."

Listening to this was agonizing. And the women stayed so late, and were so loud, and I felt so guilty each time I rolled out of bed to use the bathroom and waddled past Sharon with my huge, safe belly, that I was contracting wildly in sympathy. My routine was all off, and I felt I couldn't say anything because her situation was so dire.

On Sunday she developed an infection in her uterus. Doctors and nurses came in and out of the room and decided that she was in too much danger; she would have a progesterone gel applied to her cervix that would cause her to go into labor. The words were not spoken but implied: the baby would be born dead, or die soon after delivery.

A nurse listened to the baby's heartbeat and asked Sharon if she wanted to hear it. She said yes, and the nurse turned on the monitor so that the strong, confident thumping was audible throughout the room. I lay listening to a woman listening for the last time to her baby's heart. I listened to that tiny life, unaware of its imminent death. My face felt numb, and my whole mind was a prayer: oh no oh no oh no. Sharon was quiet. Christian was with her when a doctor came and applied the gel. The doctor told Sharon that he had ordered painkillers for her and that when she wanted one, she should ask the nurse. "Is it Tylenol?" she asked. "No," he said. "You can have Tylenol if you want it, but you'll need something stronger." I understood before he did that she was asking for Tylenol because it is the painkiller considered safe for pregnant women. Sharon was still trying to protect her baby.

"Look, this is a lost cause," the doctor said. "You should stop even thinking about it. The complications would be... There is no one in the world who can make this baby see." His voice was impatient.

Sharon and Christian were silent, my husband and I were silent. The TVs were on very loud, hers to a football game, mine to something else. After a while, she started to groan. The groaning got louder, and I could hear the whuff-whuff of her body twisting against the sheets. I contracted over and over, and kept my palm against the side of my belly, to feel the babies kicking inside.

Finally Sharon asked Christian to get the stronger drug. Two nurses came and administered it and began moving her to the ward's one private room. Her possessions were packed up, and she was wheeled out in her bed. Christian was left, gathering a few last things. I called to him, and he pulled back the curtain.

"Christian," I said, "I didn't want to bother Sharon, but I wanted to say—I'm so sorry. We're both just so sorry."

"Thank you," he said. We looked directly at each other. I felt my lips and cheeks trembling. His face was terrible with grief. Usually it is enjoyable to see your own emotions reflected on a stranger's face, but this was dreadful.

Then he dropped the curtain, and was gone.

My pleasure at the babies' presence inside me was intense. They were my constant companions, my darling playmates, whose rolls and thumps amused me. Their heartbeats were fierce and regular. The babies steadied me; they gave me a patience that was not naturally mine. I gave my body over to them. For them I lay perfectly still, pillows behind my back and between my knees. Each sonogram showed that they were healthy, always a little ahead of their growth curve, and slowly changing positions until they both ended head down, with my daughter in the A position, her head deep in my pelvis, and my son, Baby B, a little above her and on my left side.

My daughter always woke immediately after I did, squirming in response to my movements and bumping my bladder. My son was slower, more dreamy. He pushed out under my diaphragm; I pushed back; he pushed out again. I talked to the babies and longed to massage them through my skin, but that made me contract. I spent hours floating in my own thoughts, one hand lightly on my belly, the TV as background noise.

I had been afraid of having babies I wouldn't love. I loved them so much already, inside me, but picturing them skeletal, sunken-eyed, and waxy-skinned, I was afraid. Now that I had reached twenty-eight weeks, my husband and I were invited to tour the hospital's neonatal intensive care unit. It was almost certain that our babies would spend some time there, and the doctors wanted us to be prepared.

We told the nurse conducting the tour that our babies weighed about two and a half pounds each. She looked around, found an isolette, and pointed: "That baby is the size of your babies." From my wheelchair I craned my neck to see the tiny red face atop a tight bundle of blankets and knew I could love them. The baby was very small, true, but it was recognizably a baby, precious and perfect. I left the NICU happy and relieved. I was capable of a greater, more protective love than I had realized.

Now I hated having roommates. I was too tired and sad to be social, and only two or three of them were real roommates, in the sense of keeping down the television noise or sharing bathroom time. The nurses tried to help, leaving the second bed in my room empty until all the other beds in the ward were full. When they had several new patients at once, the charge nurse would ask, "Do you want a gel or a hyperemesis?", meaning I had my choice of a roommate who might go into labor in the middle of the night, courtesy of the progesterone gel that had been used on Sharon, or one who would be vomiting uncontrollably, due to severe morning sickness. Anything, I would say, except someone whose labor had started. Anyone except a patient whose water had broken. I couldn't bear to witness the loss of another baby.

Once again I woke at two a.m. with strong, regular contractions. I was thirty weeks pregnant. It was only three days after my second round of magnesium sulfate, so I assumed that my body had become completely resistant to the terbutaline.

I rang for the nurse and settled back into my nest of rough sheets and plastic-covered pillows. This is it, I thought. This is the day my babies will be born. I didn't feel the emotions I had expected to feel going into labor: not fear, not dread, not excitement. Just tired.

Two nurses appeared next to my bed holding an IV bag of glucose, an IV bag of magnesium sulfate, needles, tubing, and a catheter. I finally lost my eligibility for patient sainthood. "No," I said. I had not said that word the entire time I had been in the hospital. "I'm not going on mag again. I can't. It's too horrible."

"Honey, this is what Dr. C told us to do," one nurse said. Her name was Kim. I didn't know her well, because she worked only nights, but I liked her serious, friendly manner. Dr. C was one of the obstetricians in my group.

"Does she know it didn't even work last time?" I said. I was whining, near tears. "It didn't *work*. It's lasted three days! Call her back and tell her it didn't work!"

Kim said gently but stubbornly, "Sweetheart, we're not going to do anything against your will, but we can't do nothing."

There it was, the perfect paradox: we're not going to do anything against your will, but we can't do nothing. There was nothing better she could have said to force me to recognize the paradox within myself: I wasn't going to let them mag me again, yet I would let them do anything that would keep the babies inside me longer, even three days longer. In those three days they might gain an ounce, develop the surfactant that would make their lungs work, grow a million brain cells.

"All right," I said bitterly and lay back, smoothing the rebellious part of my mind into compliance. I couldn't feel angry at the nurses; they were only doing their jobs, and while they bustled around me, hanging up IV bags and tying an elastic band around my arm to make the veins pop, they kept up a sympathetic croon that melted my loneliness.

"Oh, sweetheart, look at your poor hands," Kim kept saying as she searched for an IV site. My hands and forearms were covered with partly healed scabs and scars from earlier IVs. "Oh, look at these battle scars. I'm so sorry." I was sorry, too, sorry for myself, but I felt a little more brave. There is nothing like knowing that someone cares about your situation to allow you to endure it a little longer.

When your day starts at two in the morning, it drags on and on; when it starts at two and includes mag, it lasts forever. This magging was worse than the others, also, in that I threw up, hour after hour, the entire time I was on it. I would spend half an hour sipping a four-ounce cup of cranberry juice; then, half an hour later, I would vomit a watery red gush. I spent the entire day clutching my little plastic sick pans, and when Dr. S came to see me, late in the day while my husband and father were visiting, I tried to persuade him to stop the mag and let my labor continue. Heavy contractions were occurring every five minutes, and I thought my water would inevitably break. Dr. S vehemently opposed that idea. "We can't just do nothing," he said. "The neonatologists would think I was crazy."

I was too dizzy and sick to argue very much, although I didn't think I would mind if the neonatologists thought Dr. S was crazy. He said, "I can't talk to you the way I would talk to my wife" (he had told me earlier about his wife's own pre-term labor and bed rest), "but if I could, I would tell you not to be stupid."

This tough talk allowed me to feel resentful of Dr. S instead of self-pitying, and I ended up agreeing to his plan, which was to inject me with large doses of terbutaline on top of the mag. Combining two tocolytics (as the drugs used to stop pre-term labor are called) could give me pulmonary edema, Dr. S informed me, but in the end nothing happened. Once again my labor slowed.

Very early the next morning, still on mag, I lay quietly crying, feeling sick and lost and hopeless. Dr. K, the obstetrician on duty, came in. She was a cheerful young woman who usually praised me for my good attitude, and she was surprised to see me crying. She sat down and told me that now we had to start thinking of my welfare and how much more treatment I could stand. "You've done a good job for these babies," she said. That was the problem; no job was good enough unless the babies went full term, which they wouldn't, which meant I had to keep hanging on until I popped.

After I passed thirty-two weeks, the change in the doctors' demeanor was remarkable. Whoever was doing rounds would come into my room smiling and say something like, "You're really coming along now!" or "These babies are going to be just fine!" The nurses came in grinning. "I've been on vacation, and when I came back and saw your name on the board, I was so glad," they would say, or, "I saw your robe hanging up from the hallway, I was so excited." I felt radiant and bridelike, basking in the attention.

It's all downhill from here, I told myself. I was still fearful, but less so. Not only were the babies safer, but I could tell by the way my body felt that I wasn't going into labor just yet. Things were too calm, too normal.

The day I really went into labor I knew it, just as I had known when I went into pre-term labor. It was the Sunday after I turned thirty-three weeks, and a friend came to the hospital bearing a baked potato stuffed with broccoli and cheese and a mango lassi she had made in her own blender. In a fit of rebellion I decided that I was going to eat sitting up, like a normal person.

We sat with a tray table between us and I experienced the unfamiliar sensation of trying to lean over my huge stomach to eat. It was wonderful to laugh and talk looking at my visitor face to face, instead of craning my neck upward. I spent an hour up, then got back into bed.

The effectiveness of the terbutaline was waning anyway, but that hour tipped the balance. Labor began once again with strong, regular contractions at two a.m., which came as no surprise. The surprise, a dreary one, was that the obstetrician on duty—again, Dr. C—was still reluctant to allow the labor to continue. She directed me to dose myself with extra terbutaline, which did nothing. I waited until the next obstetrician came on duty at seven a.m. She consulted the perinatologists, who advised her to let the labor continue; my body was wearing out, as was my resolve. My real labor progressed ridiculously slowly, as my cerclage was removed, my daughter's water broken, and pitocin administered to help me dilate. My babies were finally born that night, at 11:35 p.m. and 11:37 p.m., weighing about four and a half pounds each. I cried for the last time, feeling remorse and relief, when I saw them in the NICU, covered with breathing apparatus, IVs, and monitoring leads. I so much wished I could have carried them longer. But I had done the best I could, and they had no serious complications.

We must have seemed inappropriately gleeful, my husband and I, on our return to the hospital to see the babies. We signed in at the front desk and told the volunteer on duty that we were going to the NICU. "We have babies there," we said. The volunteer, a kind-faced, gray-haired man, looked surprised and sad. "Oh, I'm *sorry*," he said. "I'm so sorry."

"Oh no," we said. "It's going to be all right!" We were laughing as we ran for the elevator. We had learned to be happy with what was in front of us; to look at the large picture instead of the small; to take things by the week, the day, the hour, the minute.

I had gone on bed rest on August 1st; I walked again on November 27th. One hundred and nineteen days had gone by. I had lost track of the world. Although I had watched the leaves change from my hospital window, I had trouble understanding that it was nearly Christmas. I had gone into the hospital a few days after September 11th, and while I was horrified and saddened by the savagery of the terrorist attacks, I didn't fear for my personal safety as did many people around the country. My bedroom at home, my hospital room, seemed like fortresses. Lack of safety was inside my body, not outside it.

Two days after the babies were born my husband drove me home from the hospital, and at twenty-five miles an hour the car felt as if it were going too fast.

At home I saw for the first time the babies' nursery, which he had decorated in my absence. The newly refinished floor was a glowing honey color, and the walls were soft green with white trim. We had no furniture yet, but gifts began to pile up against the walls. My coworkers, in a burst of inspiration, held a shower without me, videotaping themselves unwrapping gifts and eating my favorite vegetarian foods. Thus we had everything the babies needed, and I could save my strength for visiting them in the hospital.

I found that my legs were so weak I couldn't rise from a kneeling position without assistance. To put on a pair of pants, I had to lift one leg in an effortful lunge and let it drop, aiming in the general direction of the leg hole. The bottoms of my feet were smooth and tender, and hurt after a short time standing or walking. My back ached and had a tendency to slump unless I had something solid to lean against. I had to limit the number of times I went up and down stairs every day, or by evening I was hauling myself up by the banister.

I went every day to the NICU, and walking through the hospital corridors I felt like those drawings of evolution that show a hunched-over Neanderthal eventually developing into a smooth, straight-backed modern man. I was closer to the Neanderthal end of the scale. I had the general aches and pains of birth, and I was spending most of the day in the NICU, then rising in the night to pump my breasts for milk for the babies, so I still wasn't getting enough sleep. Yet I was happy.

I felt such triumph, such power. I had accomplished the greatest work of my life. I had been tested and persevered, and had won the greatest imaginable prize. I was acutely aware of how I could have been tested and failed. The hospital chaplain and I had talked about this on one of her visits to my room. She said that she thought there was a reason some women in my situation lost their babies and some didn't. Not because of desire, because some women desperately want their babies and still lose them. It was more like steadiness of purpose, she said, a mental and physical commitment to the project. I thought my forbearance had been given to me during my fertility treatments. I was hysterical then, unwilling to accept that my husband and I were not going to conceive the way most people did. I had told only a few people about my fertility treatments, isolating myself during that difficult time. But my pregnancy problems were public knowledge, and the generous response buoyed me. Somehow, with that help behind me, I had broken through the anger and bitterness enough to endure what had to be endured during my pregnancy and to remain, despite myself, full of hope. I was grateful for that but, if I thought about it too long, pained. This was not the way I wanted my children's lives to start. Yet they had started, and three weeks later they both were home.

I saw Dr. S for my postpartum checkup six weeks after the babies were born. I waited forty-five minutes, again in a paper gown, lying on the examining table because my back couldn't support my body's weight for so long. Dr. S clearly was behind in his appointments. He breezed in, examined me and pronounced me healthy, and breezed out again. It was anticlimactic. But the last thing he said before he left the room moved me: "Send me a photo of the babies, that's all I ask. Then I can look at it and know that what I'm doing is worth it." His voice trailed away as he disappeared out the door, a man in a hurry.

I sent him a thank you card with a photo of the babies side by side in their matching car seats, both wearing sweaters knitted by their grandmother, both sound asleep. My daughter and son, Lily and Jonah. Little miracles.

judith laura
Pregnant

"It has to be a manchild," he whispered,
his hand exploring my body's questionmark.
"I know," I replied.
But in my heart I said her name.

"We'll name him John or William," he suggested.
"Michael, Benedict, Kurt, Nathaniel, Gerald,
Robert," I agreed.
Yet in my mind I said her name.

"Let's paint the nursery blue," he bellowed.
So blue, I brushed the walls
in boyish color
As my wish painted her invisible name.

"Do you want a boy or girl?" the doctor asked,
his fingers probing my ballooning belly.
"It doesn't matter," I said,
While within she pounded her name.

"It's a girl," the doctor called,
his voice bouncing in the birthing chamber.
"I know," I answered as she cried.
And aloud I said her name.

karen massey
Untitled

I've watched as the half-light arrived in its slow path, focusing silky shadows, giving way to stronger forms, and listened to the birds arrive, filling wet branches with chatter. I'm wide awake, most of the city is tangled in dreams; I'm doing nothing useful, listening to your breathing beside me and the soft rattle of the refrigerator down the hallway. Outside this window, birds build another morning while inside me embryonic cells stack together with their order and finesse. It's too soon to tell people, too early to be visible; I'll soon be swelling in the realm of midwifery care, each step so far outside the ordinary of my other life—our life *before*. I can't tell how far we'll wander, everything is altered; known roads will never seem the same. Even this rain seems new.

Six weeks along and it's still our little secret: a stranger is asleep in my body, stealing cells from my blood and keeping me awake with awe—just this unborn soul we've made a body for, this tiny being who is so early and so small and wanted wanted wanted

wende mccabe-teichert
The Orchard

This morning in the orchard
I hang secretly
among the trees
with you cradled inside
my sun swollen belly. The cherries
are so perfectly round and red,
hidden in layers upon layers of
dark green leaves. I am
stretched wide,
branches of hips and ribs reach up
forever bending and
shifting shape as
you grow. I walk heavy
among the trees, my feet
sink into the warm
morning earth. We are ripening
together
soft and sweet
like the butterfly kisses
from your tiny
eyelashes.

kristin stitz
September 12, 4 am

Dear Baby,

I chose this notebook (with a map of the NYC subway system) for your baby journal because you were conceived, and if all goes as planned, will be born, in New York City. I know that my thoughts about you and how you came into this world will always be intertwined with my thoughts about this city, and vice versa. I've been excited to tell you all about it—what we've been doing, what we've seen, how we've been feeling as we explore our new home and anticipate your birth. In my wildest dreams I never could have imagined telling you what I'm about to tell you now.

Yesterday was September 11, 2001. I wonder if you will know this date the way I know, from my parents' and grandparents' memories, December 7, 1941. Yesterday was the day of the "Attack on America," as the newscasters have taken to calling it. I'm sure you know the details—the Twin Towers of the World Trade Center were each hit by a hijacked commercial airliner. Both buildings collapsed. The Pentagon was hit by another plane, and another went down in Pennsylvania. All the work of terrorists. Thousands, no one knows how many yet, of people died here in New York City, and your father and I had an unwilling front-row seat to the whole terrible spectacle.

We chose this apartment in Brooklyn Heights because it has an incredible view across the East River to Lower Manhattan. We were intoxicated with the idea of living in the Big Apple, and nothing is more intoxicating than that view. We have a little balcony on the back of the apartment, where we can stand and gaze out at the city. I don't know many of the buildings by name, but I do recognize the Empire State Building, the Chrysler Building, and the building where your father works. The centerpiece of it all is, was, the Twin Towers. They are an imposing symbol of New York, visible from miles and miles around. Square topped and solid. Familiar to all who come here.

I was working in my office on the other side of the house when Scott called, about nine o'clock. "Look out the window," he said, "toward my building." As I walked to the back of the house, I could see what looked like hundreds of birds, flying above the harbor. They were beautiful, glowing white in the morning sun. "What is it?" I asked. "There's a rumor that a plane has hit the World Trade Center," he said. Even somewhat prepared, when I saw it I couldn't believe my eyes. Smoke was pouring out of the building, and through it I could see orange licks of flames. I turned on the TV. Tom Brokaw was already on, and he speculated that it had been a twin-engine plane. Possibly an amateur pilot who'd lost control. We all clung to our innocence for as long as we could.

As I stood on the balcony, describing the scene to Scott, I saw the second plane. For the briefest instant I thought it was a rescue plane, but it was too big, too close to the buildings. It looked so out of proportion in the skyline, so huge. I knew before it hit exactly what was going to happen, but when it took a wing dip and slammed into the south tower, I still couldn't believe it. The building looked like it had been sliced neatly in two with a thin gash, before it exploded. People below me said they heard the boom, but I was screaming too loudly. Screaming and hysterically begging your father to come home. I didn't know how many more planes were coming. I didn't know if his building would be next.

The next hour or so was a blur. I don't have the words to tell you how I felt when the first tower collapsed. I scanned the skyline for something solid behind the thick cloud of smoke and debris. It was unbelievable—that incredible, imposing, solid building that's been in every picture of the Manhattan skyline for the past twenty-five years—gone. I was crushed by the overwhelming sense of destruction, tragedy, and evil. How could such a thing happen? How could anyone do such a thing? I'm not exactly sure when or how I learned the Pentagon was hit, or when the second tower collapsed, but I do remember the moment when Scott walked in the door. He was wearing a dark blue shirt, olive khaki pants, and a tie he bought for our honeymoon. His face was red and he was drenched in sweat from his trek home across the Brooklyn Bridge, but he looked so beautiful to me.

We spent the rest of the day and well into the night glued to the television. All the networks and cable stations frantically tried to piece together what had happened, and then the beginnings of how and why. It was compelling in a horrible, gruesome sort of way. I kept turning the TV off, and then back on again. The scene outside our balcony was exactly what we saw on TV. It was a beautiful day, blue skied and sunny, but the smoke was so thick that at times we couldn't see across the river. At other times, just a column, wiping out a wide strip of sky between the other buildings. A fine white ash was falling all over Brooklyn, and the fumes were so intense that when the wind shifted across the river, I couldn't go outside without choking.

I'm sure we will learn much more about what happened in the days and weeks to come, and by the time you learn of it everything will be neatly summarized, but these are the events that will be seared into my brain forever. The thing I can't quite get my arms around is the impact this is going to have on you. What kind of world will the world be when you are old enough to take your place in it? Is this just the beginning of more violence? There's already so much, but here we've felt so protected from it all—safe in our living rooms as we watch the chaos in Serbia, Ireland, the Middle East. I feel so sad and hopeless that there is so much evil in the world. I knew it—imagine the Holocaust—but it was never right in front of me before. This is where I want to have wise words to tell you that everything will be all right. That the world will be a better place when you are born. Isn't that a mother's job, to make the world safe for her children? I wish I could find those words, but I can't. All I know is that I love you and your father fiercely, and I will do anything I can to protect you. Perhaps that love, times all the mothers and fathers in the world, will make a difference. Perhaps your generation will change the world.

I just walked out on the balcony and saw a fighter jet flying above Manhattan in the night sky. It terrified me, but I also saw a shooting star. Good night, dear baby. I love you.

brenda-fay glik
The Corridor

Down the white corridor, they chased me
the big men who decided my baby, swimming
in warm saline, would enter deformed,
who said it was time to suck her out
dismember her thumb, her nose, imperfect bowel.
Thank God for my legs that kicked
their face, raced me out of their power dungeon,
thank God I listened to my own power
unseen yet clear as their metal hands. I remember
the blank paintings on the wall as I blurred
through the exit hall, and the complete picture
of a sheer baby, the undefined love and whole
knowing that they were wrong, she would survive.
Yes her lines, her fuzzy cell, could tear with a tongue
but they would hold like a magic shaft
around her secret life, invisible destiny.
Five months pregnant, I awoke from this dream into
a nightmare. A sudden flurry of white coats
raised their charts, their dark numbers
poked my womb of knowing, fed me tonic
of mistrust. Awake or lost in their story, I fell
in fear, never let them in all the way, kept her
swallowed in my dream, close to the whisper

of silence, bones pulsing yes.
So I shut out the sounds of the white men, the cold
steel and empty screens, listened to the one floating
in velvet liquid, shielded her in my mouthy flesh, my sac
of goodness, let her love me, gave my trust to our nameless
potential, let her go if she must, held her now, learned
the moment, became the student of the wind she blew
that stormy morning when she hailed open the gates
of my bones that know who I am. I paced in labor down
the white hall with the blank pictures, warmed the corridor,
filled the frames with my own story.

lynn stearns
A Butterfly's Wings

When you were told there were four of us, that only three were likely to survive, and then only if you were lucky, I was already tired from the struggle of merely being. I was smaller, weaker than the others, and yet I was the one to feel the words, "selective reduction" pierce you like a thousand needles at once. The voices spread a venom of fear throughout your body and you held us, all of us, tighter.

The male was to be spared, they said, because he was special, unique. The decision was to be made with the three remaining, the same, except for one who was smaller than the other two. So I was to be the sacrifice, the one to give my space to the others. As I folded my limbs around my frailness and nestled in closer beneath your heart to wait, I felt your fear turn to anger.

The three seemed to forget about me as they twisted and turned, and poked constant reminders of their presence into you. I wondered if a reminder of my presence would reassure you, or encourage you to heed the words of those who said one would have to go, that there wasn't enough room for all four.

Finally, I dared to reach out to you, with hands stretched high, fingers desperately trying to caress, to convince you that the hardness of anger wouldn't help any of us. Compared to the hardy kicks of the others, my touch must have been no more than the brush of a butterfly's wings.

But as I stroked, your muscles relaxed, no longer gripping in fear or anger, and you hummed a low lullaby. It calmed all of us, though I was the only one who understood what it meant, that your decision had been made.

Against the wishes of those who in their wisdom had advised you to get rid of me, four were still present on the day when you could no longer contain us all. One girl, then the other, entered the world in rapid succession. They let out shrill complaints, echoing each other, setting the tone for how it would always be, one thinking her strength somehow was born in the shadow of the other.

The treasured boy made his entrance next, with fists clenched, feet pummeling the air. He didn't understand that he never had to fight for this moment, that no matter what, he was to be spared. There was a longer delay as the three were prodded and fondled and whisked away, and finally, your body called upon all its reserves and shoved me from my cozy cocoon, toward the light.

I was placed on your chest, across your heart, and I drew in my first breath—air that had been warmed in your lungs. It was sweet and pure, and as I exhaled, I realized that when you felt me reaching for you with tiny fingertips, your lullaby was meant to reassure me, to be a song of celebration, of what would be.

With the strength of the other three combined, I thrust my head upward to announce my arrival, and you breathed in my scent and smiled.

patricia gavin
Pickled Pregnancy Test

I think I may, I think I might
Be pregnant, but I'm just not quite
Entirely sure, because you see,
A conundrum faces me.
I bought a home pregnancy test,
Then followed directions, did my best.
I watched the stick, but what to do
Was it one line—or was it two?
One for no, two for yes
Oh, how difficult to assess,
And far too important just to guess.
I was just too emotionally involved
To see that problem easily solved.
So I renewed my anxious quest
And bought a different type of test.
It looked quite easy, no great fuss
Just distinguish a minus or a plus.
But—then there was that little dot
Indicating a valid test or not.
Once again my sight was blurred,
I was afraid that I had erred.
So—back to the store to buy a third
My palms were sweaty, my stomach churning,

Suddenly, I had a yearning.
The deli beckoned, I stopped the car,
I headed for the pickle jar.
Now I may not trust my lab technician skills,
But I accept the accuracy of dills.
My heart felt light, my nerves repaired,
I called my husband and declared
"It's confirmed, rejoice, be glad,
We're going to be a mom and dad."

cathy warner
I Knew All Along

I knew all along, but not really, that this baby I was carrying, this child who was growing large within me, kicking my ribs, shrinking my bladder, straining my back, wasn't really mine. But I didn't want to think about that because I was already so completely, thoroughly in love with this person who was coming—boy, girl, I didn't really care which. I changed for this baby. Before I even met him, or her, whatever. I swallowed vitamins the size of dachshunds and drank three glasses of milk—which I hate—every day. I gave up things I liked, like champagne at wedding receptions, and all my friends were getting married. It seemed inevitable, like catching the flu. I gave up my morning coffee, which wasn't a pretty sight. I gave up my afternoon Diet Coke, anything with caffeine. Chinese food too, after the kid spent a night doing in-utero flips on an MSG high.

The only thing I'd given up for Jeff when we got married was my apartment. I'd lived half a block from the railroad tracks plagued by shrieking trains, vomit-gold shag carpet, and too little closet space. I never missed it for a second.

This was way different. I didn't want to think about how this kid wasn't really mine. Sure it was mine to incubate, birth, breast feed, diaper, drive to soccer practice, swim lessons, and the orthodontist. Mine to rock during months of colic. Mine to teach inane songs about popping weasels and teapots stout. Mine to explain about the birds, the bees, the poison oak, nocturnal emissions, manual transmissions, and college admissions. Okay, well some of that I'd let Jeff handle. But mine, ours if you like, to pay for school pictures, summer camp, prom wear, and tuition. But not mine to keep.

And I didn't want to know this. Because I knew how much it would stab at my heart and make me want to squeeze the baby, once it was born, against my chest so tightly that neither one of us could breathe.

This is how it happened. And I suppose you could say that because I was eight and a half months pregnant, it was simply a case of raging hormones. You could say that, and under other circumstances, I'd be the first to agree with you.

A few days earlier, I'd seen one of those holiday commercials for long distance. You know, the one where the perfect mom has cookies baking in the oven and two kids playing on the swing set outside the kitchen window. She answers the phone with her oven mitts on, smiles that sweet, sad smile, sits at the kitchen table, and rests her elbow next to the flour canister. So I dialed my mother and sobbed while I told her that I was fine and did she know how much I loved her? And did I ever tell her, really tell her, that she was a good mother, despite her faults, of which there were many? Did she know that I knew, that despite all that, I was so lucky to have her for a mother?

How I wish you were here with me, I said, even though we both knew she couldn't take any more time off work and that I was so thankful she was going to fly out the second the baby was born to spend a week.

Two, she said, if I was still this weepy and unsure of myself.

In short, I was a mess.

But this was different. Like I said, it was the holidays. Christmas Eve in fact, and Jeff and I were busy being the modern couple, accommodating each other's seasonal traditions of which mine was last-minute shopping. So we were walking downtown past the outdoor ice rink, which remained a mystery to me in the fifty-three-degree evening. But it was festive and all the stores were open late and I was waddling along in my red velveteen jumper with the embroidered holly looking something like a modern Santa in the land of gender equity. Jeff was carrying packages at my side, tucking bags from the Tie Rack, Disney Store, and Crate & Barrel into the big one from Hickory Farms. I always got my grandmother beef stick and smoked cheddar. Jeff could've been an elf but he was too tall and his sweater was an olive green that actually looked pretty putrid next to Christmas red. But, hey, he was his own man, I certainly didn't dress him and there was no law that said married couples' clothing must be color coordinated, regardless of what Grandma thought.

So we were strolling, having completed the shopping, through the animated Christmas display in the plaza between the shopping center and the Hilton. Robotic reindeer and motorized Santas shook tinny bells and ho hoed while Jingle Bells and Silver Bells and Frosty the Snowman played on outdoor speakers. The tip of my nose was getting a little red so Jeff suggested we go to the Hilton bar and get some no-alcohol eggnog or hot chocolate. We ordered Warm Snugglies, mine without the peppermint schnapps, and sat at a table next to the window, stirring the hot chocolate with our candy cane sticks. We looked out at the little winky lights in the potted plants and at the stars and Christmas trees made out of lights perched atop the Fairmont and Sumitomo Bank buildings. Some of the office lights were on in a pattern that Jeff thought was supposed to be a snowman. We sniffed at the fresh pine and peppermint-candy wreath wrapped around the little oil lamp at our table.

We could make one of these and take it to my parents' tomorrow, Jeff said.

Our first Christmas as official marrieds, and we'd impress the relatives with our own brand-new holiday traditions. I licked the whipped cream off my cocoa and made a toast. Here's to the three of us, I said, and patted my belly.

Now have you ever felt a pregnant woman's stomach? There's a reason it looks like a basketball. It's as hard as one. So it doesn't bounce, and it isn't filled with air. But it's packed solid with water, amniotic fluid actually. About ten gallons, it felt like, in my case. But it felt great, too, knowing that there was this shield, the Kendra—that's me—force field around my baby. An entire womb universe where everything was squishy, red, and pulsing and my voice echoing in the baby's ears at all hours of day and night assuring him or her that he or she was perfectly loved and perfectly safe.

Then Jeff reached across the table and put his hand on my hand and looked deep into my eyes and smiled. And it would've been really sappy, the kind of thing that made me reach for the Kleenex in my hormonal state, except at that moment, the baby moved and scraped something sharp, like an elbow, across the width of my belly and we both felt it. Even my jumper twitched.

Youch, I said, and then leaned toward the culprit. How many times have I told you, no roughhousing inside? Then I shook my finger. Wait until your father hears about this.

Jeff said, That's my Sumo baby, and rubbed my belly.

My ankles feel like bratwurst, I said and slipped my feet out of my loafers and onto Jeff's thighs. He rubbed the soles of my feet. Then we settled back and looked out at the lights and watched people walk across the plaza.

Jeff said, What sort of parents keep their kids out so late on Christmas Eve? about this family who was on the sidewalk in front of us.

There was a kid, a boy I think, in blue overalls, about two, who refused to climb back in his stroller and kept stretching up his arms to be carried. We could see his mother shake her head no. She had another baby strapped to her chest in a Snugli and stroked its head. Then she pushed the empty stroller in front of her and walked away. The kid threw himself on the cement and lashed his fists and feet on the pavement. You could tell he was wailing. The mother turned around, tapped her foot, and held up one finger, then two, then three. The kid stopped thrashing, but he lay face down on the cement. He didn't move. The mother folded each finger back into her fist. Please don't hit him; please don't hit him, I thought, because you never know. You wouldn't believe what I'd seen and heard since I started paying attention to kids and their parents. I held my hot chocolate between my hands and didn't move. Jeff squeezed my feet so hard, I thought he might cut off the circulation. The piano player in the bar tinkled away on Santa Claus Is Coming to Town.

Then the mother unzipped the baby carrier and lifted the baby out of the contraption. The baby stiffened and jerked and stuck out its fists and opened its mouth. I was sure it was crying. She strapped the baby into the stroller, which was too big for it. Then she rolled up the Snugli and propped it between the baby and one side of the stroller seat. Then she wheeled the stroller back toward her son, sat next to him on the cement, lifted him into her lap, wiped his cheeks and nose on the edge of her sleeve, rocked him, and kissed the top of his head. After a minute or so, they both stood up. She hoisted him onto one hip, put one arm around his waist, and grabbed the stroller with the other.

I know I learned something from that mom and that screaming kid, although I wasn't sure at the time what it was. Anyway, that's not the thing; the thing about realizing my baby wasn't really mine, that I wanted to tell you about.

Ready to go? Jeff loosened his grip on my feet and took one last sip of his drink.

Sure, I answered. After I visit the ladies' room for the eighth time tonight.

Let me know how you rate the ambience in this one, he said.

Afterward I told him that the counters were faux marble, that there were actual Kleenex boxes and two bouquets of silk plants on a counter below a makeup mirror the length of our driveway. We held hands and walked outside, through the shopping center toward the parking garage. Then we heard bells, real bells, and the sound was so much deeper, richer than the piped-in music that Jeff said, let's find out.

So we followed the sound and ended up at a carillon outside Our Lady of Perpetual Grace Cathedral. There was a plaque in front of the bell tower, but it was too dark to read. The music stopped just after we got there.

Bummer, I said and looked at Jeff who was looking at the stone steps that led up to massive wooden doors that were thrown open. Rectangles of honeyed light seeped out.

My parents were married here, he said.

No way, I said.

Way, he said. They took me here once after my first communion.

I saw some other people walk past us and into the church. Want to go in? I asked.

I don't know, he said. What if they're busy?

Just a peek, I said.

We walked up the steps and inside. Cool lobby, I said, looking at the tile mosaics on the floor.

They call it something else, Jeff said. Vestibule, maybe.

Okay, I said and stepped toward another set of open doors.

There were small sinks near each one with wet sponges inside like they were expecting a lot of people with unsealed envelopes.

It's holy water, Jeff said, and switched the Hickory Farms bag to his left hand. You cross yourself, like this. He pressed his right hand on the sponge, and then touched his forehead, his chest, and each of his shoulders.

What's it for?

I don't remember, he said.

We stepped through the next set of doors onto a red carpet that ran between two sets of polished wooden benches that had magazine racks on the backs with *Reader's Digest*-size books tucked in them. The room smelled like lemon polish and dust burning in a heater. Before I could see anything else, a scrawny old man in a faded pinstripe suit appeared in front of us.

Let me help you to a seat, he said. The service starts in fifteen minutes.

Jeff and I started to say, No really, that's okay, we're just looking. But the man looked so unsteady we thought he'd sink to the floor if we said no. I knew what Jeff was thinking, not because I'm a mind reader or anything, but because on the way home in the car, he told me. And we were both thinking the exact same thing. Which is a good sign and one of the reasons we got married.

Anyway, the man walked us down like twenty rows. The place was practically empty. He stopped about halfway down and said, How's this pew?

This is fine, Jeff said.

The man walked away. Then Jeff did this little bob thing, where one knee touched the ground on the carpet, he touched his head, chest, and shoulders again, then slid into the pew with the bag banging on his knees and scooted across the wood. I sat next to him.

What was that?

You're supposed to kneel before you sit down, a sign of respect for God, or something like that.

You didn't do that at The Chapel, I said.

We weren't in a Catholic church, he said.

I didn't know it made a difference, I said. This was only the fourth time I'd been inside a church. Once on a grade school field trip to one of the missions. Then twice in the past year to The Chapel, a little A-frame building next to this giant church auditorium over in Orange Heights. The Chapel looked a lot like the conference rooms in my office building, same padded chairs, same patterned carpet. The only difference was that there was a piano in one corner with a small brass cross on top and lots of flowers up front. My cousin, Marla, got married there last month, and before that, in March, was my grandfather's funeral, right before Jeff and I got married.

You want to stay? Jeff asked. I haven't been to Mass since I was ten. It might be kind of fun.

What the heck, I said, wondering if we were starting another family tradition.

I looked around. One whole wall had these huge metal pipes, organ, I guessed, like in the *Beauty and the Beast Enchanted Christmas* video Jeff's niece had. There were stained glass windows up high along the sidewalls, with pictures of sheep and stuff and a bearded Jesus wearing a red toga. There were rows of candles in glass holders on either side of the stage up front. Some women knelt in front of them, folded their hands like the angels on a Christmas card, lit candles, and put money in a bucket.

Did you see that? I asked Jeff. Like God doesn't listen unless you pay for long distance?

Jeff was flipping through the magazine that was in the rack. He showed me the cover. It used to crack me up that it was called the *Missal*, but then I didn't know how to spell. He flipped through the pages. And see this, Preface. I read it wrong once. I thought it said *Pie Face*, so I told Gary and every time we'd get to that part we'd try not to laugh so hard that our eyes would water and Mom would glare at us and say if we didn't simmer down we couldn't go out for donuts after mass.

And you're always telling me you were a perfect little angel, I said.

More people started coming in. When the place was about half full, a dozen people dressed in red robes filed onto the stage and sat on two benches behind one of the podiums. There were two podiums, one on each side with big hanging banners, white embroidered with gold crosses. There was a long wooden table in the middle with two big silver cups and some trays with covers on them like they give you when you order room service.

That's for Communion, Jeff said. The priest puts these wafers on your tongue. They look like miniature Frisbees and taste like wallpaper paste. But you can't have any unless you go through catechism, and then you're supposed to go to confession. He pointed to some carved wooden phone booths in one corner.

Sounds complicated, I said.

It is.

Above the stage in the middle of the wall was a huge cross, about twenty feet tall, with a bigger-than-life Jesus hanging from it. He was just about dead with an agonized expression, eyes open and blood trickling down his forehead from the wreath of thorns stuck on his head. His head drooped toward his bare chest. His hands were nailed to the arms of the cross, a sheet type thing was tied around his waist, and his ankles were tied together. It was gruesome. It was huge. There was no escaping it. My eyes kept coming back even though I didn't want to look. I thought I might barf, like when I took my prenatal vitamin on an empty stomach.

That's horrible, I said. How can you stand to look at it?

I know, Jeff said. The one at Saint Anne's scared the shit out of me at first. But you learn to tune it out. You learn to look at it and not think about what you're seeing.

The organ started. The choir sang. Some priests came out in their fancy robes and I followed along with Jeff in the booklet. He knew all this stuff, when to stand, when to kneel, what to sing, what to say. Things that I never even knew he knew. Things that he thought he'd forgotten forever. It was strange.

Then some kids came on stage dressed like sheep and donkeys, and others came in wearing little white robes and halos and began to sing. O Little Town of Bethlehem, Silent Night, and Hark the Herald Angels Sing. Songs that I only knew the first verses of. Then, from the back of the church, Mary and Joseph walked in next to a kid in brown sweats who brayed and crawled on all fours on the carpet beside them. Now, I didn't know much about church, but I did know some about the Christmas story. I knew it wasn't all Santa and Rudolph. I'd seen *It's Christmas, Charlie Brown*. Plus, my grandma had little manger scenes at her house and I used to play with the figurines, sprinkling excelsior and moving them all around the top of her grand piano. And I knew that Mary was supposed to be pregnant, just like me, only more so, and this Mary definitely did not have a pillow in her costume.

But then I cut her some slack, because this was church after all, not Lamaze, and they probably didn't want to muck up the story with lots of groaning and an actual birth scene, because there was no way that Joseph, who looked like he was about six, was going to hold Mary—who was probably twelve judging by her gaudy makeup—under the shoulders and say, Now honey, breathe with me. Hee, hee, hee, who.

Sure enough, Joseph and Mary kneeled by the empty manger while a soloist came forward from the choir and sang O Holy Night. She had one of those voices that can make the hair on the back of your neck prickle, in a good way, and that made me think of June Allyson in *The Glenn Miller Story*, who was always putting her hand to the back of her neck to feel the tingle when Glenn played Little Brown Jug, which is definitely not one of my favorites. In the Mood is my favorite. Jeff and I won a swing dance competition to it at Tuxedo Junction, where we met. Back to the point. O Holy Night was great. She totally belted out that really high part. When she finished, I looked over at Jeff and he smiled, like church was even better than he remembered it.

Then a woman I hadn't noticed before got up from the front row and handed a baby to Mary. I could tell by the way Mary rocked back on her heels that this was a live baby wrapped in that flannel blanket, not some wet 'n wipe doll. Then the kids in the halos stood in a half circle around Mary, and the choir lit candles and stood behind them, and someone lowered the lights and shone a spotlight down on Mary, Joseph, and the baby. Everyone stood up and sang *Joy to the world, the lord is come, let earth receive her king.*

I felt a little wobbly because it had been a really long day. My bladder was feeling full again and my baby was sleeping, I could tell because all was quiet on Kendra's front. Thinking about my baby got me thinking about having my baby and that got me thinking about Mary, who by some miracle had given birth on stage effortlessly. Had just been handed a baby. Here, here you go. But I could see that huge cross in the background, against the wall, behind the spotlight, everyone trying to pretend that Jesus wasn't dying up there in plain sight.

And I thought about the real Mary and how she certainly hadn't signed up for this cross thing. The part of the Bible one of the priests read that night said something like, *An angel came to Mary and said, Low* (whatever that means). *Don't be afraid because you are going to have a child. God says name him Jesus and he will be a great king.*

Isn't it like that for every woman who is going to have a baby? Mothers and grandmothers and friends and coworkers and total strangers gather around.

Don't be afraid, they say. If natural childbirth doesn't work, there's always an epidural, and if that doesn't work, a cesarean isn't really the worst thing in the world. A healthy baby, that's all that matters. And your baby will be healthy, don't worry. And he or she will be smart and brilliant because you are giving him or her the highest quality prenatal care and you will no doubt pick the right preschool and sports programs and academic enrichment camps and AP courses, and your child can grow up to be anything, even president of our great country.

And if it isn't true, if you know someone whose kid has Downs or CP or severe ADD, or epilepsy, or lost an arm to leukemia in the third grade, or was killed by a drunk driver in high school, or became a cocaine addict and flunked out of rehab until everyone gave up, or got killed in some war in a country no one here ever heard of for a reason no one here can even recall, well you just don't talk about it. What if Mary had known?

What if she'd been standing here and looked up and saw the future, this huge cross on the wall and her son hanging from it? Would she have named him something else? Paul, John, Ringo to confuse the angel? There's been some kind of mistake. This is my son George, I've never heard of Jesus. Or would she have taken off on that donkey—leaving Joseph in the dust in case he had the urge to build some cabinets in town and accidentally let it slip—and hide out in the mountains, like some crazy hermit, living where the world couldn't find her son, where he would be safe? What would she do?

She risked it. She had this wonderful baby boy. She loved him, she treasured him and someone killed him. Who? I don't know. I'd tried not to think about it before, had pushed those ugly thoughts about my baby's mortality to the back of my head. He or she was supposed to be healthy and happy until long after I was dead.

I put my hands on my belly, my baby shield. I thought about the baby, how much I loved it, how I felt like I already knew it, how I was the entire universe to it. It won't always be this way, I thought. Someday, sooner than I think, I will push this baby out and it won't be mine anymore. The world will have its way.

And I started crying as I thought of this, and rummaged through my purse for a Kleenex, when Jeff pulled one of those little purse packs from his pocket. The thought that he'd been carrying them all night for me made me even weepier. He really did love me. And he was ready to love our baby. What if I refused to have this baby, just stayed pregnant forever, not that I really could. But if I refused to let this baby out into the world where all these bad things could happen, then nothing good could happen either. This tiny creature would never get to be loved by someone else. Would never get to be held by Jeff, or by my mother, or by my grandmother, or by Jeff's parents, or his brother Gary, or Gary's wife and daughter, or by my cousin Marla. My child would miss all the people who would love him or her in the future, people we didn't even know yet.

And that's how it came to me, suddenly, this idea that I wanted to tell you about. This idea that having a baby is the ultimate act of hope. It felt sudden, and I don't believe in sudden. I hate it when I read a book and someone writes, *Suddenly it started to rain.* Because if the people had been paying any attention to their surroundings at all, instead of being wrapped up in their own little worlds, they would've noticed clues long before the drops fell. Clouds rolling in, the sky getting darker, the barometer dropping, the temperature getting colder, wind whipping up, and the too calm before the storm. If they weren't so clueless, they would've made camp instead of getting drenched.

And so I felt that maybe my realization wasn't sudden at all. Maybe there had been clues that I forgot to notice. Maybe it was the words *Faith, Hope,* and *Love* that were gold leafed in big letters on some closed wooden doors that lead to closets or other parts of the church behind the stage. Or maybe it was because this was our first Christmas being married, and it felt like the start of a history for Jeff and me, a long history. One that I wouldn't screw up just because my parents were divorced. Or maybe it was because my whole life had been building up to this moment, up to this time when I—well, Jeff too—when we would give the most precious gift we had, our baby, and trust the world to love it.

And so, watching that preteen Mary on the stage with her dark blue eyelids closed, bopping to Joy to the World with that little baby Jesus starting to squirm in her arms, I thought about God, for about the fourth time ever, and wondered if I had the slightest clue. It seemed to me that God sent children into the world to be loved. And it also seemed to me that things hadn't worked out the way God would've liked. But we were all still here, trying to figure out how to get love right. And I guess that's hope. And I guess that's enough.

The Stitching of a Baseball Thrown at Noon

janice levy

I've been with men more often than not, a scrapbook of sizes and shapes. When I wanted a baby, one bought me a rabbit.

Oh you write, they say, but what is it you *do*?

You talk too much, one says. Your head is too big.

You tilt, says another. Your right shoulder is higher than your left.

And of course, your eyes, they all say. You know, your eyes.

I close my door in spring and summer. Others soak in sunlight, drench their muscles in pools of hot water. The days are too long. I get fat and go to sleep. I like December, before it snows. But men don't stay in winter. They squint in the dusk. They say they can't breathe.

In daylight men talk without periods. They unravel like a ripped sweater. At night when their bodies lay moist, with fingers like dewy petals on my pillow, I listen to their night noises. I learn more when they sleep.

Willie takes little gulps when he sleeps, like a kitten leaping over puddles. His breath sounds like a rusty door.

His favorite poem is:

> The trouble with a kitten is
> THAT
> Eventually it becomes a
> CAT.

When Willie sleeps his toes twitch. He is never still.

Willie comes first as a rush of warm air feathering my cheeks. His hair covers one eye, his voice hums. He rubs one boot against the other like a cat's tail flicking about your legs. He holds my book, "B.J. Bat Goes To Night School," in the fold of his chest, then asks for my autograph. I sit behind a table. I am eye level with his thighs.

Willie works as a messenger on roller blades. He gets big tips from guys in shiny suits with twisted noses. "Shit happens," he says. "I just move it around." He graduated from the University of Washington and came to Manhattan because he loved Woody Allen. He buys five copies of my book and takes my hand as we leave the bookstore. "I've never met a real writer," he says. "Do you know Stephen King?"

Willie is twenty-five. He lives sometimes with a waitress who likes orange nail polish and sleeps with cotton between her toes. She said he squished all the air out of her, that his muscles got in the way. She insisted on being on top.

She'd done all right, he says. Made my rocks slam dance around the moon.

But then she sighed, he says. And looked at me and yawned. Just like she had finished a second shift.

"It doesn't get any better than this," Willie says, his voice muffled, his mouth full of me under the covers. He pounces swiftly like a cheetah, then pulls back and savors me with tiny bites, his skin silky with sweat. For three days we stay indoors. I keep the windows shuttered, the lights turned low. Throw rugs absorb the glare from floors and table tops. The base of my spine is sore.

My clock flashes the time across the room in big, sharp numbers. We order in greasy heroes. We don't change the sheets. We don't stop to shower.

I am forty-four, but look fifteen years younger. My hair has no gray and my face is completely smooth, even at the corners of my eyes.

I show Willie my glasses, in a dozen tints of red and magenta. It's the cones, I explain. I have no cones in my eyes. My glasses change the day to night. Without them I am blind.

At dusk and when the moon and stars glimmer, I see the best.

Like the bat, Willie says. Cool.

Willie comes and goes, unannounced like a cat. He shows up with pizza at five minutes to nine to watch *Friends*. He wanders around my place during commercials, plays with the fringes of my carpet, straightens the books on my shelves.

"What are you looking for?" I ask.

"You," he says and tries on my glasses one by one.

When I was five, I say, my sister left me on the monkey bars. She threw a rock at me and made me drop my sun hat. She said I opened my mouth and blinked like a baby sparrow, but I didn't cry. Later my sister said she was just tired. Tired of pulling me into shadows.

I had a moustache in sixth grade, Willie says. They called me the Neanderthal Man. The principal wiped my bloody face and made me rest against the pillows of her leather couch. She smelled like oranges. Her palms had callouses from playing golf. She said if she were younger she could fall in love with my face.

Willie licks my eyelashes so they look like wet snowflakes. He kisses my eyelids closed. I've always been with older women, he says. I like a woman I can sink into.

Willie lived with his father, two uncles, and three older brothers in a cabin north of Spokane, behind Polanski's Pizza. His father read Ogden Nash. His uncles went ice fishing. Once a porcupine ate our outhouse, he says. Then we ate him.

Willie wears his pants backwards, his sneakers unlaced. His flannel shirts are tied like a pirate. His underwear is always black.

When I write, Willie stands behind me and traces letters on my back. His fingers spell out "wicked."

"Say it," he says and presses my hand against his crotch. He wraps his tongue around my nipples and makes them do tricks. "Now you see them, now you don't." Then he drops to his knees and swallows my lips.

My agent wants the next chapter. I whisper instead that I have stopped taking the pill. Her voice goes up an octave.

Willie comes into the room with my black nightie over his face like a veil.

"We have to talk," I say. "I have a secret to share."

"Fine," he says. "But can we do it with my hand down your pants?"

Willie sits outside my back door, his chin resting on his knees, a pizza box at his feet. He has been waiting two hours.

"It's cool," he says, fanning my apology with his hand.

"You never call," I say. "I never know when you're coming." I drop my keys twice before opening the door.

"No problem. It's not your fault."

"Of course it's not *my* fault. You just show up. I mean, what is this?"

"Pizza," Willie says, opening the box. "With extra mushrooms."

Willie stands behind me, his fingers moving lightly on my back.

"I have a life, you know."

He undoes the buttons on my blouse with his fingers and teeth.

"No, you don't," he says. "Not really, you don't."

Later when Willie sleeps curled like a caterpillar, his knuckles between his lips, I eat four slices of cold pizza alone in my backyard. I throw green apples against my ten-foot-high fence. I stamp my feet and dance.

Willie comes one midnight, panting and famished, with scratches from the waitress on his cheeks. He sucks my breasts until he falls asleep in the crook of my arm. I slip outside with headphones and dance to Debussy's three *Nocturnes*. I will dance with my child, I think. We will throw back our heads and feel the wind through our eyes. At night we will spin ourselves silly.

Willie shines his flashlight as I dance. I am like a faun caught in headlights. I cover my face and crumple. Willie lifts my naked body and carries me into the house.

I want a baby, I weep, fumbling with my glasses. I want to dance with my child.

I tell him my reasons, the plans I have made for his sperm. Willie rolls himself like an earmuff, a tight spitball of kitten fur. I can see only the top of his head.

I whisper his name until he replies:

> If called by a panther,
> Don't anther.

Then he touches my face gently, but his kisses taste like ashes.

While Willie is gone, I get a sandbox and a toy Ferris wheel that fills with sand. I tie a swing to my apple tree and buy a plastic elephant slide. At night I turn on the sprinklers and dream of flowers growing. Always I dance.

While Willie is gone, I write another picture book. B.J. Bat screeches until her teacher's eardrums burst. My agent raises her eyebrows and says we'll do lunch soon.

While Willie is gone, I wander through furniture stores with new glasses that block out blue light. I find the cardboard telescope I squinted through to see the blackboard in sixth grade. I shave off my eyebrows. My eyes pop out like Mallomars.

I turn forty-five. I call my doctor, then place my order to be spermed: He should look like Antonio Banderas and hate Ogden Nash. His eyes should see the stitching of a baseball thrown at noon.

Willie comes back the next winter. Fatter, with whiskers, a cloth hat swooped over his ears, a strip of leather around his neck. He hands me a box of cold pizza.

You face the night, he says. You stare it down. You own it.

And you? I ask.

Willie just shivers through the blankets and touches my rounded belly as if I might break.

The waitress? I ask. Seattle?

Willie shrugs and covers the scar on his chin with his fingers, as if I had never seen it before. He sleeps with his legs around my hips like a scissor. He is so quiet I put my hand on his heart. Later I wrap a scarf around my neck, put on my spotted coat and fur mittens. I pretend I am a leopard and run among the trees of my backyard, slowly, then faster, until I find calm.

I face the bedroom window and know that he is watching. I take off my coat and stand erect, for the last time letting Willie's eyes catch the white light of my naked body.

birth

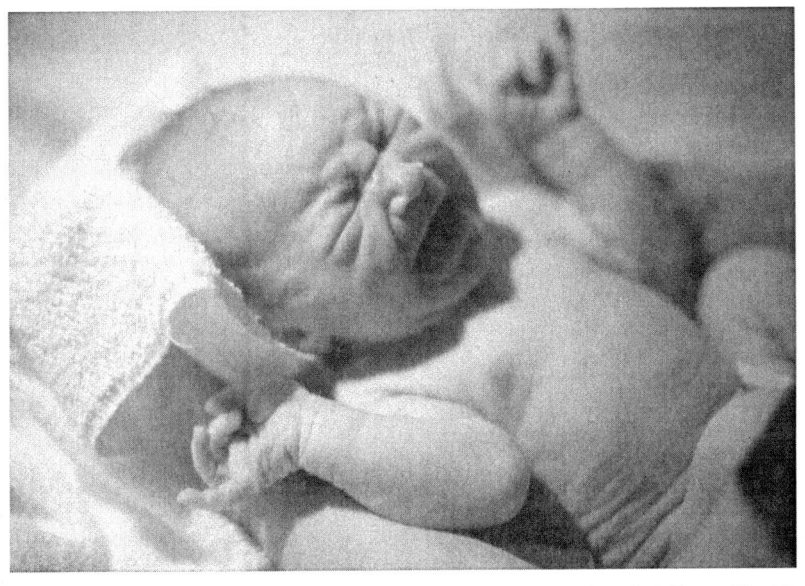

photo by jeffrey goldsmith

patricia gray
Birth

Tulips blaze yellow in the vase
as my son bursts in from school—
his fifth-grade science lesson
still glistening in his eyes. "We saw
a fetus in a jar," he says.
"His birthday was the same
as mine. I could have been
in that jar. *He* could have been
standing there, looking at *me*."
On the table behind him, a petal is
missing from one of the tulips, leaving
me a thin glimpse of stamen—like the
openings we get sometimes—like the one
my son slipped through today, blooming.

susan mckinney de ortega
from "I Married a Mexican Teenager"

There is a photo of me wandering the hospital hall, which didn't have a door, only an open entrance way, in a green gown and socks, and one of me lifting my gown to show I am wearing a diaper, ha ha. And there is Carlos on a couch in the lounge, wearing olive pants and a black button-down shirt, arms folded over his chest and looking as if someone just put a gun to his head. Then, after the pitocin kicked in, there weren't any more pictures.

The doctor brought in a backup of two doctors and two nurses to tell the crazy American lady who wanted to do everything naturally that she needed a cesarean. "*Es que eres muy grande,*" they each said in turn. "You are quite old, after all."

I was thirty-six and convinced, before they'd said a word, after five hours of laboring on my knees and vomiting into a bucket, that I did not want my baby inside of me one second longer.

"*Sáquenlo ya,*" I said, waving an arm from the bedside, where I was bent over, cheek on the sheet, taking thirty seconds of rest before the next contraction hit me like a Jersey shore wave. Take it out already. The doctors raised their eyebrows and hurried off to prepare the surgery salon.

I was out in space and there were angels all around me and one was holding my hand and she looked like Alice. Then a happy angel with a moustache *not what i expected* 53

said, "Do you want to see your baby?" and a space creature was being zoomed over my head, bloody and blinking big brown eyes. How nice, somebody clean that thing up and give me a blanket. Did I think it or say it? If I didn't get a blanket soon, somebody was going to pay. I had never been so cold in my life. Somebody had better stop that woodpecker noise in my head too. I tried to touch my face where my jaw hurt but my arm seemed to belong to someone else's body; I couldn't make it move.

"They're stitching you up now. You'll warm up soon," Alice the angel soothed. She stroked the side of my cheek and I realized my teeth were chattering so rapidly my face hurt. "Did you see? She's beautiful," Alice murmured. She? I hadn't noticed that part. I would check all the features as soon as they let me out of the block of ice they had me trapped in.

Blankets were piled on top of me and I was being wheeled through more space, and all I could feel was grateful, grateful to be warm. I thought of toast and soup and hot chocolate and standing by the hot-water heater in the basement of our house on Anderson Avenue in my snowsuit as my mother peeled my mittens off. It was nice here in space, I didn't have to think about anything, they were taking me someplace, but as long as I was warm along the way, I didn't care where it was. My ship must have had wheels—I heard them clackety-clacking beneath me. Then my blankets were being disturbed and a hand was grabbing and squeezing mine and I dropped from space, opening my eyes. Everything came into focus—some walls and closed doors we passed, a wall clock that read midnight and the face of my husband above me, wet, rapturous, trying to say many things. I could see there were a lot of words there, stuck behind his wide flat cheekbones. Tears came out in their place, until some words broke through.

"*Gracias por darme mi hija. Gracias por darme mi hija,*" my husband said, smiling a vulnerable, proud, and frightened smile as if he had just realized this pregnancy had actually produced a living creature that would require his love and care. Then his face folded in on itself again like the words behind his cheekbones were getting stuck and they turned to rain. He wiped his cheek with the back of the hand that still held mine, our fingers interlaced, like some crazy bleached-out brown and white zebra or piano keys. I forgot to notice what color the baby was. I'd only seen a mucousy, blood-streaked being flying over my head. Dora and Carmen had speculated several times in the past months about what color the baby would be.

"*Clarito*," they said in a desirous tone. "Maybe it will have blue eyes," they said as well, as if that would be the ultimate, a charm for the dark-toned family, and what envy it would inspire among their neighbors to have a clear-eyed *güero* in their midst. Carlos had said he only wanted a healthy baby, the rest didn't matter. Carlos held my hand to his chest now and kissed my cheek, my forehead. The cart I was on came to a stop and a man in white pants and a white turtleneck began to lift me from my wheeled ship. My husband slipped his arms under my legs and my back and together they moved me to a bed.

"Blankets," I said before I drifted into my first grade classroom where I was sitting next to the pinging radiator, the overhead lights bright, because it was gray outside, almost like dinner time, and snowing.

I had a child and I didn't know what she looked like! It was seven in the morning and I was fully present in the hospital room with peach and mint green curtains. There were boxes of pills on the table beside the bed and I was attached by a needle and tube to a hanging glass bottle on a pole. My husband slept open mouthed on a bench against the wall, covered only with his own jacket. I sat up, feeling the strange flaccid, bulgeless skin below my breasts and pulled my bathrobe on one-armed. I drove the pole over to the wall bench and touched Carlos's shoulder.

"Carlos, go get in the bed," I whispered. His eyes flew open. He looked like he was coming back from space, where I had been.

"I just fell asleep. They sent me out into the street for drugs for you. I spent the rest of the night looking at the baby."

"I'm going to go see her. Get in the bed."

"You can't..."

"I'm fine." I pointed at the bed but Carlos dropped back to sleep as I stood there, knees against the wall, without having moved more than his eyeballs. I took a blanket from the bed and put it over him.

There were two babies in cradles shrouded in white mosquito netting in the nursery. One had deep brown skin like my father's wing-tips and a huge head of midnight black hair like my husband's. There was black hair growing down his cheeks like Elvis sideburns and hair on his arms too, when I peeked under the blankets. Maybe that's what Carlos looked like when he was a baby, I reasoned. He turned out handsome.

The other baby was a lovely café-con-leche color with hardly any hair at all. She looked at me from enormous brown eyes laced with long, graceful eyelashes like my sister's. I looked at the bassinet nameplates, hoping for the pretty baby, already telling myself I could love the hairy one. Ortega Baby it said in black magic marker at the feet of the cow-eyed, coffee-and-cream-colored girl. She was mine.

The final photo is off-color. Carlos didn't want to startle the baby with the flash so it is taken in natural light. I am wearing the same wide smock top I wore into the hospital. I am half lying on the bench where Carlos slept, looking at the bundle next to me. A perfectly formed face shows from the blankets, the delicate, translucent eyelids closed.

"Look here," Carlos commands, camera to his face, but I can't. Only the side of my face is visible in the photo, and my arm around the bundle. I can't stop looking at her.

jacqueline jules
Prepared Childbirth

I learned every lesson in Lamaze:
how to focus on a picture instead of the pain;
how to pant and blow instead of scream.
For weeks, I practiced daily:
counting, breathing, timing, pushing—
preparing for the event which still surprised me
when the pressure of the head
crowning through the cervix,
the strangling tightness in my belly,
even blood vessels popping in my face
were nothing compared
to later sensations
of bursting inside
with love for a child
I did not need practice to hold.

viva hammer
The Demon Who Delivered Me My Daughter

Dedicated in honor of Bruria's bas mitsva and Gael's approaching the age of gvura.

Like all demons, the labor pains appeared first at night. They were so faint I barely woke; there was the sense of something pressing firmly at my back. Back labor—I knew the symptoms from the birth instructor's description, the only time I was able to use anything she taught me. As I traveled the long journey through childbirth, I found what I learned in those classes to be utterly unconnected with what I experienced. I believe a woman cannot prepare for childbirth any more than she can for death, because there is no common language between those who have passed through the gates of birth or death and those who have not yet done so.

The morning after the pains started, an ordinary Friday morning, I dutifully turned up for work, breathing deeply when the contractions came, but not bothered by them. My boss poked his head into my office and asked me to write up a memo, and for the first time in my life, I said no. Everything was left in perfect order for him, I explained, but I was in labor and it was time to leave.

None of this evoked any nervousness. There was nothing to be nervous about. The baby would come whether I exerted myself or not. No performance was being demanded of me, I would not be graded, and there would be a promotion at the end, irrespective of the standard I reached during the procedure.

If I decided to switch off, they would rip that thing out of me. There would be a thousand professionals doing their duties—I was merely the vessel for their efforts. It was a relief, really. I had been driving myself to distraction at work, proving myself in a cutthroat competitive field, desperately trying to overcome the shame of having started the job pregnant. I had stayed at work through nausea, exhaustion, depression, constipation, and high fever, imagining what they must have thought of me, disgusted with my femaleness and manifest fertility. I had transformed myself into a pregnant man, driven till my engines steamed from overuse.

The demon that had hidden its face that Friday morning returned with the darkness, and now the pressure at my back felt like a tight squeeze. My labor did not fit into any of the neat patterns the instructor had described in class. Every half hour I woke, and someone wrung my back long and hard for ninety seconds. I got out of bed each time and walked round the wall that separates the living room from the kitchen, living through the pain, knowing it, hating it, knowing that it could not be avoided, hating it, hating it. What energy it takes to be in pain.

I looked in the fridge, needing a quick fix. There they were: two fat brownies my husband Moshe had bought for a Sabbath treat. Before me sat the terrible temptations that I had fought all through the pregnancy, the desperate craving for sugar that I could never fight away, but never gave into. This time I would answer that call. I don't think I have ever devoured something with such relish, and such need. It was a powerful combination, the sugar and the chocolate and the caffeine. I fell into a deep sleep.

Relief from the pains came again with daylight. My husband was a rabbi, and that Sabbath morning he did his thing in synagogue as usual. After he came home, we smiled over how we had planned what we would do if I went into labor when Moshe was in synagogue. We do not use the telephone on the Sabbath and we weren't sure how I would contact him if I had to rush to hospital. The way things were moving at that point, he could spend two Sabbaths in synagogue before I was ready to deliver! As with everything in my life, I was a slow mover, slow and steady.

Everything I ate took a quick exit. My body was a multiuse civilian vehicle transformed into a war tank, with its weaponry trained to one target and capable of accomplishing only one mission.

More frequent visits from the demon that Saturday night, but still bearable. Round and round that living room wall I walked, as gently as I could, because the bastards downstairs had complained about my pacing the night before. That morning, the squeezer demon stayed even with the coming of the sunlight. The wring-outs continued, and I could not rest. My mother-in-law called to say that she *had* to see me that Sunday, but I told her I was busy with work, and couldn't make it. She pressed me further, and for the second time in my life, I said no.

My sister came with a truckload of baby things. I rocked on our new chair while we sorted them through, laughing and chatting nervously as the pains rose and subsided inside me.

I called my obstetrics practice when the contractions became more frequent.

"Are they coming every five minutes for thirty seconds?" the doctor on call asked, repeating the mantra we heard in the birth class.

"Not really, but it's been three days almost..."

"No, you're not ready yet if you can still tolerate the pain. I think tonight is your night, but you have a good few hours to go."

My sister went home. Ten minutes later the mucus plug slithered out, and I was seized by a pain so terrifying that I fell onto the bed. I called the doctors' office again, and someone new was on duty. She went through the whole questionnaire again about how many pains and how long they lasted, and again I failed the test.

"Look, I don't think you're ready yet," she pronounced.

"Dr. Howard, I can't bear the pain anymore. If I'm not dilated by the time I get to the hospital, I'll go back home, but I really would like to come to the hospital now."

"Okay," she agreed. "I'll meet you there at six."

I ordered a taxi, and when it arrived Moshe told me it was time to leave. I lay tightly wound up on a corner of the bed, unable to move.

"Fuck off," was all I managed. Moshe looked at me, confused. "Wasn't it *you* who ordered the car?" he asked.

When I could stand up, I limped down the stairs and slid into the car. Fortunately, the contractions slowed down with the car movement, because otherwise I would not have managed the trip without screaming. Focusing on the glove box, I did deep, controlled breathing for the two contractions that did hit me during the ride, and squeezed Moshe's hand.

Slowly, slowly I trudged though the endless hospital lobby. One foot, one foot, one foot, step, step, step. On the eighth floor they strapped me up and I waited for Dr. Howard. Only one light contraction crawled across the monitor, and she was skeptical. But when she did that critical measure, I made it: four centimeters. "I don't have to go home?"

"No, you're staying here."

We watched the monitor some more, and I writhed on the bench as the lines moved up.

"How can you ever have children after watching all this?" I asked the doctor, forever perplexed about why anyone had children, especially a woman who watched this hideous beginning every day of her life.

"This isn't a very important part of the process," she answered, and I was disgusted. How could she be so dismissive of the magisterial importance of the birth? While I sat there being measured and monitored, Moshe registered me downstairs. They gave him trouble because of our insurance, so he put me on the phone to say something lawyerly. It's extraordinary how the mind can remain tethered to earth even when the body has long gone.

Everything my friends had told me I remembered, with the heightened sense of crisis: keep going to the toilet, eat ice chips, walk as much as you can, get a birthing room, collect extra pillows, put on two hospital robes.

It was a quiet night, and both birthing rooms were empty.

"Do you want the room overlooking the Chrysler Building or the one facing east, so you can see the sunrise?" asked Valerie, the nurse assigned to me for the ordeal.

"The sunrise," I answered, because of course we would be there all night, maybe even forever, and the sunrise is so encouraging. The birthing room was attractively decorated, all wood panel, small and intimate, with a couch that converted into a bed for the significant other. In front of The Bed, hanging from the ceiling, was a television screen, and it was playing one of the *Superman* movies.

I took a few steps around the room, and a contraction came, big and round and powerful. It pressed so hard I thought I was going to burst. I gripped onto the rail at the end of the bed, put my head down, and squeezed my eyes shut. No rules here, no techniques, just survival.

"Why," I panted to Valerie, "why do I feel as if I'm going to burst?"

"That's the bag of waters, about to break."

Dr. Howard walked in "You're not moving very fast, we may have to break your waters."

"I just arrived!" I cried. "Just let me be for a while, pleeease?" I pleaded.

Always in a hurry, these professionals: get the memo out, close the file, launch the book, deliver the baby. But this time I was the client and the pace was set by me.

Moshe came in from filling in forms and having some money wrung out of him. The doctor left the room and I paced the floor once more, till the force came that pushed the bag too far and the membranes burst. Relief lasted for about a minute before the soldiers came marching in. I lay on the bed, wound up as tightly as the fetus had been before it decided to emerge. I was utterly possessed, inhabited by the contractions. All over they grabbed me, twisted my every fiber, round and round and round they twisted, and I grabbed the rail in front of me and yelled. A little time, and it started again. "Valerie! Val!" I called, and she came, and rubbed, pounded my back, fought back the demon which devoured me, breathed those rhythmic breaths, and counted the seconds till the end of the contraction.

"Only fifteen, fourteen, thirteen seconds, ten, nine, eight, oh no, here comes another one." Rolling, one on the other. I lay still on my side, and an apparition appeared, a man in a blue frock and blue shower cap, a pretty young thing.

"My name is Dr. X and I am your anesthetist," he said.

"Relax, unclasp your fingers, relax between contractions," Valerie soothed.

"Yes, that's what they say," confirmed the pretty young thing. "You should relax between the contractions."

I looked straight ahead where Superman was taking a swoop around Metropolis, and then turned back to the gentleman at my side.

"I am here to make this process easier for you. I can do a number of things. If a C-section becomes necessary, I will…" and he launched into unintelligible details.

"Valerie!" I called "Vaaaaal." It was coming again, the demon, and I needed her to fight with me. I held the rails tight and was possessed, departed from this world, yelling or silent.

"It's ending, fifteen, fourteen, thirteen, twelve..."

I ungripped the rails and watched Superman change into Clark Kent, while the man at my side persevered. "On the other hand, I can also perform an epidural. This involves threading a line through your spine and the insertion of some..."

I closed my eyes.

"I think she's checked out, doctor," Valerie said.

"Oh, is she deaf as well?" he inquired. "I noticed that her husband wears hearing aids, does she..."

"No doctor, she's not deaf. She's checked out."

It was coming again, it was coming again, it was coming all the time. I couldn't bear it anymore. I had known pain: continuous dull, aching pain; sharp, wrenching, screeching pain; I had lived with pain all my life. But this pain took the self out of me. I couldn't maintain consciousness when the contractions reached their peak.

"Moshe," I breathed slowly to my husband, "Moshe, could you ask the doctor if she could do something for the pain?" He knew that I didn't want any intervention in the labor, and he hesitated, listened to me yell once more and ran for the doctor.

Dr. Howard walked back in.

"Let me measure you," she said.

She put her hands in, felt around.

"Ten centimeters," she announced. "Get the room ready for delivery."

I had made it! Not a single alien substance had entered my body and I had borne the pain on my own. I was overwhelmed with pride.

"Get your feet onto these," someone said and they pulled me onto stirrups, while Superman flew over the Empire State, robe streaming majestically behind.

The pretty young gentleman on my left disappeared, and we were just women in the room: Dr. Howard, Valerie, another delivery nurse, and me.

There were a couple of males around the edges: Moshe, God, Superman. But while we did the work they just watched, and wrote the story.

"Okay Viva, BIG BM," the doctor ordered.

And I pushed. Oh the relief of pushing.

"Harder, big, big BM," they yelled at me.

I could feel it coming down. Now I could fight the pain, the convulsions moved with me, helped me. Pulling my legs back, squeezing my eyes shut, I pushed and worked and then:

"Viva, put your legs up here," the nurse ordered me back into the stirrups.

"No, she's got her own system there, leave her," the doctor ordered. "Viva, BIG BM."

Dr. Howard was dressed like a welder in a garage, heavy plastic curved right over her face, gloved, hair capped, not a piece of skin exposed, cutting, pulling, working quickly while the metal was soft.

Three BMs, and out it slivered. Yelling piece of sliver.

"It's a girl," the doctor said.

"Is it alive?" I asked, terrified. "Is it alive, is it alive?"

I repeated the question a hundred times. How could my horrible, twisted, malfunctioning body produce something live? How could any being survive those rolling, violent, strangulating contractions? How could anything survive my mad, anxious, hateful, exhausted, bitter pregnancy?

"Yes, she's alive, why do you keep asking? Can't you hear her?" the doctor answered, annoyed.

I pushed once again and I got rid of the real devil, that army that had invaded me and eaten me alive, that progesterone-saturated placenta. I was single again, alone, redeemed. I was like Paris in the summer of 1945, released from the noose of her Nazi occupiers.

They gave my daughter to me and I put her on my breast. For one breathtaking second we watched her, and then she sucked, and oh! for this I was born. I turned to Moshe and together we said the blessing for the birth of a girl. Then I turned my face back to watch my piece of divinity, beautiful as the day on which light was separated from darkness.

barbara a. rouillard

seeing

that evening
on the gurney to the delivery room,
I remembered I had left behind
my glasses.
had already sat up, bent over
to see the top of your head,
your dark, wet hair
between my thighs. wouldn't miss
that first clear view of your face. the nurse ran back
to get them.
you entered with wide eyes,
pale cheeks puffed out
like you were taking a deep breath
before plunging underwater. pushed your shoulders out
and then felt your warm, slippery body
slide out of me.
startled
when the doctor congratulated me
on having a daughter. I'd forgotten
you'd be a girl or a boy, seeing
I was busy
straddling some margin, teetering
on the lip of a place

free of gender, skimming
a space beyond the senses, circling, then
snapped back
with his words, "you have a daughter"
that broke in, prevented me
from seeing
the world you were just leaving.
glanced up
at the big, black and white hospital clock
on the wall beside me.
I saw it was a quarter to seven.

suzanne kamata

You're So Lucky

Dr. Nakagawa (Dr. "In the River," you translate in your head) is the man who's supposed to keep your children alive. When you first see him, the word that pops into your head is "young." He has brush-cut hair and dimples. His ample belly strains against the pink smock. From the back, you can see that he's wearing a T-shirt underneath—casual clothes when professionalism would seem to dictate button-downs and neckties. Get my babies out of here, you think. You'll take them to the Citizens' Hospital on the other side of the city, to gray-templed physicians and decades of experience. But then you see that your newborn twins are trussed up with wires and tubes. There's a long thin tube going into each tiny mouth conveying oxygen to their lungs; miniscule IV needles are threaded into their veins; there are wires linking heartbeats to monitors. Those babies aren't going anywhere. You'll have to trust this man.

Japan, the country you have lived in for ten years, has never felt so foreign as it did on the day when you were forced to check into one of its hospitals.

"Threatened premature labor," the doctor told you, and you gasped because you were only six months pregnant.

You had been planning on starting a program of Mozart and poetry in the seventh month, had already picked out a layette in the Land's End catalogue. You had just started wearing maternity clothes and ordered a gray cotton dress which hadn't even arrived yet. You had an appointment the next week with a doula recommended by your hippie friend who lives in the mountains. According to your pregnancy diary, the lungs had not yet fully developed. Your babies' eyes were still closed. One of your unborn babies is less than a pound, the other barely over two.

Most Japanese women go back to their childhood homes to give birth. They spend the early weeks of motherhood in the rooms where they first dreamed of bouquet-bearing suitors and careers in film. Their husbands go to work and make phone calls at night.

You wanted to stay near your husband, and besides, your insurance wouldn't cover childbirth in another country. You'd picked out a small women's clinic locally famous for its good food (ice cream bars every afternoon, celebratory red snapper right after the baby is born). The rooms have floral curtains and you can almost pretend you're staying at a cozy B&B instead of a hospital.

You settle in with a stack of novels and silk bed jackets. Your Japanese mother-in-law shows up every day with cream puffs and freshly laundered pajamas. She sits by your bed for hours, long after you have run out of things to say to one another.

You read, you eat, you have exams. And then the doctor tells you that you must leave. The bleeding has not abated. You'd be better off in the ward of a bigger hospital—one with incubators and a Neo-Natal Intensive Care Unit.

"I like it here," you protest. "And I like you."

The doctor shakes his head. "No. You should go."

So you are transferred by ambulance, siren singing you along the highway. Because you are horizontal, you cannot see the other cars making way.

Your mother has never seemed as far away as she does on the day you are rushed into the operating theater. A few weeks of bed rest have suddenly turned into blood running down your legs and an emergency cesarean, and you are desperate for the safe and familiar.

Fortunately, your husband is only a phone call away. He arrives shortly after the obstetrician, called in on a Saturday, still in his day-off clothes—a striped polo shirt and khakis. You see your husband long enough to tell him that you are sorry about the failure of your body to keep the babies inside. You tell him about the pain that is about to crack you apart. You press your wedding ring into his palm and then you are wheeled away.

The nurses in white run with the gurney down one corridor and the next, into a darker part of the hospital that is unfamiliar to you. There, you are handed off to another set of nurses and they take you the rest of the way.

On the operating table, you are surrounded by strangers wearing blue gauze masks and matching smocks. You look at the clock: five-thirty a.m.

The nurse tells you to curl into a ball and you do and the needle slides into your spine. You wonder if you'll be able to speak Japanese under anesthesia.

You'd expected childbirth to be something else entirely—Enya on the stereo, champagne chilling in the hospital mini-fridge, your husband's fingers kneading the small of your back. Instead, he is in another room and the obstetrician is swabbing and slicing your abdomen. There is a screen between you and the action so you can't see a thing. You feel liquid ooze and gush, and the hands of the doctor reaching into your womb. There is movement, like a fish flopping against your belly, and then a tiny mewling cry.

"*Kawaii,*" the doctor says. "Cute." But you can only imagine because your son is immediately whisked off to an incubator before you can catch a glimpse of him.

"Now we're going in for the other one," the doctor says, and he reaches for the girl who has lived beneath your heart for the past few months. And then she is taken away, too, and the worst part is over. Or so you think.

The first time you see your babies, see the swell of their eyeballs under sealed eyelids, you think "baby bird." And then you look at their thin, bowed legs and think "bull frog." Their heads, so narrow, so large in proportion to their bodies: aliens.

They have little beards, but no eyelashes. When your daughter's diaper is changed, you see that she has no labia. You can't make out the shape of their mouths which are taped to the breathing tubes.

Your husband was right. They do not look like the babies on the covers of your magazines, but you are wrenched with a violent kind of love. If you could will them back into your body, you would. You are sorry you dreaded the pain of childbirth. Let them tear you apart if they could be born again, healthy.

The nurse in charge of your boy goes about her work with the enthusiasm of a kindergarten teacher. She dances with the giant baby to the tune of Brahms's

Lullaby and takes him for "walks." She reaches into your son's incubator and waves his hand around as if he were an action figure. "*Genki da yo!*" she says in a baby boy's voice. "Don't worry! I'm fine!"

Everyone must wear a pink smock over their clothes (pink being a color found to be soothing to babies), a white cap over their hair. The parents wear masks. You have to wash your hands three times before you can touch your babies.

Every three hours, you and the other new mothers go to the Nipple Room. Okay, so it's not really called that; it has some Japanese name that you can never remember, but the Nipple Room seems apt.

All five or six of you (the number varies) sit on cushioned benches with your pajamas unbuttoned and your pink/brown nipples bared. There is none of the modesty that you've experienced in women's locker rooms in Japan. You compare and admire each others' breasts.

"Mine are so hard," one woman moans. "Feel them."

At her urging, you press the pads of your fingers against her swollen breast and indeed, it is solid.

When the nurse hands over her giant baby boy, she tickles his parted lips with her nipple, but he won't suck. "Don't sleep," she says. "Give me some relief."

You are jealous that she has a baby to suckle even if he is reluctant.

You sit there beside her eking colostrum from your own breasts. It slides into the sterilized bottle, thick and yellow, drop by precious drop. Your fingers ache. Your lily white breasts are stained with bruises.

You've heard that thoughts of babies activate the ducts, make the milk flow faster, so you think about your son and daughter.

Your boy has a slender tube through his nose going directly to his stomach. Every two hours, he is fed two milliliters of your milk. Two cubic centimeters—that's maybe a teardrop or as much dew as falls on one leaf of clover.

This morning when you sat before your daughter's incubator listening to the hum of the respirator, Dr. Nakagawa told you that she could not digest the milk. Although she, too, was fed through a tube from nose to stomach, the colostrum remains in her stomach, unprocessed. The feeding will be stopped. If she can't eat, how will she stay alive?

"I've heard that physical contact can make all the difference with preemies," your college roommate emails from New York.

You've heard that too, but you're afraid to touch your babies. You open the Plexiglas doors to your daughter's incubator and stroke her foot with one finger. She jerks away.

"I'm your mother," you whisper sadly. "I'm giving you affection."

Her eyes are still sealed shut. She cannot look at you.

You caress her arms, ever so lightly, and then her head, and then brush your fingertips over her torso. The monitor alarm goes off. You look up quickly and then snatch your hand away when you see that her heart rate has suddenly dropped from 112 beats per minute to 60.

A nurse comes running toward you, rubber soles squeaking on the floor, and then Dr. Nakagawa. "You'd better let her rest for a while," he says. Then he smiles sadly, as if to assure you that it wasn't entirely your fault.

Your mother-in-law arrives with bags of souvenirs. She has spent the previous evening preparing packages of little bean-filled cakes, oranges, and iron-supplemented soft drinks for the visitors sure to stream into your room.

"It's the seventh day," she says knowingly. "And an auspicious day on the calendar."

There is still so much that you don't know about local tradition, but you are quite sure that no well-wishers will come. Later, you will learn that the people in the office where you worked are wondering if your babies are even alive.

It is hard to decide if this is a celebratory occasion or not.

Your parents send a bouquet of flowers and a card saying "Thank you for our new grandchildren."

Your aunt calls from Michigan and her first words are "I'm so sorry."

Your mother-in-law, who has not yet seen the babies, knows only that you have provided an heir. She sits by your bed all day and puts on her social smile every time the door opens, but it is only the cleaning lady come to scrub the toilet, the handsome young intern to change your IV fluid, the nurse to take your temperature, a mischievous child who barged into the wrong room.

When your husband arrives that evening to spell her, your mother-in-law's face is heavy and sad. All of the bags that she has brought remain in a corner of the room.

A couple of days later—an unlucky day according to your mother-in-law's calendar—your hippie friend comes to visit. The nurse, with her finger to your pulse, studies him out of the corner of her eye. What must she think of this ponytailed man in a poet's blouse? Does she think that this is an assignation, a tryst? He has arrived with a tattered paperback of Anne Waldman under one arm and a bowl of salad in the other.

The nurse finishes her business and leaves and you lay against the white sheets while he feeds you freshly picked parsley, spinach, and sprouts on a fork.

You tell him about the treatment that your children are getting.

Your hippie friend who self-medicates with herbal teas says, "All those chemicals can't be good for them."

But you know that without them, your babies would die.

There is one other woman who expresses milk by hand. Her newborn son (1,318 grams and growing) is in the NICU, too. His incubator is next to your baby girl's.

One day you start talking about mothers-in-law.

"My mother-in-law," you say, "sits by my bed all day. I just want to read my book, but I feel as if I should entertain her. She's always hovering and fussing. If I so much as cough, she jumps up to throw a blanket over me even though I'm sweating. It drives me nuts."

"Mine never visits," the other woman says.

"Why not?"

"Because she blames me for this." And you know that she is referring to her own bum womb and the tiny boy behind Plexiglas.

On another day, you hear a nurse tell a story of a woman who was divorced for giving birth to a stillborn child. The husband and mother-in-law discussed it while the wife was still convalescing, still grappling with her grief, no doubt. They gave her the news the day after she was released from the hospital. You realize that the woman who annoys you so much is not so bad after all.

You walk into the NICU in your mask and smock and paper hat and the young doctor motions you to his desk.

"Your son is fine," he says. "No problem."

And then he takes out a photo done by ultrasound, shows you the blue spots that indicate blood in your daughter's lungs. He draws a picture of the heart's chambers and scratches two words above it: "ductus arteriosis." It seems that a duct in your daughter's heart has failed to close as it should have after birth. Her body has not adapted to life outside the womb; her lungs don't understand that they must now fill with oxygen. The doctor tells you that there is medication and, if that doesn't work, they can try surgery. He gives you a form to sign your consent.

You sit by her incubator longer than usual. "My little sweet pea," you say. "My darling girl." She weighs no more than a small animal—a squirrel, perhaps, or a chipmunk. You cannot imagine such a delicate being surviving cuts and sutures.

When you go back to your room, your mother-in-law is there, plumping pillows and changing the water in the vases of flowers—flowers for "congratulations" and "get well soon."

You try to smile, but your spirits are flagging. You show her the form explaining the problem and the procedure for dealing with your baby girl's heart. It is all in Japanese. You explain as well as you can that there is a duct that needs to be closed. You try to be brave and confident because you know how much your mother-in-law will worry if you aren't.

The next day when you visit your children, Dr. Nakagawa is listening to opera in his office. You can hear Italians warbling through the partition and you try to identify the music. A tragedy? A comedy? Is this one of those stories where the heroine dies consumptive at the end?

The other four babies in the NICU have been released from their Plexiglas prisons. They are given suck at intervals by cheerful moms, taken on promenades by the nurses, bathed in the stainless steel sink. If Dr. Nakagawa is worried, it's because of your children. It's because of the baby girl balanced between heaven and life on earth.

But then the young doctor emerges from his haven and smiles.

"Your son," he says, "no problem."

"And my daughter?"

"Getting better."

Yesterday's tears were tears of fear and sorrow and worry, but today's are something else altogether.

On the fourth day, the ultrasound reveals that the duct has closed completely. The treatment was a success.

So now your daughter is getting better. She is being fed breast milk. She is growing stronger.

But then the doctor tells you that although the duct in your son's heart closed on its own, it has now reopened.

"That can happen?" you ask.

"Yes, sometimes. But rarely."

You feel helpless, much like you do when an earthquake rocks your house. Everything is unpredictable, subject to chance.

You are given another form to sign. On this day you sit next to your son's incubator longer than usual.

On the day that you come home from the hospital, your next-door neighbor is weeding her flower bed. She sees you get out of the car with your little brown suitcase. She looks from your face to your diminished stomach, wipes her hands on her pants, and ambles over.

"Congratulations," she says. "A boy and a girl at once. You're so lucky."

Your neighbor had a baby just this side of forty after years of trying. She has a five-year-old girl and from what she's implied, there'll be no more children. There is an aura of envy around her.

"They're still in the hospital," you say. "They're on life support."

She waves away your concern. "They'll be fine. These days incubators are just like the mother's womb."

You reflect upon this. Inside, the body is warm and dark. The incubator is in brightly lit space. Sometimes the nurses wrap gauze around your babies' feet and hands because their extremities chill easily. Inside the body, babies are lulled by the mother's heartbeat and the sound of her voice. The NICU is a cacophony of alarms and beeps and buzzes and infants screaming in pain.

After you leave the hospital, everyone you run into asks "Why?" Why did you go into premature labor? Why were your babies born fourteen weeks early?

Your older woman friend thinks it's because you let your legs get cold. She saw you at a musical in February in a knee-length dress and nothing but nylons when you should have been wearing insulated pants.

Your boss believes it's because you walked to work each day—a five-minute saunter, if that—carrying a soft-sided briefcase containing notebooks and a magazine or two. He doesn't consider that the cigarette smoke perpetually fogging the office might have had something to do with it. You have a flashback of a cup of coffee downed at your desk in the third month and you wonder if that might be it.

Your husband thinks it's because you went to an African dance party the week before you started to bleed. You knew when you walked to the bus stop and later when you boarded the train that your husband wouldn't approve.

But he was in Hokkaido on business, and you would have been alone. Better to be among caring friends, you'd thought.

Maybe you shouldn't have moved the furniture when your husband called and said, "The new recliner will be delivered in ten minutes. Clear out a space."

But then you think about your sister-in-law who traveled to Bolivia on business in her seventh month of pregnancy, who rested her wineglass on the shelf of her stomach in between sips of Chardonnay, who actually went jogging till a few days before giving birth. Her son, your nephew, was born after two hours of labor.

Who is the freak of nature? You or your sister-in-law? And how can something so ordinary, so natural, go so wrong?

The doctor takes the tube out of your daughter's lungs. Without it, you can see that her mouth is shaped like Clara Bow's—beautiful. Until now, she has sucked on the tube for solace, but now she gapes like a fish out of water.

"Her mouth is lonely," the nurse says.

You wish you could slide your pinky between her lips.

For the first few hours, she takes regular breaths on her own. But in the days that follow, she sometimes forgets to inhale. When she stops breathing, the monitor beeps. You step aside quickly to allow the nurse to reach in and jiggle her. After a moment, her chest rises and falls, and you start breathing again, too. It takes a while to get used to it, but you do.

Soon, you are the one to reach in and remind her to breathe.

You are singing to your daughter, making up the words as you go along: "My darling child, my little peanut, my ballerina girl." Suddenly, the doors whoosh open. In comes the young doctor, a flock of nurses and a pair of incubators. Another set of twins has been born, alas, too early. You stop singing and sit frozen like a deer in headlights.

The doctor calls out for things and the nurses hand them over. Each baby is weighed. Within fives minutes, both red-skinned newborns are intubated and set up with IVs. You admire the staff's brisk competence.

This must be what it was like on the day of your babies' birth.

The new twins, you notice, two boys, are slightly larger than your son was at birth. Your daughter remains the smallest patient in the NICU. You want to seek out the parents and tell them that you know how they feel.

"But look!" you'd say. "Our boy was smaller still and now he thrives!" His mouth twitches in a smile. His hand curls around your finger.

The mother is wheeled in on a gurney, up close to the incubators. You watch her reach inside to touch each one and think, "How lucky! I had to wait till I was able to walk by myself to see my children."

But then the heart specialist is called in. He and the other doctors confer behind screens. They speak in hushed tones to the twins' parents.

When you visit two days later, one of the new twins is missing. In its place is an incubator covered with vinyl. You know that it is none of your business, but you gesture and ask, "What happened to the other one?"

The nurse frowns at you with your bad manners. She makes a stalling sound—"mmmm"—and you lower your eyes.

"Oh," you say. "Pardon me."

In that same week, another baby dies and your daughter's kidneys stop functioning.

Your daughter's face is puffy with water; her diapers remain dry. Two days ago she was delicate and slender. Now, the nurses joke that she looks like a sumo wrestler.

"We've never seen anything like this before," Dr. Nakagawa tells you. "In most cases, kidney failure occurs immediately after birth, not two months later."

"What's causing it?" you ask.

He answers with the most chilling words yet: "We don't know."

This is a country where doctors pretend to be gods, a condition that makes his frankness all the more alarming. For once in your life, you would have preferred a lie, some fake confidence.

When milk time comes around, your daughter gets nothing. She is being fed intravenously until her condition improves.

The doctor tells you that your son is almost ready to go home. You have nearly forgotten that these days will end, that you are the true guardian of the baby boy and girl in the incubators. The thought of taking care of them by yourself—the responsibility—terrifies you.

Your son begins breathing room air, unassisted. He is taken out of the incubator and installed in a Plexiglas bed. He starts drinking breast milk from a bottle and then, little by little, from the source. He cries loudly whenever he is hungry and you worry that he might be disturbing the other babies who are weaker and sicker.

Dr. Nakagawa tells you that when your baby boy reaches 2,500 grams, he can go home. He now tips the scale at 2,300.

You haven't finished preparing the nursery yet, but this news brings a bloom to your cheeks. It's been almost three months since he departed your body and you long to have him close again.

Dr. Nakagawa asks you if you'd like to schedule his release for an auspicious day on the Japanese calendar. You are not superstitious like your mother-in-law, but you know that she would be horrified if your son left the NICU on an unlucky day. You are not superstitious, but you are willing to take all the help you can get.

The medicine that the doctors prescribed for your daughter has worked. Her kidneys are functioning properly once again and her second chin has melted. Her milk intake is increased. She is getting better, but you take nothing for granted. There have been too many surprises along the way.

Every day your husband chants Buddhist sutras and you pray to another deity while on your knees.

A couple weeks later, your daughter begins to acquire the suggestion of meat around her thighs. At last, she develops labia and grows eyelashes.

By the day that your son is ready to check out of the hospital, your tiny baby girl is out of the incubator as well, engulfed in a gauze kimono and swaddled in a white bath towel. After two and a half months, she is no longer the smallest baby in the NICU. She has been breathing room air unassisted, nonstop for three days now.

You dress your son in baby clothes for the first time. The little sailor outfit is intended for a preemie, but it is roomy on your boy.

You and your husband give the NICU staff a box of cream puffs and a case of soft drinks as an infinitesimal token of your appreciation. Insurance has pretty much picked up the tab for your children's care, but you want to pay back something.

Everyone gathers round as you prepare to take your boy out. You can't speak because your throat is jammed shut by emotion. Instead, you bow and let the doctors and nurses see the tears in your eyes.

You hold your daughter a little longer than usual on this day. She looks up at you with clear gray eyes. You wonder if she will notice that her brother, her womb-mate, is no longer in the next bed, and if she will cry out in the night. Twins belong together, you think, but for now, they must separate. When she has closed her eyes and drifted into sleep, you force yourself to put her down until tomorrow morning. You tuck your son into a wicker basket with a comforter printed with a teddy bear motif. Then you carry him out the whooshing door. When you step onto the elevator with your baby-boy-in-a-basket, it feels like you are doing something illegal.

You can now hold, feed, and bathe your son whenever you want to. The nurses no longer have any say. Dr. Nakagawa's work is done. Now it's up to you to keep him alive.

It's late summer and the sun is shining on your child for the first time. Cars and trucks drive past. The grass is green. Swallows fly overhead and the sound of giggles floats over from a nearby kindergarten. Out in the parking lot, you realize that freedom can be as scary as it is exhilarating. You feel a dozen things at once, and hope is one of them.

You are beginning to think that you might be lucky after all.

dewi l. faulkner

My Daughter

Hot liquid exploded out of my body, rousing me out of near sleep. "Mywaterbrokemywaterbrokemywaterbrokemywaterbroke," I chanted at my husband. He stumbled out of bed, switched on the lamp, and began pulling on his jeans, nearly crashing face first into the dresser in the process.

"I know, honey, I know. I know what to do. Come on…up out of bed," my husband cajoled, trying to roust me out of my ranting trance.

"My water broke," I repeated, my head spinning. I could not believe how much fluid was rushing out of me. I never felt my water break with my first baby, and it took me a while to connect my sodden bed and wet thighs with the reality of the rapidly encroaching labor.

"Come on, honey. Gotta just stand up." As my husband reached over and tried to pull me out of bed by my arms, I saw two round smiling faces peeping through the crack in our bedroom door.

"Is it time?" my mother asked, leaning down to touch my face. I nodded weakly.

"My water broke."

My grandmother started clapping and laughing and doing a little victory dance, her pink nightshirt swishing against her knees as she hopped around the bedroom. It was August 8, my baby's due date, but we had all been absolutely sure she would come early. My grandma had come to stay with us for a week that turned into a month; with each passing day she was even more sure the baby would show up any minute. "Oh today Dewi, it's a full moon…today for sure." "Oh, Dewi your eyes are sparkling, tonight, I just know it." "Oh, come on! Look at you, you're ready to pop." And then finally (to my stomach), "Hey kid, what's the matter with you? We're all waiting you know!" She just couldn't bear to go home until the baby was born.

"Are we all set?" my mom asked, grabbing a bottle of massage oil. We were more than set. After three false alarm trips to the hospital, we started leaving the hospital bag and other necessities in the car. Even though I knew there was a big bath towel waiting for me on the front seat ("You're NOT breaking that water in our brand-new car," my husband had informed me, almost kidding), I grabbed another one on the way out the door; the sweatpants I had put on not twenty seconds ago were already soaked through.

"I'm so glad I was here!" my mom said, clasping her hands to her chest and grinning as we plodded down the stairs. She had driven the three hundred miles that separates my apartment in Woodland Hills from her home in Reedley a few days before, and she had almost gone back early that morning. She had missed more work than she could, and was debating going back for a day or two and then returning for a few more days and repeating this pattern until my daughter was born—hopefully not missing the big event in the process. When she had tried to leave early in the morning on August 7, her eyes had filled with tears and she said, "I just can't, I can't leave my little girl."

She wasn't there when my son was born. She had wanted to be; she had offered. But I had gotten it into my head that nobody should be at the birth except my husband and me—that if my mother was there she would just take over everything. For some reason I was on some tardy teenage quest to show my mom I didn't need her. But this time I knew I needed her. Badly.

In the car, I clutched my two towels tight against my abdomen. The contractions were coming pretty hard, and worse than that…they were coming fast.

"Here's another one!" I dug my fingers into my husband's thigh.

"Breathe sweetheart. Honey, stop holding your breath." My mother's voice was as calm as a lullaby.

"But it hurts worse when I breathe."

"Shallow sweetie, not from your stomach. And try not to wrench up your face like that. You're grimacing. That won't help."

My husband decided to chime in from the driver's seat. Without taking his eyes off the road for even a second he casually inquired, "You remember your Lamaze breathing dontcha honey?" I wanted to smack him. What did he know about breathing, or birth, or pain...or even driving?

"Jon, you do not need to go this fast!" I responded, bracing as the next contraction bathed my body in pain.

"Breathe darling; good girl! Now Dewi, Jon is only trying to get you to the hospital soon so you can have this baby. We'll be there soon, right Jon?"

"Yes we will. About another couple hours or so."

I was gonna kill him, reach right over and—

"Dewi, Jon's sense of humor is what will get you through this, concentrate on the joy and the fun in this, okay?"

"Okay. Ah! Eeeh, eeh! Yaaaa!" I belted, my spine snapping sharply toward the passenger door before recoiling back to the center of the seat.

"Good girl, sweetheart." I wanted to crawl into my mother's lap and let her take care of everything, let her make all of this go away.

On the freeway, everyone gets nervous. We're still a good fifteen minutes from Cedars-Sinai, and my contractions are thirty seconds apart. I remind my mom for the five hundredth time since we got in the car that I don't know what it feels like to have to push. When I had my son I had been given an epidural too close to delivering, and I had to "push" while I was completely numb from the waist down. "Just close your eyes and imagine you're pushing then try to make your body do what you are thinking," the doctor had said. Yeah, right.

"I know sweetie, but trust me...you'll know if you have to push. It's unmistakable, believe me."

"I think I have to push now."

At this point, Jon and my mom started speaking very quickly in hushed voices, and the executive decision was made to stop at the UCLA hospital, which was on the route to Cedars. I must hold the world's record for shortest stay in a hospital. The resident quickly examined me, after a frazzled intern had wheeled me from emergency to labor and delivery and a security guard had gruffly told my husband he "couldn't park there," and determined I was dilated to about nothing and had at least a good four hours before I would deliver.

"She had a really short labor with her first. We all have short labors in our family, are you sure it will be that long?"

"Well, I can tell you it certainly won't be before you get to Cedars…" the resident replied to my mom, her brown ponytail bobbing with med school confidence. I was wondering how old she was; I think my mom was too.

"Because her contractions are really close—thirty seconds—she said she had to push," my mom pointed out to the doctor for the fifth or sixth time. My husband stood off to the side, absently petting my hair and staring at the blood pressure instruments hanging next to the hospital bed.

"Sweetie do you feel like you can get back in the car and go to Cedars?" I looked from Mom to doctor and back: long auburn braids to pert brunette ponytail to long auburn braids.

"Okay." Back into the wheelchair, down the corridor, into the elevator, through the other corridor, past the two strung-out vagrants, out the whooshing sliding-glass doors, past the grumbling security guard, and into the car. I am completely sopping wet; my pants aren't even the same shade of gray.

In the car my mom tries to referee the blooming disagreement between my husband and me.

"Don't you remember with Brooks? You go to the ER, and then they take you up to labor and maternity."

"No, no…that is only if something is wrong! We can't go into the emergency room, it's not an emergency!"

"Honey, that is what they told us to do, I promise…"

"Jon, who is more likely to remember this correctly? Me or you?"

"Honey, you're not exactly rational right now." Probably a good thing my mom stepped in at that point.

"Dewi, dear…let's try the ER, if we aren't supposed to go there, they can just send us back to labor and maternity, okay?"

"Okay Mom."

The ER turns out to be a bust, not because it wasn't where we were supposed to be, but because we had to be "escorted" from the waiting room to the labor and delivery ward, and the "escort" was nowhere to be found. I sat in the wobbly, squeaking wheelchair silently fuming. But my mom and Jon...they quickly launched into a little good cop/bad cop.

"Excuse me, I have a daughter in active labor here. Will the escort be coming soon?" my mom asked, all sweetness and light.

"I just called him, ma'am," the slovenly front desk attendant drawled. More waiting, more horrendous contractions.

"Well, can you give us directions so we can go without the escort?" my mom tries again, with a little more edge in her voice.

"I can't let you go without an escort, ma'am, it's policy." she singsongs back, not even looking at us. Another contraction. More minutes float by. Another pregnant woman is waiting as well, but I don't see her flinching, so she is either made of steel, in very early labor, or not really in labor at all.

"Miss, my daughter is in pain here, where is the escort?"

"Let me call him again."

"Okay, look, if we were going to break your rule and go without the escort, how would we get there?" my husband shoots at the attendant, meaning business.

"I'm not going to tell you that, sir."

"This is ridiculous! Unless you get that escort here immediately, *you* will be delivering this baby," Jon shouts. The attendant ignores him; the other couple stares at us, wide-eyed, and, I think realizes we're pretty damn cool. Jon and my mom go into hushed voices and reach the third or fourth executive decision of the evening. We are going to leave the ER, cross the street, and take the long way to the maternity ward. As we are walking toward the whooshing sliding-glass doors, my mom glares at the attendant and chirps, full of syrupy bubbling sweetness, "Thank you *soooo* much for all your help."

The five-minute walk from ER to maternity is just this side of hell. I throw my head back and power walk down the halls, squeezing my eyes shut and shallow breathing for all I'm worth. I tell Jon to stop talking. Once we hit triage, I relax. Clyde is there.

"Hi Dewi! Oh! Look at your pants! This must really be it! I'm so excited for you!" the short, capable Philippino nurse exclaims.

"Hi Clyde, I think this is for real…finally," I greet her in between contractions.

"Come with me, Dewi, and we'll set you up."

My mom whispers out of the corner of her mouth, "The hospital staff knows you by name? How many times have you been here?" Jon cracks up. I try to laugh too, but can't—the contractions seem to be piling one on top of the other now, like a car accident.

"I have got to see this baby!" Clyde sings happily, "I have been listening to her heart for two months!"

Whisked from triage and tucked away in the delivery room, my mom is discussing with Jon whether or not we like the labor nurse. We all agree we wish we could keep Clyde. Our new nurse is pretty businesslike, a little cold. But I think she'll do. My mom wants her to be warmer toward me. She is trying to decide whether or not to give the nurse a piece of her mind. I don't care one way or the other; I am far too fixated on my new IV. I hate IVs; I hate this IV the most. The nurse put it in the top right side of my wrist; it hurts almost as bad as the contractions. Seconds and hours pass, my mom holds my head and brings me cool cloths, and single-handedly stops my attempts to begin divorce proceedings right there in the hospital room. I tell my mom I can't handle the pain anymore. I cry. I bite Jon's hands. I cry. I tell Jon I'm sorry I'm not brave. I cry. My mom tells me to get the epidural. She assures me there is no shame in it at all.

"But you had two children, and you never used drugs."

"I always had breaks between contractions, honey…yours are all streaming together. Get the medicine, sweetie, it's okay."

As the epidural begins to smooth over some of the ragged, searing blades of heat ripping through my insides, I let my eyelids droop and flutter and finally fall completely. When I open them again, Jon and my mom are both dozing, her balled up on the couch, him upright in a small wooden chair.

I look at Jon, who I love more than anything, who normally drives me crazy far less than my mother, but who, right now, is just making me nervous. Despite what I am going through, I feel the need to take care of him, make sure he isn't freaking out. I'm glad he is here, but I'm also glad he isn't in charge. Then I look at my mom. She looks like a wise angel; like a beautiful sage. Looking at her sleeping like that, I can't believe all the fights we have had. All the times I have been sure I have never wanted to speak to her again, *ever*. The misunderstood harsh words, the phone being slammed down so hard the console busted, the hasty recriminations flowering into torrential arguments spurred on by a smoldering stew of hormones and stress.

Looking at her that night, in that quiet room, in those precious magical moments between the beginning of labor and the birth of my daughter, I realized how much my mother truly loves me, and how much I have taken that for granted in the past. Any mistakes my mom may have made in raising me weren't due to carelessness or any sort of ignorance, as I foolishly thought in the egotistical days before I became a parent, but instead from loving me too much; weighing and choosing and debating every possible angle to the point that sometimes the wrong path was chosen. Because she loved me so much. Because all she has ever wanted, all she has ever lived for, is making the people she loves happy.

I have said horrible things to this woman. I have told her she wasn't a good mother. I have accused her of crimes of negligence, of laziness. I have said frightful things that make my skin change color just thinking about them. And yet there she was, curled up on that uncomfortable couch like a happy cat, a slight grin on her face as she dreamed happy dreams about pink dresses and lavender ribbons and baby girl giggles. My mother was like a giant salve on the raw open wound of labor. I wished I could go back in time and have her there when my son was born. I wished I could go back in time and make myself less arrogant, less stubborn...more trusting. I remember the conversation so well:

"Look Mom, I may only call you *after* the baby is born. This is a time Jon and I need together, to become a family together. I don't want anything distracting us. The labor needs to be him and me *only*. Afterward I can call you, but I don't want to have to be worrying about it beforehand. And I know this is a perfectly reasonable thing to say—I read all about it in my book."

"But you might *want* your mother there," my mom had said weakly.

And I had blown right past that statement, prattling on endlessly about statistics, and father-child bonding, and how it isn't like the old days anymore.

But what did I know about the old days? My mom gave birth to me in an army hospital in South Africa, continents away from her mother.

As misty blue light begins to dawn on August 8, the epidural starts to wear off and I can feel the final contractions coursing underneath my skin. Jon and my mom are stirring, and the kindly West Indian doctor finally makes his appearance in the room. I figure I must be close. Still unsure whether or not I am supposed to be pushing yet, I resort to begging. The doctor announces I am fully dilated and gives me permission to push. Everything changes, the doctor dims the lights, the nurse becomes nice—soothing me as I clumsily try to ease this new life out of my body; my husband stands next to my stomach, holding the bed rail and cheering me on. But it is my mother who is the star, my mother who gets me through. I catch the doctor sneaking glances at her, and I don't blame him. At six a.m., after five minutes sleep, she is glowing—radiant. Her happy green eyes are sparkling, and her dark red braids swing against a perfect, alabaster neck. The doctor doesn't say anything, but I know he is wondering if she is my sister or my best friend. Actually, she is both.

k.w. oxnard
Latitudes

Pete, a boy with shiny, wind-chapped cheeks and hair as black as his whale-skin boots, leans over her.

"It's started, Dr. Laurie."

Pete shakes her a bit more, and she waves him away with her hand. When he leaves, she sits up on the edge of her cot and stares at the wall. The thought of donning endless layers, more than the cold, makes her linger. After a few moments she begins the process that is the exact reverse of sculpting, building herself up like a clay model. Careful to work symmetrically, she starts with the silk long underwear her parents gave her as a going-away gift. They are Southern people, with only the vaguest concept of such profound cold, but they learned through a fellow Baptist that these were the best. She slides the weightless white bottoms on over her silk panties (cotton holds deadly moisture against the skin), then the top, struggling to pull the narrow collar over her head.

Next come the thin wool socks, then thick ones, and she yanks both pairs over the polypropylene liners that just cover her wide ankles. She wears the liners to bed every night in this one-room house, especially since her bout of frostbite. She looks around for her wool leggings. Originally pink, they have turned a dusty mauve for lack of washing. The temperature hasn't risen above minus ten for over two weeks, and it is too wasteful to use boiled water for laundry.

Laurie rubs the hinges of her wide, prominent jaw with her forefingers. Her face is square, with freckled, black-Irish skin and thick eyelashes. For the first time since puberty, she has given up her elaborate makeup. It bothered her for a while, even here in a village of thirty-nine. But the cold caused the oil in her liquid foundation to separate from the coffee-colored tint, and her mascara clumped from the lack of moisture. She gave it all to a few of the village children, for dress-up, but their mothers made them throw it away.

† † †

"What about some earmuffs, honey, those rabbit ones your father gave me for Christmas?"

Maureen Endicott's champagne-colored permanent shone softly in the dim lamplight of the room. It was August, and the air conditioner's hum modulated to a higher pitch. Maureen wore a powder-blue skirt and a white knit cotton top with puffy sleeves and a Peter Pan collar. Laurie always marveled at how her mother looked not ten, but thirty years younger. Maybe she thought that by dressing like a child, she could stave off the most frightening elements of life. In a way, it had worked.

"It's okay, Mama. The Indian Health Service told me hats are better," Laurie said. "You lose most of your heat through your head and feet."

"But fur is so much warmer..."

Maureen sat on the edge of the twin bed, the white eyelet cover wrinkling under her weight. Her nose was red from crying, and the puffiness around her eyes had erased the few crow's feet fanning out to her temples.

"Okay, Ma. I'll put them in."

A week later, Laurie's father drove her from their neo-Georgian brick house in the hills of Alpharetta to the Atlanta airport forty minutes away. Her fellow medical students were beginning third-year classes at Emory, but she had jumped at the chance to do a rotation in Alaska. She craved the isolation, the chance to test herself under extreme conditions. It would be the first time she'd spent out of the state. Still, her father had encouraged it.

As they approached the exit, Hank Endicott turned down the Christian radio station and tugged on his ear. Laurie had seen him do this countless times in the white clapboard church where he preached. He had told her once that at seminary they were taught never to run their hands through their hair; it made a minister look nervous. Instead, they must pinch their ear lobes, as a signal that the congregation should listen especially closely to the next part of the sermon.

Hank Endicott looked at his daughter in the rearview mirror, the tip of his long, pointy nose disappearing below the frame, and asked, "Would you please join me in prayer?"

Laurie and Maureen bowed their heads.

"Lord, our daughter is on a mission for You. She has chosen a frozen land, a land of dire poverty and great need, because she feels she can do the most good there. Help her to bring Your love to those lost souls. Please, Lord, teach Laurie that it is only You who heal, only You who drive out the evils that accumulate in our bodies. Amen."

"Amen," said Maureen.

Laurie said nothing, just nodded and watched the newest housing developments speed by. A sign said, "If you lived here, you'd be home now."

†††

It is three a.m. Laurie walks across the floor, avoiding the frigid concrete by stepping onto caribou and wolf skins—generous gifts from her Yupik patients. Two turtlenecks line the inside of Laurie's yellow sweater, and she pulls all three on in one motion, then grabs her down-filled snow pants. She is gaining speed now, sleep leaving her like a breath or sweat, quickly and not unpleasantly.

Her leather boots, lined with Gore-Tex and Thermafil, have stiffened by the door, and she winces as she laces them up and feels the after-effects of the frostbite in the toes of her right foot. It happened when she first arrived; she had stupidly forgotten one crucial layer on her feet during a quick house call on a ski mobile. Laurie drapes the stethoscope around her neck like an amulet. She's ready now, and she lifts her down parka off the wooden hook by the door. After pushing her hands into snow-stained caribou mittens, the last thing she does is grab her old-fashioned black doctor's bag before opening the door of the cabin.

†††

The acceptance letter from Emory Medical School had come on a Saturday while she was home for spring break from Mt. Zion Christian College. From her room, Laurie heard the front door slam, then the crackle of rubber on gravel as her father drove off. Her mother brought the envelope to her daughter, her expression oddly guilty.

"Laur—there's somethin' from Emory."

Maureen Endicott held the letter so taut, she looked as though she might accidentally rip it in half. Pushing the small, painted white chair away from her little-girl's desk, Laurie walked toward Maureen. She took the envelope from her mother's hands, then slit it open quickly with a painted fingernail. She leaned against the door frame, reading it over and over again and smiling while her mother just stood there, twirling the ends of her hair.

At dinner that night, her mother still said nothing as she served up freeze-dried mashed potatoes and Shake 'n Bake chicken. Hank Endicott said grace, then shook salt on his food as he spoke to his daughter.

"What's wrong with a Christian medical school?"

"Nothin', Daddy. But the ob/gyn program at Emory is world-renowned. Don't you want me to have the best training?"

"I want you to train under the guidance of good Christians. Has my ministry been lost on my own child?"

Laurie thought about all the Sundays she had helped her father prepare his sermons, proofreading them meticulously at breakfast, making last-minute suggestions. The burden of teaching the stories of Noah and Moses and Job to four- and five-year-olds, when she really wanted to be in the bio lab with her slides and cultures. The teen Bible retreats when she'd sneak away to the pond, poking a stick through algae or examining dead birds and the molted skins of snakes.

"I'm going, Daddy."

Hank Endicott, his lustrous silver hair too thin to cover a russet birthmark on his scalp, slowly finished the food on his plate. Laurie tensed the muscles of her thighs, leaning into the fight she knew was coming. But it never came. After wiping his mouth with the cloth napkin and donning the polyester suit jacket he'd hung on the back of his chair, Hank left the room. Laurie looked at her mother, but Maureen just smiled and busied herself with the dishes.

A few moments later, Laurie's father returned with a large box wrapped in gold paper and silver ribbon. He set it in front of Laurie, his small hands trembling as they placed it on the table. Laurie tore open the paper and the box, and pulled out the doctor's bag, made of dyed-black alligator skin with a brass clasp at the top. The bag was huge and anachronistic, and it made Laurie think of cartoon doctors pulling hacksaws and huge hypodermic needles out of their bags. She wanted to take it upstairs and put a few things in it, to fill its yawning insides with books and shampoo. But as she reached for it, her mother said, "No, leave it here. This means a lot to your father."

Laurie looked at her father, but Hank Endicott just prayed silently into his hands.

"Thank you, Daddy."

"It's God you should thank."

The bag stayed on the table all week, through every meal, until Laurie left to finish her senior year at Mt. Zion Christian College.

†††

The cold doesn't hit her immediately. The seal fat she has been taught to smear on her face and hands buffers her for a few moments, but eventually the wind takes effect and burns like smoke in her lungs. Laurie sees the electric light that is the only nod to modernity in this village coming from a house not a hundred feet away. She walks steadily, as careful as a mountaineer even here at sea level.

Pete hurries from the window to open the door.

"Dr. Laurie, the baby's not coming."

Laurie removes a few layers and goes over to the patient.

"How are you, Makina? Is this baby a little stubborn?"

"She knows how cold it is, Small Teeth—she's a smart one."

From the first, Makina was less reserved with Laurie than the other Yupik, bringing her into the beading circle, teasing her about her small, Caucasian teeth.

"How can you eat anything with those? You'll be hungry here. No—we must feed you like a baby, cut the seal into little pieces."

Laurie had flinched, blushing as she worked harder to complete the orange and blue earrings Makina had helped her design. As a child Laurie was teased for her plumpness, and for her loping, masculine gait, but her teeth she considered sacred. She had never needed braces, blessed with straight, even, dazzlingly white incisors. A bit dwarfed by her large head, they were her most delicate feature.

"This one is as smart as her mother, Walrus Teeth," Laurie says, laughing.

Pete is by her side, ready to hand her anything she needs. Most of the males in the village avoid Laurie. She is white, and she is best left to be cared for by the women. But Pete has followed her around from house call to house call, offering his nascent opinions, and translating for her when necessary.

"Do you feel this?" Laurie once asked Prau, an older man who had complained of pains in the lower abdomen.

"Yes, I feel your fingers."

"No, you stupid old man," Pete had said. "She means do you feel any pain?"

Prau, a sad-faced man, sat up abruptly and scolded Pete mercilessly in Yupik. When he finished, Laurie whispered to Pete, "Sometimes what the patient doesn't say is as important as what he does say."

One afternoon, Samson ran into the clinic, breathless. A short, stocky man with spiky black hair and a star-shaped scar on his left cheek, he tended the village's pack of huskies. It was Samson who rode the sled to the next town, seventy miles away, for supplies and news from Anchorage.

"Dr. Laurie, my Gresdi, Gresdi is sick!"

Laurie grabbed her instruments and was about to jump on Samson's snowmobile when she heard Pete's voice from the muddy hallway.

"Dr. Laurie, I can help. I can hand you the instruments, like on *ER!*"

Laurie stared at the boy, his snow pants already too short for his growing legs, his large, flat head cocked to one side. After a moment, she nodded.

They rode on the back of Samson's snowmobile, Pete sandwiched between them, and Laurie had to hold him down as they flew over packed snowdrifts. When they got to Samson's cottage, one of the only wooden structures in the village, Samson ran on snowshoes and opened the door. Laurie and Pete followed, and as they crossed the threshold the odor of wet fur overpowered them. Laurie coughed a bit, then asked Samson, "Which one is he?"

"She's that one, under the blanket."

It took Laurie only a minute to see that the husky had dislocated her leg, probably from straining to pull too heavy a load. As she approached the animal, Gresdi growled deeply.

"Can you calm her, Samson?"

Samson went to his dog, then crouched down and buried his face in her neck, growling himself and biting her, putting her in the submissive role. Pete stood by, mouth agape. Laurie saw her opening, so she lunged at the dog's flank and said sharply to Pete, "Pull!"

The veins in his little neck straining with the effort, Pete tugged on the dog's hind leg until Gresdi yelped in pain. Laurie felt along the socket, making sure the femur had popped back into the hip.

"You did it, Pete, it's back in!" As the three of them celebrated with some dried salmon, Laurie patted Pete on the arm. "You'll make a great orthopedic surgeon."

"What do they do?"

"They work on a lot of athletes, fix bones, backs. They make lots of money," Laurie said as she prepared a splint for the dog.

"Yeah, an orpedic surgeon."

"Orthopedic. You better study hard, then."

The pregnancy was something completely new for Pete. Yupik men didn't participate in the labor, and Pete's father had resisted the idea.

"Why do you want to do a woman's job?" he said when Laurie and Pete went to ask his permission. "It is bad for a boy to see how women work, dangerous."

But Pete had insisted, and his mother agreed.

"He'll go to school, be a doctor," Makina said, her eyes averted from her husband's gaze. "He'll come back and care for the Yupik, stay in the village. We need a doctor who will stay with us."

Larry made the decision quietly, reluctantly, nodding before he walked out of the house carrying his snowshoes under his arm.

Now Pete presides over the birth as though he has prepared for it all his young life. He watches intently as Laurie examines Makina, whose cervix is already dilated several centimeters. Makina's face is flushed with anticipation and sweat laces her upper lip. She wears her hair in two braids, which lie on her lilac acrylic sweater. Laurie runs her hands along Makina's large belly. Yes, the baby has dropped.

Laurie glances around the room, one of two in this rectangular cinder-block house. When she first arrived in Sheldon Point, these houses disappointed her. They looked like mock igloos constructed by some patronizing white architect, each block an inferior brick of artificial ice. She knew before she came that the Yupik had abandoned the romanticized hemispheres cut from the arctic floor. Still, she felt cheated somehow, like the time she went to Puerto Rico for a Christian retreat and drank a virgin piña colada made with artificial coconut flavoring.

A coal stove in the corner serves as both heater and cookstove. On the top, Pete has set a huge soup pot filled with water, just as she has asked.

"Let's see if we can't get the baby to move a little faster," Laurie says, and dips a smaller aluminum saucepan into the water to wash in. Pete brings her a bar of Ivory soap, and she smiles at him.

"Do you think it's a girl, too?" she asks.

"No, it's a boy like me. We're going to go ice fishing together, and play Batman!" Pete squats and watches Laurie intently, as though he's never seen anyone wash her hands before. When she finishes, he mimics her, right down to the way she shakes off the excess water instead of toweling them dry.

The Yupik midwife, Wanda, has begun to massage Makina's abdomen, something that no longer startles Laurie. Yupik labors are notoriously short and easy, and this rubbing seems to calm the mother.

"Which way do you think the baby is turned?"

Makina translates for Wanda, whose face has been weathered by the extreme winters into a curvilinear maze of lines. She wears traditional clothing: layers of skins that give off a musky odor. Her long silver braid is tucked into the hood of her caribou parka, which she wears even on the warmest days—a habit formed when heat came only from blubber-fueled fires, and the floors were the very tundra itself.

"She says her head will come first. She says it's slow because the head is big, and the baby's afraid to come out."

Having sterilized her forceps, a scalpel, the clamps, and surgical shears with hot water and alcohol, Laurie carries the instruments over in the rinsed saucepan and kneels at Makina's feet.

"Now, remember what we practiced? When you feel the pains, I want you to push."

Laurie says this mostly for her own benefit; she knows that Makina is in good hands with Wanda, and that she is there in case of complications only. But she reaches up and takes Makina's hand anyway, and coaches her through the next thirty minutes as the time between contractions shortens.

Pete moves closer to Laurie, and she begins to tell him about what is to come.

"Your mother's water has broken. That means the amniotic fluid that held the baby and kept it comfortable has come out of her. It's like a warm bath that you get to stay in for nine months. Then the baby turned upside down, so now she's ready to come out. Understand?"

Pete nods. "You mean he. It's a boy, remember. What are those for?" He points to the forceps.

"Sometimes the baby has a hard time coming through the birth canal. With these I can reach in and pull a little."

"Like when we pull the blubber out of the seal!"

"A little bit like that." Laurie has watched the men clean the seals after a kill. It is still hard for her to see these doe-eyed, trusting animals as food. She thinks of those awful documentaries about the bludgeonings by white fur trappers. But the Yupik hunters fascinate her, drawing out the blubber under the gleaming, liquid-like skin with one deft motion.

"Can I listen?" asks Pete, pointing to the stethoscope.

Laurie lifts the instrument over her head and places it in Pete's ears. She then takes the receiving end and lays it below Makina's navel, about where she thinks the baby's heart is.

"Can you hear?"

He shakes his head, but after a moment he jumps.

"It's so loud!"

The breaths come faster now, and Wanda has begun to chant a Yupik song.

"What is she singing about?" Laurie asks Pete, who is still entranced by the sound of his new sibling's heart.

"She says, 'Babies come from the Gods, and winter babies are the strongest.'"

Just as Wanda's voice reaches a high, sustained pitch, the baby's head appears.

"Breathe, Makina, breathe!"

Rushing over to the foot of the bed, Pete stops short when he sees the hairy, blood-covered head of the baby. Laurie reassures him with a hand on his small shoulder. In a few more minutes, half of the baby's body protrudes from Makina's canal, like an enormous chrysalis from its cocoon. Laurie won't need the forceps after all, but Pete brings over the sterilized clamps and surgical scissors as she has requested, and Wanda continues her wavering, nasal song of life. Steam rises from the baby's head, and its hands are still tucked together under its chin as Laurie knows they were in the womb.

"Sometimes, the baby even sucks its thumb in the womb," she says to Pete, who stares in awe at his sibling.

At the foot of the bed, Wanda has prepared a swaddling of furs and skins, and on top Laurie placed two clean towels. In these moments just before the birth, Laurie takes everything in: the ashy scent of the coal, Makina's steady breathing, Wanda's chants, and Pete's expectant face as he watches his mother's child emerge. After a few more pushes, the child slithers out, and Laurie holds it up by the feet, giving its back a few gentle caresses to start it breathing.

"It's a boy, Ma! You were wrong—it's a boy!"

Pete rushes up to tell his mother, then helps Laurie clean his brother. The baby is silent, writhing underneath the glare of a bare light bulb hanging from the ceiling. Laurie covers his eyes with her hand, then asks Pete to turn it off and switch on a table lamp in the unlikely shape of a mermaid. It was brought by a charity group from Anchorage, like most of the furniture in the Yupik homes.

"Are you ready?" she asks him.

"Yes."

She clamps the umbilical cord close to the child in two places, then holds it taut for Pete.

"Okay."

His small hands, already raw and ancient-looking from exposure, move the scissors steadily toward the cord. With one snip, it is done.

"Brother, you are now a Yupik." His eyes damp with pride, Pete looks at Laurie. "May I take him to my mother?"

Laurie nods. "Be careful of his neck—you have to hold his head up."

She finishes rubbing the placenta off of the baby's face, then wraps him in the skins. He is perfect, and she feels herself connected more than ever to this tiny group of people. She hears her father's words: "We are one people under God. Even those who do not yet love Him are our brothers and sisters." For the first time in her life, Laurie feels this in her bones, that shocking sameness of life here in an arctic town thousands of miles from Georgia.

Reaching under his head and buttocks, she lifts the baby boy horizontally and places him in Pete's cradling arms. Pete gazes at his brother. The baby is small and terribly red from the effort and pressure of birth. Pete stays there, not moving for a minute or so, before he walks him over to Makina. Reluctantly, he hands the baby to his mother, who welcomes him into the bed with an exhausted, radiant smile. As soon as she has guided the baby's puckered, bird-like lips to her breast, her voice changes.

"Now go and get the child's mother."

Pete answers her with a nod, throws on his parka and leaves the house. Laurie is stunned; she has forgotten about the arrangement. Her father's theories, only moments ago so reassuring, seem exposed and brittle. Feeling the sudden awkwardness of a foreigner, she turns away, leaving Wanda to tend to the spent Makina. Confused and superfluous now, Laurie cleans her instruments and rinses the towels caked with afterbirth. Before she is done, the door swings open, and a very young woman, no more than nineteen and very beautiful, walks in with Pete behind her.

"Is it true? Do I have a son?" This woman, tall among the Yupik and wearing her hair unconventionally loose around the collar of her turquoise jacket, moves anxiously toward the bed. She and her husband have no child of their own. Lately she has kept to herself, producing few of the beaded bags and jewelry needed to bring in cash for canned goods and televisions.

"Yes, sister. He's healthy, and he eats well, like a Yupik. Come see him—he looks like you."

"Hello, Bumo," says Laurie, placing a damp hand on the woman's shoulder. "He's perfect. He didn't even cry."

Wanda says something in Yupik, and Bumo translates. "She says he's good luck for our tribe—he has strength, and will know when to be silent and listen to the Gods."

The baby has stopped suckling and sleeps quietly under his skins, and Bumo lifts him gently from Makina's breast. Makina can't hold back sleep herself. Before she closes her eyes, she touches Bumo's hand and says, "Take him now, before I have time to love him too much. He's the beginning of your family. He'll make you happy." Bumo retreats as silently as she entered, taking the baby with her, and Wanda tucks the covers up around Makina's face.

Laurie wants so much to ask Makina how she can do this. How can she carry this child for so long, nurture its fluttering heartbeat, feed it by eating the seal meat and dried salmon her husband has cured over the fall months—only to give it away? She knows this practice works well for the Yupik, providing children for barren parents, relieving those with too many mouths to feed. But Laurie hears her father's voice bellowing across the latitudes, crying out against those who fail to take up their crosses, those who follow the gentle cadences of life instead of the staccato insistence of Scripture.

For a moment she feels enormous guilt. The baby is gone; the moment to protest is lost. Then she notices Pete, sitting in a metal rocking chair covered with a wool blanket. He seems unperturbed, and Laurie realizes that this child will still be like a brother to him, according to Yupik custom. Pete's knees are drawn up to his chest as he rocks back and forth, lost in the miracle that he has helped bring about tonight.

It is nearly morning now, and the two hours of pallid daylight allowed this part of the globe in winter have begun to filter through the coal-streaked window. Laurie wearily gathers the tools of her profession; they look alien in this place, too shiny and sharp-edged for the rough Alaskan life. She nods to Wanda, then enters the cold air that benefits so little from the milky rays of the arctic sun.

darcy cummings
Interphase

Even before the cord is cut, he seems
angry. Flipped on my suddenly flat gut
he threatens the air with tight fists.
The polished room echoes with reproachful screams
as I slide a timid finger along his matted
skull, feel the fierce pulse.
His cries provoke
green-masked laughter
and a tremor in my breasts.
Weary of pain,
and anxious for a smoke,
I'd like to discard him until
he's cleaned up or this weakness fades,
but he screams and shudders
until the doctor lifts him to my breast.
He nuzzles blindly.
Animal, I whisper.
The round overhead light multiplies and swings in a wide arc.
I stroke his head and whisper: son.

infertility in progress

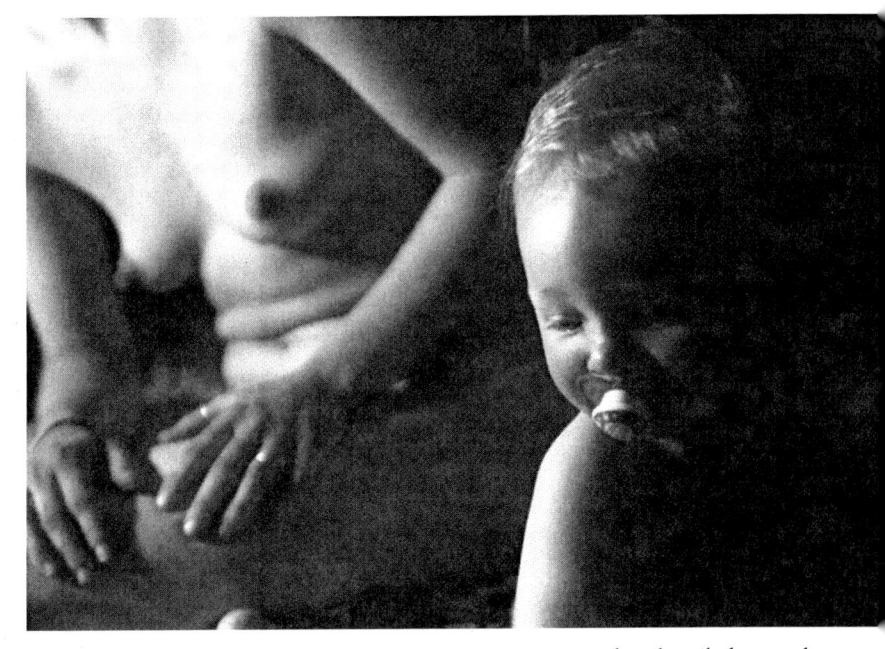

photo by mike hovancsek

anne hasselbrack
Infertility in Progress

I bought strawberries
to reconcile expectation
with failure, cycle, promise.
I did not buy the largest,
the most ripe,
a lovely cascade
of red I could not reach.
When I had another two
weeks of ghosted
sheets washing in hot water
and bleach, I bought
strawberries—
sweetness, life—
gauze tugging the crux
of my arm, and I allowed
a young man to hide them for me
in a paper sack.

tessa dratt
A Personal Relationship with God

Hadassim, Israel, 1969

I awoke to the sound of the alarm and automatically reached for the thermometer. I lay quietly on the cramped army cot supplied by the kibbutz school and counted the seconds. My daily chart had been showing a steady rise, and as I plotted my morning temperature on my graph, I realized it was now or never...

"Arnon, wake up...my temp's up. Let's do it. Hurry."

"Huh?"

"Come on, honey, we've got to do it now."

"I'm sleeping."

"You *can't* sleep. Dr. Dink told us today would be the day. Come on, let's get going."

"I'm not hard."

"Come on, Arnon, PLEASE... We've got to do it now—I need to keep my legs up for at least half an hour the doctor said."

"Five more minutes..."

"No way. Now. Here, I'll help..."

"God, I hate this."

"Don't talk, let's just do it..."

"Ummm..."

"Almost there?"

"Ummm..."

"Bingo."

I slid off my husband. Like a practiced gymnast, I flipped over on my back, lifted my legs, and propped them up against the wall. It was only five a.m., and already the heat of the day was building. No air moved in the small room, and I could feel the sweat forming on my face and under my arms. Arnon was curled up in a ball next to me, sound asleep again. I let out a slow breath and went through my ritual proposal to God:

"Dear God, give us a baby, and I promise I'll bring it up to be a good Jew. I'll keep a kosher home, I'll go to services, I'll do good deeds—anything you want, God, but just give us this baby. Look, we even came to Israel this year to work with kids—for no money—so give us a break.

"Please, God, just one little baby, and I'll never ask you for anything again."

My eyes filled as they had at this time every month for the last two years, two years of testing and fertility pills, thermometers, graphs, and sex on a schedule. Small salty streams traveled down my cheeks and over my chin to land finally on the sheet beneath my head.

Enough. I sniffled loudly, then calculated—fifteen minutes down, fifteen more to go, then off to Haifa and Dr. Dink. If we were on the road by six, with luck, and not too much traffic, we should have no trouble finding the Hasharon Hospital in Haifa and keeping our eight o'clock appointment with Dr. Jacob F. Dink, Specialist in Fertility, or was it Infertility, I always got it wrong.

For some time now, Arnon and I had been regaled with mystical tales of this good doctor's miraculous abilities. In fact, according to the wisdom of the elder kibbutz members, Dr. Dink had nothing less than a personal relationship with God. If the doctor liked a woman (and she could pay his outrageous fee), he would see to it that she would conceive promptly, with no fuss. But if, for some reason, however capricious, the doctor did not sympathize—a mole on the cheek, an unfortunately shaped nose, or an irritating manner—woe to that unhappy woman yearning for a child, because then the good doctor would not invoke his powers, and God would turn his attention elsewhere. At least, so went the kibbutzniks' stories.

Kibbutzniks, of course, had the inside scoop on just about everything—and everyone. Soon after our arrival, Arnon and I learned that there were no secrets possible here in this communal environment. Nothing and no one was safe from the serious scrutiny and concern of fellow kibbutz members. The price of a new pair of shoes was discussed with as much fervor and subject to as many diverging opinions as the issue of Shayna Leah's impending mastectomy. You couldn't sneeze in the kibbutz kitchen without having someone in the orange groves holler *"Gezundheit...Labri'ut."* If you tried to leave the premises unnoticed, Dov and Dvora, Zvee and Amitai would materialize out of nowhere to ask where you were going, what you were going to do when you got there, when you would return, and oh, could you pick up a sack of potatoes at the market or a tube of liniment at the pharmacy.

I roused myself, set the kibbutzniks aside, and shook my sleeping husband awake. We dressed quickly and hurried outside. The temperature was rising steadily, and the air was heavy and damp. Even at this early hour, the morning sun was sharply outlined against a staggeringly blue sky. As we squeezed into our battered little red Renault, Mrs. Crackapovich ran out of the adjacent house, hair askew, housedress flapping.

"Naomi, Arnon, take me to Netanya, please, and hurry."

"We can't, Mrs. Crackapovich, we have to go to Haifa and we can't make any stops."

"Oh yes, I almost forgot, Dr. Dink. Then take me only to the main road. I'll just be a minute."

"We really have to go, *now*."

We gunned the motor and took off before anyone else could waylay us. I turned my thoughts back inside, eager for signs of activity in my womb. While I knew I couldn't *possibly* feel anything happen at this stage, fertility had become an obsession. I cajoled the egg into coming down the tube, cheered on the schools of sperm swimming about eagerly, and fantasized furiously about bodily fluids mixing, matching, and mating.

Out on the Tel Aviv-Haifa road, Arnon tensed behind the wheel. Tour buses vied with communal taxis for the right of way, while drivers of ancient trucks were intently engaged in the beloved Israeli pastime of harassing the multitudes of smaller cars that swarmed in all directions like rats on the run. Curses and lewd gestures abounded, horns honked, tires screeched. I was sure that even the most aggressive Roman or Parisian would be brought to his knees on this busy Israeli road at rush hour.

By now, at seven, the heat was so intense that my shirt was pasted to the back of my seat, my hair was wet on my forehead, and I wondered if the moisture between my legs was sweat or semen. Arnon was rock silent, staring hard at the road ahead, on the lookout, I knew, for madmen on wheels. We hardly spoke. I knew better. I unwrapped a hard-boiled egg, peeled and salted it, and handed it to Arnon. I passed him a bottle of tepid *meetz tapouach*, an abomination that passed for apple juice. I, myself, could not have considered food. I didn't want to upset the precarious balance of my internal systems by initiating any major activities like digestion or peristalsis.

Arnon chain-smoked all the way to Haifa. Other than taking drags off his cigarettes, the only time he unclenched his teeth was to howl some obscenity at a passing car.

"How're you doing, Arnon?" I asked his frozen profile.

"Fine." Arnon took a last drag off his cigarette, exhaled the smoke through his nose, then flicked the butt out of the window.

"You really hate this, don't you?" I asked.

"Yeah," Arnon answered. "Yeah, I hate this a whole lot. I feel like some sort of machine. All I do these days is produce and bottle sperm."

"But...but you *do* want a kid, don't you? I mean, I'm not alone in this, right, Arnon?"

The little Renault swerved dangerously as Arnon dodged a *sherut*, one of the communal taxis, by far the worst of all vehicular hazards lose on the Israeli roads.

"Sure, I want a kid. But I want it to just, you know, to just happen. Naturally."

"But it's *not* happening, Arnon. Six years and nothing is happening."

There were tears in my voice. I caught hold of myself. If there was one thing I knew Arnon couldn't handle, it was tears.

"I'm sorry you ended up with such a defective wife."

"Maybe it's *me* that's defective, Naomi, ever think of that?"

Arnon pulled another cigarette out of the pack on the dashboard and motioned for me to give him a light.

The terrain had changed from flat to hilly, and the road had begun to climb slowly, signaling the approach of Haifa. All around us were white houses and villas, dotted with flowers and shrubs—a blessed sprinkling of color on an otherwise gray-brown palette—and soon we were able to spot the Haifa port set delicately, like a precious stone, in the turquoise sea around it. The hot air was heavy with a sweet floral scent overlaid with the sour stench of curdled milk and the fishy odor of the sea. This was the smell of Israel, and I was certain that for as long as I lived, I'd be able to summon this smell at will. It was seared into my nostrils by the heat of the Mediterranean sun.

"Arnon, slow down, we're on Hayarkon Street. See, there's the big intersection the nurse described...we'll need to take a left up ahead."

"I know, I know, I've been watching. What time is it, anyway?"

"Seven-forty-five...We're good. Now all we need to do is find the doctor's building and office. Look for Misrachi 10—a small white annex, the nurse said, right next to the large main entrance."

"Jesus, Naomi, I know. You've only given me these directions a thousand times..."

"Sorry, pal..."

At the intersection, Arnon turned to me and gave me a quick squeeze and a kiss. He was all cigarettes and sweat.

"There, honey, there's the main building. That little house must be the annex. Park right there."

"Would you just cool it, Naomi...I'm on top of this."

It was sticky inside the little annex. Antiseptic and perspiration hung in the close air. A large clock glared at us reproachfully from the wall behind a heavy-set receptionist who busily sipped her tea. She held the glass with both hands, and cradled the phone receiver between her ear and her shoulder. Eight-o-five...

"What a shame, Mamma. And how is he today?"

"Excuse me, miss, I'm Naomi Schiller and this is my husband, Arnon. We have an eight o'clock appointment with Dr. Dink for a fertility procedure...Miss? Excuse me..."

"*Rak rega, rega echad*, just a moment, one moment," said the receptionist, "Can't you see I'm busy?"

The woman continued to sip her tea cautiously, punctuating her sips with "so, *nu?*" and "so, Mamma, then what did he say?"

Eight-twenty...I stood directly in front of the receptionist, and shifted my weight from one leg to another. I desperately wanted to urinate, but was afraid as much of leaving the front desk as of losing any more of Arnon's sperm.

"Miss, please just tell us, is the doctor here?"

"*Rega*, Mamma...Mrs. Schiller, the doctor *is* here and you can go in as soon as I will be finished on the phone and take you."

"I need to see the doctor now. My appointment was for eight o'clock. Put down the phone. Call your mother later, please. Take us in."

"Mamma, I have to go. Another crazy American for Dr. Dink. Talk to you later. I love you, too. So? Yes. Yes...yes...yes, on the way home...yes. Shalom, shalom."

My desire to murder and dismember this woman was checked only by the subtle but steady pressure Arnon was applying to my right arm. Slowly, the woman got up from her chair, picked up a pink folder marked SCHILLER, dragged her bulk around the desk, and motioned for us to follow her.

We were ushered into a small cubicle, hardly large enough to accommodate the examining table and a straight-backed chair. I quickly stripped and donned the threadbare smock draped over the metal stirrups. Almost immediately, the door burst open, and a tall, spare, formidable man with a drooping mustache and a starkly bald head entered the room. His bearing was so rigid, so Prussian, that I half expected him to click his heels and salute. Smiling was out of the question.

"So, madame, shall we see how the sperm fare? Place your legs in stirrups please. Thank you, madame. Be so kind as to spread legs. Wider, please. Yes, that is good. Now, take deep breath and hold it. This will only take moment, madame."

I stopped breathing altogether as the doctor worked to withdraw a sample of Arnon's sperm. As he bent over my lower half, I checked the doctor's bald head for age spots.

"Thank you, madame. I shall study this sample under the microscope for some minutes. Please to stay and wait my return. And, please to resume breathing, madame." Something resembling a smile flashed across Dr. Dink's mouth, and he was gone.

"How're you doing, Nome?" Arnon asked and stroked my cheek.

"Fine," I said and instantly started to cry.

True to his promise, Dr. Dink was back in the room before Arnon could even light a cigarette.

"I regret to tell you, madame, they are all dead."

"Dead? What, dead?"

"The sperm, madame. We know from tests, Mr. Schiller has low count, but it appears that environment in womb is hostile. The sperm did not survive even three hours. This is not good indication. Even fertility drugs cannot fight hostile womb and weak sperm. Only remaining choice is to inseminate artificially."

"How can you be sure, doctor?"

"Madame, you will not conceive unless we inseminate. We can do this, but we must wait until next ovulation, which presents problem. Your chart shows irregular ovulation cycle. Menstruations are also irregular. Please to continue taking daily temperature. Contact office when chart shows temperature rise and we will schedule procedure. You must then remain several days in hospital to ensure good result. I regret, madame." And with a nod and a bow, Dr. Dink disappeared.

Life in the kibbutz chugged along under the relentless summer swelter, pulling Arnon and me in its wake. We had work to do, kids to teach, oranges to pick, meals to prepare, and trucks to drive to market. I banished all thoughts of babies from my conscious mind. Arnon and I had decided to wait half a year until our return to America before inseminating anything or anyone, artificially or otherwise. But night after night, I woke up abruptly, dimly aware of an infant crying out somewhere inside me. I didn't talk to Arnon about these awakenings. I didn't talk much to anyone. In fact, the kibbutzniks noticed my unaccustomed silence. I overheard them gossiping at length and in depth about my anatomy, and bemoaning the loss of enthusiasm that had formerly made me a favorite.

"Cheer up, Nomele," said Dvora one day as we stood together in the kibbutz kitchen shelling peas. "Cheer up, please. Ten years it took us, Amitai and me. Ten years until I conceived Shoshannah..."

I give her a weak smile and said nothing. Dvora's two-year-old baby was pink and dimpled and beautiful with wild blonde ringlets and round blue eyes. I'd take one of those in a minute, I thought. Why could Dvora do it and I couldn't? What was wrong with me? Even Rifka, the cripple, was pregnant, and she didn't even have a husband. I hardly recognized myself anymore. I felt mean-spirited and envious, the very kind of person I despised.

"Nomele, listen. Are you listening? Listen, Nomele," Dvora continued. "The minute you will forget about it, the minute you do not worry about it or think about it, that's when you will be pregnant. Trust me, I know..."

I nodded and continued to shell the peas for dinner.

The heat of summer burned on. Arnon and I didn't make love those days. It was too hot to breathe, let alone to touch, in our small quarters, and although I still monitored my temperature daily, the line on the graph remained as flat as my stomach and robbed me of any desire but the desire to sleep.

June and July brought the *chamseen*, a wild, punishing wind that blew off the desert, burned the skin, and filled the eyes with flying grains of gritty sand. I began to feel poorly. I was always nauseated and suffered from one severe headache after another. I lost my appetite and grew exceedingly thin. The kibbutzniks became alarmed at my condition.

By the end of August, I was so sick, I couldn't hold down anything but tea and soda crackers and could barely drag myself through my daily routine, much less cart crates of oranges or work in the hellish summer heat of the kibbutz kitchen. Mrs. Crackapovich was designated to investigate, and Arnon, who no longer knew what to do with me, gladly turned me over to the kindly, cooing matron.

Mrs. Crackapovich had served on the staff of the clinic in nearby Netanya. She arranged for an appointment with a doctor there. She sliced through the usual red tape and waiting lists like a sharp knife dicing cucumbers. Within forty-eight hours, I sat stripped and sweating on the examining table of Dr. Yarkoni, a round-faced, spectacled, internist, with the thickest, tightest, blackest curls I'd ever seen on any head.

Dr. Yarkoni prodded and poked, thumped and listened, had blood drawn, and ordered specimens of all kinds. He spoke in soft and reassuring tones when he took my history. His warmth and concern touched me and broke through my armor of listlessness. He even reduced me to tears of laughter with a long and complex tale involving a cow, a kibbutznik, and a circumcision. The examination completed, Dr. Yarkoni walked me to the clinic entrance:

"Call me tomorrow, *motek*, and I will have the results of all your tests. We cannot allow you to simply melt away. It would look bad for Israel to send you home to America in such condition. We can't afford any more bad press."

"NAOMI SCHILLER, TELEPHONE...NAOMI, TELEPHONE...COME TO THE MAIN HOUSE IMMEDIATELY."

I heard the summons over the loudspeaker system, and dropped the oranges I'd been sorting to run to the only telephone available.

"Shalom?"

"Shalom, shalom, Naomi. It's Dr. Yarkoni. Where are you?"

"I'm in the main house."

"Can you sit down somewhere, *motek*?"

"Yes, just a minute..."

"Naomi Schiller, my darling girl, I have news for you. You are not sick...you are not sick at all. You are pregnant. About fourteen weeks, I would guess."

"Pregnant? Pregnant?" My voice rang loud and shrill inside my head. "But how, doctor?"

Dr. Yarkoni laughed. "By the usual methods, I presume. Naomi, you are going to be a mama. I must see you again tomorrow with your husband, and we will give you vitamins and a special diet to build you up. You are going to have a baby—MADE IN ISRAEL."

"But, Dr. Dink...Dr. Dink said..."

"Never mind Dr. Dink. The good doctor said one thing, but God intended another. *Mazel tov*, Naomi. Now, go and tell your Arnon."

"But, doctor..."

"*Shah.* Go and find your husband. I'll see you tomorrow in my office. Two o'clock. Now go. Shalom, shalom."

I stood for a moment holding the receiver in my hand. Then the news slowly made its way from my ears downwards to my heart and upwards to my brain. I began to shout, to jump, to cheer, and to run out of the main house to the front lawn where Dov and Dvora, Zvee, Amitai, Mrs. Crackapovich, and all the others were waiting eagerly. They too had heard the loudspeaker. On the kibbutz, phone calls were no everyday occurrence.

"What's happened, Naomi?"

"Where's Arnon?"

"Here I am, Nome...what's up?"

"*Ma karah*, Nomi? *Ma karah*? What's going on, Naomi?"

Slowly, I turned round and round to look into the face of each of the kibbutzniks, one by one. My smile broadened with each turn, laughter gurgled in my mouth and joy tickled my cheeks. Finally, with all the air in my lungs, I shouted:

"I'M NOT SICK...NOT SICK AT ALL—I'M PREGNANT! Arnon, we did it. We did it, everyone—A baby—Made in Israel!"

Arnon grabbed me and lifted me up. Slowly and gracefully, the members of the kibbutz formed a circle around us. Everyone joined hands and began to sway and sing: "How goodly are thy tents, Oh Jacob, and thy dwellings, Oh Israel..."

Held up high, enfolded in my husband's arms, I looked up into the cobalt blue of the Israeli sky.

"Thank you," I whispered.

mary doroshenk
The Barren Season

Elise never thought about babies until the age of twenty-eight when she became sterile.

In the falling afternoon sun, she drifted in and out of sleep recalling memories so deeply that they felt like dreams.

She remembered the time before she knew words, sitting on her mother's vast kitchen floor shaking ice blue, green, and pink Tupperware cups, shaking the cups to see if anything would fall out onto the cool linoleum floor that stuck to her bare legs. She remembered another afternoon, her mother lifting her from the porch steps, while she still tried to remove static-charged hairs from an ear of corn, the kernels firm and smooth to the touch. She remembered an early fall evening, swaying in the baby seat on the back of her father's bike as he pedaled along the streets, the fading sunlight in her eyes much the way it was now.

Elise woke out of her trance when a cloud blocked what was left of the sun and a cool breeze brushed her arm. She stared at the darkening sky, afraid to leave her dream, but her mind wandered anyway. She went back to her first visits to the doctor's office, when he could not diagnose her condition. First, he thought it was just a urinary tract infection, then he said it was pelvic inflammatory disease, then it was cysts, then it was endometriosis. The more he wavered, the more terrified she became. There seemed to be an unspoken accusation that the pain was in her mind. The trust between patient and doctor waned, as the name of her condition eluded him. But Elise's pain was real.

The sun made a last appearance, and Elise drifted back into the past. She remembered when she was five and her mother let her hold her baby brother.

She sat holding him on the sofa, the soft baby in her arms, his gums chewing on her finger. It was a gentle, soft pressure. She could feel him breathing, and it made her calm. She colored pictures of him, with brilliant blue eyes and yellow hair.

She felt the baby kick her in the side and awoke with a start, sweat forming on her lip. The memory of the acute pressing pain cut her insides and made her quiver. When Elise was first sick, her pain lasted the whole of a morning, then it continued through the night, and extended to the next. It persisted past the end of her period—in fact, it stretched on for six months. The pain hurt to the touch, and she imagined her ovaries protruding out of her body. She sickened from lack of sleep, and her skin tone discolored like yellowed linen.

Elise thought of her mother's warmth, kindness, and softness. Words like *sterile, barren, infertile* slipped away from her mother like a changing season. She imagined trying to tell her mom that her healthy seed had stopped...that her body had rebelled against her and demanded to be removed...that the rich power of her mother's soft and loving embraces in which she swallowed her children into the safety of her body...that power had crumbled from within.

Elise closed her eyes and saw the black and white mass the size of a small cantaloupe, touching up against her uterus. Shortly after she saw the picture, that mass, along with her ovaries and womb, was removed from her body, and the aching memories, which Elise kept close, would remain in the past, never to awaken into the light of their own day.

lisa rhoades
Let's Make a Baby!

Consider the miscarriage
as a bad night of TV—
the dark oval on the ultrasound, an opening in the static
the two of us glued to the screen
and though the technician turns the wand this way
and that for better reception and I lift
my hands like old-fashioned antennae
or those folk on Public Access
who are always waving to the Lord,
the only thing coming in is this quiz show—
"Let's Make a Baby!" Our host smiles gamely,
he "sure would like to see us win,"
but the studio audience knows
this one's a bust, we've missed our one question,
and the parting gift is lame.
While Loss, the defending champion,
wants to shake my hand,
says in a couple of months we can try
again, says she can't wait
for us to try again.

robyn samuels
The Strong Pull of a Handful of Tiny Cells

It came in the mail again one day: the bill from the hospital for storing our frozen embryos. They can be kept indefinitely, as far as anyone knows, but there's really no point. Eventually they should be used or discarded.

The first year we paid the annual fee with little discussion. Our girls were only four months old. We were nearly certain that two was plenty, but what if, God forbid, something happened to one or both of them? A hundred and something dollars wasn't so much to pay to keep possibilities alive.

The next year we hemmed and hawed a little. Aren't the babies growing fast and call me crazy but wouldn't it be fun to have another? Okay, at our age it's crazy. Would we really go through another pregnancy, no matter what? It wasn't the pregnancy so much, it was getting there. When my husband and I got together, we were both well into our forties. I already knew I wasn't ovulating regularly and that becoming pregnant would be a struggle. We tried fertility drugs and inseminations. My husband is a radiologist, so we got a break on the ultrasounds. I was teaching part time and writing. I cut back to just an occasional day of subbing because fertility became a full-time job.

At our wedding, for our first dance, the band played "Just in Time," but actually we were a bit late. My hormone levels were dropping and my eggs were old. The fertility specialist told us the next step would be in vitro fertilization.

We could try it with my eggs and a less than two percent likelihood of success, or we could try donor eggs and raise our odds to nearly fifty-fifty. No chance of looking at my offspring and marveling at how they have my mother's eyes. On the other hand, no worrying that they might get my size 11A feet. At close to ten thousand dollars per in vitro attempt, we decided to opt for the egg donor. It was a painful process. I had to suppress my own menstrual cycle to coordinate with hers, which meant I spent two months in artificial menopause. I developed an allergy to the progesterone shots, leaving my hips looking like they had grapefruits attached. Would I dare put my body through such an ordeal again?

Well, we said, let's not close any doors...yet. We paid the storage fee once more. The third year rolled around and when the bill arrived, we knew we really had to talk. We didn't talk and the reminder notice arrived. Then a second notice; finally we talked. The girls are wonderful, but let's be honest, we aren't going to do this again. It's time to let go of the embryos.

When the eggs were initially harvested from our donor, she proved to be amazingly prolific. We had hoped for twelve to fifteen to give us a chance for several attempts at in vitro fertilization; she produced thirty. After combining the eggs with my husband's sperm, we had twelve viable embryos. Miraculously, I got pregnant on the first try. We were blessed with twins and left with nine frozen embryos. Our thoughts and feelings were focused on the embryos growing inside my body. Yet the others had to be contended with as well.

We had three choices on the forms we filled out at the time: When we no longer wished to store the embryos, would we prefer to: (1) Donate the embryos to other infertile couples; (2) Destroy the embryos; or (3) Allow the embryos to be used for scientific research?

Although our happiness rested on someone else's willingness to part with her genetic material, my husband did not feel comfortable giving his away anonymously. Plus, we felt like we had an understanding with the egg donor. We never met her but we spoke by phone and we knew a lot about each other. We knew what she looked like, what her hobbies were, what her family was like. She knew our ages, our careers, our interests, and our hopes.

We had selected and approved one another for this sacred three-way union. My husband and I would laugh whenever we recalled our get-acquainted conversation. "Well, I'm not sure what to say in this situation, but you can have 'em," she had blurted out in her husky voice. It seemed wrong to us to give away embryos made with her eggs. So option one was out.

We wrestled and we reasoned with options two and three; they both seemed so cold—destruction or lab research? But these were just cells, really. Tiny combinations of sixteen cells that might or might not take hold in someone's womb. They may be living, but they are not lives. Still...throw them away, just like that? All right, research then. But did we want someone picking them apart? Well, there are no real bodies, no pain. If studying the embryos can further science and medicine, at least some benefit might be gained from an act that seems so destructive. So that's the box we checked.

Three years later, when the time came to exercise our choice, option three was not an alternative; our hospital was no longer accepting embryos for research. But what about all the promising developments in embryo stem cell studies? What about the possibility we could be helping find a cure for diabetes or Parkinson's disease? Sorry. Our legal department has advised us it's too controversial.

We had to make our decision all over again. We still didn't want to give them away and we finally agreed we would not be using them ourselves. It was silly to keep spending money when we knew what needed to be done. I told my husband I would phone the next day and tell the hospital we weren't going to pay for storage anymore.

A week later I called the hospital and was connected to a clerk at the fertility center. I gave my name and proceeded to state my mission. "I, we've decided, you can..." To my complete surprise, I burst out crying. He was compassionate. He told me to think about it and call back later. I hung up, bewildered by the intensity of my emotions.

My rational mind explained to myself all over again why this was the only sensible decision, but if I made a move towards the phone, the tears would well up again. How strange is that? I asked my husband.

Not so strange. We had seen the little bundles those embryos might turn into. We had seen the results of breathing life into those cells and they were our own precious daughters. We were about to destroy the last possibility that there might ever be more of them. We were going to authorize someone to take a treasure and throw it in the garbage. No wonder my heart was putting up a fight.

One night as I lay awake obsessing about it, an alternative came to me. Couldn't we retrieve the embryos and dispose of them ourselves in a respectful way? I am a great believer in ritual for important life events, rites of passage. My girls and I celebrated their final day of nursing with a tea party featuring chocolate soymilk and popcorn on real china plates. They still remember it. I have helped heal the grief of many broken relationships and of loved ones who have passed with personal ceremonies. I have flung jewelry into the ocean, danced odes to myself in my living room, arranged photos on my mother's grave, had long conversations with other peoples' clothing, and sent written messages up in smoke.

My husband, though unpracticed in this style of coping, agreed. Neither of us had the heart to order the embryos destroyed with just a phone call, but to take them, hold them, bury them, and say our final goodbyes, seemed like something we could face.

We went to the hospital, and as we waited for the paperwork to be finished, the nurses chatted with us. It's unusual, they said, but you aren't the first to do this. Most people feel emotional about their embryos.

Finally we were handed the embryos in tubes in an envelope. How small they were! What little substance they contained. I tucked them inside a pouch around my waist for safekeeping. It felt right to be carrying them, as I had carried my babies in slings and Snuglis. When we got home, the baby-sitter had just put our three-year-old daughters down for their nap. My husband and I went to the backyard, to the place we had chosen to bury the embryos.

We didn't want it to be a spot where people might tread or the dog might dig. We made a hole. We each said our goodbyes, saying farewell to what might have been. I was sad, but not as sad as I had expected to be. Being close to the embryos, holding them awhile had given me some peace. Moreover, I was filled with love: for my husband with his readiness to go along with my plan and the warmth and simplicity he brought to the ceremony; for our children asleep in their beds.

I reminded myself these embryos were just tiny cells, not tiny people. We spilled the liquid into the ground, noticing again how small, how just like water it seemed. We didn't mark the spot. I think we were being careful not to treat the area like a grave, not to appear even to ourselves as if we were interring dead bodies or grieving over lost souls. To us, we were only saying goodbye to biological matter and dreams. We covered it and, arm in arm, walked back into the house.

My husband, who has the sort of memory that still knows Bob Hope's birthday because he read it in his encyclopedia in 1958, can't remember where in the yard we parted with the embryos. Neither can I. Do you think we're blocking? I ask him. No, he says. I think we really were finished that day. We've moved on.

I guess I think so too. And all at once, as I am writing this, I remember the spot. It was right next to the apricot seedling, to nourish it we said. As it happens, the tree is doing fine. We expect it to bear fruit next year.

teresa méndez-quigley
Cropped Roots

He gathers in his hands
the fullness of my chestnut brown waves.
Lovely, he says as he shears.
The pain shoots through
to my gut, reminded again of my not grade A eggs.
Whose mane will my child have?
Her mother's genes
running through her,
DNA of another kind, tamed tresses.
Will I love her just the same?
I recall the thickness
of my father's hair, passed down
to the few of us,
to me. No more family
trees to trace
down back beyond this moment.
How do I braid the hair
of a child not my own
borrowed
for this lifetime?

becoming mom

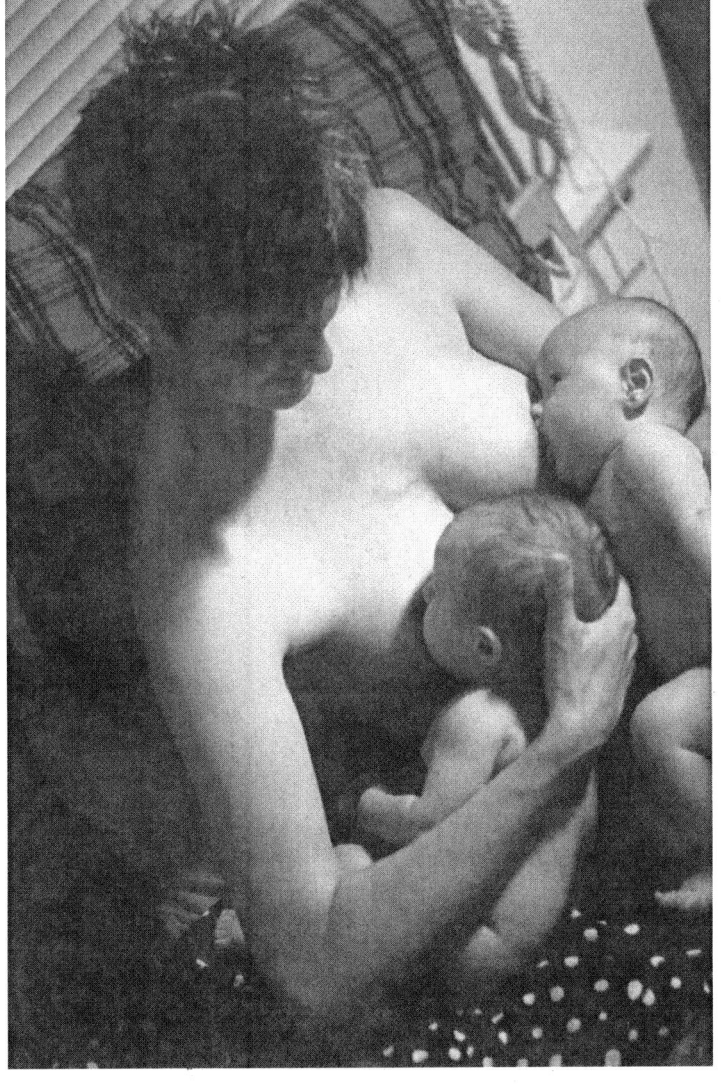

photo by david glynn

polly b. dredge
On Becoming a Mother

When I was pregnant, everyone told me over and over how Life, as I knew it, was about to change. Of course it was, I said. I was soon going to have a son to love and enjoy. I knew my husband and I would go out less often. I knew we both couldn't work late just to catch up on things, or run errands on the way home every night. I knew we would have less disposable income, and that everything—from grocery shopping to packing for vacations—would be a little more complicated.

Everyone just smiled knowingly as I assured them I knew my life was about to change, and that I was ready. I was wrong. I had no idea how much my life was going to change. I was not ready.

Some women spend their pregnancy preparing themselves for motherhood. They spend hours decorating the nursery and dreaming about their baby. They read up on the merits of breast feeding versus formula, and cloth versus disposable diapers. They buy life insurance, and start a college fund. I was not one of them.

I spent my pregnancy in disbelief. My pregnancy was a miracle. After years of waiting, hoping to get pregnant, our child finally was conceived through in vitro fertilization (a process we agreed beforehand we would try only once).

All the other pregnant women I knew were from our infertility support group and had high-risk pregnancies. Even though my pregnancy proceeded without complications, I prepared myself for anything that might possibly go wrong. I watched for the symptoms of conditions that might require bed rest for the duration. I anticipated the possibility of miscarriage, even stillbirth.

After waiting so long to actually *conceive* a child, I could not imagine actually *having* one. I protected myself from the depths of disappointment by refusing to expect a perfect outcome.

As the months sped by, however, I thought maybe I'd become the first woman to remain pregnant forever. Two weeks before my due date I decided being pregnant forever would not be a good option. I stopped working so I could "get ready for the baby." I needed to pack a suitcase for the hospital. I needed to buy a car seat, and diapers. I needed to clean out the junk room and turn it into a nursery. I went into labor that weekend. I wasn't ready.

Our son was born between two blizzards in January 1996, beheld in awe by two stunned parents and a crowd of overworked medical staff. Within about an hour of the birth, my husband seemed to complete the transition from "man" to "father." There is a picture of him in my hospital room, cradling his son in his arms, wearing the biggest, brightest smile ever captured on film. In a matter of minutes, he seemed to absorb the enormity of what had happened in our lives, and it rooted him. He stood taller. As he moved through the subsequent days, a quiet confidence replaced his old cockiness. I, on the other hand, felt blank.

Some women say they feel an instant, overpowering bond the first moment they see and hold their newborn babe. I was not one of them. I was amazed I actually gave birth to a healthy child. Amazed I survived the experience. Amazed nothing disastrous happened. Instead of feeling an instant bond, I felt...awkward. I felt what a friend of mine has come to call "the shock of motherhood." I was overwhelmed by the enormity of what had just happened to us—to me. I felt my life had just turned a sharp corner into a vast darkness and I was without a map or a flashlight. Nothing in my previous thirty-nine years seemed relevant to what I needed to know now. I had no idea how to take care of a baby. And I had no idea how to be a mother.

Now most people would say you are automatically a mother the moment you have a child. But after nine months of pregnancy, after experiencing childbirth, after holding my son in my arms, I still didn't *feel* like a mother. I felt like I had stepped into someone else's life.

Mine was not a quick, smooth transition from capable career woman to capable mother. I was in a fog for weeks. I eventually figured out how to change a diaper in record time, wrestle wiry arms and legs into rompers, and maneuver a stroller in a crowd. But I still didn't feel like a mother. I just felt like a woman who had mastered another set of skills. After six miserable weeks of trying to breast feed a voracious eater with a lock like a steel jaw trap, I finally gave up, and gave in to formula. My son gobbled and slurped and slept happily through the night. I cried. Good mothers breast feed, I thought. By surrendering so soon, what kind of mother was I? What kind of mother would I be?

I staggered into my ob/gyn's office for my final postpartum checkup, lugging the infant carrier, diaper bag, and my purse. I sat in the waiting room feeling pleased with myself for getting there on time and worrying about how long I might have to wait. My son was usually content each morning for about an hour and a half. Beyond that, he would cry and I would be miserable trying to quiet him in front of my doctor.

Mercifully, my name was soon called. I told my doctor I couldn't imagine returning to work yet, even though I had already decided to resign from my job. I felt fine physically, aside from the sleep deprivation, but I felt disoriented and confused about everything. I couldn't concentrate on anything. My brain was not available. I didn't feel like my old self.

She agreed that returning to work six weeks after delivery was absurd for many women—an arbitrary time frame. She assured me my pre-pregnancy brain function would return (after menopause), and congratulated me on my decision not to return to work. "Of course you don't feel like your old self," she said. "You're a mother now." Next thing I knew, the exam was over and I was on my way out the door just as my baby started to fuss. I drove home discouraged and exhausted.

As I drove, I longed for the days of waking to the alarm at the same time every morning. I longed to get dressed and head off to a day of meetings and appointments I planned. I longed to be in control of my time instead of being a slave to the whims of my son the tyrant. But as much as I craved my old routine, I knew I was in no shape to meet monthly goals or quarterly objectives. I could not cope with the office crisis of the week. I could not imagine *any* new mother being able to do this, although I could understand why they might want to (and I know many do because they have no choice). It seemed insane—and downright cruel to both mothers and babies—to expect mothers to return to work so soon. I felt I was just beginning to get to know my baby. I was beginning to see something recognizable in his eyes. We were beginning to find our groove. I couldn't imagine being anywhere but home, with him.

I realize, now, I was already well on the road to motherhood. Changing diapers and tying shoes and wiping runny noses can easily consume your days, and many mothers never get beyond this point. It's Motherhood 101. But motherhood on this level is, at minimum, dreary, boring, and thankless. At its worst, it's deadening. It's what causes women to flee from home, thankful that in our generation it is acceptable—in some circles, even desirable—to hire someone to do these things for you if you need or want to direct your efforts elsewhere.

For me, motherhood goes well beyond all that. It provides a far greater opportunity for self-exploration and personal transformation than any job I've ever held. I am constantly challenged, and I continue to get better with each year of experience. I am becoming a mother gradually, one bittersweet moment at a time.

My first few years of motherhood have been filled with hundreds of such moments. Sometimes I am forced to surrender some notion, some idea, some part of myself. Sometimes I am forced to just stop and watch. And each time, I always receive something in return. In this exchange, I let go of the old with one hand and grab hold of the new with the other—it's a do-si-do with change, a dance with growth.

Like the moment I gave up on breast feeding. Surrendering my most basic notion of what it meant to be a good mother was a decision fraught with peril and guilt and grief. I was putting my baby at risk for future health problems. I was admitting failure at something primal to the survival of the species, something that should be instinctual, something that I should be able to do as naturally as breathing. I was giving up on one of the few things I knew to do to make me feel like a mother. But I also felt relieved I would no longer have to endure the pain and discomfort it was causing me. I needed to be in control of my own body again. I needed to move on. I realized I would have to find other ways to be a good mother. In this moment of realization I received the most important kernel of mothering wisdom—find ways that work for *you*.

Another memorable moment came the day my son threw an award-winning tantrum in the grocery store parking lot. Hearing him made me wonder why this boy's mother wasn't giving him the help he needed to learn to express himself in a more constructive way. Then I realized his words were mine, echoing back exactly what I had been saying to him only the day before. In that humiliating moment I realized my son's temper tantrums were a direct reflection of my own inability to control my temper when things weren't going well.

Such moments of realization continue to arrive unannounced, when I'm not looking. They often arrive when I'm preoccupied with too many activities—juggling part-time work, baby-sitters, play dates, committee meetings, family crises, sick friends, housework, and a work-weary husband. My favorites are those moments of complete surrender to the surpassing beauty of watching a baby grow into a person. Like one afternoon when my son was about a year-and-a-half old and I peeked in his room during his nap to see whether I could work a little longer. Instead of going back to work, I wrote:

> *It's a beautiful autumn day—the kind of day when the temperature is so perfect you're not aware of it...I've just stolen a "Mother's Moment"—tiptoeing into Will's room, to see him wrapped up in his quilt against the breeze from the window fan, his back turned to the fan and the doorway, his hair just a little damp around the edge of the quilt, and his bottom arm outstretched across the white crib sheet. Sleeping lightly, moving into wakefulness, eyelids flickering faintly. I can hear him talking to himself now, as I quickly scribble these words. "Will's wakin' up," he yawns. And now I hear the springs in the crib squeaking as he tests out his theories about jumping and hopping—his latest curiosity...*
>
> *What makes these moments so precious?...Maybe it's the mystery of seeing him as a baby today, and knowing I'll still be seeing that same sweetness in his face ten years from now, and twenty years from now—that sense of his essential self that is taking shape now...that shows itself so purely, so sweetly, so lovely, to a mother, in such a stolen moment.*

Bearing silent witness to these moments of innocence and beauty brings me great joy. Standing steady in a storm of change brings me sorrow in equal measure. Like the morning I watched my baby crawl for the first time—away from me. I was thrilled to watch him reach a developmental milestone, happy to see him growing stronger. I smiled and applauded his latest accomplishment. At the same time I felt a twinge of sadness for what he was leaving behind, for the loss of his babyhood, and eventually, his childhood. It was the beginning of his growing up, his going away.

Each change in my child requires a change in me. Just when I've figured out how to help him through one developmental phase, he masters it and begins to work on the next one. Each new milestone he reaches means he's growing more fully into himself, taking shape before my eyes. And I am growing right along with him, learning and changing something about myself every day.

Now I know why all those other parents were smiling so knowingly when I assured them I was ready for all the life changes my son was going to bring. I had no idea that having less disposable income and going out less often were just the beginning. I had no idea I was automatically enrolling in a lifelong course of change, the most challenging work imaginable.

barbara gibson
becoming mom

i didn't carry him or feel him kick
nor did i labor for endless hours making promises to god in exchange for relief
still, he is my son
i knew it the moment i saw him—so small and alone except for nurses and doctors that prodded, pricked, and poked his tiny body at all hours without warmth or warning

he was three weeks old when the universe brought us together—flesh of my spirit, my desires—finally

just one pound, twelve ounces—he was more tubes and machines than baby
the first time i held him i did not count fingers or toes i held my breath, careful not to cross or pull the wires that sustained him

zachary left the hospital fourteen weeks and six pounds later
he is a miracle
now fifteen months we call him the brown bomber
he tries anything and touches everything
his smile is a masterpiece
a perfect combination of joy and wonder
he hides nothing
his tears come like a storm loud and raging
don't you want a child of your own? i am asked
he is my own, i answer

he is as much mine as he would be if his journey to life were etched in lines
   across my stomach

when he looks at me i can see that he understands
i am comfort
i am security
i am warmth
i am love
i am his mother

katherine mikkelson
Purple Fleece and Motherhood

I sat far away from the other expectant families, many poised with balloons, teddy bears, and cameras. I have never found solace from strangers who were experiencing the same circumstances as me. That, and the blanket, is why I almost missed Zack when he arrived.

I hardly noticed when the trickle of lanky, blonde Europeans had coalesced into a swell of stocky raven-haired Koreans. My friend jabbed me in the ribs, saying that the flight must have arrived. I stood up, but still refused to step closer to the entrance way. I stared at the faces of the adult males who passed. That's the way my son will look thirty or forty years from now, I thought. I was shocked at how foreign they looked to me. How would I ever be able to love him as if I gave birth to him? I gazed down at my sweaty hands that clutched the purple fleece baby blanket. My stomach flipped and floundered like a fish trying to make its way back into the water.

The blanket. Our social worker explained that an agency representative would meet us at the airport and would take our blanket back to Zack on the aircraft as the regular passengers disembarked. The escort who traveled with Zack from Korea would wrap the blanket around him so that when the babies emerged from behind the international arrivals door, we would immediately know which baby was ours.

For some reason, I became obsessed with the notion of the blanket. I told everyone I knew about it, as I thought the idea was quite clever. I thought about how I would react when they came to get it from me, knowing I would be meeting Zack only minutes afterwards. And for weeks Tom and I fretted over which blanket to use. Should it be the blue and tan tartan with the teddies, the yellow and blue quilt made by Grandma, or the purple fleece with his name embroidered on it? In the end, we settled on the purple fleece because it was bright and we thought we would spot it immediately.

Birth mothers cannot feel so expectantly unprepared for the arrival of their children. They have nine months to fret. But we adoptive mothers are usually given one or two days' notice that our child is ready. We go to the airport or travel to the birthplace, are handed the child, and presto change-o—instant motherhood.

Of course, it's not really so instantaneous. Criminal background checks, fingerprints, medical evaluations, writing a biography, grappling with infertility, reconciling religious views and discipline issues, and then the home study—much more preparation than most birth parents have to endure. Rather than looking at the process as a chore, Tom and I rather relished it. It gave us time to talk about how we wanted to raise our children and how we would handle certain issues if they arose. We said on more than one occasion that all parents should go through the deliberation that was required of us.

Four months after we filed our application with the adoption agency, they offered Zachary to us. At the offering meeting, we sat, staring in awe at his picture, falling in love with his slightly crossed eyes and his black shock of wispy hair. His splayed toes probably meant that he was energetic. He looked chubby, so he must eat well. For months, the balance of the world and our child-to-be hung on that one picture, and we read everything into it we could.

No one had come to retrieve the blanket yet, so I stood on the far side of the waiting area, while Tom paced back and forth, back and forth, a few hundred yards away from me, right in front of where the two metal railings stopped and opened up into the baggage claim area. Arriving passengers had to dart around him to find their waiting friends and families.

In those last few minutes of childlessness, I began thinking about the movies never to be seen, the parties missed because of vomiting and fever, the hot meals interrupted by requests for more apple juice. And then I thought about the first step, the first tooth, the first loose tooth, and the first bicycle ride without training wheels.

"Katherine, they're calling us!!" Tom yelled from across the waiting area. My reverie was interrupted as I sped towards Tom, a lump forming in my throat. The blanket, they hadn't come for the blanket, I wasn't even watching, I wasn't prepared! All at once, six or seven babies emerged from behind the swinging doors. A blondish man, the escort, carrying a chunky baby in a Snugli, called our names again. We ran over to him and met Zack, who was smiling and giggling as if he knew it was the most wonderful day of our collective lives, as if he knew he had just arrived home to his mommy and daddy. The tears ran down our faces as we hugged him, cuddled him, and told him we loved him, over and over. The crowd melted away into a fuzzy background as we laughed at the bald spot on the back of his head and marveled that he looked exactly as he appeared in his picture, the one we pored over during those three long months of waiting.

An hour later, after hearing a full report of Zack's trip, his utter lack of sleep on the fourteen-hour flight from Seoul, his eating habits and bowel patterns, we were in the car and on the way home, as a family. He was no longer an orphaned child from a foreign land whose physical appearance was so dissimilar from mine. This was my forever son. To this day, I forget that we look different and that people could question our mother and son status.

We never did find out why the blanket wasn't taken from us as promised. In the end, the blanket was such a minor detail. But like the picture, it was all we had, which created a myopia of sorts. The blanket represented parenthood-to-be and we had arrived without it, or maybe, in spite of it.

lyn lifshin

Watching Her Child Become a Work of Art

Mothers in the hallway
that leads to the dance studio.
Some knit, some nurse
babies. Most stand near the
door. Some copy the dance
steps their daughters are
learning: Miss Linda grabs a
girl's leg, molds it into
position, the child, willing
clay. At the annual recital,
that ritual that, except for
their weddings, will be the
only time they take part in
a fairy-tale existence, the
mothers come to the studio.
In the mirrored wall
They watch their children
become the work of art
they have known since
conception that they were
without intrusion of the
words stopping them
from seeing this

stephany brown
Holy Places

Oh, honey, don't hurt me. I'm too old. This is what my mother used to say to me all the time when I reached the age when girls become smart alecky to their mothers. I realize now that she wasn't old then, just prematurely gray, early silver, my father used to say as he held on to a hunk of her waist-length hair. But it worked. I wasn't unkind to her like my friend Sally was to her solidly brunette mother and Anne-Marie to hers. I figured Mom just couldn't take it, the old being much more fragile than the young.

And she wasn't unkind to me either, even when I broke all the rules and got pregnant at sixteen. I should have been smart enough to figure out that if she could handle an out-of-wedlock baby she could handle an unkind word or two. But by that time I'd lost the urge to be smart alecky. Being pregnant made me calm and content. Besides, I had other things on my mind.

Mainly Jeff. Jeff in his white Spitfire, one hand on the steering wheel, the other somewhere on me. He'd turn on the Motown station and if the top was down and we were on a country road he'd turn the music up loud and sing along with Jimmy Ruffin or the Four Tops or Mary Wells or Smoky Robinson and the Miracles. When we reached our cornfield all the sounds would stop and it would seem for a minute that we'd entered a church. And after a while the cornfield always seemed like a holy place to us, even if there hadn't been any noise on the way there.

It wasn't *our* cornfield, though, neither his nor mine. It was almost an hour away from our neighborhood and it was farmed by people we never even saw. We only went there at night. Jeff loved the drive there, the long straight road lined with tall trees and farms. When the night was bright enough, we could see the outlines of old silos. He'd go way too fast, seventy-five or eighty, but I didn't have the heart to tell him I was scared.

Sometimes there'd be straw in my hair when I got home. My mother, who'd have been reading on the couch or playing backgammon with my father, would pick some of it out and say that I'd missed curfew again, that she couldn't help worrying when I was late. And that little car is so flimsy, she'd say; it would protect you no more than a tuna fish can, what if a truck hits you. I told her once that Jeff was saving up for a Cadillac that would protect us, but I said it nicely, the old being unable to handle sarcasm.

My sweet father, for the most part, stayed out of these conversations. Sometimes he would nod and say, "Your mother's right, sweetheart," or echo something she had said. He figured it was some mother-daughter thing. Or he figured sex was involved. Or maybe he just saw my mother as wiser than he.

She was wise. She knew I was pregnant before I did and before any test had been done. She could tell by my face, she said, by the way it puffed out a little. I was horrified and expected her to be but she said she knew I loved Jeff and that Jeff loved me and that out of such love babies are born. She was so calm. I relaxed and figured she would take care of everything. But no. The next day she said she'd support me in any decision I made. But she had no advice. She'd help me find an adoption agency or she'd hold my hand through an abortion. She'd drive me to the Florence Crittenton Home for Unwed Mothers. She'd buy a new silk mother-of-the-bride dress for my wedding. She'd let me live with her and dad and be a single mother but she wouldn't take care of my baby for me. And she insisted on this: I had to tell Jeff. The baby was half his. I promised her I would but I couldn't. I was afraid it would spoil things and I couldn't stand that.

Three months passed and Jeff and I kept driving down country roads and I pretended to be carefree. By then it was too cold to lie in the cornfield. The loamy soil had gone hard. But sometimes we'd bring blankets and lie there anyway. We'd point out constellations and tell stories. Jeff liked to point to the east and tell me about Andromeda, who, in Greek legend, was the daughter of an Ethiopian king. For some offense, some boast about beauty that her mother had made, Andromeda was chosen to be sacrificed to the gods. She was chained, naked except for some jewels, to a rock at the edge of the sea. Jeff told me about Andromeda's rescue by Perseus, how Perseus beheaded a sea monster to free her, he told me how that was nothing compared to what he would do for me. Perseus's love for Andromeda was nothing compared to Jeff's love for me. I'd stare at the stars, trying to see the configuration in the shape of a much-beloved woman, and believe him. I'd imagine him slaying some monster for me, protecting me, freeing me, loving me forever.

And then one night he found my pants unbuttoned and made a joke about too many French fries. That was the night I told him. We were all wrapped in blankets.

After I blurted out the truth of it, he grew silent. He was silent for days, he pretended he hadn't heard me. This was unlike him. We'd always talked. We'd talk about constellations or we'd talk about his past or we'd talk about our future together. We didn't know when we'd get married but we knew that we would. We'd talk about which tall tower of apartments we wanted to start our life out in and how we'd decorate our kitchen. We'd talk about names for our babies—Cassandra, Vanessa, Sabrina. The first would be a boy, he'd be named Jeff. I showed him bits of leftover yarn my grandmother had given me. I showed him the pattern in her knitting book for a many-colored baby blanket, "for your trousseau, dear," she'd said and she'd promised to teach me to knit. We'd plan our wedding. Anne-Marie and Sally would be bridesmaids in fuchsia dresses. The best man and ushers would wear cummerbunds to match.

A few days after I told him I was pregnant, he told me this: he couldn't face it, he'd enlisted in the army, his father had signed for him, he'd leave for boot camp on his eighteenth birthday, only a few months away. He wouldn't even wait for graduation. No, I screamed, what about all my yarn? What about our wrought-iron kitchen table with matching chairs? What about the map of the stars that would hang in our baby's room? What about me, your beloved, the one you'd kill sea monsters for? What about the Magnavox stereo in our living room where we'd play Temptations albums and Martha and the Vandellas and the Supremes? I begged him and beat on his chest with my fists but he was steel. He didn't even say he was sorry. Or ask me what I was going to do.

"There's a war going on. My country needs me," was his answer. He turned into a stranger. He was no longer the boy who sang into the wind. Suddenly he was all involved in the Vietnam War and stopping communism. It was a subject that had never come up, all those nights in the cornfield and in the car. All that talking we did, that incessant talking, and he'd never mentioned the war or patriotism or serving anybody but me.

For a week I grieved. For some reason I spent most of that week with Jeff's mother, not with mine. We'd sit on her couch drinking Cokes and eating potato chips and she'd promise me he'd come to his senses and "do right by you, honey." And if he didn't, well, then, "God would punish him." He was acting more and more like his dad, she said, stubborn and selfish. I don't know if Jeff was more afraid of me or of his mother but he spent the rest of the time, before he went in the army, at his dad's efficiency apartment, a sordid little place full of overstuffed used furniture. It didn't even have a radio. Losing Jeff like this was a heartbreaker for his mother. She didn't even get to be with her baby before he went off to war.

I wanted to die that week but then something happened. I started to feel calm and I gave Jeff up in my mind, his music, his pain, his Greek legends. I didn't throw his picture away but I took it off my dresser and put it in a drawer, under my scarves. I ceremoniously laid all his gifts, the opal ring, the cameo brooch, the gardenia corsage from his junior prom, in a box covered with quilted ivory satin and stored it high on a closet shelf.

By then, by the time I was free to think about my baby, it was too late for an abortion so at least I didn't have to picture what that would entail. That's what my mother said anyway. Perhaps that was her way of expressing the opinion she claimed to refuse to express. Another kind ploy in her bag of parenting tricks. Another refusal to pose as the authority in my life. Another chance for me to take responsibility for myself. And I was relieved that I could check off another option, to shorten my list of choices, a list I didn't want to face.

But I did. I faced the list. I decided to give the baby up. I decided it one morning after I'd had a dream about being a mother. My brown hair was bleached blonde and stringy in the dream and heavy black eyeliner was on my eyelids. Me and the baby lived with no radio in a small efficiency full of used, overstuffed furniture. The event of the dream was this: I was using a knife as a microphone and doing an imitation of Diana Ross singing "Baby Love, My Baby Love." My hips were swiveling and I felt real cool and my baby started to struggle. I had laid him face down in a big chair and he started to sputter. The blanket under him had gotten all wadded up around his face and he couldn't get his breath. I knew he might die and I planned to get him but I wanted to finish my song first. I woke up before either the rescue or the death but I took the dream as a sign that I wasn't ready.

I stayed in school until my stomach got ridiculous. Then I made an appointment with Sister John Gabriel, the principal. I told her that my family was going to be moving because my father had been transferred. She put her hand on mine and her eyes went soft and understanding and she said she knew the truth of the matter, she had eyes to see and she was sorry. She knew this was a painful time for me. I hadn't expected her to believe me. I had eyes to see too, but I had expected her to be cold and cruel. I had expected guilt and shame. Her kindness took me by surprise and tears trailed down my face. She took me in her arms and held my head against the side of hers and I felt how stiff her starched white cap was, under her veil. It scratched my cheek. I cried and cried and she just held me. When I was done I said thank you. I said I hoped my tears hadn't wilted her habit. She offered me a bar of the World's Finest Chocolate, with almonds, which we sold every year as a fundraiser.

That was my last day at school. And it was the day I told Sally and Anne-Marie the whole truth. The story I had made up, and that they had believed, was that Jeff and I had broken up because I'd seen a cheerleader from the public school riding in his Spitfire. I had explained that the loss of him made me feel so empty inside that I was filling up with food—hot fudge ice cream cake, onion rings, Milky Ways, cheeseburgers, whole jars of olives. I couldn't stop eating. They'd given me their pity and understanding. Both confessed that grief made them overeat too. They were just lucky they hadn't blown up like I had. They were both on the basketball team. I was the sedentary one. We talked about it quite a lot. Almost every night on the phone I'd produce a litany of the food I'd consumed that day. They tried to help: when you get the urge to eat, drink three glasses of water to give you the sense of fullness; Scotch tape pictures of fat people onto the refrigerator door; always have peeled carrot sticks on hand. They were taken in by my story.

The truth floored them. Anne-Marie kept covering her face with her hands and saying she couldn't believe it. Sally called Jeff a shithead over and over. Neither of them had known a pregnant person before so they had lots of questions. Sally wondered if they should get everyone in our class to sign a petition begging Sister John Gabriel to let me stay in school.

No, I said. Just don't forget me. Without Jeff, without school, I'll really have nothing to do. I'll just be home watching *The Price Is Right* and *The Guiding Light*, I said, and reading Victoria Holt and Mary Stewart.

But that's not what happened. Our television broke and my mother said we couldn't afford to have it fixed. Even then I knew this was a lie but I accepted it. I didn't like TV that much anyway. My mother had probably broken it herself, got a screwdriver and took the back off, unscrewed a bulb or a tube or unhooked a small wire. "Well, no use sitting around here," she said. "You'll feel better if you exercise," she said, a radical notion for those days, I realize now, but I obeyed her. Every day but Sunday we went swimming at the YWCA pool. I'd move slowly through the cool blue water and imagine that my baby was doing the same thing, moving slowly in the water in my womb, waving his tiny arms, kicking his tiny legs, holding his tiny eyes closed tight. My little swimmer.

We didn't have in utero photographs in those days like we do now. But there were sketches. I checked out a book from the library called *Expectant Motherhood* that fascinated me. I learned the words for all my parts from that book, words I'd had introduced to me in sophomore biology but that had seemed to belong only to married women: fallopian tube, cervix, vaginal canal, uterine lining. I learned that bones in my pelvis were going to loosen up, that I'd be split, sort of like an earthquake, when it was time for the baby to be born.

Our library didn't have books on how to put your baby up for adoption. I don't remember where we got the phone number that led me to Mrs. Quinn, who told me all about a Catholic couple one state away. She didn't say which way. The man was a member of the Knights of Columbus and the woman was active in the Sodality. I bet the number came from Sister John Gabriel. The man was a lawyer and the woman a homemaker who loved to bake and do needlepoint. They'd been married for seven years and God still hadn't given them a child. I thought they sounded okay. I thought about this good couple for a few days and then I called Mrs. Quinn and told her they could have the baby. I filled out forms. I signed my name.

I got down my bag of yarn and asked my grandmother for the knitting lessons she had promised me. Knit one, purl one. It was soothing to sit in the wing chair in my mother's sewing room and knit. I thought the least I could do for the child was to give him a many-colored blanket for a birthday present, a going-away present.

My mother's sewing machine was across the room from me and as I knit, she sewed, humming away, making me maternity clothes. My mother made me a ridiculous number of dresses for a person who hardly ever went anywhere except to the library and the YWCA. But she kept buying great swaths of flowered material and designing me these tents. She didn't want me to get depressed.

My father brought me something just about every day, just something from the newsstand by his bus stop, a box of lemon drops, a bag of salted peanuts, a strawberry twirler, a *Time* magazine. He'd ask me how I was feeling and smile kindly but he never mentioned the baby directly. He taught me how to play backgammon and let me help him build a birdhouse down in the basement, at his workbench.

Sister John Gabriel had implored me to keep up with my schoolwork. "You must keep your mind alive," she said. I had planned to do a little algebra every day, a little chemistry, some French, religion, and English, but I got lazy. I remember reading some French plays, one by Corneille and one by Racine and one by Molière. I read each one out loud, alone in my room. The rhythm of their verses put me in the same mood as swimming did. For some reason, reading made me feel close to my baby. I felt like the poetry was a lullaby. It was soothing for me and I thought it was soothing for him.

My English class that semester I dropped out was British Literature. The only entire novel we were assigned was *David Copperfield*. I read that alone too, in my room. My class hadn't gotten to it before I left. When I first began novels in those days, I always had a dictionary and a notebook at my side. Once I got hooked I never bothered to look up a word but for the first thirty pages or so

I was alert for words whose meanings I was unsure of. "Caul" appears on page one of *David Copperfield* and that was my first entry in my new vocabulary notebook.

So when my baby was born with a caul, I knew what it was, I wasn't shocked or appalled in any way by the bubble I first saw him in through the haze of the drugs they had given me for the delivery. The doctor pulled it away, the veil, the membrane, and I could see him more clearly. He didn't look much like the graceful swimmer I had pictured during my pregnancy. He was much more wrinkled and red-faced and greasy.

The next day my mother made me visit him. She walked me down the hall to the nursery and made me look at him through the glass. His eyes were closed, his lips parted in a smile. His hair stuck straight up. My mother motioned for the nurse to meet her at the nursery door. The nurse wasn't happy with what my mother said, I could see, but she complied. She handed her a gown and a mask, which my mother then handed to me. I put them on. Then she led me into the nursery and told me to sit in the rocking chair. The nurse was mad. She told my mother she was cruel, the baby was being adopted out, wasn't it? Was she trying to punish her daughter for getting pregnant in the first place? My mother didn't seem to hear her, she just took the baby from the nurse and gave him to me. She unwrapped his blanket and told me to feel his skin, his hair, and to be sure I was ready to give him up.

"Kiss him on the forehead when you're ready to say goodbye," she said.

I put my finger on his arm and moved it up and down. A petal. I touched his black hair and studied his toes. I laid my hand on his stomach and closed my eyes. I tried to conjure up the girl in the efficiency apartment pretending to be Diana Ross. I even hummed her song, "Baby Love, My Baby Love," but I never saw the girl with the heavy black eyeliner and bleached stringy hair. She just wouldn't appear, even though I'd written about her vividly in my journal.

I kissed him on the forehead but I didn't say goodbye. I held him for most of that day and stared and stared at his face. I called Mrs. Quinn the next day and told her the deal was off. My mother got my old bassinet out of the crawl-space and put it next to my bed at home and she went to a department store and bought him kimonos and diapers and rubber pants.

A few days after we got home, I called Jeff's mother and told her my news. She was shocked. I had been so firm in my resolve to give the baby up. She wasn't at all prepared to deal with having a grandbaby. But she was kind and told me she was sure I'd done the right thing and the next day she came over to visit. She brought a little blue sweater and hat and bootie set for Danny—I had decided against naming him Jeff—and she brought a nightgown for me. She brought along Jeff's last letter. It was full of the rigors of boot camp and included a photograph. I barely recognized him, his head was almost shaved. And that day, for the first time in three years, I felt no love for him. When he looked like a soldier, he was a stranger to me.

But the love came back in a few months. I even put his picture back up on my dresser for Danny to look at. And I kept imagining that he'd come to his senses, that a grenade would explode in front of him in the jungle outside of DaNang and knock him to his senses and he'd come home and marry me and move us into our favorite tower of apartments. On Sundays the three of us would picnic in the cornfield.

He did come home before his tour of duty was completed. He was wounded by friendly fire—a buddy's gun had gone off accidentally and the bullet got Jeff in the leg. His mother called me in secret to tell me he was home. She had written him everything. She was trying to persuade him to at least visit me. He didn't have the courage, it seemed.

Danny was walking by then. I polished his white hightop shoes and dressed him cute in a sailor outfit and took him over to meet his father. I had my body back by then and my hair was still long and I thought the two of us would be irresistible, sort of. My mother said later maybe I should have left Danny with her, if I really wanted Jeff back.

I don't know if I really wanted Jeff back that day. But I climbed the steps to his mother's door with Danny on my hip. I saw through the picture window that he was there, sitting at the kitchen table with his mother. He looked anguished. His chin was in his hands. His eyes were closed. His hair was still short. I guessed that they were talking about me.

He didn't kiss me but he was real nice to me. He told me he was sorry and he even wept a little. He kept staring at Danny, looking for himself I guess, and trying to make contact with him but Danny had found the cupboards with the pots and pans and was much more interested in making a racket than in making a relationship with his long-lost father.

So Jeff wasn't the man of steel he had made himself be when he'd said goodbye to me all those months before. But he wasn't the same as he'd been in the cornfield, that's for sure. I could see it on his face—faraway eyes, set teeth, a line beginning between his eyebrows. I guess war changes a person, the way having a baby does. So by the time I said goodbye, by the time I threw my arms around his neck and told him I'd always love him and told him that having his baby was the best thing in my life, I knew that it was over, I knew that there'd never be a wedding with Anne-Marie and Sally in fuchsia.

And having his baby is still the best thing I ever did, nineteen years later. I tell my mother that, and I ask her if she had known it would be, if that's why she insisted I hold and touch his newborn self. But she swears not, she shakes her head adamantly, and says no, she thought that giving him up was the right thing to do. She thought I should have my own life. She didn't want me to be tied down at sixteen, tied down by love and obligations.

My mother is old now but there are hardly any lines in her face. Her hair is a bright white. She braids it and winds it into a bun at the back of her neck. Her skin always looks tan with her hair so white. Her eyes are a clear blue, like the water in a swimming pool. We sometimes go together now to that YWCA pool, where I first pictured Danny inside of me. We do laps side by side, slowly. It seems more meditation than swim, sometimes. It seems like a holy place, the swimming pool, like a cornfield, like a church, like a room where a baby is born.

sarah kennedy
Second Child

When I lift my shirt to offer
a swollen nipple to the baby,
my older daughter waddles
from the room. The doctor
has warned she may demand
to return to nursing at the sight
of a sister's pleasure, and the one
in my arms smiles. It shocks
me—my first never cracking
a grin before six weeks.
But now I'm twenty
and, accustomed to isolation,
haven't spent nine months
crying in bed for an education
and my parents, my old friends,
ruining, my husband frowning,
that child's disposition. But
here she comes, raising the front
of her T-shirt to press the mouth
of a stuffed brown bear
over her two-year-old chest.
A sweet picture? My mother
would say so, if she were speaking

to me. It's so perfect, I'm frozen
in this frame, breath stopped,
fantasies of freedom dissolving.
How *normal* I feel, closing my eyes,
sweating a little from the toddler
welded to my side, the new baby
locked on my aching breast.

judith h. montgomery

Night Terrors

He is standing, screaming. Shaking
the rail of the blue-shadowed crib

again. Eyes, blind wells. Glazed.
Open, but not to you or the lop-

eared rabbit or the paper-folded bird
gliding white above the nursery lamp.

His body is hostage to a phantom
horse that tangles his wrists in reins,

and drags him deep into alien terrain.
You cannot wake him to your breast.

Rush him wailing from the house,
plunge into the moon-sharp street

where elms splay black in March
and bare feet burn on frost. Talk

him back from the terror—not
knowing what he's seen. Your night-

gown whips your knees. Words
clack and shatter on the ice-slick walk.

You would do anything—
gas and flame your library of books,

renounce the earth and its green rustle
of bright sun—whatever

it takes to fetch him home.

sandra perlman
Suddenly I Am My Mother

Suddenly I am my Mother
dressed in comfortable shoes
with a towel draped over my shoulder;
and I'm not just her little girl anymore
but one much older who is called
MOTHER to some other girl who clings unafraid
just as I used to do.

molly ruskin
Ice Ages

Frozen in sepia tones
a grubby barefoot boy,
your great-grandfather,
clutches a cone of dripping ice cream
and now you sit
slurping a cherry Popsicle
syrup running in rivers
down dimpled knuckles

By the dinosaurs downtown we pause—
you at my hip,
our fingers entwined,
necks craned backward—
to behold a soaring timeline
and the dull gray mark
where human beings
dribble into the picture

Far less than a sigh in God's time

Here on the marble floor,
among the colorful, crowding legs and feet,
I pull you closer, marveling

Molly Ruskin — Ice Ages

It cannot be merely relative
these moments melting
into moments

Surely something in the particular matters,
even if the universe knows these same secrets

In your chubby fist
an acorn tightly gripped
reveals so much more

This is how I will cling to this life
I within you, you within me
our breaths nested like Russian dolls
awaiting wonders
savoring sweetness
loving
while it is our turn

kathleen walsh spencer
Slow Dance

I roll up baby socks,
folding cuff over cuff in pairs to pack
in the attic
with pink sleepers and crib blankets
boxed for Goodwill
for someone else's baby.
I wear a shawl of selfishness
for wanting another child
when I begged heaven for this one,
just one.
Now I slow dance with her in the dark,
stepping small circles,
arms on each other's backs
in an excessive embrace like seniors at the prom.
Shuffling worn slippers on the carpet of the nursery,
I stroke my daughter's angel hair
with the underbelly of my chin,
as she sleeps with a hot cheek against my neck.
I cling to what's left of her babyhood.
When she awakens she'll wrestle down
and be gone.

katy mckinney

50-50

When Molly
throws her arms around my neck
and tells me she loves me one hundred,
Ben, more worldly at seven,
allows that he loves me 50-50.
Considering our relationship of late,
I take this as a compliment.
It's scary to feel the disintegration
of that first pure love, frightening
to be swept so early into the flood
of rebellion and discipline.
Somewhere between the terrible twos
and the storms of adolescence,
I thought we'd have some peace.
But for now,
our stubborn heads collide:
he balks, I yell,
he cries, doors slam,
I sigh.
"That's funny,"
says my unsympathetic mother
when I tell her on the phone
about his fits of obstinate defiance
and his dawdling and daydreams
that keep us forever harried and late:
"I knew a child like that once."

arlene eager
Milk

Married a year,
she still can't cook.
She ought to clean the place
but she's so tired.
There's no washer
in the second-floor apartment,
and diapers are cloth,
not yet disposable,
so she washes dozens of them
in the kitchen sink in Ivory Flakes
the way her mother showed her,
then hangs them on the line
that runs from the bedroom window
to a tree in the backyard.

When it rains for days,
she drapes clean wet diapers
on the cast-iron radiators.
They dry stiff and she shakes them
and rubs them between her hands
to make them soft. After two weeks of this,
rivers of condensation run down the walls.
Hopeful one minute, weeping the next,

she wonders if she's going crazy.
The way she sees it,
there's only one thing she does right.

When the baby wakes and cries,
her milk lets down and gushes
from her breasts and soaks her blouse.
They settle down, the two of them.
The chair is soft, the dark blue eyes
in the puzzled face peer up at her
and one tiny fist bats against her breast.
The baby always looks surprised,
and gulps the flowing blue-white milk
in bliss. The thrill of love
breaks her open every time,
nearly drowns her.
She will never be this good
at anything again.

marion cohen
Bret-at-Six Remembers My Womb

It was boring.
He couldn't wait to get out.
But then, once he did, he was sorry.
It wasn't like he'd thought.
He'd thought he'd just get out of the BAG
and then go exploring in my ribs 'n' brains 'n' stuff.
He'd thought he'd get closer to me.
Not further away.

franka arabia
Untitled

I'm up early
Making lunches
And breakfast...
When I get it right
They gobble it down
And I don't feel guilty
They pile in the car and I put on their seat belts
On the way to school he asks for his permission slip
The one "that's due today"
The one
I forgot to sign
Lost somewhere in the mound of documents
Laying on my desk

hilary tham
The Naming

It all began with Mother,
Mother who called me *nui*,
word meaning female, meaning daughter,
gave me a doll to cherish, made me
addicted to tidiness, driven to fulfill
each commitment. She spoke of an imperfect world
and women its caretakers, how bulls were
like men, responsive to the gentle
tug of a nose ring, they run
from sticks and hard voices.
My husband Joe names me Wife, meaning
lover, caretaker, mother of children,
his faith and lineage, gives me
the lamp to light his way home.
Now my daughters name me, believe
I am everything, ring me with needs.
In their faces, I see the past
and future, time rippling curves of faces;
grandfather's, mother's, Isaac's, Joe's, they rise
like the wind's breath on water.
I accept their naming. I am kin
to poet Chu Yuan's self-drowned body
nibbled to nothing by river fishes.

nicole braun

Newborn Baby without the Picket Fence

Part 1.

To exorcise the demons
Inside of me
To write—
To split the world open
with my stories, life
You were inside of my womb dear baby
boy? girl? healthy? sick?
The doctors: they advise abortion
The religious groups: adoption
Your father? Disappeared; was fleeting; lasted only a moment in time.
My mother? Disappeared; was fleeting; lasted only a moment in time.
Inside my twenty-year-old self, with no home, I die
The heat of the summer kills the once green grass full of life
in
the
spring.
The stench and ruin and torridity of the inner city
spew poverty out of decay
And I, I
pregnant, poor, and alone.

Part 2.

Then: You are born.
No longer inside of me.
I leave you at the hospital, alone.
(like me)
You are a red-faced, crying, angry baby boy
You claw at the crib, your face a ball of fury
They tell me circumcision does not cause pain at birth.
I leave you at the hospital alone, faced with my own guilt
you are without a mother
(like me)
you are without a father
(like me)
I am without a partner or anyone to understand my pain.

† † †

Later: the neighbors ask: Where is your baby? They want to know.
I walk away
as if I am deaf
I have a dear family picked out for you, my child. A family that will love you. A family with supportive extended family members and a big house and they want a child so badly and they are married oh for such a long time now and much older than I and they have respectable careers and they have wanted a child for so long now they cannot wait to get their hands on you. A white baby for sale.
I hate them.
I hate. the privilege of this family. they get to have you. because they are privileged.
I don't get to have you. because of my lack of privilege.
My mother writes me for the first time in years she tells me that if I didn't want you I should have had an abortion but now I've made a commitment and I should stick with it.
The irony does not escape me. This is, after all, the same mother who kicked

me out of her house when I was a young teenager and who never invited me back. This is the same mother, after all, who kicked out my youngest sister, when she was a teenager, too, and who never invited her back. I want to tell her: you, too, made a commitment and didn't stick with it. (but I don't)
I, at home from the hospital in the crack-infested apartment in the decaying city of flint, bleeding, but forced to return to work (I am a waitress in a blue-collar bar) I am bleeding both inside and out, for my dear baby, for my mother, my mommy, for a father, for someone—
and I am no longer pregnant, but still poor, and alone.

Part 3.

The patrons at the bar I am a waitress at want to know what has happened to the pregnant girl I used to be. I serve them their cheap draft beer with a fake smile on my face, crying in the bathroom during my break, bleeding—still bleeding.
They want to know: where is the baby? A drunk couple (they are regulars) at the bar tell me I should be ashamed of myself. Why didn't I have an abortion if I didn't want you. How could I? While they lecture me in their drunken state, their five children call up to the bar periodically for hours on end wanting to know when they are going to come home to make dinner.
I have no crib. No bottles. No baby clothes. No blankets. No diapers.
I have no good parental examples, no role models, no money, no help, no
    belief
in myself.
I am condemned by everyone, except by some professionals who think I have committed a selfless act. (they identify with the adoptive couple)
I call the hospital and say: I am coming to get my baby. (I had thirty days to make up my mind before the couple gets you for good)
and: I do.

Part 4.

I cannot put you down dear baby. The privileged family is very mad and disappointed, the adopting agency angry as well; the social worker acts betrayed. I almost start a fire in the house; as I don't know how to heat the bottles; and I am exhausted from working all night in the bar; so I fall asleep; heating the bottles; I am exhausted from working all night; picking you up from the baby-sitter who I pay one dollar an hour—she smokes all night long around you, collects welfare, and complains that I spoil you because you like to be held. I figure she knows more than me, after all, she's had many children of her own.

I still cannot put you down, dear baby, despite the baby-sitter's complaints. Dear baby: you are a boy and healthy and I love you and I will be your mother and father and grandmother and grandfather all at the same time. Dear baby: I hate you I cannot sleep is there no one to help. Dear baby; I fall into sleep and fear that I will forget you; forget that you've been born; I fear that I will leave the house and leave you there. All Alone.

Dear baby: you have changed my world and my life and I love you.

judith arcana
Snow, Fall

That one time you hit the baby, that one time
out on the street when the bus was so late
and then didn't come and the snow
started falling; that time you lifted all
your food in bags, paper handles dampening
and she kept holding onto your leg, pulling
your coat and you couldn't carry her too
while the flakes came thick and wet and faster.
That's the time you remember, not all
the times you didn't, all those times when
you didn't hit the baby, times you both giggled
rolled in the grass naked of anger and fear
while the teddy bear and plastic chicken
slept on top of the rackety wooden dog
without fighting. Their toy allegory is nothing
compared to that one time you saw her small face
inside the wool scarf, her wide open eyes surprised
at the slap under the hat with knitted ear flaps;
you remember that time, sharp points on every flake, falling.

margaret mcmullan

Hurricane Season

Baby Charlie was already in the house when a woman from some office in Hancock County called to say that they had Mary's will and that it looked like she had planned ahead because it had been Mary's wish for Norma to become legal guardian. As Charlie arched his back and howled, Norma shouted out, "Are you sure?" over the phone and opened up another beer.

Norma went drunk to the funeral with her husband Sam and Charlie. In her blur, she held out hope that she would meet up with some of Mary's people—they would know what to do with the child. But the only other people there were the priest and the few women Mary had gone out drinking with that night. They all stood without moving as they watched a man in a truck lower a cable that held the pine box in which Mary lay. Norma could feel the wet grass through her shoes as she watched. The casket bumped the side of the hole as it was lowered, and for one long instant, it hung on the lip. Clumps of soggy red dirt rolled down the side. Some people left, but Norma stayed. She had heard that sometimes a crooked undertaker would dump a body out of the casket then resell the casket. Her white heels sank deep into the ground, and she stayed until the man with the backhoe had shoved the last pile of red clay on Mary.

Afterwards, they ended up at somebody's place near a fish store, and as they all kicked around the oyster shells in the driveway, they talked about how someone must have screwed up the brakes on Mary's car when she had them fixed the week before. Surely someone was to blame for this *devastation*.

The petunias all around the driveway were sticky and spent and whatever was left of anything was ghost gray. Sam sat on the porch swing smoking, watching Norma, and rocking Charlie who was wearing the same Cheetos-colored T-shirt he'd been wearing the night his mother died. Every now and then Charlie knocked against the cast on Sam's leg. Neither one of them seemed to mind. Mary had left Charlie with Norma that last night she went out, had even kissed Norma goodbye, her lips moist from beer, and said, "Wish me luck" because she wanted to meet a man. As Norma drank and listened to the talk in the driveway, she settled back into what she already knew: She didn't want Mary dead and she didn't want Mary's six-month-old baby boy, Charlie.

That night, Norma sipped bourbon straight and tried her own version of "It's a Small World After All," but she didn't know all the words, so she fixed on "Amazing Grace," a song she recalled her mother singing to her. Still, Charlie cried. Norma imagined he cried because he didn't have any words. She watched in amazement as he wailed, his lips growing plump, his dark little head turning red and hot, until at last he arched his back and thrust his face skyward in a final spasm of anger and sorrow.

"Holy hell," Sam said, looking in on them. He limped away, then closed the door to their bedroom, saying he'd sleep on the sofa.

"I know, I know sugar," Norma said to Charlie. "Maybe you and me can make a nice eggnog later on."

She knew Charlie would have no memory of his mother but she also knew his body remembered in ways that his mind could not. She did not know how she knew this, she just did. Neither Sam nor Norma had ever had any children. It simply had not happened, and by the time they had reached their mid-forties and their second marriages, it was too late. Norma put her little finger in her glass of bourbon and touched Charlie's lips. The baby stopped crying at first only because he tasted something new, then he cried more because of the newness. Norma tried another finger of bourbon, and finally Charlie quieted down. Rocking him in her arms, Norma cried and drank, hating death and hating Sam for being the only thing she had left.

It rained all day the day after Mary's funeral. It was almost October and hurricane season wasn't over yet on the Mississippi Gulf Coast. For years, people in Gulfport were predicting a bigger one—bigger than Andrew, bigger even than

Camille. By the time Norma finished setting up the crib and started a second sixpack, the rain was coming down in sheets.

"Maybe it's a blessing," she said, putting down the beer to rock Charlie with both hands. They had already gotten Charlie's things from Mary's place and the bags of clothes, diapers, and formula were all around them.

"Some way to get blessed," Sam said, scratching the skin around the top of his cast.

That night Charlie finally fell asleep, leaving Norma awake and alone, staring at her husband's back as he typed at his computer in the next room. Sam hadn't worked since he'd fallen off the roof of a video store he'd put up three months ago. He had talked about getting a job at the new casino when his leg healed, but then he went and bought a computer at a yard sale and spent $450 to take an online computer class.

Norma went over and nuzzled up to Sam. She wanted to lose the feeling of being tired, to forget about Mary and death. She concentrated on Sam's shoulders and attempted to get back the feeling of being in love. She thought about that warm, rainy night, inside Sam's first car—the blue one. They had fogged up all the windows then, leaned back in their seats, and with his big toe, Sam drew a heart on the windshield, writing *I Love U* on the inside. Norma thought about this, trying to recall that feeling she had had then when she read the inside of Sam's heart.

"You're hanging on me, babe," Sam said, reading something on his screen then copying it down on his cast. The cast went all the way down to his toes, but Sam's notes only reached as far as his knee.

"I can keep on cleaning houses. I'll just bring Charlie with me the way Mary did. You find out anything more about that casino job?"

"Leave me be," Sam said. "Can't you see I'm in class."

"We have another mouth to feed, you know."

Sam swirled around in his chair. There were dark rings under his eyes and he hadn't shaved. "Don't you think I know that? Would you leave me alone for one minute? I'm trying to do something here."

"Okay, okay," Norma said, backing up.

Sam turned back to his computer. Norma stood in the doorway, staring at her husband's shoulders, rounded like a woman's. The room he called his office smelled of coffee and unwashed bodies.

Norma got another beer. Ever since Sam had hooked himself up to the World Wide Web, he didn't look at TV and he didn't look at her. Norma wondered what they said to each other in their online chat rooms—her husband and these other people—women, most likely. She'd read about such things in the newspapers, heard about their stories on TV talk shows. Even Mary had warned her and everyone knew that Mary had some Choctaw witch in her.

If she emailed someone about her life now, Norma thought about the mountain of dirty dishes and laundry that would fill her on-screen letters. Then there were the groceries and the water, electric, and phone bills. And now there were the diapers and ointment and bottles of formula. There was and there was and there was, and these all filled whole days, weeks, and months that would make up the years and Norma wondered who would be interested in all this junk that made up her life. Changing into her nightgown, Norma wondered, momentarily, if she should start going back to church. Then she considered leaving Sam.

She lay in bed with the windows open, and even though she didn't mean to, Norma caught herself thinking back to the times she'd spent with her first husband. His fingertips smelled of shrimp shells and she had liked the tobacco taste of his mouth. But after she left, she had to put a restraining order on him, then he landed up in jail anyway for a handful of DUIs. He was a freckled, brown-haired man who did drink too much and who did hit her once or twice—it was true—but he was always trying to make Norma laugh.

Hot and tired, Norma got up out of bed. She had a taste in her mouth now for bourbon and Coke.

The following morning, all along the waterfront people were closing up their houses, hammering fitted plywood over windows, and locking their shutters. Miss Betty was yammering on about how she just loved the tail end of hurricane season and how it seemed to her such a lovely, dishonest time. Miss Betty had had a party the night before and the house smelled of fish, perfume, and alcohol. There were crumpled napkins and dirty glasses still in the living room and Miss Betty told Norma to recycle any empty bottles from the liquor cabinet. The bottles were standing on a marble side table under a picture of Miss Betty's great-grandfather. Miss Betty had the good stuff and there was a lot still left. As Norma passed, following Miss Betty to the back bathrooms, the floor rumbled and the bottles shook and clinked against each other.

Sometimes Norma walked into a house with just a little mess and she'd wonder why the woman couldn't clean up herself, why she had to hire someone to do her cleaning. Mary had explained it once and Norma figured she understood as well as anyone: There were times when a person needed somebody's help to get back to ground zero just so they could get on with their lives. Some did their own dishes, stripped their own beds, bothered about their own laundry, but it always took people like Norma and Mary to know that behind every microwave lay cobwebs, under every refrigerator was dirt.

Most people along the Mississippi coast weren't entirely comfortable with white maids. They figured something was wrong with a white woman who would be a maid, but Norma could tell that Miss Betty had gotten used to her and to Mary, maybe because they did not look at all like Miss Betty. Norma and Mary could have been mistaken for sisters. They both had heavy, hanging breasts, narrow hips, and dark hair. Norma often told Miss Betty that she and Mary were like Laverne and Shirley from that old TV show—always laughing and getting into trouble, spending more time with each other than with anybody else.

Cleaning other people's houses was better than working third shift at the shirt factory, a dismal place with no windows and no air conditioning. The outside of the building was painted with pretty, false windows and planters, and wisteria bloomed eternally over fake open doorways. The other girls who worked there were all younger than Norma, and they reminded her of all the mistakes she had made. On breaks and at lunchtime, she sat outside in the shade, smoking and watching them eat their hamburgers, going on and on about plans that would never materialize, houses that would never be bought, men who never were what they pretended to be. These girls still laughed and their laughter still sounded like giggling, and even if they smoked, the sound of their giggles came out clear and sing-songy. Norma had met Mary at the factory. They were about the same age and they were put to work side by side—Mary doing buttons, Norma zippers.

Norma put Charlie down in his car seat, then she set to work on Miss Betty's bathroom. Norma was tired, but she was used to waking up feeling heavy and hung over, working and waiting for the end of her shift, waiting for another drink to give her a few hours' worth of light-headedness. She thought everyone worked through their days this way. She could not remember spending the waking hours of her life any other way and she felt she had finally become what she was meant to become—a tired old woman. At least she knew who she was and what she was.

Miss Betty had already packed her bags. She was dressed up, ready to go out, trying to hook a gold bracelet around her wrist. All summer Miss Betty had felt smug, telling everybody how good her bone density was ever since she had been shopping at that expensive health food store downtown.

"I was sorry to hear about Mary," Miss Betty said, looking up from her bracelet. "How's Charlie?" Without touching him, Miss Betty bent over to examine Charlie in his car seat on the bedroom floor. She neither smiled nor frowned. Miss Betty did not say so now, but she was of the belief that the reason there was so much *E. coli* in the world was because there were too many people with too many pets and too many babies and there was just too much "dookie." She had used that word—dookie—when she told this once to Norma and Mary before there was Charlie, and later, over a pitcher of beer, Norma and Mary had laughed long and loud, repeating the way Miss Betty had said "dookie."

"Charlie's doing real good," Norma said, on her knees, scrubbing out the tub. She went on to tell Miss Betty what a wonderful woman and good friend Mary had been, how such a thing ought never to have happened, how she hated to think of Mary all alone out there on the highway in the middle of the night, it raining and all, and Miss Betty interrupted and said, "I know, I know. Why on earth didn't she just take a cab? Drinking so much then driving. All those times she used to call in saying she was too depressed or too tired to work. What was it last? Oh yes. She said you were both laid up with sick headaches." Miss Betty shook her head and Norma thought she saw her smile. "Now we know, don't we? We know all right. She was just hung over. It could make a person livid."

The bathroom cleaner stung Norma's eyes, and even though the air conditioning was on, she had to open a window for air. Norma tried to think of something to say back to Miss Betty then, but already Miss Betty was going on now about her *evacuation* and how she'd be out for the day and for all week that week staying with relatives somewhere around Magnolia, *inland*. Do be careful not to touch a Louis-something chair, Mrs. Gillespie sat in it and broke it last night, and could Norma get rid of those sunflowers over there, wilting in the corner? They smelled like dog piss. Miss Betty swore at the clasp she still could not clasp, then stuck out her arm towards Norma, who without a word, fastened the bracelet.

"I hope you have a place to go," Miss Betty said, her breath smelling like mangoes. It was understood: Miss Betty was getting out and she wanted, no, *needed*, Norma to look after the house. Norma had her own key. Mary had once confessed to Norma that she wondered about Miss Betty and her kind—those women who lived closest to the water, women who talked about teas and lawn service and "building" their wardrobes. Mary had wondered out loud how such women spent the minutes of each day and what all they thought on. They had time to take naps and sit in a fancy chair to just think about the seasons or the way the wind blows curtains and changes the shadows in a room. They had time to forget their sadnesses, to be happy and to laugh.

"We're not down low. Did I ever tell you my great-grandfather built this house? See that rise out front? I like to think he knew it would save us from Camille," Miss Betty said, smiling, as if only poor people got killed.

Norma cleaned quickly that day, thinking about Miss Betty's party alcohol, telling Charlie all a person could do with baking soda and Windex, and wondering all the while what Mary's last thoughts had been, if she had thought of Charlie or even of Norma herself. Norma couldn't help but wonder about the details of Mary's accident, what exactly lay broken in the street and how much blood there had been. As Norma stripped the beds, then made them back up again, she hoped that an angel had come down with the rain to hold her friend's broken head while she lay in all that wet, twisted wreckage.

Miss Betty liked her bottles dusted before they were put away, and as Norma worked through the bar, she could hear herself thinking as she drank: You deserve this drink because your head is numb and you've lost your best friend. And you deserve another because your husband's out of work and another because you don't want to go home.

Norma and Mary always saved big houses like Miss Betty's along the waterfront for the end of the day, because afterwards, they could go down to the beach and walk on the flat part of the shore. Already Norma missed looking at Mary's bare feet in the salt water—her toenails painted red for the winter. They'd wipe the sand from their feet, then go up a ways to a bar at the corner of the street. It was then, after work, with Mary, waiting for drinks, when they smoked and talked about how bone-tired they were, that Norma would think to herself how much she needed to laugh again just to wake up, just to feel alive. Then the drinks would come and they'd toast something or somebody and they'd take their first sip and there would be a moment of silent, forgetful relief and it was in this quiet, holy second that Norma would always let go with a laugh because she felt safe then—like with Mary and with that drink under the canopy of their cigarette smoke everybody and everything was going to be all right.

Norma couldn't clean any of the other houses that week. They were all too big and lonely without Mary, and before she went to work her shift at the factory, Norma went back to Miss Betty's house every day, not to clean, but to sit outside on the porch with Charlie. When she saw Sam it was only to say she'd already eaten or not to wait up or Charlie needed more diapers. She never waited around long enough to hear his response.

It was raining every afternoon now, and one day, outside on Miss Betty's porch, Norma held Charlie in her lap, and feeling heavy and light-headed, she rocked him and told him about Camille. Norma had been fifteen when Camille hit. Some said the worst part was all the noise, but for Norma, the worst part was afterwards—the boats and bodies hanging from all those naked trees and the enormous effort it took to keep on living just when you didn't think you had anything more left in you.

It was like that now. It felt like after Camille. Ever since Mary had died, Norma felt as though the world had stopped and she didn't know how to get the strength back to start it spinning again.

Sitting out on Miss Betty's porch that day, Norma took another sip from her drink and looked out at the Gulf that was the color of Miss Betty's slate roof. She knew then that it really was the end of her friend Mary's life and that there was no getting her back, but it felt so much like the end of something else too. Drinking had killed Mary, and Norma knew at one point she would have to quit. But she did not want to quit, not yet, not now. It had been a month since the accident and Norma realized she had not laughed. Mary had said once that not being able to laugh was like being too weak to think of strength. Norma looked at Charlie, asleep in his car seat on the porch, then she rocked him awake and lifted him up to show him the dark, bourbon-colored sky, explaining to him why he would never be able to drink it all, even though someday she knew he would want to.

Norma woke up to the sun going down. It was windy out and the air felt yellow with the cool, but it didn't smell like rain.

Charlie was gone.

The tomato sauce smell coming from Miss Betty's kitchen filled the house with a warm, dark odor and Norma thought of how she would have to remind herself to open all the windows to air the place out before Miss Betty came back. Charlie was asleep in his car seat on top of the kitchen table. Plastic grocery bags ballooned all around Sam's feet as he stood at the stove, stirring.

"You just left me out there?" Norma said.

"You deserved to be left outside during a hurricane, Norma. You put that baby in danger. You think about that."

"I need something to drink."

Sam put a glass of something in front of her.

"Iced tea," he said.

They both looked at the glass.

"You can snap out of it now, Norma," he yelled. "Don't you see?" He spoke quietly then. "You've got to give the three of us a chance first before you go on and give up on everything and everybody."

Norma didn't say anything as she stood without moving. The TV in the kitchen was on and the local weatherman was standing out on the beach without a raincoat, saying that strong winds were headed that way and a hurricane might not be far behind.

Sam cleared his throat, then he told her how he had driven by Miss Betty's in his pickup and had seen Norma passed out in the rocking chair on the porch.

She had managed—just barely—to keep hold of the baby, who, with a soggy, dirty diaper, had been crying for who knew how long.

"I'll make a deal with you," Sam said finally. "I'll quit drinking too, right now, if you quit your drinking."

"It's not that bad. I just wanted to feel good again."

"You can't let yourself fall apart, Norma. You're not even trying." Sam looked at her then. "Not with me and not with yourself." She thought he might get a beer then, but he did not.

"Charlie needs you. I need you and you need us." Sam paused and looked at Charlie asleep. "We'll do what we have to. Meetings. Whatever. We got Charlie to think of now. I ain't never had a kid, and I'm not fucking up like I seen some do."

"So now you think I been fucking up." Norma felt her face get red.

"That's not what I meant."

They both stared at each other. Norma wanted to leave the room, the house, get in her car and drive to Alabama—anywhere east or west, it didn't matter, but the storm shutters were shut and the rain was coming down hard.

Sam limped over to her. She felt sticky now with a cold sweat. He said he would kneel down if he could, but with the cast and all, he couldn't. He awkwardly held her hand instead. She thought that she would not like that, not like the feel of Sam's rough palm, but it was warm and dry and she allowed herself to fall into a chair.

"You know when I fell off the roof that video store and didn't die, I felt like I got a second chance. Now I think I might be getting me enough computer skills so I can get some decent work. I've already got a lead on a job selling water systems. I won't have to keep killing myself putting up crappy little stores and you won't have to work at that factory."

"I need a cigarette," Norma said, looking around the room.

Sam put a cigarette in his mouth, lit it, then gave it to Norma. She took a long drag and considered the possibilities.

"Mary." Sam shook his head then. "She didn't get another chance."

A reporter was on TV talking to a woman at the grocery store. The woman was saying how much energy she had, knowing a hurricane might hit. She'd cleaned her house and now she was polishing all her silver.

Absentmindedly, Norma touched her own hair. The roots were coming out gray. She hadn't done anything to it since that day she and Mary took off and colored each other's hair in the kitchen sink. Mary had died that night, a blonde.

"I look like a raccoon," Norma said.

"You look damned good," Sam said. "And you know what else? You're strong enough for what's ahead. You might not know it, but I do. What's that the Brits say? Chin up."

Norma sipped from her glass. The sweet iced tea made her think of God and the coast. She bent down and kissed the top of Charlie's head. His hair smelled of everything.

Norma wanted to tell Sam to screw it all, to sit back down with her and drink and laugh for the rest of the evening, till the storm blew the pretty little roof off of Miss Betty's old house. That's what she and her first husband would have done and he would have called it their own private hurricane party. But the time would come after the storm and Norma didn't want to be sick or passed out or in need of another drink.

Norma sat staring at the black and blue computer instructions Sam had scribbled up and down his cast.

"I'll go put some towels under the doors," she said, getting up slower than usual. "For the leaks."

The electricity went out, the rain came down hard, and Charlie woke up crying. All the noise spooked him and he howled louder and longer than ever. Norma rocked him until he calmed down, and over his whimpers they could hear the rain on the roof and against the windows and the shutters shook. Sam got out flashlights, batteries, and candles, then filled up all the bathtubs just in case they lost the water too.

They ate by candlelight in Miss Betty's big dining room as Charlie watched the flickering light from Norma's lap. Norma hadn't known how hungry she was.

"That's one of my favorite sounds," Sam said as Norma chewed. "The sound of you eating something you really like."

The dark house and all that rain made them both nervous and polite with each other, like they were on the first date they'd never really had.

Finally the storm blew past. Sam found a battery-operated radio, and when he turned it on the weatherman was warning everybody that hurricane season wasn't over yet and that there were predictions that the "big" one was still to come. Fate or luck had turned this hurricane into a nasty storm with gale winds.

They brought Charlie into the living room and they pulled open the shutters to have a look outside. Tree branches littered the yard and the Gulf looked choppy and gray.

"Maybe this time next year, you'll be an assistant manager somewheres," Norma said, sighing, beginning to think now of wanting another drink.

"Maybe we'll get us a house of our own. A brick one," he said. "We've had a string of bad luck is all. But I can feel it changing. I can."

They were both of them looking out the window and Norma hoped they weren't just dreaming. Then she felt Sam's lips touching the back of her neck. Tentatively, she breathed out and settled her head back on his chest.

She recognized the vast stretch of white beach before them, the two sprawling Live Oaks, the telephone wires and the slick highway and the possibility that her life would never really change no matter what new job Sam got or where they moved, would in fact, always be just what it was now. She was born on the Gulf, lived on the Gulf, and would, most likely, die here. Norma had never thought much about why she lived where she lived just as she had not thought much about being with Sam all these years, not until Mary died, not until now. But standing here, looking out Miss Betty's window, Norma felt just then a vague sense of relief that at least she and Sam were not landlocked. At least here there was always something or at least the chance of something wonderful, terrible, or dangerous coming at them and it was up to them to see it through. She knew she did not really need a drink just then—didn't quite yet have to have one, and all at once, for just that moment, she felt less heavy.

Norma's breath was fogging up the window and she made a mark with her finger. She thought how funny it was that just standing there breathing could make an actual mark, as though by just being alive she made some kind of difference. She knew there was a chance she would forget this moment, this good feeling of not needing but of just being. She hoped she would not forget. Sam reached over, and with his index finger, he drew a heart. Just then, Charlie stirred in his car seat on the floor, and Norma and Sam stared at each other with the same expression on their faces as though they had finally gotten the same joke. Sam picked Charlie up and held him towards the window. Norma breathed again then she made another heart next to Sam's, then another and another, and with each heart Norma made, the baby kicked and giggled, and as the window caught the last bit of light from the sun going down, Sam smiled at Norma laughing.

dianne smaniotto
Dancing Partner

A little child
who cannot sleep
awaits our midnight rendezvous
becomes my dancing partner
before the night is through.
The living room, our dance floor
a lullaby minuet
our hearts beat with the melody
a mother and child duet.
It soon appears before her
the shadow on the wall
an audience in silhouette
captivated by it all.
We trace the same familiar steps
lost in tranquility
I serenade her sweetly
she becomes my harmony.
A little child nestled in my arms
there is no other love so deep
now dancing in her dreams
she waltzes off to sleep.

lost children

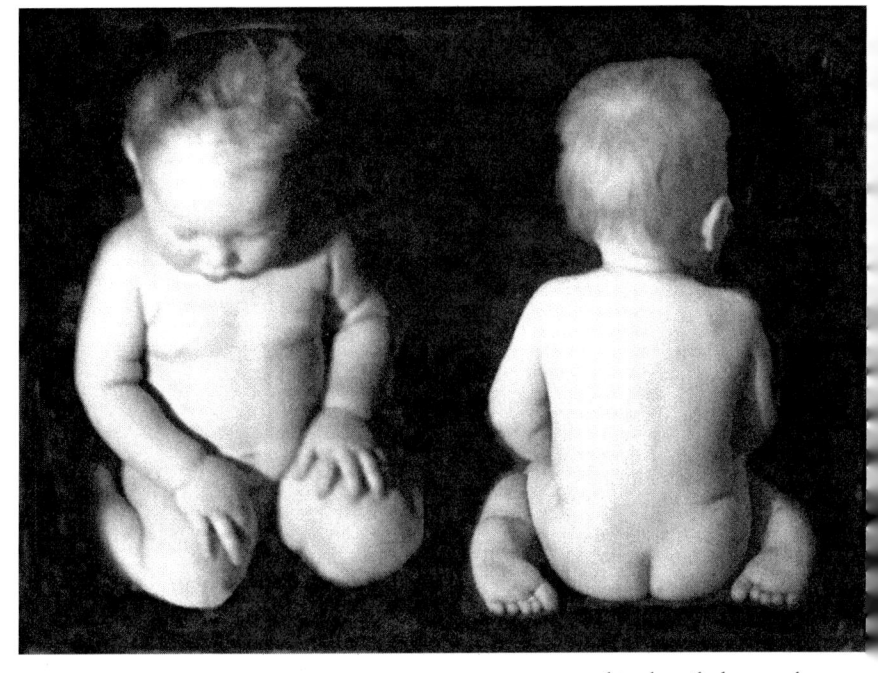

photo by mike hovancsek

jacqueline jules
As Soon as the Baby Moves

I remember having to sit down once from doing the dishes
'cause such a battle was going on inside.
The warm funny feelings I had then
holding up my shirt,
watching my big belly wiggle. So different
from what I felt a month later
when I realized
the wiggling had stopped.
Of course at first I told myself I was crazy—
I'd just been too busy to feel anything,
till that Thursday night
I sat on the couch in front of the TV
both hands folded on my belly
telling myself
I'd get up and go to bed
the minute I felt the baby move.
My husband found me on the couch in the morning.
But I didn't say anything to him
or the doctor, either.
I just sat up on that table, watching the black round circle

of the stethoscope move from one end of my belly to another—
back and forth, back and forth—
the doctor's young face turning grayer and grayer.
He never said it out loud, never asked me to call my husband.
Just told me to go to the hospital:
"For a test," he said,
looking away from me and down at his charts.
I drove to the hospital alone,
parked the car in the very back of the lot,
folded both hands on my belly,
and made a deal with myself about going in:
"As soon as the baby moves," I said.
The police found me in my car late that night.

kate banigan-white
First Child

In the weeks leading up to my daughter's birth, I filled the freezer with sweet breads for guests coming to see the glorious new arrival. I made banana chocolate chip, pumpkin, whole-wheat honey, and lemon poppy seed cakes as the McGarrigle sisters and Lucinda Williams crooned in the background. Sweet sugary smells of cinnamon, cloves, vanilla, chocolate, and fruit filled the house. I cooled each loaf on a round wire rack, and then wrapped it tightly in shiny tinfoil. I was joyful and proud. This was nesting at its finest.

After my daughter died the day she was born, the guests came. The sweet breads were retrieved from the freezer, thawed, and put on blue ceramic plates. Hot tea was served. Heads bent forward, towards my husband and me.

† † †

The morning of the birth, David and I wake up, telling each other with fear and excitement that this could be our last Saturday, just the two of us. We decide to clean our small two-story house "one last time." I take the kitchen and bathroom; David dusts and vacuums the rest of the house. As I scrub the bathroom sink, I imagine the trepidations I will soon encounter with Baby's First Bath. I smile at my reflection in the water-streaked mirror. A mother. Backing away, I turn to the side, raising myself on my toes to glimpse the large bulge that encloses my child. I can feel her move in the familiar way: rounding her back, then stretching her legs. I have been told it could be any time. "Your body's working well, doing what it needs to do," the obstetrician said the afternoon before. I wrap my arms around myself. *I love you*, I think, *I'm ready.*

It begins with the pain and blood that sends David and me rushing to the hospital late at night. We had been having dinner at our friends' house when the symptoms started. Moments after arriving at the hospital I am curled, knees to chest, feeling the sting of spinal anesthesia, preparing for an emergency cesarean section. Nurses, physicians, and technicians swirl around me, and David is instructed to change quickly into scrubs. My limbs shake and my teeth chatter and I ask the nurses if I am going into shock. "You're afraid, honey," one says.

The words "It's a girl!" are exclaimed, just as I'd always imagined. One doctor looks at me through plastic goggles, eyes wide. It is so bright in the operating room. I breathe deeply into my oxygen mask to steady myself. I scan the room, searching for her. I see a baby on a table, people all around her, performing CPR. *That's my daughter*, I say to myself. She's motionless and silent. I tell myself that everything will be all right but I watch David, hovering beside me, as the doctors are sewing me back up. He looks over his shoulder a lot, face tight and reddening. People circling the CPR table turn around and look at us: the gray-bearded man, the older woman with curly brown hair, the African American woman. I look over at her. "Oh God this is so sad," I say softly.

Two nurses back away from the CPR table, palms open, up. The anesthesiologist leans over me to say, "I'm sorry, she has died." I already know. David's mouth is open and low sounds escape. We huddle together. I put my hand over my face and attempt to use language. "I am so sad," I say. How many times? How loudly? Faces look at me, crying faces, concerned and sad looks. There is a lovely Latino man in bright green scrubs sitting and looking at us, silently. An African American nurse with long black hair brings our baby to us. "Do you want to see her?" she asks, her words echoing. Our baby has a head of dark brown hair, and her lips are pursed. She looks peaceful, and so beautiful. "She's very cute," I say meekly. Hospital staff remaining in the room stand with bowed heads, as if in prayer. As I am wheeled down the hall of the childbirth center to my recovery room, I cover my face, ashamed.

Doctors and nurses move around me, asking me questions to which answers don't come. A nurse hugs David for a long time, smoothing down his hair with the palm of her hand, like a mother. The pediatrician who attempted to resuscitate our baby approaches my bedside and touches my shoulder. He says he's sorry, asks if we have a church, and if there's anyone who needs to be called. When he tells me he'll come by tomorrow to talk more, I acknowledge that he wants to discuss having an autopsy performed. He nods his head. He is so sorry.

The recovery room nurse brings our baby to us again, wrapped in a blanket with a pink hat on her head. I am afraid to see her again but David says we'll be glad we did, and he wants to hold her. We ask the nurse to stay with us. We name this child Elizabeth Story, after my mother, as we planned. She is ashen, but lovely. Do we want to see her little hands? No, I say, and later regret it. Of course I want to see her little hands. I want to hold her, observe her hair color and texture, memorize her features, feel her weight. David holds her, and I stroke her arm, saying, "poor little baby." Why don't I take the time to hold and memorize all of her, and tell her what I'm feeling? I am terrified to face life without her.

A nurse tells me to press my right index finger down to make a print. The day we leave the hospital I will see my fingerprint by Elizabeth's footprints—little baby feet we're told were slightly clubbed. I would have loved to take care of them.

† † †

I wake up crying in the childbirth center as if I'm picking up where I left off the night before. David's hand reaches up to mine from the roll-away cot beside me and I take hold of his forearm. Sun emerges in slivers through venetian blinds.

We have been told that I had a sudden and complete placental detachment from my uterus, and Elizabeth was deprived of oxygen too long to survive once born. A pediatrician called emergency code upon her birth, and CPR performed for twenty-five minutes could not revive her. I hear this and feel I have failed. Was it my anemia in the second trimester? The blood transfusions that followed? How could I not have known in time? Did I not believe enough in my ability to deliver a healthy baby? I pull cotton blankets to my chin and turn my curled body towards the window.

The pediatrician from Elizabeth's birth comes by my hospital room early each morning. He's a man in his forties with a rosy complexion, a kind face, the weight of loss pulling his lean body towards me. In a community hospital situated in a college town it is rare for a pediatrician to preside over a dying neonate. Higher risk pregnancies are cared for in larger medical centers, in bigger cities.

After we attend to necessary issues—arranging an autopsy to confirm the cause of death and determine if an underlying cause can be found for the placental abruption—the pediatrician continues his visits. I am not sure why he wants to do this: is it for us? To comfort us and make sure we have the information we need? Is it for him? Is he afraid we might blame him for Elizabeth's death? Does it soothe him to remain in touch with us? I stare at his hands: now clasped in his lap, hands that once placed our breathless baby on a CPR table, administered a plethora of medications, pumped her heart, later gestured, *no more*. I watch them, now resting, perhaps remembering touch and movement. I remember constant light, a plastic mask, breathe in, breathe out.

My parents fly into Northampton from Louisville the morning after Elizabeth's death. I know they hold a double pain of losing a grandchild, and their daughter into a sea of grief. I see this when my mother first enters my hospital room and swallows hard, moving quickly towards my outstretched arms. *Oh, sweet baby*, she says. I had dreamed of telling her, tearfully, happily, that I named my daughter after her. I imagined her crying with joy.

Before we leave the hospital after our five-day stay, David and I gather the strength to ask for the three Polaroid pictures the nurse took of Elizabeth the night she died. At first I had thought looking at the pictures would be morbid; I was incredulous that they were taken and annoyed when people reminded us of their existence. But we are already forgetting what she looked like. The hospital social worker hands the pictures to us, along with a clipping of her hair and the hat she wore after death. We cry at the memories but they are a relief. The pictures don't show her as we remember her, held for us in the operating room, or in David's arms; she doesn't look as beautiful. They do show us that she was real and we decide to keep them.

The day of my discharge, I tell the nurse who cared for us nearly every day that I don't want to be wheeled out of the hospital, without my bundle wrapped in homemade blankets. This nurse has worked at the hospital for many years, and confidently breaks the rule that says all new mothers must be escorted out of the building in a wheelchair. She has tight curly brown hair, is very thin, and moves with efficiency. She leans into the open window of the car and asks us to send the nurses at the childbirth center a letter some time, "even if it's just to say: 'we've planted the daisies and we're doing okay.'"

The front door to our house opens into quiet. I walk to the places I'd pictured her in: the room that was to be her room, now without her crib, bassinet, and drawers full of clothes and diapers. Only a few weeks ago I filled the top drawers of a dresser with many items on our layette list: a thermometer, cotton swabs, rubbing alcohol, nail scissors, baby soap and shampoo, baby wipes. The book *Little Cloud* rests on our bedside table; David read it aloud days before, our bedtime ritual. The cover is blue and white with cardboard pages for a small child's learning hands. I press it to my chest, sinking into quilted covers.

† † †

I drive with my mother to take my father to the airport after his five-day visit, and my father and I embrace outside the terminal. When I first moved far from home, I used to cry privately after saying goodbye to my parents—I'd hug them at the airport and let the tears flow as soon as I turned around to board my plane. Now I can't help but sob in my father's arms. He calls us every day. My mother remains at our house for a second week and tells me she'll stay longer if I need her.

It's too soon, but David returns to work ten days after Elizabeth died. I get up with David as he readies for work; I want to face the day together. I wake, body heavy and slow, walk down the stairs, and kiss my husband hello. After David leaves, I stand at the kitchen sink and wash breakfast dishes. Thick, gray water fills the basin. I imagine it spilling all over the house, down the hall, down the staircase, sloshing up onto the kitchen table. It runs through the cracks of the front door and I'm sure that even those who *don't* know we've lost our baby can see it.

My mother has the gift of making things seem possible. Her tie to ritual and routine helps me to keep moving. We sit down for healthy meals each day and have a schedule of sorts. Even my mother's way of dressing—her elegant, tailored pantsuits and dresses—reassures me. Each day, we plan an excursion—just a small one—to keep us going. We visit a bookstore in a neighboring town, have fresh waffles at a local restaurant, and wander through the not-yet-bloomed gardens on a college's grounds. So that I can recover from my surgery, we take progressively longer walks down a bike path and through a wooded park.

Occasionally a small fraction of peace stands before me. It is a glimpse of what I know is there but I can't touch it. I try to remember this when I'm drowning, treading water, or when I wonder at the intensity of my emotions. "You've lost a child!" my mother reminds me. I pull myself off my bed or the living room sofa and peer into my puffy, red-rimmed eyes in the bathroom mirror, searching.

I sometimes think I can still feel her moving inside me—a small kick or that familiar rounding of her back. I have read that this is very common after a newborn baby dies, or a stillbirth. Some parents hear phantom crying after their baby dies. I hear nothing, but I do feel movement for several weeks.

What evidence is there? Breasts leaking, aching. Three color photographs. A plastic bag with clippings of dark brown hair. Developed film from weeks ago revealing a robust pregnant woman in a plum sweater, feet propped on a coffee table, reading the newspaper.

After my mother leaves, my friend Ruth comes out from Boston for a couple of days; I'm still afraid to be alone. Ruth drives me to my first postpartum checkup, after we take a long walk on the bike path behind our house. I put on my boots because it has snowed, and remember the day I bought them on sale, nearly eight months pregnant. I pranced gleefully out of the store, wearing them, saying over and over to David: "I love my boots! I love my boots!" I stomped into icy puddles, making him laugh as we crossed Main Street, and navigated Old South Street, towards our car.

I am eager to see my delivering physician; I still have questions about what happened. I walk into the pine-colored waiting room, so inviting with its homey decor and coffee tables covered with *Parents* and *American Baby* magazines. I cry as I step on the scale, and as the nurse asks me routine postpartum questions. She never acknowledges my loss and I stare away from her, at the rack of medical pamphlets on the wall.

The physician comes in. "How are you?" she asks and looks into my eyes. She has short, light brown hair and gold-rimmed glasses. She's not much older than I am and I suspect she's never overseen a case like mine. The morning after Elizabeth died, she had entered my hospital room just before dawn. The doctor on call that night, she left my recovery room to attend the births of others. She stood, head bent down, confessing a delayed reckoning with our daughter's death. "I just saw her again," she said, shaking. I reached for her hand. She was there.

We review again the night of Elizabeth's birth and death. I have many questions. Did you know when you saw her low heart rate on ultrasound that she could die? Did she suffer? Was I in danger of hemorrhaging to death? How common is placental abruption and how likely is it to recur? When can we attempt pregnancy again?

She takes her time with me. She is thorough in her responses, and refers to Elizabeth by her name. She tells me that in discussing my case with a colleague she had said, "When this woman has a baby again, I want to be there. I was there on the worst day of her life and I want to see her on the best day of her life." I thank her for saying that, and I feel that sense of hope flash near me. I note it despite my grief, despite its distance from my present life.

† † †

David and I leave for Mohonk Mountain House, near the Catskill Mountains, on a Tuesday—three weeks and three days after Elizabeth died. We pause several times backing out of the driveway, apprehensive about the impending distance. As we enter the parking lot of the expansive resort hotel, we stay in the car for a while, staring at the rolling hills set against overcast sky. Eventually we make it into the hotel lobby and are whisked up to our room, which overlooks Lake Mohonk and the hills behind it. The hotel was built in 1869; it is run by a Quaker family. It is large with Victorian-era decor and many private sitting areas with views of water and mountains. We learned about the place through a song in which it's featured, written and performed by favorite musicians of ours. The hotel is sparsely populated because it is March and it is midweek. It gives us the quiet and privacy we need.

The structure of the resort helps us. Continental breakfast is at eight-thirty, lunch at noon, afternoon tea at four o'clock, and dinner is at six-thirty. All we need to do is fill in the spaces. We take long walks on the lakeside paths; the lower path is flat and wooded with the hotel across from it. The upper trails are on an incline with increasingly glorious views of the mountains, rocky cliffs, and sparkling lake water, all surrounding the vast old hotel. Wooden chalets dot the trails and we sit in them, letting the sun warm our backs and shoulders. We also walk to the greenhouse and look at the plants and flowers growing in the enclosed humidity. After dinner each night we light a fire in the fireplace in our room, and we sit there until we're ready to fall asleep.

All of the meals at Mohonk are served in a large, wooden dining room with a view of the mountains in the distance. Each table is set with a vase of fresh flowers, resting on a white linen cloth. We are seated at the same table by the window at each meal. At our first meal we ask to be reassigned tables because we are placed next to a family with a baby. It hurts to see babies. During our last dinner there we plan our ceremony for Elizabeth—something simple, in a couple of weeks, unencumbered by visits from afar. I imagine myself at home with my baby, rocking her within ivory walls bathed in moonlight. A window is open and wind blows through me, and over me. I attempt to focus on making a meaningful tribute to Elizabeth. Not suppressing wishfulness, just letting go in that moment. I want to find some peace, letting my suffering feel like a soft breeze sometimes.

†††

After David and I return from our retreat, I do little with my days—I read what I can focus on, go on long walks to get my strength back, see friends who come for visits, write in my journal. Cooking a meal by myself still feels like too much of a challenge. I also have a difficult time talking on the phone and can hardly take in much beyond my own crisis. I am used to being a present, attentive friend and family member, and it is painful to be now limited in what I can give. I rely a great deal on my friend Ginger, who was with us just before I was rushed to the hospital. She comes to our house often in the weeks after

Elizabeth's death and she offers her full self to me, listening to all of my sadness, my fears and anxieties, my uneasiness about the future.

There is a kind of crying that makes me feel as if I'm drowning. I've never been in such dark waters, not knowing if I can catch my breath long enough to survive. The first time this happened, my mother was still visiting. We were watching *The NewsHour with Jim Lehrer* and I noted that I was simply staring at the television, not taking in a single current event. I walked silently up the stairs to my bed and lay down. A sudden rush of panic ran through me, and I sobbed so violently I scared myself. David came up and curled close to me on the bed. "Oh poor baby," I heard myself saying. "I'm dying, Dave. I can't do this, I really can't."

† † †

I wake at dawn, shower, walk downstairs, and listen to the song "Talk to Me of Mendicino," by the McGarrigle sisters, several times. I played it often during the last weeks of my pregnancy. I sit on the floor, staring out the window which is covered in frost, like delicate lace. A little while later David and my sister Caroline, visiting from New York City, get up. We all put on formal clothes, instinctively. This is a memorial service. We meet two friends at the entrance to the mountain, and an employee, whom we've lined up in advance, opens the gate. We drive to the summit of the mountain, walk to the right of the summit house, and stand on the rocks, facing west. The morning sun glows and cuts the pre-spring chill. I am nervous and make a few jokes about finding the best place to have the ceremony; no one laughs.

We spot the exact location where we will commemorate Elizabeth and move to it. Ginger reads *Little Cloud* and Caroline reads a letter I wrote to Elizabeth, beginning, *Before you were born you were already part of our family*. David and I walk forward together and scatter her ashes on the rocks and trees below us. I stare into the dust floating downward and back onto us. The valley and river shine in the distance, and we stand silently for a while, saying goodbye.

laurie king-billman

Miscarriage

On a freezing day in July
My little one passed soundlessly
Into a world he could not feel
A soft outline on a blank page
Written in invisible ink the words
Who were you?
A year later on a warm day in April
I went to see a counselor
To heal my broken womb
In her notes she wrote "woman suffering from prolonged bereavement"
In November I went to the hospital support group
A woman in our circle spoke of a dream
She would be making baby clothes on a black sewing machine
They shrank smaller and smaller until they disappeared
Her fingers aching from the tiny stitches
Her words hit me like a heavy stone plunging through
The ash-covered pond of my face
I got up to go
One lady said "wait you need to cry your sorrow out"
But I wanted to hold my sorrow to cradle it
"No," I said "why water a dead flower"

carole burns
Changing Color

I am sitting in the garden watching my tulips grow. There are ten tall stalks whose flat leaves turn a deeper green each day. I planted them two seasons ago then forgot them until the first leaves pressed through the icy mulch, poked through dried leaves and sticks and grew despite me. I discovered them splayed against the ground, draggled but alive.

Planting them was a small pleasure, then. I knelt on the damp earth, grass sticking to my bare feet, my swollen knees. Leaning over as best I could, my bulging stomach pushed warm against my thighs, I cradled each papery bulb in my hand before laying it carefully in the hole I had dug for it. I placed each one in the dirt, pointy side up. They looked like brown garlic, like lumpy onions. Then I gently pushed the earth over them, leaving them to winter. You kicked. I remember you kicked, right then.

Not all of them came up. Perhaps I crowded them in too small a garden; perhaps I knocked one on its side. But I root for them all; I try to take care of them all.

One is especially tall and strong, her leaves wider and greener than the others, her stem thick yet resilient. She was the first to lift her heavy leaves toward the sun, the first to bud. Though none of them have flowered, she is already the queen tulip, reigning at the center of her bowing ladies, feeding off their beauty and generosity. I am appalled by her, and enthralled.

I spend an inordinate amount of time sitting alone by my tulips. My neighbors are beginning to wonder. I start to bring out a chair with me, a book. I turn a page occasionally so they think I'm reading. But I cannot. I soak in the late spring sun; I take off my sandals and burrow my toes in the grass, in the dirt. I watch my tulips. I want to see them flower, to see their orange or red petals blossom. I want to witness their moment of grandeur, their triumphant debut.

† † †

"She's so beautiful," he said.

I held you in my arms. You were ugly and old-looking, wrinkled and supernaturally red. All tummy, you had skinny arms and legs, bent like a crab's, that wriggled around you. You smiled and stopped, smiled and stopped, your muscles not strong enough to form a grin. But your gaze was steady, tiny blue eyes that wouldn't let go. They squeezed my heart.

"Isn't she?" I said. I could barely breathe.

Elizabeth. A long name for such a small entity. We wrapped it around you like a blanket. We had planned on shortening it to something cute and modern—Bethie, Lizzie, Zee. But we never could. If anything, your name ended up longer. "Elizabethie," we said, tucking the extra syllable around you.

Your cries and whimpers and squeals filled up the house. Your slightest sound sent us running. Even when you were napping, we listened. On the monitor, your gurgles sounded alien, a radio broadcast of static-laced slurps, tiny sighs, and delicate coughs. Sometimes you giggled in your sleep. Sometimes you woke up screaming; there seemed to be no pause between sound sleep and pure terror.

† † †

"And what did our princess do today?" he asked. Still in his suit, he bent over your crib, catching his tie before it dangled in your face. You smiled for him, moved your arms about in a circle, as if you were swimming. You gurgled like a mourning dove. Performed. You were happier than you had been all day. "Eat a little? Nap a little? Poop a little?" he asked.

"Exercised her lungs," I said. "A lot."

"Oh, are you making sure your lungs are big and strong?" He smiled at you, nodded his head encouragingly. He seemed enormous next to you, as bulky and awkward as King Kong. "You make sure you do that during the day, for Mommy." He wagged a finger. "But not at night! There's more oxygen during the day."

"Gee, thanks," I said. I walked over and wrapped both my arms around one of his. It was meaty and muscular beneath his starched blue shirt. His free arm reached toward you. He placed his thick finger in your skinny, wriggling hand and you squeezed. I watched him watching you, watched him tickle your double chin with his thumb. "I wish you would tickle my chin," I whispered.

"Oh, does Mommy want her chin tickled?" he cooed in the same voice.

†††

"She's a difficult one," the nurse said cheerily.

You were whimpering as I put you to my breast, as I put my breast to you. You wanted no part of it, you thought. At a few hours old you already seemed to know what you wanted. I placed my nipple near your mouth but didn't put it in—I wanted you to come to me. For a moment I felt your tiny lip on my breast, wet and warm, and then you jerked your head away as if on purpose. More new cries. Everything a first.

The nurse stuck her raw, chafed finger between us, turned your head and pushed my breast so my nipple filled your mouth. I almost pulled it out—it looked like my breast could smother you. But then you sucked, so hard it hurt; I knew we'd done it right. "Can't be shy," the nurse said. I felt reprimanded.

Sometimes I still needed to force it into your mouth—you often fought the breast. I'd let you fuss first. Difficult. I wondered if you'd always be difficult. But then you'd suck, pain and relief at once. Who would think you could suck so hard, my nipple pulled long and taut, like the umbilical cord we had to cut.

†††

You slept on your belly, your limbs curled in around you. So quiet, so peaceful. I was going to look only, watch only. But I didn't see your back trembling, your blanket shifting; I didn't see any sleepy spasms in your fingers. You weren't supposed to be on your stomach. Had you rolled over already? I leaned into your crib, trying to place my cheek near your lips, to feel your hot angel-breaths. I felt nothing. I leaned my large face closer: still nothing. I was about to panic when you sneezed, woke, cried. I patted your back to soothe you, but you wouldn't quiet down. You screamed. I picked you up. Aaron poked his head in the nursery, a towel hugging his waist. "What did you wake her for?" he asked. "Why do you make it hard for yourself?"

†††

My tulips are beginning to reveal the secret of their color. Their brilliance is peeping out beneath the enclosing bud, which for so long was dark and protective, sheltering their vibrancy and life.

In just a day they are fully in bloom. I marvel at the speed of their opening, the medley of color. Three tulips are deep fuchsia, gorgeous and sad as promise. Two are a tropical Miami orange, with a deep summer shine. Several are striped two colors—pink and white, yellow and orange.

Yet something about them looks weak-kneed and limp. At least compared to my centerpiece. Although plain yellow, she has the largest blossom, the sturdiest petals. If I had to name her I would choose Jane, or Sue. There is nothing elaborate about her, yet her fragile power affects me. Plain Jane. Sensible Sue.

Aaron walks by me sitting in the grass. I listen to his heavy footsteps passing me, for the hundredth time, it seems. He's early—the first time he's home before dark in weeks. Or maybe the days are getting longer. The sun sends weak light in our direction.

"What are you doing?" he asks. We never ask "how" anymore, just "what."

"Nothing." I don't open my eyes, don't move.

"I bought some bread for dinner," he says. "And wine."

Though the sun is dipping dangerously close to the hills I feel warmth like candlelight. I remember the round of a wineglass cupped in one hand, his fingers cupped in my other, as we sit cramped in our small kitchen. But the light flickers. We haven't eaten dinner together in weeks.

I hear him clinking dishes in the kitchen, setting the table for two. "Honey, come inside." He uses his authoritative voice, the one he must have been saving for you.

"I'm not hungry," I say.

"Keep me company," he says, changing tactics. I pretend not to hear him. "Hon. C'mon!"

I shake my head so slowly I can feel my muscles creak in my neck. When I open my eyes to peek at him he is gone.

†††

I needed to put on your coat for a walk. You'd been crying and fussing and I decided we both needed air. Round and round the park we'd go, several sets of mother-and-carriage. Some talked to each other but I always said an overly polite hello so they wouldn't bother me. I had a disdain for stay-at-home moms, although I had become one myself.

You weren't in the mood for anything that day. You raised your eyebrows, puckering your forehead as I put on my sneakers. "You're going to get premature wrinkles," I told you. "You shouldn't have such an expressive face." You looked at me blankly then, wondrous, all creases suddenly disappearing, and I laughed. "Silly."

As I approached with your coat you scrunched up your nose and scowled. I gently took one of your arms and you squirmed. You let out quick breaths that I recognized as the prelude to a tantrum. You began screeching as I succeeded in getting arm number two into the lavender windbreaker. "Damnit!" I screamed, banging my palm on the counter next to you, startling you, for a moment, into silence.

You screamed even more loudly, started shrieking as my palm began to smart. I zipped your coat up to your chin, slowly, trying not to lose my temper. "Shit!" I hissed again, irrationality building within me then dipping back down. I watched you calmly. Your brow was doubly wrinkled; your nose twitched. "Why do I have to do all the bad things?" I asked. "Put on your coat. Change your diaper. You won't hate Mommy for it, will you?" You were hysterical now, your face purple red. "Is that a yes or a no?" I asked, then answered for you. "Yes, Mommy, I won't hate you."

By the time he came home you had fussed, nursed, napped. It could take you an hour to wake up, groggy and grumpy as a forty-year-old. Then, for him, you were all grunts and grins.

"She's been crying all day again."

"You're kidding." He lifted you higher, bounced you until you seemed as light as a doll. "Are you giving Mommy trouble? Elizabethie? Or is Mommy pinching you again?" You squealed and squeaked. Then his adult voice, mock-accusing. "Once she starts talking," he told me, "you're going to have to stop pinching."

###

I have decided to cut down my tulips. Beauty is worth nothing. Their sweet faces bob in the breeze, nodding, agreeing. I kneel on the grass with the scissors, grasp them in my hand. My knees graze the dirt of the garden. I will cut the healthiest flower first. The scissors squeak open. Their metal touches the thick stem of my yellow star.

I cannot cut. The scissors squeak open but I cannot move to sever the green stem. It is too strong. It holds too much life.

I think of the fresh milky-green sap, the life-blood, inside the stems. I put down the scissors. I fill up an old plastic garden pitcher and water them instead.

###

The house was silent and dark. We lay still as if the slightest noise would wake you, as if the monitor were reversed. You were in your room but we whispered like stowaways, not wanting to get caught. We were talking about you, of course. After crying all day, you had been sleeping an hour, and we hoped for several more.

Finally, we hushed, prepared for sleep ourselves. He patted my fanny. His fingers grazed my bare thighs. I reached for him and we were suddenly alone. "You," he said. "I remember you." I don't know how long it lasted but soon I was bearing the weight of him. He had just maneuvered inside me when I heard you, waking. A complaining old invalid, you were insistent, persistent, your whine pathetic and helpless. It seemed like you knew what we were doing, and disapproved.

"Shit," I said. He laughed, was suddenly hysterically laughing, barely breathing as he rolled off me. "Shut up," I said, sitting on the edge of the bed, bare feet searching for slippers. His guffaws increased, but he eked out a few words.

"I can get her."

"I'm so freaking tired," I said.

###

I would sleep out here if I could. I would sleep in my bed of tulips like a girl lost in a fairy tale. But something prevents me; a nagging sense of appropriateness filters through my madness. So I wait shivering in the cool May night, damp with dew, until he has gone upstairs. I wander inside then, turn off the lights as if I'm going to bed, and stray through the darkened rooms as if my house were a museum. Except there are no pictures to look at, just blank walls subtly lit by the moon and the domes of streetlamps, her apostles. I rest occasionally in a couch or chair, curl onto the floor by the chair where I rocked you, the wood hard against my bones. This way, I never experience the shock of waking up—the shock of memory after thinking everything is normal.

I am roused by a gentle shaking of my shoulder, a warm hand on my arm and on my hip. He leans down, whispers. "I'll carry you upstairs," he says.

I stiffen, jerk away. I lean sleepily on my arm. "No—don't. You'll drop me."

"Come upstairs," he says.

I shudder, suddenly cold. "I'm not tired," I say.

† † †

I was wearing a purple silk dress with a red sash, preparing for our first outing alone since we became a threesome—our (his and mine) anniversary. I click-clacked to the bright lights of the bathroom, makeup bag in hand. You were in your bouncy seat—bungie jumping, we called it. I strode past Aaron to the bedroom for my eyeliner, and noticed you watching me. I sidestepped in front of you; you followed me the only way you could—with your eyes. They shined light hazel, flecked with green some days, yellow others, so large they made you look skinny, though you were a bouncing cherub, in the ninety-fifth percentile. Your gaze fell about waist-level—my red sash.

I shuffled to the left; I shimmied to the right. Your eyes were wide and alert, as if you knew you would see only so much, as if you knew that you had to pay attention. I tap-danced in a wide circle around Aaron, my arms flailing back and forth like Gene Kelly's. Both pair of eyes, now, bright and adoring, followed me closely. You squealed with delight.

I scanned the babysitter for bloodshot eyes or burned-out hair or the faint afterwhiff of pot. But she seemed more efficient than I did, asking where the diapers were and the time of your last feeding, details I'd forgotten to tell her. Everything about her was tidy and calm: her pale folded hands, her tucked-in ironed T-shirt, flowers embroidered on her breast pocket.

We guiltily slunk out the door. I felt naked leaving you behind. At dinner, I fingered the red silk beneath my white linen napkin. I was reluctant to hold his hand; it meant letting go of the sash. It meant letting go of you.

⨱⨱⨱

Black is fashionable any time, necessary only a few. Convenient, actually. I had several dresses to choose from: long and flowered, long and plain, short and flowered, short and sexy. I fingered another dress, bright purple silk, red silk sash. Inappropriate but it's what I wanted to wear. Then I could know you'd be watching me.

I chose the long, plain dress instead, sober and fittingly tragic, then took the red sash and wrapped it around my neck. The end of it trailed down my back.

⨱⨱⨱

We were trying to get to sleep early—adult time for reading or renting a movie, another habit we seemed to be giving up. Instead, I listened to the silence. "Do you think we should check on her?" I asked.

"You'll wake her up."

Not a gurgle. Not a sigh.

"She's never this quiet."

"That's good, isn't it?" he asked, sensibly. He turned to hold me, to warm away my worries. He wrapped one hand under my breasts; he slipped the other beneath the elastic of my cotton underpants. The silence was drowned out by his hardening, the slow, increasing caresses of his hands then lips. We didn't get to sleep early, but, eventually, we slept, and peacefully.

⨱⨱⨱

He discovered you. "How's my princess today?" he sang as I filled the coffeepot with fresh water. "How's my sleepyhead?" He opened your shimmering white blinds. I took the coffee out of the freezer, measured out the frozen grounds. "Elizabeth?" His tone was unusual. Something attracted my attention. I heard, "Elizabeth—Oh my god!"

I ran to your door but I felt like I was not moving at all, as if the room, your crib, the light from your window, were moving around me. He was holding you to his shoulder, patting your back, as if you needed burping, then rocking you with his arm. Your entire body fit into the crook of his elbow. I went to hold you, to take you, but something told me to think. "I'll call 911," I said, my voice sounding outside me. I found myself in the kitchen listening blankly to the dial tone. I didn't remember what to do. Then I hit three buttons, heard them say, "Mrs. Josephs?"

I was excessively polite. I said, Please and Thank you. I said, Please come. My baby isn't breathing. Please hurry. Please.

He was kneeling on the floor then, curled over you, as if in an extravagant bow. "Let me see her," I said. I wanted to find a minor problem, a minor glitch. Like I could switch the batteries around; like I could fiddle with the plug. "Let me see her." Slowly he stood up, stretched out his arms, holding you, extending you to me like an offering.

I learned the meaning then of stone cold. I cradled you in my arms. I pushed you underneath my breasts. It was always warm there, even warmer since you. I wanted to warm you; I wanted you to be warm. When the medics arrived I refused to give you up.

My eyes were dry until the night of the funeral. Wind pierced my eyes; no tears soothed them. I watched you, my still infant; nothing closed my eyes. Until we were trying to sleep and I could hear only silence.

After I was crying for ten minutes, after I began heaving and gasping, he held me. He placed his hand under my breast; he slipped a finger beneath my underpants. "Don't," he said. "I don't—" Don't think don't feel don't know what happened don't cry. By habit he grew hard, but we pretended not to notice. Don't. When I woke, I was lying on the very edge of the bed.

† † †

Overnight, Elizabeth, a transformation. I find my Yellow Sue, my Plain Jane, is changing into a tiger, a jungle lily. A Suzanna, a Janette. Black stripes now charge up her petals. I miss her simplicity, but I am in awe of her brilliant sophistication.

The next day she has changed again, her yellow deepening into a velvet orange, sweetened by a tinge of pink. Yesterday's brazenness turns into today's beautiful regret. She is my flower, after all.

† † †

I don't turn to look at him but I listen. Aaron's steps don't pause, though the sun is hours from its end; his steps scrape busily by me, thin dress soles whistling against the cement walk. The afternoon is extra quiet now; even the tulips have stopped their chatter. A breeze picks up for a moment and maybe that is why I don't hear him stepping off the porch. "How is my princess today?" he asks. I look up and he's standing with your quilt, rolled up and stashed under his arm, as if he's taking it a long way.

"Where are you going?" I ask.

"Picnic," he says, oblique. He loosens his arm, catches the quilt with both hands, and throws it into the wind. Its sturdy cotton takes up the sky for a moment, clouds become patches of yellow flowers and blue dogs, which land so softly on the grass the blades barely bend. It is the first time the quilt is used; you never graduated from your receiving blankets, soft as your skin.

He has my attention now. He steps quickly down our walk, turns the corner. I hear the car door open and shut, and see him return, three grocery bags dangling by his legs. He eases them onto the quilt, goes into the house and comes out with plates, silverware, wineglasses, corkscrew. He sits sideways on the quilt, pours two glasses of wine. "C'mon," he says. "Sit with me." He brings out cheese spread, crackers, tiny grapes the size of dewdrops, shrimp salad, and bread.

I leave the comfort of the beach chair for the quilt, carefully cross my legs so I am Indian-style, back as straight as I can make it. I clasp the glass he offers.

"Look," I say. "She turned."

He gazes at the tulips curtsying at the border of the quilt.

"Is that the yellow one?" he asks.

I nod, as if we've been discussing the tulips all along, as if I knew he'd been watching them too.

"That's amazing," he says. "I didn't know they changed colors."

"Me neither," I say.

"You know," he says, "in the morning, they're closed up." He holds his glass up to the sun, cups the curve of it in his hand like a tulip. "Like you." Shadows flash through the golden wine.

"Am I going to change color?" I ask.

We sit on this patchwork of white and blue, green and yellow, linked by thread so thin it's invisible, laden with holes made by a prickling needle which stitches together as it pokes, opening circles then filling them.

"Three months," he says. "Three months today."

"Is that all?" I ask, after a moment.

The fresh light of spring is deepening to summer as I sit in my garden, not wanting to leave the sun, not wanting the sun to leave. These are the things I wanted to teach you: Tulips. Grass. Red. Yellow. The sun sets, the moon is full. I am here.

corrine de winter

Premature

For every thousand babies born
Nearly a dozen
Will need tubes
The size of fishing line
To carry nourishment or medication
Into their palm-size bodies.
Some will not survive
For a first feeding
Or gather enough time
To be named.
It is then the anonymous
Volunteers are called on
To help patiently fashion
Soft cloth into tiny gowns
From a doll dress pattern,
Creating the premature shrouds
No one sells
Or talks about.

kirsten swain rogers
Our Beloved, Jacob

The first thing I see is the baby's head. The doctor takes measurements—skull, abdominal circumference, thigh bone length. She takes her videotape out of the ultrasound machine and replaces it with the one I have brought.

As she records the rest of the procedure we see the baby's hands, feet, face, heart, nose, eyes, a perfect little ear, and a full bladder, the work of healthy kidneys.

I am twenty weeks pregnant. The doctor tells me my baby will arrive in mid-February. Everything looks really good. The doctor is pleased. I am pleased, amazed, awed at the good news, so much better than the last time I was pregnant.

When I was a girl, I fantasized about having a family and being a mom. I wrote a "letter to my unborn children" to tell them how much I wanted to have them. As I got older, I dreamed of my future. I knew I would have many children. I enjoyed baby-sitting, teaching, and being around them, whether it was one, two, or ten.

Years went by, high school ended, college began, then ended, and soon I felt I was "comfortable" enough to afford a child. I had a stable income and a job I liked, but I didn't have any prospective father. I wanted the old-fashioned getting married and then having children, but as I started feeling my biological clock ticking, I considered becoming a single parent.

Another year passed. My prayers to meet the right man started to get desperate. One night I was praying, and I didn't just cry, I sobbed, begged, and pleaded to God to give me the right man. If I didn't have a prospective man by my next birthday, I would look into other alternatives—I wanted a child. I knew that giving our higher power an ultimatum didn't mean an answer would be given, but that was how desperate I felt. I wanted a family.

Two months before that birthday came, my job sent me overseas into a new and stressful position where I encountered a whole bunch of new people, including Michael, the man who would someday be my husband. Meeting this wonderful man distracted my brain and slowed down my biological clock. When the relationship became serious, I knew who would be the father of my children, so I knew I could wait a little longer. While we courted, we wrote letters. One of the questions I asked him was how many children he wanted. When he wrote back and replied with the same number I wanted (it was six), I knew we'd have many children.

As time went by, we got engaged and then married. At the end of our first year of marriage, a few days before Christmas, we received an early present. We were pregnant. At first, we didn't tell anyone, but finally our excitement burst through, and when I was eleven weeks pregnant, we told our family.

Two days later, I started feeling cramps in my stomach. As the cramping continued, I tried to lie down to make it go away, and when it didn't, I tried to move around. The cramping got worse. I started sweating. I felt like I was going to throw up. I needed to call my doctor. Since it was after normal work hours, I had to call the answering service and wait. As I waited, I sat on the toilet and had a bucket nearby, just in case. The pain heightened, and as I sat there praying for it to stop, the phone rang. It was the doctor. After I explained what was happening, he told me to get to the hospital. He would meet me there.

I was in so much pain, I was unable to move quickly, and since it was winter, I had to dress warmly. Before I could finish getting my coat on, I had a very intense pain, and then I knew I was no longer pregnant. No more pain. I drove myself to the hospital. I went to the admittance desk, explained the reason I was there, and started crying. I was sent to an exam room, and when my doctor arrived he checked me over. I was given medication that sent me to la la land. There was no "fetal material"; I had a "blighted-ovum."

Only a couple of days after I got out of the hospital, I realized I still wanted to be pregnant. So after waiting a few months for my body to recuperate, my husband and I began again. A month later we found out we were pregnant. We immediately told our family and friends, just in case. We were anxious and scared of another miscarriage, but we held our breath, and when we got past the eleventh week, we exhaled a sigh of relief.

As weeks passed we became comfortable with this new wonder. My husband had to go out of town on the day of my ultrasound, so I took a VCR tape to record everything I got to see. The figure on the screen became visible; little hands, little feet, an arm, and finally, the whole body. I could even see the tiny heart, beating away. The doctor started taking measurements while I stared in awe at this amazing being inside me. When the doctor mentioned that the size of our baby's head was smaller than its belly, I didn't understand the implications. The doctor didn't seem concerned. She said "go have a Level II ultrasound." This procedure would help rule out a couple of things. I didn't ask any questions. I wasn't worried, just curious.

I had the Level II at a genetics center a week later. The technician prepared the equipment, took measurements on the monitor, and then left to get the doctor. When the doctor came in, she looked over the measurements and proceeded to explain them to me. She first described normal growth patterns. A fetus's skull fuses together at six months, and during that time the brain has room to grow. My baby's skull had already fused. I was only four months. At the very least, my baby would be severely handicapped. There was also a high probability that the eyes, nose, and other facial features would not develop any further. Currently, they were not to be found. The formal name of this defect was holoprosencephaly. The doctor suggested a second look at the heart, since defects are normally paired.

When the doctor left the room, the genetic counselor came in and asked if I had any questions. I didn't know what to say.

"Is there any hope at all that my baby would survive outside my womb?"

She looked at me like she wished she didn't have to answer the question, but said plainly, "No." The tears started falling.

I had to tell my husband on the phone that night. We cried together as I tried to explain to him all the developmental problems our little one had. Holoprosencephaly sequence, a midline deficiency, which occurred in the third week of fetal development, was the disability of the brain, and truncus arteriosus was the defect of the heart. With all this news, my husband planned on coming home for the weekend for our mutual support and for an appointment with the geneticist.

The next day I went to Arkansas Children's Hospital. Once I was in the exam room, the technician hooked up the echocardiogram, and the doctor came in. After applying cool gel to my belly, she placed the scope and tried to locate my baby's heart. She was able to see a little bit of it right away, but then my baby moved, so the heart was impossible to see. After that it was like a cat-and-mouse game played between my baby and the doctor's scope. This continued for over an hour, and since there was still not enough evidence to get a good reading, the doctor continued. She explained to me there was a surgical procedure that could fix the heart defect if there was enough material, but most times there isn't. Finally, the doctor was able to get some evidence to support the geneticist's conclusion of truncus arteriosus.

I went home, called my husband, and cried. When he came home that weekend, we went to see the geneticist who told us we had a very important and difficult decision to make. Since our baby, whom we knew was a boy and had named Jacob, would not survive birth, we had the option of either interrupting the pregnancy or continuing for the remainder of the nine months. Either way I would have to be induced for delivery because the hormone that causes normal delivery would not be developed in Jacob. We asked all sorts of questions about interrupting and also about the stresses of waiting.

My husband and I took this information home with us to make our decision. We were silent in the car, both thinking of what we should do. How does a person make this type of decision? I wouldn't wish it on my worst enemy.

We only had a little while to ourselves before we had an appointment with our reverend. During that time, we shared our gut instincts on what we should do. I told my husband that I didn't think I could mentally live through the stress of carrying our baby for another four months, since we knew there would be no life at the end. My husband also said he didn't like the idea of having to wait for death. I then realized that I would be going through labor sooner than I or my body was ready for.

At our appointment with our reverend, he listened to us explain what had been happening with us, then he asked us one question,

"What do you think Jacob would want you to do?"

That question gave us our final decision. We knew Jacob wouldn't want us to go through four more months of waiting for his birth/death day.

We called our family, and they were all supportive of our decision. We wanted them to understand there was a big difference between interrupting a pregnancy and having an abortion. We were not having an abortion, and that term highly offended us when we saw it in some literature we read. An abortion is firstly not a delivery, and normally, an abortion is done to a child that is not wanted. We wanted Jacob and were going to have him, just a little earlier and sadly, not alive. We wanted his birth and death to be with dignity, and this was how we were going to deal with it.

On September 13th, 1999, I went into the hospital to be induced, and to give birth to my son. We were told the process could take anywhere from twenty to thirty hours. So we planned on Jacob being born on the 14th. I was going to be given two types of medication, one to thin my cervix and the other to induce labor. I had also decided to take full advantage of an epidural if I felt I was in too much pain.

After the first medication, a pill placed behind my cervix, failed to thin the wall, another dose was put in. During this time, I was not allowed to eat anything but ice chips, and since I was hooked up to all these tubes, I only had enough leeway to get up and go to the bathroom. After about five hours, my cervix had thinned enough for the doctors to give me the second medication to start the contractions. This medicine was in a drip, another tube.

After about ten more hours, labor was causing a lot of pain, and I requested the anesthesiologist; I needed the epidural. Once the epidural was in, my legs felt like they were five hundred pounds each, and I was unable to get up anymore. Sleeping was something I would have liked to do, but it was hard being in a strange place and undergoing something I had never experienced before. Michael was great through it all; he stayed in the room with me the entire time. Finally, after thirty-five hours or so, we were both able to sleep.

I suddenly awoke with a start because I couldn't breathe. I quickly sat up and started coughing and fought for my breath, and it frightened me. I tried to stay calm and sat up to help alleviate my pain and the pressure in my chest. Michael woke up out of a sound sleep, and I urgently told him that I could not breathe, and to help me. He pushed the "panic" button for the nurse while I continued to fight for my breath, not go unconscious, not to panic. When the nurse answered, I yelled,

"Help, I can't breathe!"

While I waited for someone to come in and tell me why I couldn't breathe, I knew my job was to focus on my breathing—I was afraid I would go unconscious, faint, or die, and I did not want that to happen. Just breathe, in and out, in and out.

The doctor and two nurses came in and asked what was wrong. I again tried to explain that I couldn't breathe; I didn't know why, but my chest was tight, and it hurt. They started to go through their routine of figuring out what was wrong. They took my blood pressure, then placed a nasal canulla on me, giving me needed oxygen through my nose, and took a blood sample to find out what percentage my blood gasses were at.

This whole time they were focusing on me until my husband notified the doctor that he saw some liquid between my legs. Then the attention was focused on the baby inside me. The doctor checked my dilation, found I was at seven centimeters, and my water sac was ready to come out.

I had already been given an epidural thirty-five hours before, so I had no feeling below my waist. Besides concentrating on my breathing, I had to open my eyes and listen to the labor instructions the doctor gave me. The doctor told me the water sac was right at the exit of the birth canal, and if I pushed, she could get to it easier. I pushed, and then all of a sudden I heard a noise that sounded like a pumpkin-sized water balloon popping. The next thing I was told was that the baby was really close to coming out, and I had the choice of either letting my body do the work or pushing the baby out. At this point, I was breathing a little better, but with being in labor for over forty hours and feeling I was close to the end, I needed to push. I needed to get this over with.

not what i expected 211

The doctor told me how to correctly push to get the baby down the birth canal. The next time I pushed, she told me I was doing it right, but hold my breath and push immediately, then again. I couldn't tell how well I was doing, but I continued to do as she said. I took another breath, as deep as possible, and pushed as hard as I could, and then I felt something leave my body. My son was out.

I immediately started crying, my baby was born. My poor little baby who had so many things wrong with him. This little boy we named Jacob Halia'a Swain Rogers. Halia'a meant "to remember fondly" in Hawaiian.

Then something happened that Michael and I were unprepared for, I started to shiver. No one noticed at first, including myself. When it was noticed, a blanket was put over me and my husband put a warm washcloth on my forehead. The shivering became violent and uncontrollable; the nurse brought in two more warmed blankets and asked for a "bear hugger." My whole body was shaking and both my husband and I started to get worried. I could not control the shivering and I also felt clammy and sweaty on my skin, but within my body I was extremely cold. I realized I must be in shock. After fifteen minutes the "bear hugger" came in and we found out that it was a hot-air machine which blew air under the blankets to warm me up.

While the doctor and nurses were trying to help me, I saw my husband go to our nurse, who was working on Jacob, and heard him ask,

"Do you have a hot lamp for babies? Could you put Jacob under it so he stays warm?"

The nurse very willingly said she would and then Michael came back over to be with me.

My husband then continued to stroke my hand and my forehead, changed the warm washcloth, and told me what a good job I had done and how wonderful I was through it all. After approximately fifteen minutes, my shivering lessened, my breathing was more under control, and the "emergency" seemed to be over. The doctor and everyone else left except for the nurse who was cleaning Jacob.

I stopped shivering. I asked to be sat up so I could see and hold my son. I asked Michael if he had seen Jacob and when he said he had, I quizzed him on what he looked like. I needed to be prepared to know how "bad" he looked since we had been told all the terrible things that were wrong with him. My husband said he looked good, but he didn't have a nose and didn't have any eyes. So we asked the nurse to bring Jacob in to us. He was so small, he fit completely in only one of Michael's hands. He was such a little boy, no one could have helped but cry. Then he was placed in my arms and through my tear-stained glasses, I gazed at my son.

My baby. Such a wonderful gift from God, Jacob was with Him already. He was perfectly formed from the neck down, but sadly, he didn't fare well from the neck up. Our little guy didn't have eyes or a nose, just indentations where they should be. He had only one, perfectly formed, ear, and a tiny mouth. We could see teeth buds on the bottom, and a cleft palate. We held Jacob, took pictures, and cried. We told him how much we loved him, that we would miss him. He was, and always will be, our baby, even if he was only with us for such a short time.

sharon winn
The Not Named: Mothers Who Grieve for Lost Children

How many women carry grief from loss of a child? One in five mothers has experienced the death of a child through miscarriage, illness, accident, or stillbirth. The percentage of mothers who grieve over a lost child is much higher, perhaps one in three, including those who have lost a child through adopting out, estrangement, or abortion.

†††

Samara came as a surprise to us. After three years of trying, at thirty-seven I became pregnant. When the amniocentesis showed she was a girl, we named her Samara. Three months along, our doctor announced that leaking fluid meant complete bed rest for six months. I stayed home for two weeks and then abandoned this enforced solitude. I knew I'd hate this child if her birth required my "death"—giving up career and time outdoors.

Our daughter—the size of a man's open hand—died in the operating room moments after her premature birth. My husband watched. Samara and I had shared over six months before her birth—plus six hours of labor. In the operating room, when I heard the doctor ask if I wanted to hold my child, I did not hesitate. Firmly I said, "No."

So Samara disappeared. I didn't touch her. I didn't see her. No picture. No funeral. The hospital staff kept me overnight in the medical-surgical ward for observation. No visitors. No flowers. I was discharged the next day.

That same day, I went to work wearing an old maternity outfit, a stone gray sack-like jumper that hid my girth and loss. Within the week, fifteen of us women in business suits sat around a stone brown table, a meeting of our professional association. I don't know how many knew about Samara's death, but I do know that no one turned to me and said, "I'm sorry." Few sent cards.

I thought I had killed her, our first and only child. Complete bed rest might have saved her. I think that's when my husband and I started to end every day with a bottle rather than a glass of wine—red or white, it didn't matter—to numb the horror of the unasked question: what right did I have to kill this child?

No one told me how important it might be to join a support group of bereaved parents. Without place for honor and expression, this loss of Samara burrowed deeper and deeper. My husband and I stopped drinking long before I stopped grieving. Twenty years later, I heard anger in my voice as I told a friend of an upcoming funeral for a seventy-year-old man. The funeral Samara never had.

Around and around my friend Beu and I circled on a gravel path close to playgrounds and play fields—empty of the children who were in school. She listened as I explored the source of my anger. She then shared the story of her two miscarriages. Two women walking and talking. Our stories are the stories of many.

We call ourselves the not named. There is no word in the English language for parents who lose children. Children without parents are orphans. Spouses who survive each other are widows and widowers. But this horror of losing a child runs so deep that we name it not. Many bereaved parents bear two burdens. First, loss of a child. Then isolation if they bear that grief alone without funeral or memorial service.

So, twenty years after my loss, Beu and I decided to create a memorial service for our dead children. We invited other grieving mothers to join us. I called a woman whose story was well known in our community. Linda had lost two grown sons in three years—one through suicide and one through drowning. She willingly joined us. At the first gathering, we three sat on overstuffed chairs in front of a large flip chart covered with my writing. Scared of my feelings, I provided way more structure than needed, but they forgave me. Next we sent an email to Molly, an artist who works in stone, asking her to become the fourth member of our team. She had lost her infant son Peter in a car accident. Although it was scary to email an invitation for such an intimate venture, Molly's response was one of deep sharing. Another woman, Jean, heard of our ceremony, and called to offer her services. She wanted to use her art to honor her grown daughter's death. So she became member number five.

At the first meeting of this group of five, we decided to hold the ceremony on the day before Mother's Day. We agreed to invite mothers who had lost children through any means: abortion, stillbirth, miscarriage, accident, war, suicide, and estrangement. We knew that some wouldn't be ready to come, but might find solace in knowing such a ceremony existed.

We rented space in an old wood-frame community hall, once home—many years ago—to a family that had lost house and children to a fire. We did not want to ask for donations. So the five of us together paid $150 for room rental, decorations, posters, and mailings.

At the next monthly meeting we decided on a simple nondenominational service. The third month, the month before Mother's Day, we mailed typewritten letters to local pastors for use in their church bulletins and personalized invitations to mothers we knew who grieved lost children. We arranged for a pianist and violinist and placed a notice in our community newspaper. Seeing that notice, a reporter called from our local cable TV station to interview us.

Beu, Molly, and I gathered and cleaned multicolored stones from a beach on Bainbridge Island, where Indians had a sacred sweat lodge. Molly brought forget-me-nots and a stone-encased candle to mark the center of the circle. Linda came armed with bouquets of flowers—daisies, lilies, larkspur, and roses—that poured over and perfumed each window ledge. Beu covered the round table at the center with a purple-and-red-bordered Ethiopian cloth, a *gabi*, a memory of her eight years there with her husband and mother. Jean's delicate photograph of a rose-colored rhododendron hung at the entry.

Just before three p.m. on a warm cloudy spring Saturday before Mother's Day, twenty other women appeared. Some came dressed in long flowing skirts with gauzy shawls, two in jeans. Beu and Molly welcomed these mothers as, tentatively, they climbed the stone gray stairs to the entry hall. Each bent over the beach stones on the table by the door, and searched for the one that best captured her own particular loss. One young woman took five stones—four children lost to miscarriage and one shortly after birth. Although we had practiced twice, I stood immobile in that wood hall. But it didn't matter. Molly walked over and greeted new arrivals. Beu and Linda did the same. Surrounded by these women—the not named—there was plenty of room to be vulnerable.

We started with a brief meditation. Then, one by one, we stepped forward and named our loss. Some shed the quiet tears we all held inside. We told no more of our story than each child's name—if there was one—and the date. More was to invite a very long ceremony. Less was to say and do nothing. A musician rang a delicate chime as each mother returned to the circle.

It was done. Linda offered the closing meditation. We walked out of the hall single file, back down those stone gray steps, each holding our stones as tightly as our memories. Then, as if held by a common hand, we stood on the gravel drive and talked quietly for an hour under gray clouds. No coffee. We stayed, clusters of three or four women sharing our stories, breaking apart, then joining another group to tell our stories again. One woman knew two of the other mothers. But never before had they spoken of their loss. Few chairs. It didn't matter. What mattered was we were together. In this way we prepared for Mother's Day. Many wrote in our guest book:

- This was the first ceremony I had in which to grieve.
- Thank you for coming together in circle with stones—close to my son's heart as a lover of nature, and a collector of rocks and crystals.
- It feels like my heart will never mend…being with other mothers who have lost a child makes the sadness less lonely.
- Perfect timing…just before Mother's Day.

Today, nearly a year later, Samara's small smooth white stone sits on the windowsill above our kitchen sink. Seeing it there reminds me that she died and that there was honor in her death. And that she lives.

a mother's needs

photo by david glynn

jacqueline jules
A Mother's Needs

Danny would stand at the door:
"Don't go, Mommy! Don't go!"
and I'd drive to the firm in tears.
It took months of negotiation
till terms we accepted appeared:
I didn't love the law more than him
as much or instead—
I simply loved my work, too.
Like the plants
we watered at the windowsill
in need of soil and sunlight, too;
it made sense for a mommy to need
more than one thing in her life to grow.

hildie s. block
Just Talk

She used to speak in whole sentences. Long, meandering sentences. Paragraphs too, sometimes. Occasionally an entire monologue. A rant, they were called. At happy hour, as a younger woman she would occasionally hold court, a cheap yellow beer in one hand, and spew off the sweat and blood and insult of the day at work. And people would look at her, amazed, and laugh. Then raise their glasses and drink.

This seems like a fantasy. This seems impossible, like something that maybe never happened, or a dream, or a fictitious imagining. Like an exaggeration.

But she reminds herself, no. Once sentences existed, not just in her head, not just on the page, but flowing out of her mouth like a river. Someone once said her writing had the breathless quality of someone who could say it all without taking a breath. This too seems like a past, distant fading lie.

Now she limits her speech, mostly to one word. If she's lucky it's heard. If it's responded to, her day is made.

No.

Stop.

Please.

There are a few times "Put it down" is heard but rarely.

Go.

Come.

Now.

Her husband interrupts himself when there is a moment, a pause in the noise and starts talking to the baby. She tries to jump in and tell him something right over him talking to the baby. Runs over him like a freight train, like labor through a pregnant woman. Not stopping, not pausing, not noticing. And it was not something totally frivolous, but something that she herself thought was important. Maybe she's wrong.

Do it.

That's two words technically, but it's really run together. Doit, doit, doit. Now.

Potty.

Shoes.

Teeth.

Even at baby group she's truncated, if not by herself, being distracted by the leaf getting caught in the baby's throat, then by the other mom, who has to catch the toddler just before he hits the ground. And by the time the tears have stopped, it's on to another topic.

Look.

Okay.

Whatever.

I don't care.

That's three words, but it's easier than trying to say what she thinks. She can say that and she's done, but to explain that maybe she could go either way or that there are other issues at stake or that the answer is longer than a sound bite, by then the audience has moved on.

And as her voice is quelled, silenced, squashed, she hears the words she didn't speak rattle in her head. As she tries to sleep at night, the sentences flow back to her. They dance. They jitterbug. They try to get her mouth, but it is dark. For every unfinished sentence, every unfinished thought, there is an end result.

I didn't know.

You never told me.

Why didn't we...

So she starts to tell the baby, but the baby is more interested in the cat, who is furry and has a tail. The baby says "cat" and not "mama."

And then came the day she locked herself in the bathroom.

Anyone who was listening might have heard it coming.

No one heard it coming.

The lock on the bathroom door makes a click when you turn the knob. You can jimmy it from the outside, with a Phillips head screwdriver, but you'd have to want to do that. You'd have to not respect the lock to do that. You'd have to have exhausted asking her to open the door.

No one asked her to open the door.

Because they didn't want to interrupt.

They couldn't interrupt because she did not stop.

Not even to catch her breath.

Instead, they gathered like the tiny animals dressing Cinderella, magically, silently sat on the carpet outside the bathroom door. They stared at the door, at the knob that would not turn, marveling at what was inside.

They heard.

For what started as a quiet noise from inside now rose and fell. It was a sound that they remembered, but had not heard in a long time.

She stared at her reflection and spoke. All of the unfinished sentences. They tumbled out of her like soap bubbles overflowing out of a misfilled washing machine; they spilled on the floor and under the crack.

At first no one heard them, they were too busy at the table, making their own noise, telling their own stories and she just got up and left and went to the bathroom

And

Locked

The

Door.

And she looked in the mirror and said to her reflection, I will listen.

And she proceeded, at first, only to finish the things she tried to say at dinner. And no one yet had noticed. Then the baby cried, and the other one couldn't find something, and the husband picked up the phone and called a friend, and eventually, the noise got so loud because the precious thing was still undiscovered and the friend on the phone was quiet, but the husband went on and on and on about some sporting event that NO ONE, not even the husband, really cared about and the baby wailed louder and suddenly, at once they noticed that she was gone.

Not far. Ten feet only. But she had locked the door and she wasn't coming out, not until she'd said all she'd come to say.

And
Not
Even
She
Knew
When
That
Might
Be.

holly smith
Untitled

Three a.m. and the baby's awake
all the time it seems like I haven't
slept in six months old and teething
for the past twelve weeks of
morning sickness during the middle
of the semester is a lousy time for
having a baby changed my life
so much money for diapers
are bad for the environment
might be ruined by the time she's
twenty is so young to be a mother
is the greatest role I could ever play
peek-a-boo and the itsy-bitsy spider
constantly worrying about the money
for the pediatrician is in the mail I
swear I'll go nuts if I don't get some sleep
between me and Daddy always wake
up at three a.m. you want to eat
from my tired body is amazed that
it can feel so much love.

terry scheidt
Sunday, Four O'Clock

So. She boots up her computer and is trying to open
a document while nursing a baby so she can do the assignment:
write a poem about having three kids, when her daughter calls
from the bathtub "Mo-om can I get out?" Yes, if you've washed
your hair, she answers and *I've got it now* the first line *I've got it*
when her son comes up and whispers in her ear (softly
so his sister won't hear), *can I have an Oreo?* Yes, she says
go ahead, the baby's sated now and might lie on the floor
if she gives him a pacifier. She'll try to get something down,
some high-blown crafted crap about motherhood. It'll be
poignant, touching, even noble "Which towel?" her daughter's
yelling. Any towel—isn't there one on the door? she calls back
and *Christ! Can I get ten minutes to myself to write one lousy poem
show a roomful of writers how brilliant I am?* When the baby
starts to fuss, his whimpers escalate as big brother comes back
wanting to know "What's for dinner?" and her daughter stomps in
completely naked and wet, puts her hands on her hips and shouts
"You <u>said</u> you'd take us to the mall" and That's it! she says, *I give up.*

rachel hall
On Mothering and Writing

"It was as Mother that woman was fearsome; it is in maternity that she must be transfigured and enslaved."—Simone de Beauvoir

"Because young humans remain dependent upon nurture for a much longer period than other mammals, and because of the division of labor long established in human groups, where women not only bear and suckle but are assigned almost total responsibility for children, most of us know both love and disappointment, power and tenderness, in the person of a woman."—Adrienne Rich

Sometimes looking at my daughter's face I am reminded of photos in my family album—is it me she looks like, though my face was longer, my hair darker? Photos of my mother show a chubby dark-haired baby, darker even than me. My daughter is blonde and petite, but her forehead and nose are my mother's. Because I've studied these old photos so often and for so long, when I look at my daughter, I have the uncanny feeling I've seen her somewhere before.

There is a photograph of my mother from some time in 1938. She appears to be tooling around in a wooden walker—a contraption with a seat and tray on wheels. My mother's infant legs are shiny sausages. Her feet are encased in stiff pointy booties. Both fists are crammed into her mouth, and her eyes show concern, perhaps from the noise of the camera or the lights necessary for the photograph. Behind her there is an ornate fireplace grill, a dark cabinet, and a settee covered in a geometrical print fabric. My eye goes repeatedly to that upholstery, though I try to train it on my mother. The fabric is so bold, so dark in contrast to the infant's light smock and bloomers. Who chose that couch,

I wonder. What else was in this room? What did these things mean to these people? What did they want for this pudgy, dark-haired baby, my mother? I hope they sang to her, rocked her by the window, watching rain fall on the Parisian street below. But none of this tenderness will prevent what happens next.

The baby doesn't know that her mother—her whole world!—will die in a year, that a war will break out, that as a Jew her life is at particular risk, that her father will be murdered in a German prison for his work with the French Resistance, that after losing all that, she will lose also her country, home of her mother tongue.

Really, the story begins even earlier: When my mother's mother was newly pregnant, she and her doctor husband decided not to have the child. My mother's aunt, Alice, came into the apartment my mother's parents shared, where she found them with a syringe filled with an amber liquid. "What are you doing?" she cried, though she claims she knew immediately.

My mother's father knew what Hitler's plans were. "It is not a good time for a child, Alice," he said. "You must believe me."

Alice grew hysterical, crying, flailing herself about until they agreed to stop. In this way, she takes credit for my mother's birth. She doesn't tell me why she reacted as she did; her stories have been told so many times the ambiguities, which once may have driven the telling, are smoothed to stone. I know from another story, though, of her clandestine abortion in Paris. She is afraid, a foreigner in this country, a girl with one leg several inches longer than the other, and she says the wrong word—abortion instead of D&C. For this slip, she wonders, was she punished? She will never be pregnant again.

France enters the war. My mother's father is stationed at the Maginot Line. Her mother is dying in Brive-la-Gaillarde. Alice receives a call to come immediately. When she arrives, her sister-in-law is screaming, "I don't want to die!" Beside her bed, in a dark back bedroom there is a bookshelf filled with medicine, but not the penicillin which would have saved her. In the front bedroom, my mother, still chubby, reaches up to her aunt with glee: "*Maman!*" she says, "*Maman!*" As she bends down to pick up my mother, Alice is crying. She has always wanted this child, always felt that she was hers, and now she is. How horrible she feels, how glad.

I am reluctant to tell this story of unexpected motherhood, this legacy of guilt and desire, bad luck and bad timing. But of course it informs the way I was mothered and the way I mother. How could it not? The dark apartment, its heavy furnishings, my own mother's many losses weigh on me even as I move around my daughter's bright bedroom straightening her toys, folding her soft garments.

I am pregnant at the same time as Madonna and Helen Hunt's character, Jamie, on *Mad About You*. The celebrity magazines play with the inside-out irony of Madonna-as-mother and print a special request of Madonna's to her fans and well-wishers: Please no more gifts. She has received an outpouring of baby clothes and stuffed animals. This season, it seems, pregnancy, motherhood, and infants are cool. And noteworthy, too: Several weeks after my daughter is born, the White House holds a press conference on speech development in infants. A panel of experts says that parents should sing and talk to even the youngest of infants, because verbal stimulation is crucial to thinking and language skills later. A photograph in the local paper captures Bill Clinton, his eyes cast down, his hands clasped together as if in prayer. The First Lady says parents should talk and sing to their infants because "it lays a foundation for the child's life, and in turn, our nation's future." As I read the articles, I'm uneasy. Of course I will chatter at my daughter, sing her ridiculous rhymes, learn to speak out loud my thoughts, though I am a person accustomed to quiet and introspection. But the limelight is perplexing, the attention misleading. At the time, I can't put my finger on why exactly, but it feels like additional pressure, a new theory to add to all the other theories of how a mother ought to behave. While I am absorbing all these theories, dealing with sleep deprivation and the monotony of life with an infant, a silence descends on me, though I don't yet recognize it as such. All I know is that I am too tired to write more than a few sentences in my journal, and this only sporadically. Even the journal entries look self-conscious to me now, as if I were thinking of audience: who would read these entries? Whose life was I charting here—my own or my daughter's? And there is a tension, too, in the entries, between my desire to keep track of things (nursing times, number of wet diapers, hours slept) and my desire to make sense of things.

A scene: When my daughter is six weeks old, I need to go to my office at the college where I teach to turn in some independent study grades. I have to time the forty-minute commute around nursing times. This is my first visit to my office, my department, as a mother. I'm self-conscious, unsure of the rules—both wanting and fearing the attention and fuss. The drive goes well and it instills confidence. I'm entering the department when I run into a former student, a fiction writer whom I appreciate for his honest, subtle language and his intuitive sense of how to plot a story.

"Hey, Chris," I say.

"Hi, how are you?" he asks, slowing to look into the baby carrier.

"Good," I say, "but exhausted."

"So this is your little bundle of joy," he says.

I check his face, expecting his ironic grin. *Bundle of joy?*

I can't allow my daughter, who is at two months already a personality, with particular gestures and squeals, to be turned into a cliché, anymore than I can stomach the implication that the experience of motherhood is wholly joyful. "This is the hardest thing I've ever done," I tell Chris, perhaps a bit too fiercely, for he begins to back away.

It would be untruthful to the profession of motherhood, already so underrated, to say it's a breeze. And yet, if I don't say it's great, I'm great, my baby is great, then I'm perceived as unnatural, unmaternal, perverse. I know, vaguely, that I'm up against more than Chris here, but I push on. I tell Chris how consuming motherhood is, how filled with worry and fear and the unknown, how chaotic, before I notice he's nodding politely, his eyes glazed over, thinking of his next class or how he'd like to smoke a cigarette.

Months later a friend mentions that television sitcoms suffer a drop in ratings after an infant is introduced into the story line, a fact she's acquired from an *Entertainment Weekly* she perused in the pediatrician's office. Yes, I think, that's part of what was happening that day: mothers and babies are uninteresting beyond some temporary slapstick or cliché. I'd been offered a script that day too, and I rejected it, though it would be a long time before I knew how to say what needed to be said.

In *Of Woman Born*, Adrienne Rich writes that

> women have been both mothers and daughters but have written little on the subject; the vast majority of literary and visual images of motherhood come to us filtered through the collective or individual male consciousness. As soon as a woman knows that a child is growing in her body, she falls under the power of theories, ideals, archetypes, descriptions of her new existence, almost none of which have come from other women (though other women may transmit them) and all of which have floated invisibly about her since she first perceived herself to be female and therefore potentially a mother.

The result is what she calls "The Great Silence." Twenty years later, Jane Smiley, a mother of three, makes a similar comment in her essay "Can Mothers Think?" Writing about literature, she asks, "Where were the mothers? Why didn't they speak up? Can mothers actually think and speak?" The absence of mothers' voices in our literature, Smiley and Rich assert, is detrimental both for the individual mother and for the culture. I'm beginning to see that my silence might be temporary, bolstered as I am by the writing of other women writers who found ways to face their silence—I'm writing this now, for instance. But I suspect that the silence is tenacious, rearing up again as thick and tightly woven and as startling as the first time. And I wonder what might be done to prevent it from descending at all.

Becoming a mother involves what psychologists call "role adjustment," and it is easy to imagine the visuals for this process: the young woman tossing aside her dark suits, her attaché case and heels in favor of jeans, a stain-hiding turtleneck, Keds, and a quilted diaper bag. Drumroll, please: Ladies and gentleman, a new mother! In my case, I gave up vintage dresses of delicate fabric—old rayons and silks, dangling earrings, velvet scarves, sheer beaded blouses—and donned the standard-issue stretch pants and loose T-shirts, things quickly pulled on and off, lifted for nursing, and easily laundered. How strange it felt after years of artful dressing to encounter the world in this utilitarian costume.

The psychological shift is more nuanced and gradual than the physical shift I've just described, but just as dramatic: What I once knew, I'm no longer sure of, what I once liked, I no longer care for, things I yearned for, hoped to achieve, seem like someone else's dreams—remote, slightly foolish, pie-eyed. Recently I gave my students in a writing workshop a journal-writing exercise. "Write me a letter," I said, "telling me what you believe in." This was a tough assignment, I thought, so I was surprised to see them writing without hesitation, their heads bent over their notebooks. I tried then to write such a letter myself, but the only thing I found I believed in was that pediatricians overprescribe antibiotics for ear infections. When I collected my students' letters, I was surprised by how many of them had written that they believed in love. Of course, I thought, why didn't I think of that?

When I sat down to write before becoming a mother, I was accustomed to a certain degree of self-doubt and insecurity, but I didn't doubt my material. After my daughter was born, the material that I was most interested in exploring in writing—the physical and psychological and emotional demands of caring for a child—had been both trivialized and romanticized to the point of myth. And that myth, I was learning, wasn't to be messed with. If one can't write about her passion, what is there to write about? Put differently: why write?

My head throbs as I try to write this—I have literally pounded my head on my desk in frustration trying to make my ideas cohere, stack up to something meaningful, probing, instructive. Why is it so hard to make sense of the silence that descended on me? How can I unravel cause and effect? Understand chronology? Is it because I'm living these issues even as I try to write? This essay is my foray back to writing and there is risk involved both to life and to art. After writing all day yesterday, I raced to pick up my daughter at day care. She expects a snack in the car and I provided her one—some cheese and a sippy cup of apple juice—but forgot, I discovered when we arrived home, to buckle her into her car seat. As for art, I violate other laws when I take on this material—I am sentimental, self-indulgent, small-minded, and light. Why mention that the snack is apple juice and cheese? Is that significant? Yes, yes, it is, to the thirsty child, her blonde curls tight at the nape of her neck. For the mother, children are never abstract.

I don't mean to say that motherhood is the only life event that is intensely unsettling and transformative. Certainly life is full of shifts and readjustments: adolescence, widowhood or divorce, death of a loved one, old age, war, no one more predictable than the other. And perhaps there are people for whom these events are a breeze, but that is not my experience.

As an adolescent I felt utterly betrayed by my body and wore wool sweaters all through the steamy Midwestern summer to conceal my developing breasts.

I resented the way my body elicited proprietary and invasive questions and comments from even strangers: "Look at your figure!" "You're growing up!" "Do you have a boyfriend yet?" It may be even worse for the pregnant body, with all that belly touching one is subjected to, all the predictions of gender, the tales of thirty-six-hour labors or babies born en route to the hospital, of failed epidurals or knotted umbilical cords. The public scrutiny and judgment are powerful and loud—I found it hard both as an adolescent and as a pregnant woman to escape the assumptions and the demands.

It is a dreary February afternoon in western New York. Melting snow and mud pool by my students' booted feet. The plastic stapled to the classroom windows to keep the cold air out snaps and billows in the wind. In this beginning creative writing class, the students, in two groups of twelve, are turning in their first fiction-writing assignment. We have to distribute them to each other quickly in order to get to the discussion of two published stories. As I do every semester, I have given the class explicit directions about coming prepared, with the right number of copies already stapled and labeled. But in one group only two people are prepared. The rest are madly collating on their desks' lima-bean-shaped top. At eight months pregnant, I can no longer wedge myself into these desks and have had to ask a student to bring me the armchair from behind the lectern. Papers slip off the students' desktops, sail through the air, and land on the scuffed wood floor. Someone asks if I have a stapler on me.

I'm tired from carrying around an extra twenty-five pounds, from waking every couple of hours at night to pee. "No, I don't have a stapler," I say measuredly. "I thought I asked you guys to come prepared."

I catch the eyes of one student, a young man whose writing and comments in class show promise. I intend to encourage him to take more writing classes. But his eyes startle me; they are steely, contemptuous. I imagine he is thinking, "Pregnant bitch," "Cow," "What's the big deal?" Behind me the heater grinds loudly and clicks on. When I look back, the student is bent over his papers again. I don't know what to say. I am no longer who I think I am. My new girth, the loose smock, and stretch pants are speaking for me, telling people who I am, what I am, and in this role I am supposed to be patient and undemanding, uncritical, and unconditionally loving. I'm aware of something else, too, another transgression: I have brought my body—my clumsy, swollen, female body—into the classroom, called attention to the fact that I am a woman in a place where man is still the norm.

Fortunately or unfortunately, there are plenty of "experts" who will happily tell me who I am, what I should expect once I am expecting. I study these magazines and books, just as I mooned over *Teen, Young Miss, Seventeen,* and *Mademoiselle* in junior high, absorbing the guidelines, the fashion dos and don'ts, the credo of young womanhood. Both the magazines for teens and mothers have articles and regular columns on relationships, diet, and makeup tips. Both are laden with advertisements and checklists of things the reader needs: things for the nursery, things to take to the hospital, the layette, that lovely French word co-opted by American materialism, comes to mean a confusing assortment of little cotton items, some with snaps, some without, some with booties, some with hoods and drawstrings. I buy them all, checking off the list efficiently as I go. And just as the magazines recommend, our freezer is packed with soups and sauces for easy meals after the baby is born. It doesn't strike me then, as it does now, how I was groomed for motherhood by those teen magazines. Nor do I note the revealing fact that the word teenager became popular in the fifties, as did this particular—and tenacious—incarnation of motherhood. I can't think this because I am too busy preparing and later I am too busy deciphering my daughter's cries—is she gassy? Hungry? Tired? Wet? Generally alarmed with the sharp edges, the hard realities of the world after nine months suspended in a watery pouch?

I'm looking around for a story to add to a class packet when I come across Alice Munro's "Labor Day Dinner." The protagonist, a children's book illustrator and mother of two girls, wonders why she hasn't been able to get to her work. "Roberta meant to keep busy illustrating books. Why hasn't she done this? No time, nowhere to work: no room, no light, no table. *No clear moments of authority, now that life has this grip on her.*" (My italics.) These words have a kind of grip on me—this is how I feel. I can't get to my writing because I have no clear moments of authority. The lack of time or energy are real concerns too, but more easily grappled with. This lack of authority is the real obstacle.

For days, I tell anyone who will listen about this quote. An artist must have clear moments of authority, I say and know it to be true. "What do you mean, 'authority'?" people ask. I know what I mean, but can't quite explain it. It is a bit like confidence, the knowledge that people will listen and will respect what you have to say. But it also has to do with being in control, in charge and comfortable in that position. How is authority earned? Who gives authority, anyway? Are we simply trained to give it over to certain people? Doctors, say, or lawyers, or within the family, to fathers, "the authority figure." I check out the dictionary definition and am not surprised to find that authority is linked to the masculine: it is "the accumulated weight of the expressed opinions of the great men of the past. Tradition and authority." How then does the mother/writer garner authority? You can be sure that what she has to say will complicate, if not contradict, the expressed opinions of the great men of the past. And without authority, will she speak at all? A tautology, a vicious circle: Without authority, she can't speak, won't be heard, and without speaking, she can't be an authority, an author.

I read the opening of this piece to my father, a sociologist, and he tells me the term for my experience: Altercasting. How vindicating to have a legitimate word for this, to brandish in my argument, to lend me some authority. It's like the sick person's relief upon hearing her ailment has a name, something to make concrete all her murky complaints and symptoms. Altercasting, my father tells me, is when someone else, usually someone in power, gives identity to his or her subordinate, disregarding the other's announcement of self. The altercast person feels alienated, devalued, and inauthentic.

"Yes, yes, yes!" I say. With the self assaulted as such, denied its complexity, it is difficult to sustain one's voice and to raise it over the cacophony of voices dictating the mother's behavior, critiquing her methods, finding her lacking or too indulgent.

In the grocery store, I watch a new mother and her infant waiting in line to return bottles. In five minutes, no less than six people stop to remark about the baby. One woman suggests that baby is too warm, and the mother obligingly unzips the infant's sweater. Another woman approaches the cart and moves the bag of cans away from the baby's hands. The mother, now stacking her returnables on the counter, thanks the woman. The other people only coo at the baby, tell the mother how cute she is. The mother looks a little frazzled by the time her bottles have all been returned, but she smiles or nods at each comment. The baby is not exceptionally beautiful or charming; it is simply a baby, a clear ribbon of drool on her chin. This unextraordinary child and her mother have unwillingly, perhaps unwantingly, solicited all this attention and scrutiny. Perhaps they enjoy it, see the people's comments and coos as a representation of our feelings of hopefulness, our reverence for the innocence, the possibility in a baby. Or perhaps the mother finds this scrutiny daunting. Perhaps it makes her self-conscious, aware of an audience always gauging her thoughts and behavior. Perhaps she has become uncertain of her words, her authority. Perhaps, like me, she edits every thought before it's complete and can't finish a sentence without questioning it, recasting it, stumbling over words. Like now, for instance, I imagine an audience, impatient, a bit embarrassed for me, thinking of their own mother's talcum-scented bosom, her selfless love. "This essay is idiosyncratic," the audience chimes, "and whiny." "It's your problem," they say. "The great minds have always operated outside of social norms. If only you were smarter, less sensitive, worked harder...What you need is more focus, more child care."

My own therapist said in response to this project— "What about Grace Paley? She wrote stories after her children were born. What about Tillie Olsen?" I am thankful for these women writers who found a way to write about the mother's lot, and I don't want to suggest it was easier then, that mother's voices were more welcome in literature or on the Senate floor or in department meetings, because clearly they were not. But different standards apply now to mothering. When I read my daughter the children's books I loved as a child, I'm surprised by what appears by current standards to be negligent parenting—children left in strollers outside the corner grocery or spoken to sternly: "Run along and pick your own berries." We believe that the world is a more dangerous place, and contending with those dangers—real or perceived—is the mother's responsibility. This perception of the world as dangerous and the mother as protector has only increased since Adrienne Rich wrote that the mother is thought to be "the source of angelic love and forgiveness in a world increasingly ruthless and impersonal...in a world of wars, brutal competition and contempt for human weakness."

If we cannot solve the world's problems, we can make our homes safe for children. There are a number of catalogues and stores that are entirely devoted to this goal. One can purchase outlet covers, Lucite stove guards, toilet seat clamps, foam tape to affix around tables with sharp edges, heat-sensitive bathtub nozzles which turn red to indicate water that could scald a child, a "choke tube" to test small items that might be swallowed, cupboard locks. One could go crazy, could spend hundreds of dollars as some people do on consultants who come and baby proof entire homes. All this well-executed market research and paranoia despite falling home-accident rates.

In a recent issue of *Mothering* magazine, Alice Munro, who rarely grants interviews, agreed to speak on the subject of writing and mothering, because "it is important for people like me to say what it's like, give comfort and courage to younger women." How did she do it? "She put her one year old daughter in a play pen and let her four year old play with the neighborhood kids." That was forty years ago. Today manufacturers call playpens "play yards" to distance them from the experts' criticism of them as cages for children. Mothers are cautioned against using them as baby-sitters:

> Start using the playpen for emergency duty only, for those times when he needs to be <u>penned</u> in for his own safety or briefly and infrequently for your convenience—while you mop the floor, put something in the oven, answer the phone, go to the bathroom, or straighten up for last minute company. Limit the time he is <u>sentenced</u> to the <u>pen</u> to no more than five to 15 minutes. (My underlining.)

Do I have to be a bad mother to be a writer? How hard it is to completely dismiss those voices when so much is at stake. Annie Dillard writes of the writing life "your work is so meaningless, so fully for yourself alone, and so worthless to the world, that no one except you cares whether you do it well, or ever." But the opposite might be said for the mothering life: Everything you do is for someone else and all the world cares how you do it and will hold you responsible for the results. How difficult then, to disengage from one's child to write. For Dillard her realization is liberating; for the mother it further complicates.

Recently I consulted *What to Expect: The Toddler Years* for help with toilet training, and this is what I found:

> Reduce the likelihood of accidents by having your toddler use the potty before leaving the house; by limiting prolonged outings, when possible; by being well-versed in the locations of toilet facilities wherever you go; by stashing an inflatable or regular potty chair in the car trunk...or by tucking a foldable potty seat in your tote bag... by dressing your toddler in easy off clothes; by watching your toddler carefully for signs of urinary urgency and by suggesting a trip to the toilet at frequent intervals. Avoid (as much as possible) restaurants, stores, homes, and any other destination where floors are covered with expensive carpeting or where the only seating is upholstered.

This is the good mother, the standard to which all others are held up. She is organized, prepared, utterly attuned to her child's needs, self-sacrificing (perhaps she'd like to go to a restaurant or to a friend's house, but no.) Barbara Christian writes of American mothers "only sacrifice counts as goodness." But can this woman, with her constant vigilance, participate in adult conversation? Can she write? By my desk, I have a postcard of Virginia Woolf. Beneath her serene profile is a quote from her journal: "It is in our idleness and dreams that the submerged truth sometimes comes to the top." There is no idleness for the good mother, not a second free from the concerns of her child. This prescribed vigilance is not only consuming and exhausting; it is, of course, loaded with implied criticism and threat for the mother.

Barely pregnant, I am awarded a fellowship to attend a prestigious writers' conference. I'm nervous, not because of all the famous writers I will meet, the reading I will be required to give, but because I have morning sickness all day long. I want only to sleep, eat Saltines, and drink seltzer. Not sleeping isn't an option—it's as if the part of my brain that considers consequence is turned off. My body says sleep and I do. When I'm not sleeping, I'm able to hobnob with the big-shot writers, something that has never come easily to me even when I could have cocktails. Now, of course, I'm not drinking because of the baby. At the time, I thought my calm and confidence was the result of the pregnancy hormones, and perhaps they helped. But now I think my calm derived mostly from the fact that I'd already abandoned my writer self. I could talk easily with the authors because I didn't care anymore. I watched the events as if from some distance, even the workshopping of my story by an author I very much admired. I was, I thought, done with this racket.

At one of the many cocktail parties at the conference, another writer, the father of four and a college professor, repeats a dictum someone told him: "Pick two—writing, teaching, family." I didn't like the message, but I suspected it was true. Something had to give, to go, and it was pretty clear to me what it would be. I'd already seen an interview with Sarah Jessica Parker in which she claimed she would give up acting when she has kids because she was the kind of person who could only do one thing at a time. Yes, I'd thought, me too.

While my juggling of mothering and writing and teaching isn't always graceful or easy, I've come to see it as worthwhile. And really it's only a recent phenomena that mothering be exclusive of other duties. A recent study shows that working mothers today spend more time with their children than mothers did in the 1920s. Even the 1950s mother was aptly called a housewife, denoting her primary allegiances—to hearth and husband. Interestingly we've replaced housewife with the clunkier, more judgmental "stay-at-home-mom." The mother who works is then called what? "The blow-off-mom?" "The hit-the-road-mom?"

What I'm learning is that writing and mothering needn't be set against each other. They can coexist—they do coexist, as life and art always have. While I read a bedtime story to my daughter, warm and dewy from her bath, I'm thinking of this essay or a story I'm drafting, so that when I reach the end of her book, I can't remember reading the middle. I am both engaged and idle; I am a mother and a writer.

All the daily ministrations of motherhood aren't, as I originally felt them, distractions from the world. They have reconnected me to this complicated world. The early spring flowers I noticed while pushing my newborn daughter in her stroller, were so exquisite, so dazzling and of such variety and color that I had to learn their names—snow glories, white star of Holland, winter aconite, grape hyacinth. How, I wondered, had I never noticed them before pushing through the sooty snow?

Driving yesterday, the autumn leaves on the thin white trees by the side of the road are dabs of gold floating, floating on a slate gray sky. The radio news recounts the gruesome beating of Matthew Shepard and I find myself crying. Someone's child, I think. And when the defendant's lawyer presents the sad facts of his client's childhood—abuse and molestation—I think again, a child ruined.

At the mall on a rainy Sunday, we watch a walk-a-thon for all the local agencies that care for mentally and physically handicapped adults and children. We see an enormously fat girl waddle by in stained sweatpants, a quartet of middle-aged women in thick-lensed glasses holding hands, another woman pushing a baby doll in a stroller, a thin man whose mouth moves continuously in a sort of toothless chew. And this family I won't ever be able to forget: A young, blonde mother and father each pushing a daughter in a reclining wheelchair. The girls have their parents' fair hair but their bodies are twisted, their limbs all points and angles. In the mall's fluorescent light, their eyes roll and twitch. There are so many ways for things to go dreadfully, dreadfully wrong. I want to look away, to shop for tennis shoes, but I can't. I keep looking, saddened, cataloguing defect and damage, absorbing it as I did the first shoots of spring.

Mothering has made me more fully present in this world, deepened and enriched my vision and sensibility. My daughter has made it all possible, and she has made it all difficult. These statements no longer seem at all contradictory to me.

jill stein

At the Waterloo Poetry Festival with My Daughter

A poet must write every day,
they say, but here I am,
her cries slicing me like meat
at the deli counter
into the measured functions of a mother.
Her legs hang frog-like down my back.
I pace behind these rows of heads
all still with focus,
and bob to coax her into silence.
I am trying to seduce her back in time
but she has moved out past me.
She is discovering her first joke—
a matter of juxtaposing
her self on mine.
She tugs my hair and
shifts her weight
inside her saddle,
galloping me through the canvas flaps of tent
into the light,
and yelping with the thrill
of the newly powerful.

maureen egan
A Sweet-Loving Mother

I don't think I could be a mother if it weren't for the perk of being able to make brownies, lick the batter off the spoon, and eat as many warm ones right out of the oven as I want. Thankfully, cookie-baking has given motherhood a good reputation, among children at least, Hillary Clinton's unfortunate "stay home and bake cookies" remark notwithstanding. So as long as staying home and baking cookies is morally superior to staying home and eating bonbons, I'm in good shape.

For all the baking I do, I have never been the idealized version of a sweet, selfless mother slaving away in the kitchen whipping up sweets for her little dears. I'm in favor of mothers being loving, self-sacrificing, generous, and nurturing—to a point—and the point is that once the cookies come out of the oven, they're mine. I refuse to hide behind the "I'm making chocolate cookies for my kids" excuse; instead I hide behind the fridge hoping my kids don't find me eating cookies for breakfast. No offense, Betty Crocker, but I don't bake as if the love of my children and desire of my husband depend on it. I bake the good stuff for me.

In the good old days when my kids were little, I could eat a cookie anywhere in the house with impunity—even as they were sucking soggy Cheerios. Anytime I overcooked the Toll House squares, I pawned off the burnt-edge ones on the youngest kid around. I'm not proud that I've stooped so low, but the alternative was wasting perfect, chocolatey moist ones on a toddler content to eat melba toast.

Now that my children are old and experienced, I can't sneak a batch of anything good by them. They have every item in the shopping cart catalogued.

When my son sees unsweetened chocolate, he's on the lookout for brownies; oatmeal means expect chocolate chip oatmeal cookies to my daughter

Sadly enough, they don't fall for my attempts to keep them away from the kitchen at a critical juncture anymore. Their sense of smell works altogether too well.

And when they catch me eating say, the last four or five chocolate peanut butter cookies a moment before dinner, I get in much bigger trouble than I did when they were small and easily deceived and distracted. The yelling and whining start as they converge on me and admonish me to share. I wish I could say that they do the whining, *but I don't want to*. No doubt my deceptions have affected them deeply, and someday a therapist will hear how I tricked them into tasting unsweetened chocolate, hoping it would scare them away from the good kind during their formative years, but at least I got mine.

Often, it so happens, I get theirs, too, as when several years back, I made a wonderful chocolate cake with a luscious vanilla icing from scratch, so I could eat lots of it. I dreamt about sneaking downstairs before breakfast to eat a slice, but I don't think I did that—laziness and gluttony go hand in hand. At any rate, over the course of a day, I sliced myself several slivers, and inhaled them without need of forks or plates. (I hate doing dishes.)

Still, I made sure the rest of the family had their chances, even giving my six-year-old son a piece in his lunch box. That evening before dinner, I needed an hors d'oeuvre, so I gobbled what cake remained on the plate. While looking for a pick-me-up a few minutes later, I remembered to my delight that my son hadn't touched the cake in his lunch box. So much for the sweet, selfless mother.

Yes, I ate his piece, and I had no qualms about eating it until he announced after dinner that he would have cake for dessert. Guilt pangs twisted my stomach, but when I broke it to him gently that it was all gone, I cleverly omitted any pronouns or active verbs that could have pointed to me. When he looked over towards the counter and saw that the cake had vanished, it was clear that he thought no one, not even his own mother, could have eaten that amount of cake so quickly, and he ran off crying. Did I feel like a crumb.

I was trying to think how I could comfort or bribe him, when he reappeared happy a minute later and, to my dismay, headed straight for his lunch box. When

I realized how he had trusted me, how very much he had underestimated me, I 'fessed right up. I can still see the look of disbelief on his face, but I don't think I'm kidding myself that there was also a look of awe, even a glimmer of pride there, too. What kind of mother would do such a thing? His and his alone. And I don't have an eating disorder or a weight problem, which is worse: I'm culpable. I'm fiendish. I'm conniving. I'm hungry.

So how did I get him to forgive me? Easy. I promised that I would make him an angel food cake (with a fabulous chocolate glaze, of course) the next day as my penance. And being the sweet, loving mother that I am, I kept my promise.

peggy garrison
Mother Notes for Elaine

"I keep forgetting things," I told one of my students,
"sometimes I can't even remember
what I've been saying
a few seconds before.
Is it cuz I'm getting old?"
"No," she said
"it's because the mind thinks parallel thoughts,
we rarely think one thing at a time."
"So that's it," I said as I saw
the P.S. 128 anthology still unedited,
snowpants my son still needs,
a strange fast-talking man
from a dream I can't quite reach,
chicken or sausage
for my sweet or sour husband,
Mother leaving me alone in the car for hours
in Schuster's parking lot (did she ask
the attendant to keep an eye on me?)—
all *that* stretched across my mind
like lines in a music-paper notebook,
chords and chimes that can't chime
cuz like a class full of children
they're all ringing at once—

not what i expected

what I need is
a one-note solo, not lines
but a dot the size of
and as interesting as
a clitoris—
(when you play with yourself
all imagery and action
move toward one goal)
so during these blessed twenty minutes
between picking my son up at the baby-sitter
and macaroni & cheese for dinner
let me crouch down
undistracted
unrefracted
in my peanut-shell chair
tiny and folded
like an unborn child
to write this poem...

annie farnsworth
Nightcap

It is stolen time, this
few minutes after husband and son
have been coaxed to sleep,
the dog and cats curled
into their own furred oblivion.
Under pretense
of tucking in the rabbits,
adding midnight bits of straw
before closing the hutch,
I've really just come to anchor here
in the driveway gravel,
to drink in the moon,
the full moon, grass moon,
pink moon. There is plenty,
and I will sleep on it,
will make mother's milk
of this solitude; I will need
something to pour back to you
tomorrow.

donna d. vitucci
Tug and Pull

On a calm day in late March, following a windstorm in the spring of 1959, Jane was born.

Mama said she'd stay with Annette and the new baby a week once they were released from the hospital. It was such a comfort to sleep and be taken care of. Annette had forgotten how, when she was sick and had stayed home from school, Mama had set tea and buttered toast on the bedside table for when she felt like eating. The baby's birth washed the slate between them clean, as if her teenage years and the tug-of-wars she and Mama had been through had never happened.

Mama put Jane down for her morning nap, then she'd bathe Annette. The sponge soaked up the hot water she'd drawn into the big soup kettle and brought to the bedside. Annette let her lift and wipe and nudge her clothes around, as spineless and undirected as the Raggedy Ann that Curt had brought to the hospital the first day he'd held Jane.

If not for the stitches, Annette could almost forget she'd given birth. Mama hushed the baby and walked her, only brought her in to be fed. Mama stroked Annette's breasts when she showed her how to help bring the milk down. Such a surprise, her mother's hands on that part of her body. At night Mama sent Curt to the bedroom with a glass of beer for Annette to drink during Jane's last feeding, but the baby never slept through the night. Jane's howls cut the walls, trailing out into the night and back in through all the other windows on the street. Annette imagined her neighbors shook their heads, all their suspicions confirmed. *That girl's too young to take care of her own baby.*

At the end of the week Mama had to show Annette three times how to do up the diapers before she got it right. She hadn't changed one since they'd come home.

With that one glorious week gone, March flipped into April.

How time got away from Annette when none of the outside world mattered. Not television news or neighborhood gossip, not even the growth of spring grass and buds. Jane sucked all time and attention from morning to night. Annette's every thought centered on the baby, what she needed, what she wanted, what she might be thinking or learning. Annette didn't wish to miss a thing. Even exhausted, in the woozy limbo of dreams, she could anticipate Jane's first whimpers (like Curt never could—a triumphant thought!), and she'd stand at the crib's edge ready to pick the baby up before she worked herself into a tantrum. She checked the diaper, then offered the breast, and when hunger didn't seem to be the problem, she rocked her or walked back and forth along the creaky wooden floor of the baby's room, shushing and bouncing her in her arms, Jane's wailing mouth open and wetting down the shoulder of her nursing gown against her skin.

Curt called her a martyr.

When Seagram sent him on a sales trip through Indiana and Illinois, the first since Jane's birth, Annette felt she'd been awarded her test. Not yet convinced she could be a mother, even though she held Jane in her arms as evidence, she was glad to at last be on her own, without Curt dogging her, offering his solutions to whatever might be bothering Jane.

Curt had been absent only a few hours when, surprise, Mama Sophia arrived in a taxi. Looking down on the commotion in the driveway, Annette first thought, Take the baby and escape. But to where? At the wedding Mama and Daddy had made it clear that her decision to lay down with Curt had set her on her own path. So as she watched Mama Sophia stumble up the driveway in her high heels, followed by the driver straining with the weight of her luggage, Annette silenced her objections. Alone, she knew she could not stand up to the woman, and she could hardly send Mama Sophia back to Cleveland. She was Jane's other grandma.

With the baby snug in the crook of her arm, she waited for her mother-in-law at the top of the stairs. She tucked her hair behind her ears and smiled.

Not a typical grandma, Mama Sophia dressed in the sexy style of Sophia Loren. Though she was born too early to actually be named for the movie star, she played up any small resemblance. She accentuated her bosom and her trim waist. She was a divorcee, a woman alone, just like many of Loren's movie characters.

Mama Sophia managed to cluck her disappointment, even with shortened breath from climbing the stairs. The driver dragged her suitcase up behind her to the second floor.

"Ah! What are you doing still in that nightgown? Go wash your hair for heaven's sake. I'll take the darling."

The woman whisked Jane from where she'd lain so warm and quiet against Annette's breast. Mama Sophia prodded her into the bathroom and closed the door, leaving Annette cringing at the sight of herself in the harsh mirror light. Her hair hung filthy, with hardly a hint of its usual curl. Had she even washed it since she'd been home from the hospital? The loose pouch of belly embarrassed her, and she wouldn't dare bend over to examine where the nurses had shaved her pubic hair. Already she itched from the wiry black stuff growing back.

Voices—Mama Sophia cooing at Jane and a lower rumbling line of syllables. Was she entertaining that taxi driver?

Annette washed her hair and used a lemon juice rinse, then sank into a lilac bubble bath and dozed. In her dream, Mick O'Donnell knocked shot glasses on the smooth slick wood of the Twilight bar. In fact all the customers who sat there, whose faces remained hidden, pounded their glasses, probably irritated because she couldn't serve them fast enough. Dread and inadequacy enveloped her, which seemed to be the point of the dream.

Mama Sophia's knuckles on the bathroom door startled her awake. "Are you staying in there all afternoon? Some of us might have to go, you know. And this baby's ready to eat."

In the hallway, Jane's rooster cries were piling up. Mama Sophia's high heels clicked across the wooden floor as she walked and tried to shush the baby.

With her hair still in a towel, Annette took Jane and sat her between pillows while she climbed in the bed beside her. Her stitches pulled, burned, slowed her down. Jane's screams were using up her breath so she couldn't settle down to suck.

Annette yelled into Jane's squalling face. "Will you just cool it a minute?"

She surprised the baby into silence. A string of regret tugged her inside, right between her lungs. Jane's deep blue and unfocused eyes sought her and Annette shoved the nipple into her mouth.

From the doorway Mama Sophia warned, "You get that baby so worked up she's going to have colic for half the night." She pivoted on her high heels and stalked out, so ridiculous a sight that Annette didn't know if she could stifle her laughing before the woman disappeared down the hall. In the kitchen Mama Sophia banged pans and the oven door.

Annette shoved her free fist into the rumpled bed sheets so hard Jane bounced and popped off the breast. The baby didn't scream, but her hands were curled in the same tight way.

Annette cried and laughed, both. She cuddled Jane up to her cheek before she put her on her shoulder to burp her. "We'll fight her together, you and me, you hear? And we'll win because you're mine and I'm all you've got."

Jane spit up clots of breast milk and Annette first cleaned the baby, then herself. Some of her tears plopped right into Jane's open mouth.

Curt called on Monday, and Annette could hear from Mama Sophia's response that he was surprised to hear his mother. The woman listed Annette's faults in a petulant, throaty voice, sometimes transposing words in her sentences so she sounded like she'd just come over the ocean from the Old Country. Mama Sophia wouldn't even let her speak to her own husband. It was agreed, without her consideration, that once Curt returned at week's end, he would drive Mama Sophia to the airport. That promise carried Annette through Mama Sophia's criticism at breakfast each day as she nursed Jane and tried to spoon dry cereal into her own mouth, sometimes spilling it in the baby's face. Somehow they made it to Friday.

In the twilight they rocked in chairs downstairs with Mrs. Weller on her front porch, Annette with the baby in her lap as they watched for Curt's maroon Olds.

Jane slept, her back against Annette's belly, her head slumped over to one side so she appeared to have no neck. When Mrs. Weller went inside to refill their iced tea glasses, Mama Sophia leaned over and touched her on the knee below her skirt hem. Annette had bought it two sizes larger to get her through the pregnancy, but these days she had to keep it up with a belt. Since Jane's birth the pounds had melted away, leaving her with her former waistline. Besides Jane, it was the one thing she could be proud of.

"I want you to take that baby to the doctor once Tony gets home."

Mama Sophia still called Curt "Tony."

In her mind, Annette tunneled back from whatever Mama Sophia had to say. From the moment she learned she was pregnant, she dreaded facing a crisis, some infant illness or deformity. She played the game that if she acted as if Jane didn't matter, then nothing bad would happen to her. She had tried to trick herself, pretending to slough off her layers of care for the baby, but each day Jane grew more rooted in her life.

Her voice wavered. "Why?"

"Look at that baby's head." Mama Sophia ran her fingertips along Jane's fuzzy scalp. "Something's not right. Look at this dent." She touched the center triangle area above the almost invisible hairline.

Annette laughed. "That's just her soft spot. It'll close up in a few weeks."

Mama Sophia shook her head. "There's something not right, I tell you."

Annette's skin prickled as if a breeze had blown, but the tree leaves lay flat and still. "What do you know about it? You're not a doctor." She cuddled Jane. "Just leave her alone. She's fine."

"If you don't get that baby to a doctor, my grandchild's going to grow up to be a freak."

She pointed a blood red fingernail to make her point. Mama Sophia had done her nails twice during the five days she'd been there. Each time Annette had found her at the kitchen table with the polish remover, and the bottles of topcoat and various shades of red, she'd retreated to the bedroom, closeting herself and Jane away from the fumes.

She considered slapping that accusing hand just as Curt pulled up.

"My Tony," Mama Sophia announced.

She wobbled, so ridiculous in her high heels, to meet him in the driveway. Annette hoped she'd stumble and turn her ankles.

"Give your mother a hug and kiss." Before he could get out of the car, she snuck her head into the open window to smear lipstick on his cheek.

"Hi, Ma."

Annette heard him kiss his mother. The car door groaned open and closed. She couldn't wait until they left for the airport.

"How are my girls?"

Curt stepped onto the porch and bent down to put his face inches away from Jane, who still slept. That little blister on her top lip she got from sucking puffed gently with each breath she exhaled.

Even in the dusk Annette noticed Curt's bloodshot eyes. Was he sleepy from the drive or had he been drinking? Inside, the car always smelled like a cordial factory. During pregnancy, Annette couldn't look at sweet fruits like cherries and oranges without feeling sick. The smell was on him all the time, but with him selling it, always being around it, she never knew if he'd been sipping or not. Until he put his tongue in her mouth.

"Hey, Annie."

He kissed her. Mint.

"How have things been?" He withdrew his lighter and cigarettes from his pants pocket.

"Fine."

Mama Sophia blew out Curt's lighter after he lit the cigarette. Annette wanted one herself, but wouldn't speak and risk Mama Sophia criticizing her for all those ashes and the possibility of flammable clothing while she held an infant.

"That girl's got her work cut out for her," Mama Sophia started in. "She lets the baby nearly starve before she'll sit down and nurse her. She says she needs a schedule. Ah, I don't know! When we were young, a baby was hungry, you fed the darling. Common sense." She raised her hands to heaven, then dropped them.

Mrs. Weller rocked in her chair, her eyes on the peony bushes that would bloom in a month or so in the side yard. Annette followed her gaze. Once they opened, here and there flecks of red, like blood, would stain the white petals. No matter how much she knew it beforehand, the red always surprised her.

Curt smoked, leaning against the peeling white paint of the house's clapboard, his eyes closed, his face shadowed. Annette saw his exhaustion, the way the wall helped keep him standing. Well, she was tired, too.

She stared at the top of Jane's head. Did the baby's skull show its lines and slopes more than usual or was it a trick of the twilight? Damn Mama Sophia.

After Curt left with his mother for the airport, Mrs. Weller said, "She means well, honey."

Annette made a face. "Sure she does."

Jane sighed on her lap, then startled herself awake, ready at once to cry. Annette shushed her, crooned baby talk as she unbuttoned her blouse and prepared to nurse.

Dark had stolen in so only the moon and the blue glare of Mrs. Weller's TV in the living room provided light. While Jane sucked, Annette stretched her legs, stiff from so much bed rest. She would take a walk tomorrow, no matter how painful the stitches. But what about Mama Sophia's prediction about the baby? No walk. She'd have Curt drive her and Jane in for a checkup first thing in the morning, as soon as she could get him out of bed. After she guessed maybe seven minutes had passed (she couldn't make out the time on her wristwatch in the dark), she then switched sides to keep the milk coming in both breasts. Jane nuzzled in closer, and she had to pinch the heavy flesh of her own body away from the baby's nose so she could breathe.

The baby gulped and Annette stroked her soft cheek. Jane was a hearty eater. During these first weeks it was all nursing and doing for the baby. Jane had colic, especially at night. She rejected a bottle and even a pacifier, as if to say nothing and no one but Annette would do. How satisfying that Jane preferred her above all others.

First-of-the-season moths bounced against Mrs. Weller's screen door. Drawn by the inside light, they fluttered, then crashed at the screen time and time again.

"Wouldn't you think they'd know better after a while?" Annette said.

Mrs. Weller's voice came to her out of the shadows. "You'd think so."

Jane was colicky, fussy, irritable, demanding, needing lots of sucking and little sleep, but other than that, a normal, healthy month-old baby. The doctor said the soft spot would close up on its own, it was nothing to worry over.

He suggested formula might help fill Jane's stomach so they could all sleep through the night, but Jane had already established a schedule that included Annette on demand. Now needed more than she'd ever been in her life by a being so helpless and beautiful, down to her perfect tiny fingernails, Annette gave herself over like a slave.

Curt called it a female conspiracy. He took every out-of-town assignment he could to escape the squalling. Annette didn't miss him when he was gone, except when the handle on the toilet broke and when one of the bedroom window screens fell two stories down to the backyard grass. Each of those times she called Gene Sheeter, the landlord. Self-conscious about allowing the man into her bedroom to replace the screen, she also imagined he saw her as an adult, as an equal, as she stood in the hallway, with Jane straining from her shoulder. Together, she and her daughter watched this stranger put the square of wire and wood back where it belonged. In those first months after Jane's birth that's really all she needed Curt for, the odd household jobs.

While other girls her age were still finishing up their junior year of high school, Annette made it through the day on three or four hours of sleep, with maybe a bath around seven o'clock on a good night, if she put the baby on a comforter surrounded by pillows on the bathroom rug where she could see her. Even when she washed her hair under the faucet, kneeling naked in the tub, she kept her eyes open and turned on Jane. She couldn't bear not knowing what the baby was doing. If she put her fist to her mouth, if she screamed so loud and long that she lost her breath, if she marveled with her beautiful blue baby eyes at the bulb above the medicine cabinet mirror, Annette wanted to see it. She used the baby shampoo on her own hair so her eyes wouldn't sting when soap ran into her ears and over her face. While she rinsed, Jane batted herself in the face with her hands, fat little mitts that she didn't yet have control over. She waved them in the air, and back at her cheeks, then out again as if asking to be picked up. She was still too young to know how to ask for what she wanted, and yet she put her open hands to her head and pulled the little bit of brown hair she'd been born with until she screamed from hurt.

Annette couldn't help laughing. "Well, you're definitely mine," she said. She stood, with the bath water streaming down her seventeen-year-old body, which unbelievably to her, had given birth to this wailing baby, and she wondered what would become of them.

† † †

Annette cut her hair. She began styling it like Jackie Kennedy's, with poofy bangs in the front, the rest curled in a flip at her shoulders. While Curt was away, she kept the house spotless—no small task with Jane walking now and into everything. Annette sang, "*Chains, my baby's got me locked up in chains...*" above the roar of the vacuum sweeper, a round flying-saucer sort of machine. She dragged its tentacled attachments around the house behind her.

On the TV news she watched the astronauts, with all their tubes and hoses, getting ready for their launches into space. Jane was like an astronaut in a bubble suit, tied by a lifeline that allowed her to bob and weave and explore, but always homing back to Annette. The little girl nursed for nearly a year and a half before Mama Sophia, during one of her long-distance checkups on her Tony, said Jane's dependence stretched beyond normal.

Mama Sophia couldn't possibly understand how Annette delighted in Jane's very existence. The job of mothering so used her up that she had nothing left at the end of the day for Curt. No one had told her that marriage could lapse into this dullness, that looking just to her husband could make everything, to Annette, seem like an obligation.

He'd want sex in the middle of the night after she'd finally returned to bed from pacing the floor with Jane, who was prone to earaches and nightmares. Weary to her bones, Annette went limp so he could finish. She no longer enjoyed this. When he wrapped his arms around her from behind, she wore silence on her shoulders like a coat. Sometimes she thought she'd fly apart, splattered to bits across the bedroom ceiling. Her soul had to be hiding out in the corners of the hallway because it was not in the room.

She thought of when she and her brother Jack had played hide and seek in the barn. She hid in corners then, half believing she could flatten herself so thin that she'd disappear from sight. They did dangerous things, like stabbing pitchforks into piles of hay to see if enemies lay hidden there. With eyes closed, they jumped from the hayloft, pretending to parachute over North Korean lines.

If Jack played the spy, then she'd be the interrogator. She shoved stiff twigs under his fingernails, forcing him to disclose classified information.

"I'll never give up my secrets," he'd whisper and then spit at her, usually missing.

She'd have to get rough, twist his arm behind him and sneer into the back of his neck. "Just who do you think is in charge here?"

A quick jerk on his already twisted arm made Jack give in. She would only free him when his knees buckled. Easy to get carried away with the game, her face on his neck, his hair shaved short for the summer. Freckles burned on his shoulders, his shoulder blades breakable as bird's bones. The faces of brother and sister blurred. There was Curt's hot breath on her neck, his hand twisting hers, force barely held in check.

This was the way to get what she wanted, and she gave in.

She was anxious to get pregnant again. When she'd find the spots of rusty brown in her underwear each month, urgency nagged at her. She'd adjusted to Jane, could hardly recall what glamour the days held before her baby so thoroughly consumed her. As much as she loved pretending that she alone could provide Jane the answers to her every question, she recognized the necessity of stumbling, the trial and error of getting along with others. Jane needed a sibling so they could, together, face each treacherous day.

There'd been too many years between Annette and Jack. The opportunity to play the vicious older sister had taken her over with the least effort. For Jane she wished a closeness that brothers and sisters brought with them to the playground and to library story time. She'd seen families, tight knit in a crowd of strangers, the children holding hand to grubby hand. These children skimmed around corners, falling maybe, but always just missing scraping their foreheads. They had a confidence in their stumbling that she wanted for Jane.

She and Jane would spend all afternoon on their backs watching the clouds change shapes, Jane's brown hair nearly down to her shoulders and spread out on the grass next to Annette's. If they turned to each other, they'd trade Eskimo kisses, Annette breathing in the scent of clover and baby shampoo from her daughter's sweaty hair. If Curt happened to be out of town, they'd have applesauce and Cheerios for supper, a picnic for two on the backyard patio Gene Sheeter had put in.

Curt's sales territory required his travel for days at a time. Annette had never given up the rock and roll that caused trouble between her and Mama when they lived in the same house. She bought 45s by the Everly Brothers and the Four Seasons from Woolworth's in the Hill and Valley Plaza. When Curt was gone, she played those records loud and long.

In late October, she decided to take Jane to Hill and Valley. She suspected she might be pregnant, her belly bowing like it did into that low, slight slope. Shopping would be her reward. Burning leaves hung their salty smell in the air as she pushed the stroller to the bus stop across from St. Charles. Curt was gone; she needn't return to cook dinner. She intended to have a good time, to run her fingers along the perfectly knitted stitches in some of the tiniest baby booties at Woolworth's.

When the bus pulled up, exhaust stirred the candy wrappers, bits of yellowed leaves, and empty cigarette packages in the gutter. She pushed Jane's face into her own jacket to escape the smell. Jane insisted on taking the three tall steps into the bus herself, gripping Annette as she swayed with the effort of stretching her legs high. While the bus pulled into traffic, Jane screamed her high-pitched wail after Annette had slipped the nickels into the change box though she'd promised Jane she could do it. She swept Jane up with one arm, hooked her shoulder bag and the push-rail of the collapsed stroller onto her other arm, and took an open spot at the end of the first long seat that ran lengthwise on either side in the front of the bus. The rest of the seats, separated by a center aisle all the way to the back emergency exit, faced the front. In this first front-facing seat, and perpendicular to them, sat a man in a gray raincoat.

With her feet, Annette held the stroller halfway in the aisle. She adjusted the loose bobby pins that kept Jane's navy beret on her head, a beret that matched her navy knee socks and the navy blue collar and cuffs of her red corduroy dress. Annette's heart was full up with love at the adorable sight Jane made as she sat sucking on her bottom lip.

When her daughter smacked the soles of her red patent leather shoes together, the man in the raincoat smiled and said, "Hello." His hair was black and grainy, as if it had been shoe-polished, while his sideburns bushed gray along his jowls. A sweaty odor wafted from him, though the fall day was comfortably cool.

"Hi," Jane said, chewing at the inside of her cheek, a nervous habit she'd just recently started.

The man's smile nagged at Annette. Something not quite right about it, but to get up and move would admit her discomfort. She gently lay her hand on Jane's skirt, a reminder to stop knocking her shoes. "You'll get scuffed up."

Jane sat still, but continued staring at the man. Their seats were so close she could have climbed into his lap without touching the floor of the bus.

"You're mighty pretty," he said.

Jane tried out the manners Annette had practiced with her. "Sank you," she said. She looked up for approval.

Annette smiled.

The man grinned. He had no teeth. His blank gums reached smoothly to where that pink thing hung down at the opening to his throat. What did they call it? Annette used to know.

Jane tried to climb up onto her lap, but Annette already had trouble balancing the stroller with the braking and accelerating of the bus. She placed Jane firmly in her own spot.

"You sit here until it's time to get off." She smoothed the wrinkles of Jane's dress.

"Teef?"

Annette blushed as Jane mentioned the man's deficiency.

He laughed and opened his mouth wide. Annette pretended to check the stroller's wheels. Were they too far in the aisle?

"I ain't got any in there, honey." He put his face next to Jane so she could take a close horrible look. He expelled his sour breath on them.

Jane hid her face in Annette's side and the beret fell from her hair.

"They're here," the man said. Out of his raincoat pocket he brought a jar, the size that might have held peanut butter. A set of false teeth floated in the clear liquid.

Jane took a peek, her hands still clutching Annette's jacket. The jar reminded Annette of high school biology, vague ideas of organs and half-formed animals in formaldehyde. She held back sickness, recalling her possible pregnancy in that weary nausea.

"You can hold it." The man offered Jane the jar of teeth.

"Me?" she said, reaching for it.

Annette began to object, but Jane was asking his permission, not hers. Jane held the man's teeth in her lap. They swished back and forth, first full at one side of the jar, then the other.

"Just hold on tight and don't drop it," Annette said.

When the bus braked, the man stood as if to leave, then sat again. "Not my stop." He smiled his toothless grin.

Annette averted her eyes, concentrated on Jane, who watched the teeth in the jar as if they were alive, but in peril, like the goldfish Curt had won for her at the church festival last summer. She had sat alone in the car's back seat, exclaiming over the fish and their frenzied swimming, two of them captured in a plastic bag of water with a twist tie. One corner leaked and Jane screamed over the water dribbling on her lap. They only lived a mile from the church, but even as fast as Curt drove, by the time they pulled into the driveway there wasn't a tablespoon of water left in the bag. The fish had flopped on each other and suffocated.

An overhead bus placard announced registration for the School of Court Reporting. Annette thought maybe she'd like to walk into a court of law as her daily job, once her babies grew up and moved away. The idea of her babies gone, all those that had not yet even been born, stoppered her throat. She had trouble swallowing. Jane still attended the jar of teeth.

The bus pulled into the Hill and Valley Plaza parking lot, and strangers bumped shoulders with one another.

"I'll take those now," the man said.

As the bus stopped, Annette stood to adjust her hold on the stroller and her purse.

"In my lap," he said.

She glanced to make sure Jane had obeyed. With her two hands clasping the sides of the jar, Jane leaned over the seat and put the teeth in the man's lap. The man patted her on her head. Jane had lost her beret. While the man in the gray raincoat touched her daughter's hair, Annette saw his penis next to the jar where his raincoat flap had been drawn aside. It sat there alongside his hairy inner thigh.

She grabbed Jane and pulled her from the seat where she'd made her sit so quiet and obedient. At the bus door the stroller got away and clattered down the three tall steps to the sidewalk. Jane cried from being wrenched so roughly, and oh the commotion once she realized her beret was lost. Annette recoiled from the exhaust fumes of the bus. Then she vomited into the curb, taking a good look at the dented bottle caps, crushed cigarette butts, and tattered leaves the color of blood.

† † †

It was true. She found herself pregnant again.

Jack came by when Curt was out of town. He stacked his 45s along with Annette's high on the stereo for a dance party. He twirled Jane over his head, tossed her back and forth on either side of his hips, until she shrieked when he spun her. He held Annette in a slow moving jitterbug, his hands grazing over her palms, her shoulders, her swollen waist, as if he were afraid she'd break if he grasped her firmly. They talked about the weather, about Jack's wish to drive a Wonder Bread truck as soon as he got his license, and about Jane's latest phrase. They never mentioned Daddy's heart condition, how he'd given up cigarettes on doctor's orders, how he might have done it too late.

When she had a minute to think about her life, Annette barely recognized the sassy Twilight waitress she'd once been. Working at establishing a happy home, she embraced Curt's heritage. Everything Italian seduced her—blood red roses, Dean Martin, the unspoken code of chivalry, the dusky taste of Chianti. She asked Mama Sophia for recipes, intent on recreating the family atmosphere, or at least the favorite food, of Curt's boyhood. Dinners held allure. The very words slipped off her tongue like olive oil—veal parmigiana, spaghetti carbonara. Mama's fried chicken and potato pancakes paled in comparison.

In a month, Jane would turn three, and by mid-summer they'd welcome another baby. Jane was bent over on the kitchen floor, coloring in some of Curt's outdated AAA maps of Midwestern states. Annette rubbed her belly and then Jane's back, as she paused on her way from the ironing board to the sink. She was taking care of herself this time, resting when Jane napped, drinking plenty of water instead of the Coke and black coffee she'd swilled while she waitressed pregnant at the Twilight.

She dreamed of naming their next children, if they were girls, Veronica and Angelina, but Curt insisted on American names. He even began calling her "Annie." Annette sounded too exotic, he claimed. He had named Jane, and if the second child was a girl he wanted to call her Susan. A boy would be John.

†††

Susan Marie arrived in the midst of that humid June in 1962. Daddy had retired from his Hudy truck route and spent more and more time playing solitaire at the kitchen table, in his plaid cotton bathrobe over long underwear, tattered slippers on his thin bony feet. Mama telephoned apologies to Annette. She just couldn't leave him, she said. Mama Sophia had booked reservations on a ship to Italy, so she could visit cousins and the old graves of relatives. Jane stayed with Mrs. Weller when Annette and Curt went to the hospital, and the girl didn't give her a moment's worry, she told them.

This new baby was blessed with such a sweet disposition that, had she been born first, Annette could only wonder how life might have been different if fussy, colicky Jane had been her second child. Susan slept as if she were still being lulled by the murmurs of voices she'd heard while she'd grown strong in Annette's belly.

The first nights home from the hospital, Annette would stand at the edge of Susan's crib, watching her sleep. She turned her head in the dark to reassure herself with the rise and fall of the baby's back under the thin sheet. She had always had to endure Jane's screams between her feedings to give her body the chance to produce more milk. At only one week old, Susan slept through her first night home seven continuous hours, until Annette wound up three music boxes and the musical mobile of the stars, the moon, and the planets to gently wake her. She worried about starvation, but Susan slept seven to eight hours every night, and nursed a good half hour six times through the day, on a schedule so regular Annette swore she could set the clocks by her. Her strong appetite brought Annette's milk in full and constant.

Through the night her breasts grew lumpy and tender. By the medicine chest light in the bathroom, she wanted to express some milk into the sink, but without the baby's cries to spur the let-down reflex it was hopeless. She tried to massage as Mama had taught her. With Jane there'd never been a question that she was ready to suck. Now Annette's breasts were so engorged that she couldn't stand the smallest touch. The flimsy weight of her summer nightgown pained her. She undid the front laces that kept it closed.

The bedside clock read four-thirty. She turned her head and lay barebreasted in bed, listening for Susan, awaiting the milky light of morning that would bleed through the venetian blinds and reveal the bedroom furnishings. She smelled the diluted scent of Prell from her own pillow, the sweet aroma Curt carried with him, and the musky scent of his unwashed body.

He rolled over in his sleep and flung his arm to her side of the bed. The back of his hand, all rough knuckles and hair, skimmed her right breast. Her whimper hung there in the bedroom dark.

Curt awoke, straightened, facing her. "What's wrong?" He kept his words soft.

"Nothing." Her voice matched his.

"Annie?"

She couldn't speak.

He brushed his fingers along her cheek and brought them away wet. "Is it the baby?"

She shook her head. The mattress shuddered with her.

"What?" he insisted.

Swallowing twice, three times, she wiped her face with the sheet's edge. Her voice was stuck. It might float away if she let herself cry out loud.

"The baby hasn't nursed since last night," she said. "And I'm full up." She paused. "It hurts."

Curt drew closer to her, reached out to touch, ever so lightly, the side of her breast. The mew sound of a kitten escaped her mouth.

"Should we wake her up?"

Again she shook the bed. "I checked her. She's sleeping soundly. I hate to break that."

She heard his long exhale as he shifted his body, pulled the covers more closely over them both.

"Well, what can we do?"

She shrugged and the act made her wince.

Curt, curled alongside her, began stroking her thigh where the leg of her panties arced up her hip. His voice snuck past the range of whisper, into the baritone that was his daily speech, part growl. "I could suck them for you."

Her blood left her feet, hands, and head, as if her heart had expanded to rise right out of her body.

His fingers drew wider circles, reaching from her hip to her inner thigh. She knew what he had in mind, and her womb cramped.

"I can't," she whispered. "The stitches..."

"I know," he told her. "But I could suck them. So you'd be more comfortable. Just until the baby wakes up."

She'd been his wife almost four years. It wasn't as if he'd never taken her breasts into his mouth, had never run his tongue and the blunt edges of his teeth over the dark brown nipples, but it sickened her, the idea of him swallowing what was meant for the baby.

"No. I just can't." She turned away so his hand slid off her body and lay on the mattress between them. The dull dawn showed it there, a ghostly thing on the gray bedsheet.

She rolled slowly out of bed to check on the girls. Jane spoke out something garbled from her dream. Susan slept quiet in the crib beside her.

Mr. Sheeter had installed a shower in their bath while she'd been in the hospital, and now Annette undressed in the morning dark, regulated the water from the tub faucet. First birds chirrupped outside.

She felt grit under her feet on the bathroom linoleum. Maybe she'd wash the floor later if the weather didn't turn too humid. Nothing more disgusting than scrubbing a bathroom, the air of the day wet on her skin and mixed with her own sweat, the odor of Pine-Sol hanging like the smell of a raincoat.

She flipped the metal latch to direct the tub water through the shower nozzle. Under the tiny separated streams, she shut off nearly all the cold so hot water pulsed down her breasts. Her tears mixed in with the shower, making her think, absurdly, about washing with her own body fluids. She saw the weak, blue-white liquid leaking from her nipples, two slow rivers in the gush of the shower. It all slipped over her still-swollen abdomen, down her thighs and shins, over the bones in her feet. The tub filled with water up to her ankles.

† † †

While in the middle of Curt's two-week sales trip up and down Indiana, the Strangler claimed a fifth victim in Boston. A copycat stalked their own area, and folks on Bonner Street locked their houses up at night all summer and into the fall.

Annette feared letting the girls out of her sight, even for the few minutes it took her to hang up wash on the line out back. When Maggie Sandor, the little girl next door, offered to sit with Jane and Susan, she took the opportunity to drag the sheets out of the washer. Maggie had just begun second grade. Annette could trust her with the girls as long as they were simply pushing Susan in the buggy up and down the driveway.

She tasted the brown flavor of the wooden clothespins she held in her mouth as she walked down the clothesline to hang the sheets in the early September breeze. A wind gust slapped the nearest wet sheet into her face so the Clorox smell burned the inside of her nose. Her muscles, aching from carrying and hanging the sheets' white length, tingled with relief when she brought her arms down to her sides.

As she came around the side of the house, she stopped short at the sight of the three girls, two of them hers, against a backdrop of startling blue and green. Maggie pushed Susan up and down the driveway in the buggy. The girl sang that pilgrim song about *"turning, turning, we come round right."* Jane propelled her trike-bike to keep up with them. She hummed along, but out of tune. For many minutes, Annette kept herself hidden in the side yard. Someone else could take care of her girls. She had weaned Susan after only three months of breast feeding when she'd begun to bite.

She'd be missed, but in her absence they could go on. Such relief flooded her that she had to sit on the porch step before she gave the neighbor girl a dime and took over the buggy. A long time passed before she asked Maggie to watch Jane and Susan again. Once she trusted Maggie enough, maybe she'd lose her one good reason to come back.

andrea potos
The Calling

My child's murmur breaks open
into a cry I can't ignore.
I lay pen and notebook down,
last images leaving like bright streamers
trailing behind me
from a party I must leave too soon.
Her cry keeps calling
like a mother's voice in the summer dusk
ordering her child in
from the generous lawns
where the child lingers—claiming
it can't yet be time to go in,
it's much too early for sleep. The fireflies
have only just appeared
leaping their messages of light.

kathryn leenay
Night Vision

I run to the rhythm of the lullaby I sang to my baby last night. My uneven strides try to conform, but I end up running to a lopsided waltz in three-quarter time. I've gone out for this run to "get away," but being alone takes more energy than caring for my new baby. The sun is coming up behind a papery film of harvested cornstalks and the dew is so heavy it runs in streams down the leaves of the trees I pass.

My baby is all of me. She wraps me inside her so that I am nothing without her. I run faster to feel something outside of me. But all I remember is my husband, holding her, trying to soothe her through the night while I sit on the bed next to him, half fallen into my pillow so that after a few minutes my right side is numb. He is stronger at night than I am. Once it passes midnight every cry and wiggle becomes a nightmare for me. The night is the hardest time because without the light I feel I have no control. I want to cry too. Tell my baby that I'm scared. I'm scared that I won't see the sign of some danger. So after I lay her down each time, I ask God to watch over her. But it's more like a deal than a prayer, and I wince at my own instinct, wondering what it is I have really done. Once the morning comes and I no longer have to turn on the light, I feel I have accomplished something; making it through the night becomes an achievement.

The moon is still out as I begin my run. It lingers like a doubt. All I hear is the sound of my feet on the pavement, and I think that if I stop long enough I can also hear the dew as it drips from the tree limbs. Maybe I could see myself in the watery mirror that forms only for that short time between night and dawn. But I don't stop. Not like I used to. I can't remember what it's like not to have her in my life, although it's only been two weeks since her birth.

Last night, my husband sat with her on the bathroom floor while I took a bath. She was quiet in his arms, her eyes dark olives and the only sound was her breathing. I wasn't talking so he asked me if I wanted to be alone. After they left, I splashed my face with water until I stopped tasting the salt of my tears.

I came across a journal entry from when I first found out I was pregnant:

> He sits on the couch with his fingers kneaded so that his skin looks like a candy cane; all white where he is pressing so hard. Perhaps trying not to say something wrong. "Sometimes it's all too much," he says, not looking at me, not looking anywhere because his eyes are like two small pools of water, and the edges are creeping inward like water evaporating.
>
> I stand in the middle of the room, an upstairs bedroom that I have made into an office. Only you can't even see the floor because all my paperwork is laid around. Nothing matches and I press my forehead to remember the colors I once liked. The green curtains in the store had looked so shiny, an inspiration, and now next to the dark woodwork and the dirty white walls they stick out. Something new and beautiful in my old and dull.
>
> My body bends to support my crying. "I wish I could cry too," he tells me, his face like cut stone. It is white in the overhead light. He can't touch me, I know, because he would never find me. That makes me cry more and I hold my stomach to stop my insanity from spreading to the baby inside me.

I still hear her cries from last night and the sound of his voice as it changed from confident consoler to beaten prisoner of her discomfort. I had slept, or tried to sleep, while he took her downstairs "for a walk," he said. Between my dreams I heard his voice first singing, sometimes pleading, and finally barely audible as he lays her to sleep between us. Later, when I got up to run, they were sleeping on their backs with their bodies slightly aligned. They seemed out of place on the large bed, but oddly comfortable like a tree that grows around some foreign object, taking it for its own. They both wore the same half-gapped smile found in sleep that is well needed.

"It only lasts a short while," my friend told me. "There's a moment when you stop thinking she'll break. When you let her take her own tears if even for a moment. It's the moment they gain strength and the moment you realize the cord was not broken."

My mother told me that there is no love like the physical love you have for your child. I didn't understand her when she told me this on the phone, five minutes after Audry's birth. "Not sexual love," she said. "Physical."

But I feel it now as I run harder and try to stop my breaths like I tried to stop her cries last night. I'm running away into something.

It seems like I've been running forever, but my watch says six a.m. Only a half hour since I left. The lights are starting to go on in our neighbors' houses. My house is still dark and the cat greets me at the door with a tired stretch. I climb the stairs to our bedroom in silence, holding my breath, because there isn't a sound coming from the bedroom. They are sleeping as I left them. Audry's hands are thrust out to her sides in softening fists. I hear her breathing; first in fervent dream breaths and then silence.

"How was your run?" Tim asks, his eyes closed.

I crawl between my husband and daughter, and pull the covers to my neck. My body is moist with sweat and this new-found warmth. I dig my body deeper until I feel Tim's hips against me. He puts his arm on my leg and I listen to his breaths as they go deeper into sleep.

She wakes with a start. Her face the heavy red of sleep, soft patches that mark her like her dreams. Clumsily we hold her, singing the songs that we never thought we knew. Under the yellow light of the lamp, we examine the dog-eared baby book, and swear beneath our breaths because there is nothing in the index under "night crying." So we think of other headings, shouting them out like answers to a Trivial Pursuit game.

ethney mcmahon
Nap Time

Your naps are never more than 40 minutes long
so once I close the door to your room
I become a mad woman
a lightweight boxer taking jabs
at the jaw of the clock
forget the laundry
the dishes
the floor
the bills can pay themselves
I am a petty thief on the subway
of motherhood
stealing time
in the pocket of a poem
but inevitably you call me
MOMMY
as if it were being said for the first time
abruptly
as if I could not hear you
in the jungle of living room
where I have cut a path with my pen...
MOMMY
tugging at the compass of my heart
I make headway into your room
into the empty cocoons of your dreams
a lifetime away
from the chores
I left behind

katherine grace bond
Not a Poem

I am supposed to be writing a children's story on a deadline and instead
the poems are clamoring like a lapful of thick watercolor coins and they are
   falling
to the ground between my knees.

When the words start to come, the baby wakes and pulls
long draughts of milk from me.
I watch the towels hanging stiffly on the bathroom rack
and it is twilight and the birds outside chatter to each other and I think to
   myself, "This is not a poem."

Back in my room my drawing board has a stale smell and now it is dark
and the light comes in the glass door from the neighbor's kitchen
and I pour myself a cup of coffee and think,
"This is not a poem."

I shift on my chair and overhead a plane trumpets by
and on top of my computer the plastic Quasimodo my son gave me for luck
   kicks his feet in the air and I feel sleepy behind my eyes and I think,
"It's still not a poem."

I am poem-starved,
ready to stuff myself with images like ripe berries, greedy
as the Steller's jays that land on the peach tree in the yard.
The words come rattling down like hail,
like shards of ice,
like manna
and I have no bucket to collect them before they melt away.

katherine grace bond
Stopping by the Bathroom on a Busy Evening
(With apologies to Robert Frost)

Whose brush that was, I think I know.
She's busy doing laundry, though;
She will not see me standing here
Watching the toilet overflow.

My dinosaur must think it queer
To swim with Rubber Duckie here,
Between the tub and potty chair,
While I smear toothpaste on the mirror.

He splashes on the sloshy floor
And asks if we can play some more.
The only other sound's the swoosh
Of water running out the door.

The toilet's wondrous, cold and deep.
I'll leave the dinosaur to steep.
I've much to do before I sleep;
Yes, much to do before I sleep.

carol carpenter
A Fine Day

The nurse rubs Vaseline on Juanita's swollen finger, twists the wedding band over the knuckle. Juanita moans. She isn't ready for the next contraction, can't remember any of the Lamaze class lessons, doesn't want to remember.

Pinching her arm, Richard tells her to breathe. "Why do you make everything so hard?" He sticks out his tongue, pants. "Like this."

She wants to yank out his tongue with forceps.

"Goddammit, breathe right."

She scratches at the starched sheets, holds her breath against the pain.

"You can do it," her husband says as she begs for the needle. "Bite on this." He slips a sponge between her teeth.

Her teeth close on his finger.

"Goddammit." He squeezes his sore finger, rocks it between his knees and back to his chest. "That hurt, goddammit."

When the nurse comes with the needle, she holds out her arm.

"If you only tried," Richard says from the flowered chair by the window. Newspaper pages crackle as he turns them; his voice floats above her, reading the baseball scores.

After the doctor drops the baby on her abdomen, after he stitches the wound and washes his hands, she is alone in a room. Curtains are pulled around her and she sleeps.

Her breasts that leaked for nine months go dry. Her daughter cries against her and the nurses bring her less often. Juanita is glad. Her daughter reminds her of the chicken in her freezer—feathers plucked, skin puckered.

In the middle of the night, the new mother in the next bed bites into apples and sucks the juices from oranges. She whispers through the curtains; Juanita feigns sleep. In the morning, the woman buys pictures of her infant. Juanita orders none.

When Richard visits, the woman is nursing her new son. Her face, like her exposed breast, is smooth, full. She laughs at Richard's jokes. Her son's feet straddle her breast as she burps him against her shoulder.

Richard turns away, hands Juanita a potted geranium he is holding. "Spot of color for the front porch."

"I'll keep it in the bathroom."

"Not enough light there." He kisses Juanita on the forehead and takes the apple the woman in the next bed offers.

"Want a bite?" he asks Juanita.

Juanita shines the apple on her nightgown and takes a bite. She gags and spits the half-chewed pieces into a Kleenex. "Wormy," she tells Richard.

Richard holds the apple close to the light on her headboard, examines it. "Just your imagination." He bites and the juices glaze his lips.

"What are we going to name her?" Juanita asks.

"Who?" Richard closes the curtains and turns on the television.

"Your daughter." She pushes the off button and moves the control box to the other side of the bed.

"I don't care. The mother is supposed to choose the daughter's name." Richard pats his pockets for a pack of cigarettes. "Can I smoke in here?"

Juanita's mother parts the curtains. Her fleshy arms jiggle as she moves forward, holds out two packages. "For the new mother from her mother." She hugs Richard until his body is lost in hers.

In the first package are nursing bras, the front flaps folded down so the back tag shows.

"Thirty-six D," her mother says, winking at Richard. "Didn't I tell you pregnancy would make a woman out of her?"

"Mother, please," Juanita says. "I can't breast feed. There's no milk."

"Nonsense. The women in our family always have enough to feed triplets." Her mother unties the second box and removes the cellophane wrapping. She eats the caramel in the center and picks out a chocolate-covered cherry for Juanita.

"Let Mother pick the name," Richard suggests.

Juanita shakes her head.

"You got something against your name? Juanita is a nice name. Don't you think so, Richard?" Mother picks caramel from her back molar.

Richard does not answer. He's pushing in the tops of the candy to find a soft center.

"All a girl needs is a pretty name. I read your name in a book."

"What book?" Juanita asks.

"One of those detective magazines. Your name was right on the cover."

Richard's laugh is too loud for this room of mothers. A nurse pokes her head through the curtain to remind them that visiting hours are almost over.

Juanita closes her eyes and rests her head against the pillow. She does not want to walk her visitors past the nursery where they will stop and try to pick their flesh and blood from the other pink bundles.

Richard leans over and kisses her cheek. "As soon as you get better, we'll start working on a baby boy," he whispers.

During the eleven o'clock news, Juanita uses her cuticle scissors to cut the nursing bras into strips. She cuts each thread holding the hooks and eyes. Some seams she rips apart with her hands. The weatherman predicts sun and a high of eighty as she puts the cotton strips into their box and dumps it in the wastebasket by her bed.

She dreams names of childhood playmates—Lori, Judy, Cindy, Katherine—but none seem right. Through breakfast, she says names aloud: Esther, Ruth, Mary, Sarah, Hannah. In the book of names the hospital provides, she finds Amanda, worthy of love. This is the name she writes on the birth certificate. The meaning of the name, she repeats to herself—over and over, a litany.

Amanda develops jaundice and is kept from Juanita. Through glass, she watches her baby. Although Amanda sleeps and does not open her eyes, the nurses assure Juanita that she is doing fine. Juanita points her out to other parents and grandparents. Tells them Amanda is starting to gain weight, is losing the yellowish color that made her look like a chicken. Juanita studies the nurses' movements as they bathe and feed other infants. She watches how they pin diapers and is sure she can do just as well.

Back in her room, she waters the geranium. Water leaks through the clay pot, onto the congratulatory cards. The card from the office is on top; the signatures smear as Juanita blots them with tissue. Their card is the kind with a chubby baby smiling, pinks and whites blending in the pastel borders. At the bottom, they tell her to hurry back.

Juanita reaches for the ringing telephone, knocking over a carnation arrangement. The white milk glass breaks on the carpeted floor. Storks with pipe-cleaner legs and babies in yellow blankets are lost under carnations and glass.

Yes, her boss says, they miss her. The new girl puts figures in the wrong column and flirts with the married men. Not to rush Juanita, but if she finds she can come back in a month instead of six weeks... No need to decide now.

The baby is fine, she is fine, everyone is fine, and maybe in a month...

A nurse bustles in. She takes a white cup from her tray and rattles the pills against the paper sides. "Hang up, dear," she says. "Time for our medicine."

Glass crunches under the nurse's feet as she moves toward Juanita's bed. She sets the tray on the foot of the bed and bends down. "Poor things," she says, straightening a stork's leg. She pushes the button for an aide and the red light glows above Juanita's bed.

The nurse gives Juanita pills and water, and turns, almost tripping over the aide who is sweeping the glass and carnations into a dustpan. The nurse swivels on her foot and says to Juanita, "We really must learn to be more careful with a baby in the house."

The nurse closes the door quietly. The aide leaves without looking at Juanita.

The same nurse brings Amanda for her evening feeding, checks the mother's and baby's bracelets. She tucks in the neckline lace on Juanita's nightgown and says, "We don't want to irritate the baby's skin, do we?"

In her sleep, Amanda wrinkles her forehead. Juanita watches. Without warning, Amanda opens her eyes and cries. Juanita sticks the bottle in her mouth, rocks her back and forth. But the baby hits at the bottle with her fists, drinks, instead, her own tears.

"Hush now," Juanita says. "Pretty baby sleep, sleep."

Holding the baby against her shoulder she sings, "Mama's going to buy you…" The baby's tears run down her neck, between her breasts. The wails are trapped in her ear canal, bounce against the bones.

"Stop it." Juanita shakes her and tries to force the rubber nipple into Amanda's mouth.

The toothless gums set against her. She cannot pry them apart with her fingers.

Juanita rings for the nurse, again and again, until the nurse comes running, her crepe soles silent against the carpet.

In the nurse's arms, Amanda burps and is silent. The nurse says nothing as she walks out.

Juanita bites through the cotton pillowcase, sucks the plastic covering until pine Lysol stings her tongue. The roof of her mouth is clean. She sleeps with her hands tucked under her chin and dreams of spruce forests, of pine cones nestled in branches.

At home, Juanita is alone with her daughter. No nurses with sterile hands stand waiting behind glass. Richard at work all day, into the evening. Later every night. Friends at their desk or at home cooking for their own families. Her mother at the hardware store, counting out nails for men. Only herself in the mirror every morning, her skin parched, peeling around the lips.

She vacuums to drown Amanda's cries, watches soap operas on television. Sometimes she rocks Amanda in the darkened bedroom and cries. She tries to sleep with Amanda next to her in the double bed, but the baby kicks against her, keeps her awake.

Richard says Juanita is too tense; the baby feels it. "Girls cry more than boys anyway," he says one night at the dinner table. He takes Amanda for walks in the buggy while Juanita sleeps.

Her mother calls and says it's colic; Juanita was the same way as a baby. "Is her stool runny?" Mother asks Richard over the phone.

Richard relays the question to Juanita.

"I don't know," Juanita shouts over the television voices.

"Yes, it's runny," Richard says into the phone.

Richard goes to the drug store and buys a case of Enfamil. "Mother says this is better for colicky babies," he tells Juanita when he gets home.

The doctor tells Juanita that most formulas are the same, says Amanda is a normal, healthy baby. "You just spoil her," he says. "Let her cry. She'll stop eventually."

That night, Juanita calls the doctor's home number.

"Dr. Feldon speaking." A calm voice, warmer than his office voice.

Juanita lays the receiver in the crib next to Amanda's mouth. The cries grow louder. She waits one minute exactly and picks up the receiver. It is dead.

When Amanda cries again that night, Juanita dials the doctor's number and listens for his voice before putting the receiver near Amanda's mouth. On the third call, a distant voice identifies itself as Dr. Feldon, tells the caller to leave a message when the beep sounds. Amanda cries through the entire tape.

Exhausted, Amanda finally sleeps. Juanita falls asleep on the couch watching the late movie. Sunlight wakens her and she puts her hand over her eyes, pulls up the blanket that Richard put over her before he left for work. The television is off and everything is quiet.

Juanita jumps up and stumbles on the edge of the blanket. She tiptoes to Amanda's room, stares at her daughter whose face is already filling out. She stands there until Amanda whimpers in her sleep.

By the time Juanita warms the bottle, Amanda is crying. Juanita changes her diaper and wraps her in a blanket. She rocks Amanda and tests the milk against her forearm before putting the nipple against the baby's lips. Amanda sucks. Suddenly, she chokes on the steady stream. Juanita lays her across her knees and pats her back gently.

Again she holds the bottle to Amanda's lips. Amanda will not drink more.

"An ounce isn't enough. Come on. Just a little more." She squeezes the nipple so milk beads on the baby's lips.

Amanda turns her head. Milk drips onto Juanita's arm, sticky against her sweating skin. Juanita wipes her forehead with the back of her hand, all the time making clucking sounds with her tongue, coaxing Amanda to drink.

Amanda's cries grow louder. Juanita hurls the bottle against the wall. The plastic sac breaks and the milk drips down the blue walls, behind the framed print of the little drummer boy.

"Stupid baby!" she screams. "Why can't you act right?"

The muscles in Juanita's arm twitch as she lowers Amanda into her crib. She runs from the room, slams the door. The wood is cool against her forehead.

"Dumb, ugly, little baby." She pounds the door with her fists. Pounds until her fists hurt. "Why don't you leave me alone?"

Juanita runs cold water over her bruised flesh. "I'm leaving until you stop that crying."

Juanita pours a glass of orange juice and picks up the morning paper from the breakfast table where Richard always leaves it for her to read. She shuts the heavy front door behind her and sits on the top porch step, the concrete warm through her shorts. It's the first time she's read the paper since she's been home. By the time she reads the comics, she is laughing.

As much as she hates to admit it, her mother and Richard are right. She needs to get out for a while, talk to other people.

She opens the front door and is surprised at the quiet. A good sign, she decides as she puts on her makeup. She takes her time and blends the rouge, wipes away the mascara smudges.

Even when she opens the bedroom door, Amanda does not wake up. She stays asleep when Juanita puts her in the buggy, stays asleep as the buggy bounces down the curbs and up.

Two mothers are sitting on the park bench rocking buggies. The first mother wears a peasant blouse with intricate embroidery on the front and on the sleeves. The second mother wears a halter top and moves her position occasionally to catch the rays of the sun on her shoulders. They are talking about a rash on the second mother's baby.

Juanita aligns her buggy with theirs and sits down.

"Looks like diaper rash," the first mother says.

"Can't be. I've tried all the ointments on it."

"What do you think?" the first mother asks Juanita. She reaches into the other buggy and points to a rash on the inside of the baby's thighs.

Juanita leans over and looks into the buggy where the baby makes soft noises sucking at the nylon blanket binding.

"Diaper rash," she agrees.

"Try baking soda," the first mother says. Then she looks over her shoulder at a small towhead on the monkey bars. "Be careful!" she shouts.

Amanda wakes up and begins to cry. Juanita rocks the buggy harder. She picks up Amanda and rocks her against her shoulder, offers her the bottle.

"Let Ruthie try," the second mother says. "She has a way with babies."

Juanita hands over her baby, watches her baby snuggle into Ruthie's shoulder.

"Your first?" Ruthie asks. "My fifth. A boy," she says, pointing to the baby asleep in the buggy. His light hair stands on end and his fair skin is flushed. The blue stretch pajamas pull tight across his fat belly. "Girls are tougher," she reassures Juanita.

An ice cream truck rings its bell on the other side of the playground. Three children jump from the sandbox where they've been digging underground roads and run to the park bench.

"You promised," the towhead says to Ruthie. "You promised." All three children nod their heads.

Ruthie puts Amanda back in the buggy and winks at the second mother. "We promised." To Juanita, she says, "Do you mind watching the babies while we get the kids ice cream?"

"'Course not," Juanita says.

"Bring you anything?" Ruthie asks, tying the red ribbon at her neckline.

Juanita shakes her head and Ruthie laughs. "Good thing. Probably melt before we got back here."

Juanita watches the mothers and children walk under the slide. She brushes a fly from Ruthie's baby. While she's up, she wheels Amanda's buggy next to the boy's.

Juanita does not think about it, just wheels the boy's buggy along the path. She pushes faster until the path curves in to the center of the park. She pushes over bicycle ruts and sings, "Mama's going to buy you a mockingbird."

Concrete dolphins rise out of the fountain ahead of her. Water streams from their mouths.

"And if that mockingbird don't sing," she hits the right notes, holds them.

Juanita leans over the concrete edge and washes her hands in the water. She rubs a moist finger along her lips.

She pulls the buggy back from the fountain, sits on the cement bench next to an old man.

"Fine day," he says.

"Yes, a fine day."

"Your baby is sure enjoying it." The old man looks into the buggy.

"He's a good baby. Sleeps all night and eats good." Juanita takes a handful of popcorn from the box the old man offers.

"Reminds me of my son when he was a baby." The old man reaches into his pocket and pulls out a wallet. Behind the scratched, plastic frame, a blonde, middle-aged man smiles.

Juanita has no pictures to show. In the distance, she hears the ice cream bell.

sharon charde
Whiteout

It started simply enough, a flurry of seed
pearls sown on peau de soie. Veiled
with lace, the pure bride stood
among flowers. Happen of white juice
in her next, mixing with egg, making
a baby. Silence. Snow muffles. The boy
slips out too small. She holds it in morning
in the circle of stove, sink, refrigerator,
her tools for the storm. Cook, wash,
package, store, there is more than milk
that comes then, yellowfat sweet nippled
into the baby mounded on her chest
with those breasts, out of him into diapers,
sheets. Bleach, scrub, bring back the first
white, she tries, the blizzard begins, another
boy, the wild of men around her feeding,
wearing whites starched to the stiffness
of drying sperm. She begins to fight
the white, wears weaves of it in patterns,
a sweater her sister sends her, not knowing
the Irish stitches made different so each
drowned man could be found in the sea.
She tries browning her face in the sun

but the men are sick and need her. She
creates a cave from thick wet snow. Blank
in her body she breathes in the blizzard,
freezes the storm, becomes ice,
a whiteout of wife.

worry

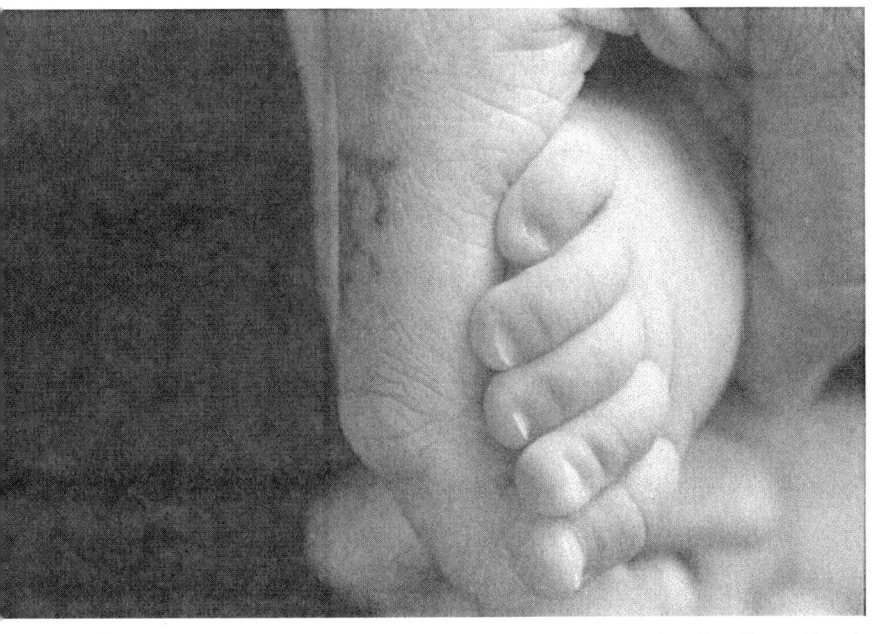

photo by jeffrey goldsmith

judith h. montgomery
Card Party

For Alex

Now pause, as mothers everywhere do pause,
one hand to curtain, knob, or nursery door,
to listen for the breath that lifts before
the silence of the heart stopped without cause.
Anyone may chide us: we turn and laugh.
Of course the baby's fine, we say, and sip
our wine, poke the fire, paint a redder lip,
refill the nut dish, play a heart, or pass.
And yet, the househeart beats elsewhere, above
the merriment, the card-bright air, the din.
We slip away to listen, certain of
a pillow slipped, a choking toy—our sin—
and, bent like tardy angels overhead,
we breathe again with him to heal our dread.

bonnie jo campbell
Natural Disasters

Gravity is wrong for babies. They fall earthward and into coffee tables with too much force in houses where the smallest earthquake dislodges glass mixing bowls from high shelves. Books too become missiles poised to tumble from heights at the slightest tectonic shift. The bookshelf I made after college is now all edges, corners, and metal screws. Honor society pins, lubricated condoms, lapis lazuli earrings, wine corks from France slither in my dreams from the dresser top toward Baby's throat to stab and choke him. And the appliances! The oven is a crematorium, the refrigerator a suffocation chamber. Every outlet hisses with vipers of electricity.

Baby's tendrils have already reached from my uterus to my brain, implanting a vision—a cushioned, babbling world of foam rubber, cotton balls, and warm air, a world whose walls are covered with quilted fabric, soft and washable, or coated with a high-density gel like those shock-absorbing bicycle seats. If only there were a way to make the wall supports themselves bend and curve in response to pressure. Give me sagging Claes Oldenburg typewriters and central processing units capable of producing only nursery rhymes and simple, hopeful sentences; beanbag chairs poofing with Styrofoam dots; hot-water heaters set to tepid, and stoves with smooth, flame-less burners made to warm food only to the temperature of breast milk. Even in hurricanes such furnishings will blow about harmlessly. In case of flood, Baby and I will use the pieces as rafts.

I have begun to dislike my bones—ribs as inflexible as jail bars, sharp elbows and scapulas, axe-blade pelvic bones, long hard femurs. And what about this spine against which Baby will continue to be pressed, as if crucified, for months?

I dream of making incisions in my skin through which I can slide out these bones in case of a tidal wave, to flow atop the currents like a jellyfish.

The plastic blocks, crib beads, and even that stuffed fish mobile are so wrong with their cartoon separation of blues, yellows, and pinks. Colors should bleed into one another the way they do in rainbows following sudden and torrential storms. Let reds dissolve into purples, then blend through a thousand blues to blue-greens, to true-greens. I will take these doors off their hinges, because, once born, Baby must be free from the violence of boundaries. And from gravity. Once I find a way to free Baby from the terrible pull at the center of the planet, he will float through rooms and glide helmeted through bumper-car doorways as if swimming. Thus ungrounded, Baby will be safe even from strikes of lightning.

donya currie arias
Baby Dreams

Rayna dreams her baby is a boy made of spun glass, and when she gets up in the night to change his diaper, she trips on the rocking chair and drops the baby, shattering him into thousands of shards of glass that wedge in the carpet. All the shards have tiny, crying mouths.

"Hmm, weird," is all her husband ever says. He's never been the reassuring type.

By the time Rayna is six months along, she alternates the glass-baby dream with one that scares her as much. Her baby is born a year old, popping out of her womb wearing a top hat and twirling a cane, a tiny charmer ready to star in a commercial for Huggies or Michelin tires. Then the baby ages backwards, at the speed of one month a minute, shrinking to the size of a sperm and egg. Rayna screams and tries to hold on to her baby as it curls into a fetal position and disappears. The last thing she sees is a tiny finger, pointing at her and then vanishing like the rest of her child.

"I can see her, it's always a girl, and she is at first all chubby cheeked and giggly," Rayna says at breakfast, looking desperately at Mark as he stares back at her, chewing his Frosted Flakes. "Then she gets smaller and smaller, her head gets too heavy for her neck, and her eyes cross, and she is shorter and shorter. She stops making sounds and just sleeps, then she curls up and is gone. It's terrible."

"Honey," Mark looks worried, like the pregnancy crazies really are as bad as he's heard. "It's just a dream. Try to remember that." He pats her hand and stands, walking to the sink to fill his cereal bowl with water. He doesn't bother putting the bowl in the dishwasher, just leaves it sitting in the sink.

Mark doesn't want to tell her that he, too, has been having baby nightmares. He dreams of holding his retarded son's hand while they cross the street. He pushes his little girl in her wheelchair and stops at a street corner, bending to wipe the drool from her chin. Mark keeps telling himself that the majority of babies are born perfectly normal.

"My wife smoked the whole time she was pregnant, and there's nothing wrong with my kid," Mark's friend Josh says. The two men are outside, pulling old bushes out of the ground in front of Mark and Rayna's house. Some of the junipers are so old they have to tie a rope around the thickest part of the bush and yank it out with Josh's pickup. Josh's son is spying on them through the downstairs bedroom window.

"He thinks we can't see him," Mark says, laughing at the little blonde head bobbing up and down beneath the windowsill.

"I think he knows we can, and he's wondering how he can get in on the action. Marge won't let him outside while we're doing this because she's convinced we'll run him over. One more trip to the emergency room this month and she'll go off her nut."

Broken arms, bleeding head wounds, Mark starts thinking of all that can go wrong even once a perfect child is born. He remembers biking home from the grocery store, a bag of apples in one hand, handlebar in the other, when he hit an uneven spot in the sidewalk and crashed chin-first onto the pavement. Still has the scar from the eight stitches. Still thinks he could have saved his face if he'd just dropped the bag of apples and caught himself with his hand. The apples ended up wasted, anyway, rolling all over the street and promptly squashed into applesauce puddles by passing cars.

A man riding a motorcycle pulls out in front of Rayna as she merges into traffic on the way home from the grocery store. Making a mental dinner menu out of the ground turkey, crushed tomatoes, fresh mushrooms, and angel hair pasta she's just bought, she is pulled from her meal planning by the man's canary yellow shirt billowing in the wind as he accelerates. I'll never ride a motorcycle again, she thinks. Parents can't do such things. Parents can't take risks like that. It'll be years before we can take a vacation.

The last vacation she and Mark took was their honeymoon, a road trip to the Florida Everglades where they camped at the tip of the National Park where palm trees lined the shoreline just yards from giant mangrove hammocks. They had never seen an alligator in the wild and were fascinated at the commonality of them, like bumpy stones scattered everywhere. Mark almost stepped on one as he waded in shallow water searching for fish.

"Alligators are so common here, it's like seeing a sparrow," said a ranger who led Mark and Rayna on a guided hike with a cluster of other tourists. She thought he was cute, in his khaki pants and forest green shirt. She thought, if I wasn't married, he'd be just the kind of guy I'd go for. Mark seemed to read her mind and slipped his hand in hers, kissing her on the lips just as the ranger turned toward them.

"I know you've probably all heard about this recent unfortunate incident," the ranger said, passing out laminated copies of a newspaper clipping. The story was about an eight-year-old boy who fell off his bike in the Everglades and was snatched by an alligator. His mother freed him by beating the 'gator over the head with a tire pump. "We want to publicize it not to scare you, but to remind you that the Everglades are one of the few bona-fide wilderness areas left in the United States."

At the time Rayna couldn't imagine the mother's bravery, attacking a six-foot alligator to free her son. She wonders now if she'll be that kind of mother, or one who freezes in the face of danger.

When she pulls into the driveway, Mark and Josh are still outside, bare-chested and sweaty and working furiously at a tree stump with two shovels. She sees deep tire tracks where they've tried pulling the stump out. A rope runs from the stump to the back of Josh's truck, and the side yard is annihilated, all the grass buried in loose dirt that's been dug from around the stump. The stump wasn't so bad. Just a little stump, she thinks.

"Hi, honey," Mark calls, then trots over to take her grocery bag.

"No, I'm okay," she says, turning her head so his kiss lands on her cheek. "I can get this. Just finish what you're doing."

She clicks the front door shut behind her, careful not to slam it like she wants to because Josh would tell Marge and she'd call and say something soothing and Rayna would just burst into tears and feel stupid for crying over a mess in the yard. She makes her way slowly up the bare wood floors to the kitchen. She remembers being thin, limber, able to skip up these stairs without thinking.

While she peels garlic cloves and turns on the front right burner, she thinks, when the baby is walking, I'll have to use the back burners. And turn the pot handles to face the back of the stove. And latch the bottom cupboards and move the knives and plastic bags and breakable objects all to the upper cupboards. Mark walks in sweaty with pieces of bark stuck in his hair.

"Smells good," he says. She is irritated that Mark is lifting the lid on the pot where she's just put water on to boil for the pasta, but she bites her lip instead of blasting him.

"Man, you look so tired," Mark says, taking Rayna's hand and leading her toward the living room. "Come sit down with me for a minute."

She wonders how he can stand her moodiness but lets herself be led to the couch and lays her head in Mark's lap, careful to lie on her left side. This is the optimal position for placental blood flow. She misses lying on her stomach and her back. She misses painting her toenails and running until the sweat soaks her shirt and drips into her eyes.

"I'm sorry. I'm worried all the time and tired and mean," Rayna says. "Just tell me it's worth it."

"It is," Mark answers, watching a slow-moving swell in her belly that looks like a sea creature emerging from the water, then diving back down again. "Really, it is."

Rayna falls asleep with her head in Mark's lap and dreams of a sunny day. She is sitting in a field of yellow flowers, and her baby girl is crawling toward her, smiling. The baby has two teeth. She laughs at Rayna and stops to grab fistfuls of grass.

Mark looks down and sees Rayna smiling in her sleep. He hears the water boiling on the stove and wonders if he should risk waking her to put the pasta in the pot. As he inches his body lower on the couch, he sees Rayna's belly swell again and rests his hand there, feeling his baby pressing against him like an answer. He sits still and listens to the water boil.

jody bolz

Croup

When our children were very young, we lived in Guatemala one summer so that my husband could study Spanish for his work. During the first six weeks, we boarded with the family of Hilda and Magno Perez on the outskirts of Antigua by arrangement of the language school. The Perezes had three daughters—two full grown (one with children of her own, the other working in Guatemala City) and the youngest, Raquel, still at home in high school.

Antigua itself is a spring garden, a small city nestled among volcanoes in a high valley, and a showplace of Spanish architecture. But we were stuck on the edge of town, a long walk from the central park with its surrounding arcades of shops and cafes. Worse yet, the Perezes lived across the street from an active tannery that stunk of uric acid and from dusk to dawn, except on Sundays, produced a dull hammering. We registered each thud in our ribs when we lay down to nap. Despite these facts, despite the insurgent winged ants in our bedroom, the oversubscribed bathroom, and the overabundant, unfamiliar food, we felt at home with these people. Señora Hilda, a handsome woman in her late forties, was wonderfully gracious to us. The chance to learn each day from her clear Spanish was well worth the inconveniences.

One day in late June, a month into our stay, our two-year-old daughter Jessie began to cough—an ancient barking—and lost her voice entirely. Her fever was minor compared to the long fever our son had endured earlier that month. We'd stayed up nights testing his pulse, terrified it would slow as his fever rose, a sure sign of typhoid. We'd begun to blame ourselves for taking risks, for choosing adventure over safety and comfort at our children's expense.

It was a simple case of dysentery from which he fully recovered. With Eli's return to health, we gained confidence, and so we weren't worried about his younger sister—a wide-cheeked comedienne with ringlets and an appetite. But for some reason our hostess was: Even though Jessie seemed strong, Hilda tracked her every movement, frowned at every cough. I wanted to make light of it, but my Spanish was too new, and I was newly awkward in this woman's home.

The Perezes' house was built in the traditional fashion around a rectangular courtyard, only this courtyard had been defiled—paved as a makeshift driveway for the family truck. No bougainvillea here; no hibiscus bushes; no banana palms. All of the bedrooms, the bathroom for guests, the open kitchen, the pantry, and the dining room faced onto this dreary concrete yard. We crossed it over and over each day en route to meals or the bathroom. We washed our clothes in a plastic tub there, gave the children baths there, lined up chairs to construct "trains" there with Hilda's young grandsons. It was the common space for the family and their several language-school guests.

A couple of nights after Jessie got sick, she woke up at two in the morning to pee. I carried her to the toilet, stopping to point out the full moon above the open courtyard. I didn't expect to see anyone, so I nearly screamed when I spotted Hilda standing near the kitchen—staring back at me, ablaze in her white nightgown. She must have been cleaning up after Recuerdo, her husband's hunting hound.

¡El aire es peligroso! ¡Cuidado! she was ranting in a whisper. How could I have failed to protect my child from the dangerous night air? I felt she was angry at me for the first time—for the first time not polite—as she covered Jessie's head with a towel and patted it down. What could I say? Should I apologize? The words she'd taught me thickened in my throat.

The next day, after an oddly silent breakfast, Hilda called the best pediatrician in town, a doctor well known throughout the country and a family friend. She made an appointment for Jess. I was embarrassed but grateful, and that afternoon we took a taxi into town. We spent a half hour or so in the waiting room, witnessing hare-lipped children file in and out (the doctor was famous for corrective surgery) and listening to worse coughs, watching the effects of higher fevers. When he called us into his office, I did the best I could to describe Jessie's symptoms in sketchy Spanish. He asked questions, nodded yes, and prescribed an antibiotic and something to relieve her breathing. He told me to steam her twice a day in the shower and insisted that we keep her quiet for the rest of the week.

I took Jessie home, gave her the medicine, tucked her into her cot (our beds were tight as piano keys against the back wall), and sat down on the floor with Eli to play Crazy 8's. Oblivious by now to the tannery's thud, we listened to the courtyard sounds of scouring, sweeping, mopping—the cadences of Hilda's household. Jessie slept fitfully for two hours, her mouth wide open, her breathing raspy and irregular.

After dinner that night my husband took the children to our room, and Hilda lingered at the table as she never had before. Buttoning her sweater, pulling at the pockets of her smart gray dress, she asked me how I thought the baby was doing. I said that Jessie seemed fine, that we called this "croup" in the States and it was common. Hilda's face changed: she looked old and exhausted.

"I see," she said in Spanish, watching her own hands as they gripped the table's edge. "Well, *I* have been worried about Jessie. When one of our daughters was two years old, she had a cough like this for a few days." She turned to me gravely.

"When the fever broke and she seemed well, we decided to go ahead with a trip to the countryside to see my in-laws. It was a warm day, and we left the truck's windows wide open. She loved to ride with her head out, breathing the country air. That night, the cough came back." She stopped. Why was she outraged, her eyes full of tears?

"The next day her throat closed up, and our daughter died."

I didn't move. I'd forgotten I was listening. When I realized where I was—what I'd heard and understood—and that I was crying too, I placed my hand around hers on the sticky plastic tablecloth.

"You didn't know about her—but she was Anna, our third daughter—before Raquel."

We stood up and embraced, the heavy chairs scraping the cement floor as we crossed the line that had kept us as we'd been: polite and separate. Hilda had moved towards me, a mother towards a mother, blaming herself after twenty years—missing the daughter our daughter had raised from the dead.

cindy dale
Early

Day seven. It's before eight a.m. when I get to Mercy, and already there are two women ahead of me in line for the breast pumps—Nancy, who looks as zombied as I do, and a dark-haired woman I don't recognize, someone obviously new to our select little sorority.

"Hi Nance. How's Jeremy?" I ask. It is always what you ask. How's Jeremy/Marissa/David/Keyshana/Tara/Julia/Austin/Elizabeth/William/Dakota/Mary Jane. Just fill in the blank.

She shakes her head. I can see the exhaustion in her eyes. I don't think she's slept in a week. "He had two bradys last night," she says. Brady is short for bradycardia which means, in a nutshell, that Jeremy stopped breathing. Of course, he is hooked up to so many machines, and there are so many nurses, one for every two babies in the green section, which is where Jeremy still is, that it's not really a crisis. Or that's what the perpetually cheery nurses tell you. The goal is to get Jeremy to yellow (one nurse for every four) and then to pink (one for every six) and then out these God damn doors once and for all. But who knows how long that will take. And, of course, not all of these babies leave by the same set of doors. There's a back door right down the hall that no one much talks about.

I want to say something to Nancy, but there is nothing to say that will make her feel any better and she knows that I know that, so I turn to the new woman instead. "Kassie Crayton," I say. "Mother of Sarah and Luke, born six days ago at thirty-one weeks. Two pounds eleven ounces and three pounds three ounces respectively. Sarah's in basinette D over in yellow. Luke's in green. He's still on the ventilator, but the chest tube came out three days ago."

At least I think it was three days ago. You lose track in this place. It is not like your typical hospital waiting room where there is always a discarded newspaper to confirm the day and date. People don't read here. They pump milk. Corner doctors. Sneak peaks at cryptic charts. Cry silently, and not so silently, in the bathroom stalls. Spill out their story, again and again, to anyone who will listen. Measure out hope gram by gram.

"Stella," the new woman says. A name I haven't heard in ages, don't even recall from those countless baby name books Sam and I spent months poring over. Wasn't there a Stella on *Perry Mason* I think? Or was that Della? *Streetcar Named Desire*. There was a Stella in *Streetcar*, for sure. You think a lot about names here, names and the way things didn't turn out.

"My son was born two days ago at thirty weeks. He's over in green, down from your son I think," Stella says. She still looks stunned, like she doesn't quite know how she got here or what's happening to her. She's wearing the regulation Mercy candy-cane colored robe, which means she's still on her paid-for hopefully-in-full four-day post-C-section stay on second floor south, the wing where they stick those of us who had "complications," the ones who won't be taking home a baby when they re-pack their colorful overnight bags once Prudential or Travelers or Mass Mutual decides the party's over.

I am about to ask her more—we're ambulance chasers all of us, wanting to know the gory details—but just then Lizzie, mother of the unit's only current set of triplets, three tiny, identical little girls, comes out from behind the curtain, clutching a plastic container of thin milk. Her eyes are red, her face drawn.

"I'm next," Stella says, standing. She manages a faint smile and disappears behind the white curtain. I can hear the click of the breast pump as the motor whirs into action, and imagine it sucking full force at Stella's hard little breasts. Another thing no one warned us about is this breast-feeding business. How, I wonder, did the cavewomen and pioneer mammas manage without breast-feeding classes and electronic pumps? Why doesn't anyone tell you it doesn't come easy?

"Hey Kassie," Lizzie says. "How's things?"

"Status quo," I say, which I've learned is a very good thing. Two nights ago Lizzie's Madeline, the second of the triplets, had a "neurological event," i.e., a brain bleed. No one knows why it happened, if it will happen again, or what it means long term. Lizzie is doing the best she can to cope, pumping like crazy, giving all the milk she can eke out of her swollen breasts to Maddy, hoping like mad those fabled extra antibodies will do the trick. She's here eighteen hours a day and spends all of her time next to Maddy's isolette, rocking back and forth, back and forth in a big white rocker donated to the unit in memory of one Leonardo Jones III. Bart, her husband, won't go near Maddy anymore who, of course, is still in green, just like Luke. Bart spends all his time across the room in the yellow section where the other girls, Michele and Monica, are, right next to Sarah. What a small little world ours is!

When Lizzie told me about the episode yesterday, I hugged her hard and let her sob into my shoulder. "I love her so much," she cried. "How could I have done this to her?" Way back when, at twelve or thirteen weeks, the doctors had gently suggested Lizzie consider "reducing." Had offered to magically make one of the growing embryos "disappear," so Lizzie might have a safer pregnancy, perhaps go to term, deliver healthy babies without neurological problems. Of course, Lizzie hadn't. (Could I have in her shoes?) And now she feels responsible. Guilty in the first degree for putting poor little Maddy through this with no guarantees. We all want crystal balls. Peripheral vision to see around the corner a day, a week, a year. To know how it all ends.

I feel for Lizzie, but must confess that what I also feel is a palpable sense of relief that it is her baby and not mine. Everything is a crap shoot. Odds are better than even that all these babies won't make it, or if they do, they will have massive problems, and I want like hell for Sarah and Luke to be on the right side of fate's fickle coin flip.

"How's Maddy?" I ask, sincerely hopeful that the news is good, that she's spent a peaceful night, maybe gained an ounce.

"The same," Lizzie says. "Bart won't touch her. He's written her off. Says we should concentrate on the healthy two." And with this she bursts into tears, her whole body heaving and shaking beneath her husband's oversize workshirt. Some milk has leaked through and left a large wet circle under her left breast, right beneath her heart.

"She may be okay," I say. I pat her gently on the back, this woman I hardly know. "She's in the best place. They've got the best doctors here, you know that." It all sounds so hollow. As for Bart, what can you say?

My own husband Sam has already shown a distinct preference for Sarah, our perfect little child. When he comes to visit, he goes directly to her isolette, lifts her out tenderly and rocks her for a good half hour before he ventures down to green to see how Luke is doing. If I point this out to him, he'll deny it. Say it's my postpartum hormones raging, making me imagine things. But I know it is true. I've been observing, making mental notes, and already overcompensating in return, always heading first to Luke.

Poor little Luke. He had a tough time of it. His placenta rupturing like that, me still at the office, wrestling with yet another spreadsheet. I remember the wetness, the immediate knowledge that something was very, very wrong. There were phone calls. To the doctor, whose service picked up twice and never bothered to call back. To Sam at work. To 911. There was the ambulance ride, an endless eternity crawling through grid-locked Midtown traffic. The oxygen mask and IV. The urgency in the medic's voice as he phoned ahead and said we were coming in. Then papers, jammed in my face. Sign here. No time. Emergency C. The room. Five, maybe six people in dull green gowns hovering around my body, strapped on a stainless steel table. The cool, iced air. Me thinking "Where's Sam?" then nothing, nothing at all. Waking later, thirsty. More thirsty than I can ever remember being. Dry, parched mouth. Worse than the worst hangover. Me begging a nurse for an ice chip, just one little ice chip, please, please. Just one. The same nurse (or another?) showing me two little sets of footprints. "Your babies are fine," she said, which is what she says to everyone, I am sure, regardless of whether it is true. No need to tell the truth to someone on morphine. No need to break the bad news on her shift.

Later, downstairs on two south, two different nurses told me what a beautiful daughter I had. "But what about my son?" I cried. "What about my son?"

Sam came in shortly after the nurses. His face was drawn and pale. I had never seen him look so scared, not even when his father was dying. He took my hand, squeezed it hard, bent down to kiss my parched lips. "They're fine," he said. "Small, but fine. And Sarah, Sarah's a real beauty."

It was all it took to break my heart. I needed to see Luke, to see my son with my own eyes, to know that he was okay, but it would be a full twenty-four hours until they let me up to the neonatal unit, and another three days until I could hold him, tubes and all. The enormity of what we had gotten ourselves into hit me. It was too much to bear. Too much to shoulder, the responsibility for these two little creatures' happiness and well-being.

Suddenly, I wanted to rewind. To go back, way back, to that stormy Tuesday night in June five years ago at the LaGuardia airport bar where Sam, his flight to Atlanta postponed due to weather, and me, early—always early—for a flight to Pittsburgh that, ultimately, too, was delayed, sat on adjacent stools and ordered the first of several overpriced beers. I wanted to be single again. To have no husband, no children, none of this! Because if something is wrong with Luke—

And this is just the beginning! There is everything that lies ahead, all the danger lurking between the Kodak moments. The broken bones. The schoolyard taunts. All those things you never see until it is too late—fast cars, cancerous cells, thin ice. I can't do this! I want to scream. I simply cannot do this.

If you could dissect this place, you would find more love, more fear, more faith, more despair, more sorrow, more joy, more anger, more courage crammed into one space than is humanly imaginable. None of us intended to be here, and each of us has a story with one common denominator. We were all early, preempting our own baby showers and nursery set-ups, leap-frogging at least one astrological sign, and sometimes two or even three, expecting Geminis or Cancers and getting tiny, fragile Pisces and Aries instead.

Every baby's isolette is heated like a sauna and has a pink or blue sign over it with three pieces of information: the baby's first and last name, the baby's birth weight in grams, and the baby's original due date. Walking past, you can't help but do the arithmetic. There's a nameless little black boy down from Luke who wasn't due for ten more weeks, and the nurses tell me he's already been here twenty-two days. Since we've been here, I've seen someone visiting the boy only once. She stayed less than twenty minutes. A woman my age, possibly younger, who the nurses tell me is his grandmother. The nurses here are amazing. You must need a very big, very resilient heart to work in this place. Though no one says it, we all assume he's a crack baby. When no one is looking, I sometimes poke my finger through one of the side portals of his isolette and gently massage his tiny black leg.

At last, there is a breast pump available, but my breasts aren't cooperating. I have taken the breast-feeding class twice, but still I can't get more than an inch or two of milk to come, even after half an hour on these damn machines. I'm ready to give up, but the nurses, the other mothers, all make you feel guilty for not trying just a little bit harder, for the babies' sake.

So I take my inch of milk, put it in a plastic container, label it with my name and the date and give it to one of the nurses at the main desk. Then I go to see Luke. Sure enough, Stella's son is next to mine. She is standing beside his isolette, looking down at him.

"He's beautiful," I say.

She looks up and feigns a smile. These are not Gerber babies, and we all know it.

I glance up at the sign to get his name, but all it says is "Baby Boy" Rosen.

As if reading my mind, she says, "We don't know what to name him. We're waiting. To see—"

I nod. Again, there is nothing to say.

"How's Luke?" she asks.

"Fine," I say, which is only partially true. Until yesterday, we weren't sure he would make it at all. But today, today things are looking up. All the blood he swallowed in utero has been drained, and the doctors say he may come off the respirator tomorrow or the day after. He's still listless and doesn't respond when you touch him, but he's hanging in there, making progress. So although he's asleep, the green lines on the machine monitoring his vital signals zigzagging along nicely, his little chest rising and falling, rising and falling at a steady reassuring rate, I flip open the top of the isolette and reach down through the maze of brightly colored wires patched to his tiny body and touch his wrinkled fist.

They say that once you have a child nothing will ever be the same again, and they are right. But it is not about the sleepless nights or the cost of diapers or how in hell you'll pay for college. It is about what happens to your heart, how it will never be the same.

Day eight. Sam and I have fallen into a routine. The alarm sounds at six. Sam showers first, then me. My stomach is still puffy, the scar from the C-section still red and raw, but there is no time to dwell on this, no space for vanity these days. We have a quick breakfast. Juice, coffee, stale bagels. Sam leaves for work, and I head for the hospital.

As usual, Nancy is already there when I arrive. So are Stella and Lauren, mother of Alexander, and Jocelyn, mother of Cleo. I don't see Lizzie, which worries me. Lizzie is close to the edge. Maddy is not responding to the drugs and she has lost fifteen grams, and Bart is of no help.

The husbands have receded. They come after work, occasionally before, and sit five- and six-hour vigils on the weekends. But they have jobs. There is money to be made, money that will be needed to pay the mounting hospital bills, bills that none of us allow ourselves to think much about. Sam and I joke that, at two thousand dollars a day per baby just for the isolette, this is the most expensive hotel these kids are ever gonna stay in.

"Guess what," Joceyln says. "The doctors say Cleo may go home today. She's up to 1,610 grams." Jocelyn is beaming. She is a tall, pretty woman with softly streaked blonde hair. Her husband is an investment banker, someone whose name, were you looking for it, you would see quoted in the *Wall Street Journal*. They live in a big sprawling apartment on Park Avenue. Under other circumstances, it would be easy to be jealous of Jocelyn, but not here, not knowing what we know. Cleo has been here forty-seven days. She has had two surgeries, one to repair a tiny hole in her heart, another to stop a brain bleed. I am sure there were times when Jocelyn never thought she would see this day, the day that Cleo is going home.

"That's great," we all say in chorus.

Jocelyn starts crying, and I can't say that I blame her.

"We're going to miss you," Nancy says, wrapping her arm around Jocelyn's shoulder. Nancy has been here far longer than I, going on twenty-seven days today. But even she can't rival Jocelyn for longevity.

Today turns out to be moving day here on the fourth floor. Cleo is indeed being sprung, as are two other babies in pink. Jeremy is being upgraded—at last! Moved from green to yellow, having spent, to Nancy's relief, a brady-free night.

Monica, the biggest of the triplets, is moving from yellow down to pink. And so, surprise!, is Sarah.

Later, when Sam comes after work, I watch him head to yellow to see Sarah. You can see the terror in his face when he realizes she's not there. Then the relief when Georgia, one of the nicest nurses, says something to him and turns and points him towards pink. Now the distance is even greater back to green to see Luke.

Day nine. There are good days and bad days here. Today is a bad day. Maddy had two more brain bleeds in the night. Lizzie and Bart are meeting with the doctors now to go over their options. And the little black boy is gone. At first, I think maybe he has been moved up to yellow, but when I go down to yellow with Nancy to look in on Jeremy he is nowhere to be seen. There is no need to ask what happened. All I can hope is that he was not alone. I pray one of the nurses, preferably Georgia or Jasmine, the large black lady from Grenada, was there at the end as his sweet little soul surrendered. I call Sam in tears from the pay phone in the hall and he tries to comfort me, but what can he say?

It gets worse. Quadruplets are born at twenty-seven weeks to an Italian couple from Brooklyn, but one of the babies, baby "B," doesn't make it. The missing baby is little a phantom limb that we all can feel as we walk through green. There's Rosetto baby "A," Rosetto baby "C," and Rosetto baby "D"—but no baby "B." The doctors pull off miracles, perform magic, here every day. But they are not God. Sometimes the rabbit doesn't come out of the hat.

It is on this worst of all days, at five-fifteen in the afternoon, that Luke finally comes off the respirator. Sam and I go home that night and drink a bottle of champagne, but it is hard to feel too festive. Even as we are toasting Luke and our own good fortune, I can't help but think about all that has happened on the fourth floor that day, especially about Maddy. Still, Luke, our son, is now breathing on his own!

"What would you do if you were Bart and Lizzie?" I ask later in bed.

"I'd let her go," Sam says.

"How could you?" I say. "How could you not want the doctors to do everything possible?"

"How could you put her through 'everything possible'? Hasn't she been through enough?" he retorts. We are lying next to each other under a sheet no one has had time to wash, but we are not touching. In a way, Sam's right, but it's not what I want to hear.

"If it were Luke—" I say, unable to finish the sentence.

"It's not Luke, okay? Luke's fine. He's breathing on his own. Go to sleep, Kassie. It's late."

Four a.m. that very same night. The phone rings. I am groggy with the champagne, creeping up on a hangover, but somehow find the receiver. "Hello?" I say.

It is the hospital. Sarah has had an episode. A seizure of some sort. They don't know exactly what it is, or how bad, but they thought they should call us, let us know.

"Are you sure you heard right? Sarah?" Sam asks. He has one leg in his jeans already.

"Yes, Sarah," I say, pulling a sweater over my head.

"But Sarah was fine. I don't understand—"

"Come on. Let's go," I say.

The ride over Sam and I hold hands. At first we don't say anything, but then I blurt out what I have been thinking. "You wish it were Luke, don't you?"

"Jesus, Kassie. Don't be ridiculous," Sam looks at me like I'm insane and I know immediately it was a stupid thing to say.

"I'm sorry," I say. Tears start—tears for Sarah and for us and for all the babies over there and all their mommies and daddies.

"What I wish," Sam says, "is that the fucking phone had never rung."

Sarah is hooked up to all sorts of new machines and there are four monitors going. She is stone still, the tiny little creature dubbed the aerobics queen by the nurses because of her perpetual tai chi gyrations, is not moving at all. Otherwise, she looks the same. The same little upturned nose. The same rosebud mouth. The same perfect little fingers.

Sam and I pull up chairs and start the vigil. We cannot hold her. Nurses come by every ten minutes, a doctor every hour, to check her signs. No one knows what happened or why. The doctors don't think any permanent damage was done, a thought that throws me for a loop. I had considered the best and worst case scenarios, but not the middle ground, not a damaged masterpiece.

The next twenty-four hours are key, they say. That will tell the story. At some point, Sam squeezes my hand. "I'm going down to check on Luke," he says. "I want to see my son."

The night creeps by. The next morning, for the first time, I beat Nancy to the breast pumps.

It is now some sixteen months later. A drab November day with cool, crisp air and dead leaves scuttling at your feet. Sam is home with the children and I have escaped to run a few errands. I am in Barnes & Noble, looking for a gift for my niece who is turning five. My fingers touch the classic *Madeline* and I can't help but wonder about Lizzie and Maddy.

We took Sarah home after seventeen days, Luke after twenty-two. They are both fine. Sarah's episode was never repeated, and never explained. Just one of those things, the nurses said with a shrug. When we left with Luke, two of the triplets had been sprung, but Maddy, of course, was still there. I don't know how Lizzie managed it, splitting herself like that, between two at home and one still in green on the fourth floor of Mercy. I called her twice and left messages, once a week after we took Luke home, and again towards the end of the summer, but she never called me back. Maybe Maddy made it. Maybe she is fine, just a third pea in a pod, and Lizzie is just too busy to call. I understand busy. Or maybe she isn't fine, or isn't even here anymore, and talking to anyone from that time, especially someone who took home two healthy babies, is too much to bear. Or maybe we were just the cliché two ships whose paths crossed on a very stormy night, each en route to our own distant port of call. What does it matter? In the end I pass on *Madeline* and opt for *Babar* instead.

Downstairs, I stop at the fiction section briefly, kidding myself into thinking there is time to read a novel, even a very short one, when I hear, "Hey—"

I turn and there is a woman pushing a big navy stroller, someone I recognize but can't quite place.

"Stella. From Mercy—" she says, and I'm back there in a flash.

"How are you?" I ask, looking down at this mini-Michelin man crammed into the stroller. The baby has chubby, apple red cheeks. He grins and I can see a row of little white picket fence teeth.

"Benjamin," Stella says. "You remember Benjy."

"He's huge," I say. No need to remind her that, back then, Benjamin didn't have a name.

Stella laughs. "Yeah, seventy-five percentile weight-wise, the pediatrician says. You'd never guess he was a premie. How are your guys doing? Luke and—" she pauses.

"Sarah," I say, rescuing her. "And they're fine. Happy. Healthy. A handful."

"I wish you had them with you. It would have been fun to see them again. Pictures?"

I whip out the requisite half a dozen photos, and Stella oohs and aahs.

"You live near here?" I ask.

"No. East Side. We're over for a birthday party."

There is nothing much else to say. Had she lived in the neighborhood, I might have suggested exchanging numbers, gone through the motions of proposing play dates, a rendezvous in the Hippo park. But she doesn't, so I didn't. Besides, neither of us really wants to go back and revisit the place where our lives once, briefly, intersected. That was then, and this is here and now.

"Well, nice seeing you," Stella says. She bends down and tucks the blanket in tighter around Benjy. She looks up at me suddenly. "We got lucky," she says.

after

photo by kendra shafer

marilyn rauth

After

Imagine waking each day with only yourself to consider. After years of raising children, it sounds so lovely, no one to wake up, to help dress or direct. No eggs to fry, no milk to pour over cereal. No rubber boots to shove over shoes in the winter, no caps or gloves or scarves to quickly find, to pull on and tie up. No lunches to make or monies to pass out. No reminders to return home right after dismissal; the hugs and kisses, the shrieks and shouts and sometimes frowns as they go.

A quiet interlude ensues, a cup of coffee, time to read the paper or call a friend, or even a few minutes of sitting and staring out the window, like a victim left in the path of a hurricane.

Then begins the cleaning and putting away of clutter, the floors to vacuum or scrub, furniture to dust, grocery shopping, school meetings, the planning and execution of dinner. And before you know it the hours have slipped by and there they are again: cold cheery faces, smiling or teary or indifferent faces looking up, saying, "Hi, Mom." The pleas: "I want..." or "Can I have...?" or "May I go...?" And me, like time, slipping away from the strain of it, not quite myself, trying to stay "up," to keep everything balanced, the children's lives, the husband's. Mine. HA! How much time was there really left for me?

Not much, really. That's why living alone always sounded so lovely, especially when the children were young.

The years slip by and the scenario changes. As they grow, some of the demands lessen, others expand. There's the nightly vigil for returning teenagers. Homework that you can no longer help with; they've already surpassed your academic knowledge or you've forgotten. The dating game, the nice boys or the bizarre boys who step over your threshold to take your daughter out on a date, or your son leaving for one, nervous and sullen. The worries: their driving, teen pregnancy, drugs, and nowadays that is not the worst of it. The hunt for the "right" college and the money to pay for it all. By the time they make you an empty nester, you feel like a leftover balloon from a birthday party—empty, wrinkled, stretched out, and cast aside. The party is over. Oh, they call now and again, they say I love you and thanks for everything.

Alone now, you rest for a time. You slowly begin to enjoy the beauty of a day, the sunrise, the sunset. You begin to appreciate the small things more. Soon you realize you're not really all that shriveled up and emptied out. You fill up on new or old work, more time with your significant other, fun with friends, walks in the park. Perhaps you take up yoga or Tai Chi, a class in painting, a writing workshop, or a part-time job. You try out one of the kids' leftover bikes and ride it around the neighborhood—the wind in your hair, your legs pumping fast, your heart. It takes you back to your childhood and its promises, your dreams. You begin to feel young and interested in things. You ask yourself, what *was* it I wanted to do with my life when I was thirteen, fifteen, and sixteen?

You ruminate around in your brain. Oh, yes, I remember. I wanted to fly, to travel the world, perhaps be a stewardess. I wanted adventure and excitement. Who knew whom I might meet up with, but whatever or whomever, the point then was to have fun—drink champagne and dance in Paris, cruise the Rhine or see Windsor Castle from the deck of a barge. The list is endless.

And now I realize I'm back at that point in my life again—a new starting point—a little bit older and wiser. Life suddenly seems thrilling and full of possibilities.

susan kushner resnick
Vasectomy Saves Woman

The night I became a woman, I stood in front of a mirror in my dormitory and beamed. I had just lost my virginity. But instead of thinking about the boy, I imagined my parents and thought this: *Hah! Wouldn't you disapprove!* And this: *Now I am mine.*

I held onto myself for eleven years. Then I had a baby.

I felt close to my essential womanhood while in labor, as if it were some kind of grand finale. I growled and screamed and gave forth life with the same equipment women have used for millions of years, give or take a few hot showers and a mauve and teal birthing suite. I felt for those hours that I was a member of a pack, a person doing what she was born to do, a real woman. And then my daughter emerged and I was nowhere to be found. Motherhood can be degrading, in the true sense of the word. A lovely young lass becomes utilitarian. A fully functioning intelligent human being becomes a thing.

A thing that nurses. A thing that wakes and sleeps by someone else's schedule. A thing that can't read without interruption for seven years. A thing that wears magenta exercise suits in public.

Not all of us fall that far. But we each lose ground in the beauty arena. It's a part of nature. The red breasts of female robins aren't really red at all. They're faded, to the pink-gray shade of medium-rare roast beef, so it is easier for the mother bird to seek camouflage and protect her babies. Human mothers fade, too. Exhaustion whitewashes our skin. Gray strips the shine from our hair. Curves get too soft or too angular.

Those of us who stay home with our children often feel like kids ourselves.

My friend Kelly and I were sitting on the floor of her family room when we realized how much we'd regressed. We sat on the floor with our babies instead of on the furniture, like children. We wore playclothes—jeans and sneakers and T-shirts—everyday, like children. We ate cold, bland lunches, earned no money of consequence, and waited impatiently for our grown-up to come home every night. Sometimes one of us would jump into his arms in gratitude.

Kelly's kitchen held the only evidence that an adult spent the day at the house. Five empty beer bottles sat lined up on the counter at the end of the week, one drunk each afternoon as her son howled with colic.

Let me stop here to tell you how much I love my kids. I love when my daughter leans against my arm while I read her *Little Women*. I love when my son kisses me fifteen times on each cheek before I leave him at preschool. I love when she makes a joke and he lets out the glorious sound of giggling. I love that she read for 260 minutes the other day and that he spent close to an hour playing with his pet ladybug. I love making meatballs with him. I love that she keeps a notebook for all of her inventions.

I love being their mother.

I hate being their mother.

I hate going to the playground. I hate breaking up fights. I hate herding them out of the house and into the car. I hate when they drum on my head as I tie their shoes.

Enjoy these days, older mothers say. They'll be gone before you know it. And I know they're partly right. I'm sure there will come a time, when my boy has hair on his chest, that I will miss when he begged me to carry him from room to room. I'll walk into a neat room that was once my daughter's and pine for the days when the floor was covered with doll clothes and magic markers. Sometimes, even now, I wish I could freeze them where they are, self-sufficient but still innocent. But mostly I feel relief as they get older.

It's a tunnel, these childbearing years, and there is an end. Diapers go, then strollers. They learn to pour their own juice and put on their own socks. They spend hours at friends' houses and eat grapes whole.

Time expands. You can take a shower. You can wear clothes that won't be spit up on. You can be vain.

I started my Vain Campaign the year my son turned four. Before the campaign, I wore a little makeup that I never put on thick enough for anyone to notice, and I occasionally got a massage. During the campaign, I did this: put mousse in my hair and blew it dry every day, paid someone to cover the gray with chemicals the color of cinnamon, paid someone else to pour hot wax on my inner thighs and use it to yank off the hairs, bought three different shades of lipstick, started carrying a compact of pressed powder in my pocketbook, covered my skin with foundation in the winter and self-tanner in the summer, and subscribed to fashion magazines.

I would laugh at myself for taking all these measures, because they were so foreign. *Who is this person powdering her shiny nose?* But sometimes the costume makes the character, and the person I needed to be appeared in the mirror one morning. She was fixing her hair with care, like a woman. She was tending to her morning routine in private, like an adult.

†††

My husband, like most men, refused to get a vasectomy at first. "No way," he said. "I'm not letting someone touch me down there."

It's a macho thing, you see. Family jewels, and all that. But then he realized that all forms of birth control, including the major surgery required for tubal ligation, are detrimental to my health. And he realized that he didn't want more children with the same intensity that he *did* want to have intercourse without a condom some day. So, like most men with a relatively secure sense of their masculinity, he consented.

He also procrastinated. We began to hear about more and more guys tampering with the jewels, with mixed opinions on the sacrifice. At the end of a dinner party one night, an elated couple arrived for dessert. The man had just had a vasectomy the day before and he felt great! He passed around his urologist's name. He explained how he kept his kids from jumping on his crotch. "You tell them Daddy had a mole removed from his upper leg!" I was surprised he didn't set down his plate of chocolate cake and scoop out his privates to show us the incision.

Another friend reported less jubilant news. He said the pain of the vasectomy was worse than childbirth. A third told my husband about the hematoma that migrated to his leg after the procedure. He could have died!

Procrastination turned to terror. I needed to beef up my offense. It was really quite easy, sex being a more potent drive in men than fear. One afternoon, we stood in the kitchen while the kids played outside. "You know," I said. "If you had a vasectomy, we could have sex right here, right now."

He made the appointment.

My only job was to drive him home. I hadn't been to the hospital in four years, since we walked out with our fresh-off-the-cord son. I hadn't navigated the maze of elevators and corridors that lead to the various clinics in five years, since we visited the miscarriage doctor on the third floor. This was like graduation day. First they get you pregnant here. Second, they give you the baby. Third, they take the resources away. Grab your diploma on the way out.

I read a book on puppies while someone cauterized my husband's vas deferens. A few worries ran through my mind. What if a blood clot shot to his brain and killed him? What if—oh, it's so cliché—the surgeon's hand slipped?

I imagined the doctor as I imagine all of them: either too short or too tall, with glasses and a bald spot and a paunch in the middle. When he emerged from the surgical suite and the nurse introduced us, I saw a man who had been clearly cast against type. He was tall and broad-shouldered, with thick gray hair and strong hands. He was dashing and debonair in his white coat. He was Heathcliff and Cary Grant and Richard Gere. Dare I say that the man who took away men's virility was doggone the most virile man I'd seen in ages?

He shook my hand and told me the procedure had gone well. My husband was resting until his blood pressure rose to normal, but he'd be fine.

"Thank you," I said and he understood what I meant: *Thank you for keeping my husband safe.* And he didn't understand what I meant: *Thank you for taking away the chance that I will ever have to be pregnant again. Thank you for freeing me. Thank you.* I wanted to wrap my arms around his handsome neck.

† † †

I sat in my reading chair next to the fireplace while my husband read to our daughter. Occasionally, he'll come into this room and sit across from me on the couch. Usually, though, he settles into his own territory. At the kitchen table with a file in front of him. In bed eating cereal and flicking from channel to channel to channel on the television. It wasn't always like this, of course. Before children—before marriage, even—we spent every evening magnetized together on a couch. If it was cold, we took off our clothes and put on our bathrobes. Robe Night, we called it. Then we became parents and had to take turns lounging.

When he came down the stairs, I called out to him. I wanted him to spend time with me.

"Hey," I said. "What are you doing?"

He walked in with a file in one hand and a bowl of cereal in the other.

"I'm coming in here," he said.

I moved to the couch and asked how he was feeling. The results of the procedure were not immediate. A certain amount of residual sperm must be released before it's safe to have unprotected sex. There's a plastic cup to be filled before he's deemed clinically sterile.

"I think I'll survive," he said.

We kissed. My husband, who had a crush on me for years before I appreciated him, has always told me he adores me; that he still can't believe he's married to me. I love to hear it, but sometimes it scares more than reassures me. Maybe I'm just a victory to him, I think. Any day now he'll realize I'm indeed not a prize. But this reassures me. This operation feels like more of a commitment than the diamond ring or the vows or the kids ever were. It means he's done. He's not saving it up for his second wife. He's not hedging his bets in case a better life comes along. This is the life he's chosen and I am at the center of it.

"It feels weird that I'm done having my kids," he said. "My evolutionary usefulness is over."

But I also knew he felt the same relief that I did. Making a family is like building a house. First you construct. Then you decorate. Finally, you can settle into the comfortable chairs and enjoy it.

There was grief, of course, but it only smarted for a second. The love I feel for my children is the strongest I've ever felt in my life. I won't, I realized, ever fall in love like that ever again. I won't ever give a person a name. Or know who that third child would have been.

But mostly there was triumph. I didn't need to look in a mirror to see it this time. I felt it in my arms. I wanted to pump them in the air and declare victory. As I read and wrote and put on my lipstick, this is what I thought: *Now I am mine. Again.*

lynn tait
Mother and Son

I remember times he held my hand,
insisted on it,
though no longer a baby
or even a toddler.
Regret the times
I insisted he walk
unfettered by my fingers.
Fail to see why,
now that I miss those cheeks
that once fit into the palm
of my small hand,
why I wished his high-pitched whine
would break into deepening tones.
Was I preparing myself
for the cut ties,
the growth that leans away?
Am I nothing more than a loose string
unraveling at the slightest tug,
a wayward strand of hair
pushed back in annoyance
or without much thought?
I'm tempted to shake him back into my life
like a furious snow scene trapped in glass.

At the same time, want to close my eyes
plug my ears, wish for ignorance
and ground him when flashes of myself —
ripples in the gene pool—wash over me
in a cold shudder like an October lake.
I'm afraid history will repeat itself;
afraid he will swim in a sea of delusions
reaching shore too late,
waterlogged with regret
and blaming me
for the lateness of the hour.

mary ann larkin
On a Son's Leaving after Thanksgiving
for Andrew

I put your napkin in the hamper,
think what to do with your sheets.
I wonder what you've left behind,
where I'll find it.
I put away the yogurt and apple
you had no time to eat—
marvel at your speed:
rush of shower
gulp of orange juice
thud of duffle bag,
your final admonition
to my final admonition,
the last wave
and honk of horn.
Now only the sun
and the cat
wandering from room to room
as if wondering how
it all happened so fast.

grace cavalieri
Children

Do you really think there is anywhere
you can go where they will not leave you?
Any continent that's safe
without old bowls, a half-cracked
pan?
    The tangled wilderness of their
bodies just beyond
           this field of night?

This is not something I went out to find:
the sun in the apron
the torn pocket with a picture
           of them.

Yet once there was love,
        scarring as red as an open
           pulse.

Can you see them?
Those who faced us? Then walked toward
the distance
        and did not return
although we waited on corners.

Please understand,
they never knew what it was like

without us so of course they
                went to find out.

I studied their leaving
day by day,
                faces like flowers ready
                    for winter,
until I could hear them heaving up stairways far away
perfecting love on their own.

What we prepare for is
the silence after sound,
the cold after fire,
the single moment for when
                        we are spirit.
How will I hold them then?
How will I open the door? And
                in whose heart will I rest?

Today I must really find those things I've lost—
                my grandfather's stickpin,
the single pearl earring.

The treasure box looks strange when empty
I always think it
should be fuller than it is.
If we give up loss
                what will we have left?

Listen. I can hear them at dinnertime
sounding like nothing ever dies.
The last I saw
they were walking toward me—
time
breaking open into their little forms.

terri watrous berry
On Guard

She boiled all of their nipples.
She boiled the bottles and the caps
plus the brush used to scrub
the bottles and the caps and the nipples.
There were long nights and high fevers,
hot little bodies under alcohol rubs,
medicine minutely measured given round
the clock, and baby aspirin scored
midnights at the twenty-four-hour
pharmacy. Bee stings poison ivy broken
bones hearts, ear-nose-throat infections
pinkeye. They had all their inoculations
and she spent her summers counting
bobbing blonde heads at the beach:
one two three, one two three,
one two three, ad infinitum.
She held tightly to their hands in public
places, discreetly stood outside of
countless men's room doors when
the boys were old enough to pee alone.
(She showed the girl how to do it
without touching the seat.)
She taught them to cross the street,

to ride a bike, to drive a car,
and they have and they did and they do,
their circles ever widening
beyond perked ears and straining eyes,
rarely does she get to count
them all at once anymore:
one two, one two, one
two three, one two, one two
three one two one two three...
Twenty-odd years a vigilant sentry
without a rest, with no relief.
Blow out the porchlamp, Mother, and
know that your watch has ended.

amy unsworth
How to Hold a Son

For a newborn, the bend of your elbow
supports the head, the untrained neck.
Note the bunched face, the pulse
visible at the crown. Prop your arms
with a pillow. Don't sleep.

At two, pretend to be a zebra,
prance on all fours. Become
accustomed with carpets, grass.
Rediscover your knees, sitting
cross-legged. Laughing, he'll
collapse into your arms. Hurry.

The five-year-old will bring tulips,
stemless. Or a ladybug. Find a bowl,
a stool, a magnifying glass.
Stand behind, peer at the dusting
of pollen. Hold the glass steady
to see spots and wings. Inhale.

At nine, tousle hair.
Carry the backpack, tuck in
an extra chocolate. In front
of friends, smile. Read about
dragons or mummies. Sneak
your arm around, let it settle.
Pull him close.

In the teens, persist.
Wrestle, slap backs. Knock first.
Attend ball games and cheer.
Say it's for your own sake.
Recall the ache in your arms,
the throb of his heart.
Let him leave. Learn to sleep.

lessons

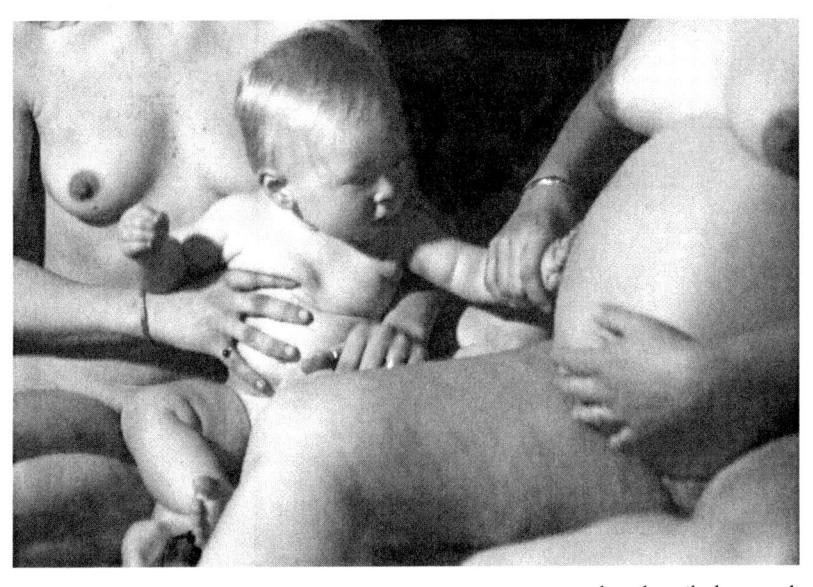

photo by mike hovancsek

margaret grosh
Today We Learned to Blink

Once I burned the midnight oil, proved myself, went beyond my dreams. I wrote books, gave speeches, counseled ministers, hoped to help the poor. I bought a house, made it home, arranged, enlarged, landscaped, be-decked and jacuzzied. I scubaed, biked, hiked, kayaked, skied.

This morning I nursed my child at dawn. I blinked hugely, sleepy and loving. She blinked hugely, mischievous and grinning. I blinked back, she blinked back. Eyelids as semaphores of joy, love, discovery.

I used to nourish my body and brain with an hour or two of gym time and NPR at dawn. Now I nourish her body, her brain, my soul.

phylis warady
Pearl in a Foul Oyster World

"You found it, Kevin?" Doubtful eyes combed the gold stingray bicycle. "Where?"

"At school."

"Take it back right away!"

Kevin squinted up at her from where he rested on his haunches, while he worked to loosen a bolt with his grandfather's wrench. "You've got it all wrong, Mom. Nobody wants it. If they did, they wouldn't have left it laying around the school ground for days."

"You may be right," she conceded. "Just the same, I want you to take it back. Immediately."

"Gee, Mom, do I have to? After all the work I've done?"

"Bikes are expensive, son. It has to belong to someone."

"You think that because it's beginning to look like something. You didn't see it when it was all wrecked out. Seat hanging off. Sissy bars loose. Please, Mom, can't I keep it?"

"The fact remains, it's not your property. Don't you see, taking what doesn't belong to you is stealing."

"Stealing?" Angry tears squeezed from the corners of large smoke-gray eyes. "But Mom, I didn't *steal* it. I *found* it!"

His lips set in a grim, determined line. Everything about her sturdy son struck her as stubborn. Even his hair. It grew in clumps that kept popping up every which way—no matter how often it was brushed into a smooth line.

"Kevin, you'll have to make an honest effort to find out who that bike belongs to."

Renewed hope flickered in her son's eyes. "You mean if I turn this bike into lost and found and nobody claims it, I get to keep it?"

"If it works out that way, yes."

"Oh boy!" The grin he cast her was the epitome of jaunty exuberance.

Kevin whistled confidently as he wheeled the bike off toward the school. Her heart went out to him. He truly believed the owner of the bike wouldn't claim it. But she knew better.

A few nights later, Kevin sought her out.

"Um," she said, "you smell like soap."

"'Course I do. Just took a shower." He frowned. "You know, Mom, I've been thinking."

"About the bike?" It had been reclaimed soon after Kevin turned it in.

"Yes, but about other things, too."

"Oh? What other things?"

"That bath mat beside the tub. The one you took from the motel where we stayed last summer. I've been thinking over what you said the other day, Mom, and I don't think it was such a good idea." Kevin spoke hesitantly, watching her facial expression with trepidation as though he were walking a tightrope and one false step would send him tumbling.

"What I mean is, in a way, it's like me taking the bike."

Stunned, she stared at her son fresh and clean, his stubborn mop of hair still damp from his shower. She choked back a startled laugh.

He's only a kid. How dare he presume to judge her? His mother. Everyone collected souvenirs, didn't they? In all likelihood the motel hadn't missed the bath mat. Or if they had, they'd deducted it from their income taxes.

A searing light pierced her flabby defense. Did she consider herself an exception to the values she was trying to instill in Kevin?

"I'll bet," he continued, in a tone of kindly understanding, "you never thought taking that bath mat was stealing, did you, Mom? Just like I didn't think bringing home a wrecked-out bike was either."

Because he took such infinite care not to hurt her any more than necessary for her own good, she managed to forgive the trace of triumph in her small son's voice.

"You're right," she admitted, once she had managed to swallow a painful obstruction at the base of her throat. "I should never have taken that bath mat. It wasn't my property. Guess I talked myself into it like you did that bike."

Kevin's face reflected profound relief, as though at last he had it all sorted out. "That's what I thought, Mom."

She reached down and gave him a quick hug, acutely conscious that the day would soon come when Kevin would feel too grown-up to allow it.

clarinda harriss
Arabic

Hubbub, I say. *Hubbub*. The baby
pats my lips. He loves the funny

word. He loves today's repairman,
postman, the dogs howling at them,

the pasta boiling over,
the phone machine's someone-or-other—

the hubbub. We stop at the mirror,
stare into my eyes, Berber-

dark under the pale-blonde hair
gray age earned me, stare

into his baby-blue baby eyes,
already the shape and half the size

of his father's grown ones.
Abracadabra, my daughter's son

changes a bit of Kleenex to mothwings
with a touch of his fingers.

(He seems less surprised than I
when the white scrap flies.)

Clarinda Harriss — Arabic

I prattle him to sleep
with piggies and baa-baa sheep,

one-two-three. With
Arab numbers and pretty words: *zenith*,

hashish, assassin, cous cous.
Old stuff has its use.

amy hirshberg lederman
There's No Place Like Home

When my son Joshua was born, I was given more unsolicited advice than baby gifts. Family, friends, friends of friends, and total strangers took the liberty of counseling me on everything from nap schedules to nipples. I'd shop at the grocery store with Josh nestled into his Snugli like a baby kangaroo and inevitably some self-proclaimed baby expert would approach me shaking her head.

"Too much contact at an early age will turn him into a momma's boy," she warns shaking her finger at me. Josh is not yet three weeks old at the time.

Generally, I hate being told what to do. I have elevated this tendency into an art form, refusing to follow even the simplest of directions. Recipes are as much of an irritant to me as a clogged drain, which is why my soufflés fall more often than my two-year-old nephew.

When it comes to instruction manuals, I am a total loser. I think of this as a good thing, that my spiritual awareness is so elevated that it knows better than to mess with anything not originating in nature. But rather than the respect I deserve, I am the brunt of most jokes around our house.

My family thinks it's hilarious that I own a cell phone but have no idea how to retrieve messages, that my car radio is set at stations that only they like because I don't know how to de-program it, and that I still haven't figured out how to change the font color on my email from magenta to black. I calmly remind them that I have two graduate degrees from prestigious universities and that it is not kind to make fun of an unfortunate with an affliction.

I don't want to give the impression that I am totally resistant to the counsel of others. Generally, I am more inclined to heed the printed word, which is how I came to follow this sagely advice in the "How to Travel" section of a working mothers' magazine.

"Avoid air travel with a toddler. Take all your trips to see relatives and friends before your baby can walk. A baby is content to sit on your lap, cooing, sucking, prodding and pulling for most of the trip. A toddler believes that the only reason you are on the plane is so that she can explore every square inch of inhabitable space while in the air."

I'll admit it. I had a definite motive for following this advice—pure, old-fashioned guilt. My parents live three thousand miles away and never let me forget it. Since Josh's birth, our weekly phone calls sound something like this.

"So, how's our darling grandson? You know, the one we never get to see since you decided to leave your real home in New Jersey and move to that God-forsaken cow town in Arizona?"

On a good day, it goes like this.

"Tell me darling, does Joshua look like me? Everyone asks but of course I can't really give them an answer because in the last picture you sent me he was a month old and still had that monkey face. He's how old now, six months?"

I'm angry at the moment, but I let it pass because deep down I know they're right. It's horrible living so far away from your grandchildren. You miss all the special moments. Josh spitting his creamed corn at the camera, Josh teething on my flip-flop, Josh biting the dog. I admonish myself to send them more pictures and head straight for the phone.

"Mom? Hi, it's me," I announce before she starts in. "I'm coming—next month—for a week—to visit." The words are truncated by my efforts to untangle the phone cord from Josh's chubby foot.

She gives herself a minute of sheer joy at the thought that we are coming before she begins to hassle me about the logistics.

"How will you fly with a baby? Where will he sleep? Should I get the diapers now, they're having a sale at Kmart. Do you have a car seat? I don't see why you need one. We never used one when you were growing up and look how you turned out. What does he eat? What do you eat? Are you still doing that crazy vegetarian thing?"

I'm exhausted from trying to save Josh's foot from a phone cord amputation and sound more impatient than I mean to.

"Oh Mom, just don't worry about it. I'll take care of the food and the car seat. Just roll up the oriental rug and put away all your breakables. Gotta go. Love you, bye!"

I hang up and sweep Josh off the floor, foot intact. "I hope we know what we're doing," I tell him brightly. He smiles and sucks on a piece of dog food he found on the floor.

Packing for the trip is a breeze. Three large canvas bags for Josh, one small carry-on for me. The list of things to bring on the plane is arm's-length: car seat, umbrella stroller, baby bag stuffed with a week's worth of clothing, food, diapers, and amusements. The novel I recently purchased remains on my night stand giving me dagger looks. I pick it up and optimistically tuck it into the side pocket of my carry-on. Maybe he'll sleep, I pray silently as we head out the door for the airport.

There's a mix-up with the seats. The bulkhead I desperately fought for on the phone has been given to another family, a mother with twins who sound like they have turned crying into an Olympic sport. She looks even more frazzled than I, so I acquiesce in exchange for a free drink coupon. Is eight a.m. too early to start drinking?, I wonder to myself.

"He's really very good on a plane," I mutter to no one in particular as I buckle us up. Then, as if on cue, Josh starts to cry. Not his standard fussiness-before-bedtime cry, but a full-blown wail.

"What's the matter, sweet boy?" I ask, desperately trying to distract him with the contents of my purse. Only then do I notice that the clip on the seat belt is pinching his thigh. The glare from the man in 14B tells me all I need to know. I have been indicted and convicted in less than fifteen seconds as an incompetent, abusive mother by a man who probably never traveled with his own kids, if he even has any.

Once Josh has been released from the grips of the seat belt monster, he settles down nicely and begins to explore his surroundings. This includes two lipsticks, a Tampax container, and the toupee on the head of the man in the seat in front of us. I apologize profusely to an indignant backside bending over to grab his carry-on in search of another seat.

God is clearly on my side. An unsuspecting college girl offers to exchange seats and I can tell right away that she loves babies. I store that information in my mommy Rolodex, knowing that at some time during this four-and-a-half-hour flight I will have to use the bathroom.

Within less than an hour, I am attempting to remove a mixture of ranch dressing and pasta sauce from the front of my T-shirt, the new one I bought to avoid hearing from my mother how washed-out and unfashionable I look since I've had a baby. Josh is finger painting the pullout tray with applesauce and instead of disciplining him, I am grateful for this self-directed art project. I take this as a sign that I'm beginning to lose it and ask College Girl if she wouldn't mind rescuing me for a few minutes while I freshen up in the bathroom. She covers herself prophylactically in an airplane blanket as I hand over a sticky, soggy Josh and scurry up the aisle.

Just about the time that the pilot comes on and tells us that we are beginning our descent for landing, Josh falls asleep. I am coated in dried sauces and drool and look as if I haven't slept in a week, which isn't too far from the truth. Josh is in desperate need of a diaper change but there's no time for that, so I wrap him up in the baby blanket my mother made and douse him with talcum powder. I smile wanly as my mother rushes over to hug me, her excitement turning to horror as she gets within smelling range.

"Oh my God, you didn't actually travel smelling like that, did you?"

I suck in my breath, bite my tongue, and think of how nice life would be if I had an evil twin to blame all my nasty thoughts on. I hug my mom and dad, holding a sour-smelling Josh between us. He spontaneously reaches up, holding out his baby hands to my mother, and I can tell, in that instant of connection, that she's hooked.

"It's great to be home, guys," I say to their backs as they march proudly off to the baggage claim with Josh held high on my father's shoulders. In those first few minutes after arrival, I notice things I never saw before. My father's forehead and how it slopes the same way that Josh's does. My mother's delicate ears, which I have kissed numerous times on my own son. An unconditional love that I thought only my husband and I could feel for our child permeates the baggage claim area.

Josh is reaching towards my mother, who is playing a game of peek-a-boo with him, hiding behind her oversized pocketbook.

"Look, look! He knows me, he knows we're family," she practically gloats with pleasure. "He can smell it, I tell you. It's in the blood."

It really is good to be home.

mary-sherman willis
The Vine

A daughter is the vine that climbs the mother
Like honeysuckle on the apple tree
While the mother grows to light within the other—
The growing daughter—who, threatening to smother,
Twining even as she's breaking free,
Knows herself to be the vine that climbs the mother.
The daughter does not crush the mother, rather,
She takes up the slack reflexively,
As the mother grows toward light within the other,
Reaching up as if she had discovered
That sky and air engendered liberty,
While the daughter, vine that climbs the mother,
Using limber tendrils, is bending to recover
The backbone needed for security
In a mother growing light within the other.
In time they will resemble one another,
Although in season each blooms differently,
The daughter vine assumes the shape of mother;
The mother glows, a light within the other.

katy mckinney
Lessons from Ben, Just Turned 3

Ben sits on a basket piled high with laundry
and announces, "I'm a cloe!"
What else would you be
if you were only one of the many
clothes in the basket?
He putters around the kitchen
waving my spatula, and tells me
he is spatching.
Ben teaches me about nouns and verbs.

Ben stretches his father's tape measure
out against a board
and tells me, "Sixteen pounds!"
We weigh tomatoes at the store
in a hanging produce scale.
He asks me how fast they are going.
Ben teaches me how to measure things.

Katy McKinney — Lessons from Ben, Just Turned 3

Ben tells me the reason
he likes lima beans so much
is because they have mashed potatoes inside.
He kisses me awake
as I try napping on the couch;
he tells me he's Prince Charming.
Ben teaches me to open my eyes.

Ben cradles his doll gently
as I feed baby Molly; he nurses it
from his bellybutton.
We tell him of all the things he can do
now that he's getting bigger.
He tells me that when I get little
he will take care of me.
Ben teaches me about loving.

claire tristram
Camping with Lucy

My daughter Lucy began to walk on October tenth, her first birthday, leaving me weepy and in awe of the huge journey she'd just taken from the sofa to her father's knee. The next morning, Lucy and I started off on a week-long camping trip, for what became a huge journey for us both. Our destination, the Pacific Coast of Northern California, is one of my favorite places in the world. I wanted Lucy to like it as much as I do.

It wasn't Lucy's first outdoor experience. She first slept in a tent when she was six days old. An intrepid traveler, she doesn't seem to mind weather, bugs, or dirt. Not so her mom. Living outdoors doesn't come naturally to me. I crave plumbing. A telephone. A word processor. In many ways I'd planned this trip because I wanted my daughter to be more at home with the world than I am. But what I'm continually surprised about, when traveling with my daughter, is how much she is teaching me.

###

We camp the first three nights at Salt Point, four hours north of San Francisco. It's one of the few wild and desolate places in California that you can drive to. It's a place where sandstone cliffs and jagged rocks plunge straight into the sea. Occasionally a chunk of the highway falls into the sea, too, closing the route for days or weeks and making the area even more desolate than before. There's no town at Salt Point, only a lone general store where the closest thing to fresh produce is a can of chili. There's an occasional luxury home built on a bluff, a scattered hotel or two in the heavily wooded hills, and the biggest Buddhist temple in the Western world, Odiyan, on the hilltop a few miles above our campsite. That's about it. It's mid-October. Definitely off-season, unless you're an abalone diver. We're the only people camping in the entire park.

None of these things matter to Lucy, of course. Her perspective on the world is far more immediate: whatever she can grab. Because I can't childproof the whole outdoors, and don't want to confine her to a playpen, I've spent hours teaching her not to put things in her mouth that might choke her. We've developed a unique communication, she and I. Instead of shouting "No!," I yell "Ah-ah-ah!"—a sound, I'm embarrassed to admit, that was taught to me in dog obedience school for my Samoyed. It causes some confusion in my dog on this trip, but my baby responds immediately by dropping whatever is in her hand.

This afternoon, our first in camp, I don't need to say it. Lucy says it for me. She prowls around our site on all fours, earnestly searching out every small stone and shouting "Ah-ah-ah!" before crawling over and handing it to me with great ceremony.

Finally, the pile of stones next to me growing out of control, I pick Lucy up, put her in her carrier, put the dog on a leash, and take them both for a walk through the woods near our camp. Deer, quail, and what-just-might-be-a-fox cross our trail. I point to them with great excitement—my daughter is getting a great look at nature!—but it's unclear to me whether Lucy sees any of them, because she's busy looking at the ground for more stones.

The next day I hike down to the beach with Lucy, hoping to get out of the October wind. I've layered Lucy's clothes until she resembles a miniature fullback. The waves are rough and more than fifteen feet high. It's peak abalone season, but no one is going into the water. A few glum divers sit on the beach in their wet suits, complaining about the weather.

I've brought along a new pail and shovel. Lucy ignores them, preferring instead to play her own elaborate game with pieces of driftwood. She picks up a piece in each hand, throws them into the air simultaneously, and watches them earnestly as they drop. Again and again. After a while she crawls up into my lap and falls asleep under my down jacket. I decide to wait until she wakes up before moving her. The wind dies. The tide goes out. I wonder why the only reading material I've brought is Sesame Street books for my daughter. I wonder if Big

Bird is a man or woman, if Bert and Ernie are TV's first same-sex marriage. I wonder if my daughter will ever wake up. Lucy wakes up and smiles.

On the fourth day we break camp, heading north on California Highway 1. The landscape grows more civilized almost immediately, as the craggy outcroppings of Salt Point smooth their way into flat farmland. At Stewart's Point General Store, we stop to get a book to read for me, and groceries for both of us. I discover that Lucy has learned her first word. As we get out of the car, she shouts "Hi!" to a gruff old man in a battered cowboy hat. The wrinkles in his face realign themselves in a thousand smiles. Later on, behind us in line at the register, he gives us three cents so we can pay in exact change. "I knew I'd get rid of those pennies someplace," he says, looking only at my daughter.

Driving north again, we pass Sea Ranch, a huge and depressing development of luxury homes, before passing a real ranch, where a man is driving a tractor draped with two newly butchered cattle. We pass a llama ranch, too, just in time to see two llamas mate. Lucy has fallen asleep in her car seat and I decide to keep driving, all the way to MacKerricher State Park, north of Fort Bragg, which is the largest town on this stretch of the California coast. The campsites are large, sunny, and a stone's throw away from a wide and wild beach.

While setting up camp I must keep Lucy confined somehow, because I'm too busy to watch her. I usually leave her in her car seat, or put her in the portable high chair I've brought, along with a few new toys for her to play with. After the tent is up I let her roam free, keeping her always in sight.

Today Lucy crawls to the next campsite, inexorably drawn toward the sound of another baby. My God, the baby is dressed in white. She sits in her playpen like the Emperor of the Forbidden City, remote and wise and oh, so clean. My own daughter, whose favorite game in camp is to make mud by throwing dirt into our dog's water dish, looks something akin to an invading barbarian.

The other mother comes out of her mobile home, looking alarmed as my baby approaches hers.

"How old is she?" she asks in a voice that's just a little strained.

We learn our daughters were born within days of each other. I look at the two of them, looking at each other, one clean and civilized, the other dirty and wild, and I wonder what I'm teaching my daughter, and if she'll ever recover from it.

We visit Mendocino the next day, eight miles to the south. It's a coastal town so cute that it has been the location of more than three dozen feature films and countless television series and commercials. Even in mid-October the town is bursting with tourists.

Lucy says "hi" to a rough-looking woman in a flannel shirt and jeans. That's how we meet Mary, a woman who makes her living as a "water witcher," dousing for wells in the area.

"My partner uses a coat hanger," she tells us. "I have a more complicated method, involving piano strings."

Mary shows us her plumb bob, too, about the size of her thumbnail, dangling from a fine chain on her key pocket. She tells us that the plumb bob is connected with the spirit world, and will answer any question Mary asks it. She holds the plumb bob absently over my baby as we speak. It swings wildly. I'm afraid to ask Mary what it's saying.

Lucy's "hi" entices people to speak with us all day. It's a loud "hi," and lusty, accompanied by a wave and a six-toothed smile. It's the perfect traveler's vocabulary, and all she needs to say—the people she says it to invariably take up the conversation from there. Lucy's "hi" stops a bent old man dead in his tracks. He looks at her in wonder, then tells her, "Look at you! Living for today! No thought for the future! Don't ever forget how to do that!"

I want to ask how he got all of that out of my daughter's single-word vocabulary, but he has already walked by. Next Lucy stops a middle-aged couple with Mendocino written on matching sweatshirts, who are holding hands as they pass us. They both wave and say "hi" back again for several seconds, giddy with smiles, before moving on. All the people here in town seem somehow typical of this stretch of coast. Grizzled hippies, real estate agents, pot growers and cattle ranchers, water witchers and curmudgeons and people just passing through coexist peacefully, with a grudging respect for one another. Thanks to Lucy's one word, we meet quite a few of them.

The problems you have when traveling with small children always have something to do with time, and what you'd rather be doing with it. You don't have time to read the book you've been meaning to read, because the baby won't nap when she's supposed to. You can't finish a meal, because she's getting too tired and needs to be nursed to sleep. You can't just relax and do nothing for a while, because she's demanding that you pay attention to her. You can't have fun, damn it, because your child just won't cooperate.

On the sixth day of our vacation, Lucy explodes. No more cute smiles—she screams constantly, a grating sound that leaves me on the edge of calling our vacation quits and going home. No more minding me—at our campsite she's grimly determined to put anything into her mouth—dirt, grass, bugs—that will cause her mother to leap up in horror to rescue her. No more napping on schedule—she stubbornly refuses to sleep that afternoon, despite my best efforts to get her to nod off so I can have some time to myself.

Finally, at four that afternoon, beaten by Lucy's stubbornness and sheer force of will, exhausted from trying to get her to sleep, I give up. I carry her to the beach, just over the dunes from our tent, and put her down on the sand.

She scrambles away from me as if she's driven to put as much distance between us as she can. Amazing how quickly she moves. I scramble after her.

Something happens then. A shift in the breeze, and in my perception of the world. I discover that my daughter, who barely has taken her first step, can clamber over sea rocks like the most nimble crab. My daughter, who knows only one word of English, can imitate perfectly the cry of a seagull, or a barking dog down the beach, or the drone of a passing airplane. My daughter, who is just a year old, can show me things about the world that are too subtle, or too familiar, for me to notice myself. She points to the barest whisper of a moon in the sky before I see it. To a dragonfly high above our heads. To a jet trail, lit up in the setting sun.

I didn't know she could do any of those things.

The next day it rains. Our vacation becomes a series of knotty problems to solve: how to keep Lucy warm and dry; how to keep the dog from tracking mud all over the back seat of the car; how to prepare and eat hot meals. This last problem we solve by giving up on the outdoor eating experience and going frequently to Denny's in Fort Bragg instead.

But nothing—not the rain, nor the mud, nor the sudden chill that tells me winter has finally come to the California coast—can get in the way of this shining memory: Lucy, on the beach at MacKerricher, at sunset, at the moment when I first felt her growing away from me.

patricia gavin
Postpartum Day Two

I feel slender, oh so slender
Oh so slender and tender and fine,
And I can't believe this figure is mine.
I feel fragile, oh so fragile,
Oh so fragile, yet agile to beat
Looking down I can now see my feet.
I feel narrow, oh so narrow,
Like a sparrow who's narrow and small,
And I can't believe it's me at all.
I feel meager, oh so meager,
Oh so meager, yet eager to say
That I'm going home today.
I feel depressed, so depressed
So depressed getting dressed for I can't
Possibly zip up my pants.
I feel defeated, so defeated,
So defeated and cheated by chance
As I change into my maternity pants.

jacqueline kudler
Spock Addendum for Maura

The hard part is not
doing. That will come
easier than you know:
the first stipple of
milk, the meteor shower—
the bouncing, balancing,
rocking. All the troll
costumes, lemon bars,
birthday cakes—the
staying hand, the stilling
voice—I tell you
who do the doing part
so well, how ably you'll
oar the small craft of
each morning forward
through all the pools,
eddies, backwaters, past
shoals and quagmires,
the lift and dip of your
paddle steady,

systolic.
The hard part is
not doing, a movement
downstream that may
look like drifting from
the far shore but has
nothing to do with
drifting. Not steering
and not saying either
but a way of responding
to the current under
you—a question of
balance, really—the
cells at full attention
to each surge, each
shallow, each ambient
breeze: a weight shift
here, a small adjustment
there. No matter the day
is glass, the visibility
splendid—you'll never
exactly know what lies
behind the next
turning.
Sit still. Listen.
Don't hold too tight.
It will be the best,
the wildest, ride
you'll ever have.

christina daub
Domestic Bliss

After another night of waking and nursing,
    waking and nursing,
morning splinters like a ship and I bob
    among the once white sheets.
The clouds are milky, the pillows,
    even the dream I am now forgetting
where the Nile turned white, and the Atlantic,
    and Atlantis rose

like a carnivorous mouth to suckle the oceans dry.
    Milk stains on my gown,
I'm La Leche's poster girl, I'm Dairy Miss,
    Heidi, Helga *mit die* buckets
coming back from the barn.
    The baby squawks.
Heavier than a Thanksgiving turkey,
    he bobs along on my shoulder

as I stumble into my first son's room
    where some castle door or Lego man
cuts my foot, and because he knows
    what I'll say for the zillionth time
about toys left on the floor, Son One
    dives under his covers and won't get up.

And as if this were not enough, I go downstairs
    where the cat's back from an all-night bender

and has splatted the living room in vomit,
    stippling the rug, the floorboards, a chair leg
and pooling a great lake, say Erie, under the piano,
    all of which my husband navigated right by
on his way out to work, as if he floated over it
    not noticing, and because it's a new millennium
and *Ich bin keine Hausfrau,* I'm thinking
    forget Domestic Engineer, I'm Domestic PhD!

For in the middle of all this,
    I have to make the breakfast, pack the lunch,
nurse the baby again even though his head now
    is a raging pomegranate
and it's so loud I think my ears
    might blister, my thoughts snaffle,
though everyone knows when you have a baby,
    part of your mind goes...

when Son One tromps downstairs barefoot
    and slips in a cat pool, and between amp-loud
nine-year-old expletives like, "GROSS!" and "FOUL!,"
    he tells me he can't find his homework,
he'll have to stay in at recess
    to which I'm tempted to reply,
at least you get recess, but don't because
    now I have to jiggle the baby

and focus on food because it's not like
    when I was a kid and ate Lucky Charms
or Sugar Pops or those cardboard things
    you slip in the toaster and pinch the jam out of.

In the age of balanced breakfasts,
>   I'm boiling eggs, slicing open a grapefruit,
a bagel, a gash in my thumb

and screaming, scaring Son One
>   who won't eat a bite, not one,
due to the "DISGUSTING" smell deviling in
>   from the living room, but who for once
does not protest going to school this morning
>   despite his recess loss,
the hated gym coach, and the dreaded Mrs. P.

And if I am finally able to perch my mouth on the rim
>   of a cup of already lukewarm coffee,
and latch the baby's mouth firmly onto my nipple
>   as I sink yawning and bandaged back into bed
though it's not even 8 a.m., and the day's chores
>   hang like a wet rag waiting to be wrung,
I guess you could call this bliss...yes.

Our Contributors

Franka Arabia lives in Toronto, Canada, with her two wonderful kids, Jacob and Gloria, and husband Murray. She works in an advertising agency and writes poetry in her spare time.

Judith Arcana has written two prose books and a collection of poems (*What If Your Mother*, 2005) about motherhood. Her web profile is at womenarts.org.

Kate Banigan-White lives in western Massachusetts with her husband and second daughter Charlotte, age six. Kate has had work published in *Patchwork Journal* and the *Daily Hampshire Gazette*.

Terri Watrous Berry didn't begin to write full time until her three children were almost grown. Her work has since appeared in several publications, and her poetry has received awards from Still Waters Press, Sky Blue Waters Poetry League, and the Poetry Society of Michigan.

Jody Bolz, mother of two, is the author of *A Lesson in Narrative Time* and an editor of *Poet Lore*. Her work has appeared numerous journals and anthologies, including *Her Face in the Mirror: Jewish Women on Mothers & Daughters*.

A mother of four, *Katherine Grace Bond*'s books include the best-selling *Legend of the Valentine*, a story of the civil rights movement, and *Considering Flight*, a collection of poems.

Nicole Braun earned a college degree and then a master's degree from Rutgers University after her son was born. She is still a single parent. Her son is a teenager.

Our Contributors

Stephany Brown is the mother of three daughters. Her stories have appeared in *Blackbird*, *Other Voices*, *Brain, Child*, and other publications.

Carole Burns's book, *Off the Page*, based on her interviews for washingtonpost.com with writers such as Alice McDermott and Paul Auster, is being published by Norton in fall 2007. She's at work on a novel.

Bonnie Jo Campbell is the author of the novel *Q Road*, and the prize-winning story collection *Women & Other Animals*. She lives in Kalamazoo, Michigan.

Carol Carpenter (Livonia, Michigan) enjoys the fruits of her labor: two adult children, a son and daughter. Her work has appeared in over a hundred publications.

Grace Cavalieri's four children and husband have made her writing career possible, by taking into the family the foundling "poetry," sharing, nurturing, and caring for it all through the years. She has written fourteen books of poetry and twenty produced plays as part of this venture.

Sharon Charde is a wife, mother, grandmother, family therapist, and teacher of writing. She is the author of two award-winning chapbooks, *Bad Girl at the Altar Rail* and *Four Trees Down from Ponte Sisto*; four of her poems have been nominated for a Pushcart Prize.

Marion Cohen, a published author who has taught mathematics part time at several universities, is the mother of five children, four of them living, and the grandmother of two. Her new book, *Crossing the Equal Sign*, is forthcoming from Plain View Press.

Darcy Cummings's book of poetry, *The Artist As Alice* (Bright Hills Press, 2006), examines the struggles of the artist as a child and as she later tries to create work while tending marriage and children—those challenges that often follow childbirth.

Cindy Dale lives on the barrier beach on Long Island with her husband and ten-year-old twins. She has published short stories in many literary journals and has twice been nominated for a Pushcart Prize.

Christina Daub is schussing along with three boys ranging from diaper age to dating age. When the slopes aren't too steep, she manages to write and teach poetry here and there.

Rocky Delaplaine is a yoga instructor, poet, artist, and activist. Her daughter Olivia was born in 1997. Her photos have appeared in the *Sun* and *Quest: A Feminist Quarterly*.

Mary Katya Doroshenk holds an undergraduate degree in English from the College of William and Mary and a master's in writing from Johns Hopkins University. She and her husband live in Arlington, Virginia, and have a baby daughter.

Tessa Dratt's writing has appeared in over forty of the small presses and in numerous anthologies, and she has received three Pushcart Prize nominations. She is the mother of two adult children and a new grandmother who has been married, for forty years, to the same man.

Since becoming a mother, *Polly Dredge* has edited three books and is working on her first novel. She and her family live in Fairfax, Virginia.

Arlene Eager and her husband Bill live in New York. She leads an advanced poetry workshop at SUNY, Stony Brook. Arlene's work has appeared in the *Hudson Review*, the *Gettysburg Review*, and other publications.

Maureen L. Egan's work has appeared in many publications, and she currently teaches English at VCU in Richmond. Her two teenagers continue to provide fodder for her writing, much to their chagrin.

Annie Farnsworth lives on the Maine coast with her two children and a bevy of adopted animals. A poet, artist, and student of the metaphysical, she works in an acute care mental health facility.

Dewi L. Faulkner has always loved writing. Her children, Brooks and Gabrielle, are her muses, and give her the courage to call herself a writer.

Peggy Garrison juggled writing, teaching, earning an MA in English, raising her son—exhausted, grateful for all of it! Four poetry books—most recent, *Ties* (P&Q Press, 2001).

Patricia Gavin is the mother of eight young adults ranging in age from twenty-one to thirty-seven and grandmother of ten. She has had several articles and a short story published in magazines.

Barbara Gibson works with survivors of domestic violence. She and her partner of eleven years parent three children. Barbara enjoys freelance writing and reading whenever time permits.

Our Contributors

Brenda-Fay Glik is a poet in St. Louis, a counselor in private practice, and a mother of two. Her poems have been published in several literary journals, and she has authored two books.

A godfather to his brother's son, **David Glynn** comes from a family of artists. He does digital prints as well as painting. Glynn has a book available. www.glynns.com.

Jeffrey Goldsmith grew up in New York and lived in Mexico, Japan, and France. The father of two now writes and photographs people and places in San Francisco—and around the world. He shot the photographs for the book *Cafe Haiku*. www.jeffreygoldsmith.com.

Patricia Gray's book *Rupture* was named one of the best books of poetry for 2005 by *Montserrat Review*. She received a 2006 artist fellowship in poetry from the D.C. Commission on the Arts and Humanities.

Margaret Grosh: guru of international welfare programs and author of several books on same; bureaucrat and long-standing workaholic, recently turned mother, champion nurser, and now, to everyone's surprise, poet.

Rachel Hall's award-winning fiction and nonfiction have appeared in numerous publications, most recently in *Water-Stone*, *New Letters*, and *It's A Girl!: Women Writers on Raising Daughters*. She writes, teaches, and mothers Maude in western New York.

Viva Hammer (vivahammer@aol.com) is an Australian-born writer working in Washington, D.C. Her writing has been published widely, including in the *Rio Grande Review*, *Potomac Review*, *Washingtonian*, and *Forward*. She also mothers two children.

N. LaQuis Harkins is an actress/writer/hobby photographer from Chicago. The Howard University alumna can be reached at nlhphoto@yahoo.com.

Only-child **Clarinda Harriss** has published three collections of poems. Her children Lisa and Andrew and their spouses have given her a sizable collection of grandchildren.

Anne Hasselbrack's poetry and nonfiction have been published, and her novel was performed on stage. After years of unexplained infertility, she now has a son and daughter from Archangel, Russia.

Mike Hovancsek is a licensed psychotherapist. His work challenges the messages in our culture that lead to guilt, shame, low self-esteem, and unhealthy body images. Contact him at point@neobright.net.

Jacqueline Jules is an elementary school librarian and the author of six children's books. Her poetry has appeared in sixty publications. She is the mother of two grown sons. www.jacquelinejules.com.

Suzanne Kamata is the editor of the anthology *The Broken Bridge: Fiction from Expatriates in Literary Japan* (Stone Bridge Press, 1997), and mom to twins Jio and Lilia. She lives with her family in Aizumi, Japan.

Sarah Kennedy is the author of four books of poems and the co-editor of a Virginia poetry anthology. She has received grants from the NEA, the Virginia Commission for the Arts, and the NEH. She teaches at Mary Baldwin College.

Laurie King-Billman is a mother of two who works part time as an adolescent therapist and is finishing a book of poems entitled "Personal Western."

Jacqueline Kudler's first full collection of poems, *Sacred Precinct* (Sixteen Rivers Press, San Francisco), was published in 2003. She has two fine sons and two dear granddaughters.

Mary Ann Larkin is a poet and teacher living in Washington, D.C. Her poems have been published widely. She is the mother of three grown children.

Judith Laura is mother of one daughter. Her poetry has been widely published in journals and anthologies. Her latest novel, *Beyond All Desiring*, is a finalist in the 2006 Word/Work Book Awards.

Amy Hirshberg Lederman, a published author, Jewish educator, public speaker, and attorney, lives with her husband and two teenage children in Tucson.

Kathryn Leenay is a mother of three living in Ontario, New York. She works out of her house as a writer and piano teacher.

Janice Levy is the author of ten children's books. Her adult fiction has won the Writer's Digest Magazine Competition for Literary Short Story three times. www.janicelevy.com.

Lyn Lifshin has written more than a hundred books and edited four anthologies of women writers. Her poems have appeared in most poetry and literary magazines in the United States.

Our Contributors

Poet and artisan *Karen Massey*'s work has appeared in numerous Canadian publications and anthologies, and her chapbook, *Bullet*. She has an MA (creative writing) and is the mother of two sons.

Wende McCabe-Teichert is a poet and the mother of three children. Her poems explore border crossings, which include motherhood and connections to the natural world.

Katy McKinney lives in Trout Lake, Washington. She's published poems in the *Sun*, *Windfall*, *Pacific Magazine*, *Manzanita Quarterly*, and elsewhere. The "Ben" of her poems has just graduated from college.

Ethney McMahon lives in New Hampshire with her husband and two children. Her passion is poetry and video editing.

Margaret McMullen is the author of three novels including *In My Mother's House* (St. Martin's, 2003) and *How I Found the Strong* (Houghton Mifflin, 2004). Her son James was born in 1996.

Teresa Méndez-Quigley's poems have won awards by *Mad Poets Review* and appeared in *Philadelphia Poets* and *Drexel Online Journal*. In 2004, she was named Poet Laureate for Montgomery County (Pennsylvania).

Katherine Mikkelson is a freelance writer, recovering lawyer, and adoptive mother. She lives with her husband and two sons outside of Chicago.

Judith H. Montgomery is the mother of two sons. Her first book, *Passion*, received the 2000 Oregon Book Award for Poetry; *Red Jess* appeared in 2006.

Ruth Neubauer, MSW, has loved being a mother since she was twenty-four. Writing soothes her soul and de-clutters her mind. Taking pictures is her unconscious love affair with the world.

Former television news reporter *Susan McKinney de Ortega* lives with her husband and two bilingual daughters in Mexico. Their second child was born at home with a Mexican midwife.

K.W. Oxnard feels that motherhood transports women into a foreign country, a place with its own language, culture, and expectations. Her work has appeared in literary journals such as *Story*, *TatlinsTower.com*, and *Reed*.

Sandra Perlman is an award-winning playwright and poet who lives in Kent, Ohio. She and her artist husband, Henry Halem, have one incredible daughter, Jessica.

Andrea Potos's daughter has been a continual source of wonder and inspiration for her writing. Her full-length collection of poems, *Yaya's Cloth*, is published by Iris Press.

Marilyn Rauth, mother of four, began writing to voice frustrations. She has written a novel, several short stories, and is at work on a memoir. She lives in Bloomfield Hills, Michigan.

Susan Kushner Resnick lives outside Boston with her husband and two children. She still enjoys the kids more and more the older they get.

Lisa Rhoades is the author of *Strange Gravity*, published in 2004 by Bright Hill Press. A postpartum and pediatric nurse, she gave birth to her first baby in July 2003.

Elizabeth Roca's essays have appeared in the *Washington Post* and *Brain, Child: The Magazine for Thinking Mothers*. Her three kids keep her continually on her toes, in literary and other matters.

Kirsten Swain Rogers is a graduate writing student and a very busy mom of two highly active and smart boys. In her spare time(?) she is a Tupperware Consultant and loves it!

Barbara A. Rouillard is a teacher and writer from Springfield, Massachusetts. Her work has appeared in over eighty-five publications, and she is the mother of a thirty-one-year-old daughter.

"Ice Ages" is the first poem *Molly Ruskin* has submitted for publication. She lives in Kensington, Maryland, with her husband and three children.

Rooted firmly in feminist theater, *Robyn Samuels* branched off into teaching then bloomed late as a full-time mother, part-time writer, and budding storyteller.

Terry Scheidt is a poet (*Red Rock Review*, *pms*, *Mudfish*) who wouldn't trade her three kids for anything, except maybe an uninterrupted afternoon.

Kendra Shafer is a mother of two girls who writes and teaches in Fernandina Beach, Florida.

Our Contributors

Dale Shimato's artwork is a combination of expressionist influences and unique metamorphic narratives. His aggressive yet introspective art has appeared in newspapers and magazines nationally.

Dianne Smaniotto is the mother of a teenage son and daughter, whose love has inspired her to live in the moment, laugh often, and write honestly. Her poetry has been published widely.

Holly Smith has three children, none of whom sleep enough. She's an editor at *Maryland Life* magazine, and her writing has appeared in the *Washington Post*, *Salon*, *More Mirth of a Nation*, and other publications.

Kathleen Walsh Spencer has poems in many journals, including *Clackamas Review*, *U.S. Catholic*, *Red Cedar Review*, and *Rosebud*, and in several anthologies. She lives with her husband and nine-year-old daughter in metropolitan Detroit.

Lynn Stearns is a grandmother of three and instructor at the Writer's Center in Bethesda, Maryland. Her work has appeared in the *Bitter Oleander*, *descant*, *Thema*, *Wascana Review*, and other publications.

Jill Stein is a psychotherapist and the mother of a fifteen-year-old son and a twenty-year-old daughter. Her writing has been published widely, and she has received three New Jersey State Arts fellowships.

Kristin Stitz has published essays and short fiction in parenting magazines, literary journals, and online. She lives outside of Philadelphia with her husband and two young sons.

Lynn Tait, a poet from Sarnia, Ontario, Canada, has a twenty-three-year-old son. Her work has appeared in *Owl Creek Review*, *Re:al*, *Night Roses*, *Sophie's Wind*, *Quills*, *Concrete Wolf*, the *Windsor Review*, *Contemporary Verse 2*, and various U.S. and Canadian anthologies.

Hilary Tham, mother of three daughters, is the author of nine books of poetry and a memoir. She passed away in 2005.

Claire Tristram is a novelist and short story writer. Her novel *After* was published by Farrar, Straus, and Giroux in 2004. Her short fiction has appeared in many publications and anthologies. She lives with her husband and two children in northern California.

Amy Unsworth teaches literature and writing at Kansas State University and is an editor for *Three Candles Journal*. She lives in Manhattan, Kansas, where the wind buffets the Flint Hills, with her husband and three sons.

Donna D. Vitucci has two grown sons, and her fiction has appeared in several journals, including *Mid-American Review*, *Southern Indiana Review*, *Faultline*, *Natural Bridge*, *Hawaii Review*, and *Kennesaw Review Online*.

With three children under the age of five, *Phylis Warady* began to write to save her sanity. Her award-winning short stories regularly appear in literary journals and magazines.

Cathy Warner lives in Boulder Creek, California, with her husband and two daughters, eighteen and fifteen. Her fiction has appeared in several literary journals. Her spiritual writing can be found at http://holyink.blogspot.com.

Mary-Sherman Willis is a writer living in Rappahannock County, Virginia. She teaches creative writing at George Washington University and is the mother of two, a daughter, twenty-four, and a son, twenty.

The twenty-five weeks of *Sharon Winn*'s motherhood birthed this award-winning story and her memoir, *In Service to the Soul: 100 Ideas for Women in Transition*. SWinn614@earthlink.net.

Corrine de Winter was nominated twice for the Pushcart Prize. Her poetry, fiction, essays, and interviews have appeared worldwide in publications such as the *New York Quarterly*, *Yankee*, and *Sacred Journey*.

About the Editors

Donya Currie Arias, mother of three young children, holds a degree in journalism from the University of Florida and was an award-winning newspaperwoman for many years, most notably with the *St. Petersburg Times*. Specializing in health issues, she currently writes for the American Public Health Association, the AARP, and her local paper, the *Fredericksburg Free Lance-Star*. Wearing her more literary hat, she has a master's in writing from Johns Hopkins, and her short stories have appeared in many literary magazines and have been widely anthologized.

Hildie S. Block has done a variety of marketing style/catalogue copy writing, but these days teaches writing at American University in Washington, D.C. She's also taught at George Washington and lectured at Johns Hopkins. Aside from the requisite papers at conferences, her fiction has been published in *Gargoyle*, *Cortland Review*, *San Francisco Review*, *E2K*, and elsewhere. Her essays have appeared in *PopMatters*, *In the Fray*, *Strata*, and elsewhere. She lives in Arlington, Virginia, with her husband, two daughters, and a finicky cat. Her novella, "Oh, and She Has a Dog," is set in a group home in Washington, D.C., in the early 1990s.